# Kindred Spirits

By the same author

*The Heart of the Rose*
*Rooks Nest*

JUNE BARRACLOUGH

# Kindred Spirits

St. Martin's Press
New York

Library of Congress Cataloging-in-Publication Data

Barraclough, June.
    Kindred spirits.
    I. Title.
PR6052.A716K5  1989       823'.914       88-29900
ISBN 0-312-02597-1

First published in Great Britain by Severn House Publishers Ltd.

First U.S. Edition

10 9 8 7 6 5 4 3 2 1

# Contents

# PART ONE

# 1823
# The Springtime of the Year

A springy motion in her gait,
A rising step, did indicate
Of pride and joy no common rate,
   That flush'd her spirit:

I know not by what name beside
I shall it call: if 'twas not pride,
It was a joy to that allied,
   She did inherit.

'Hester'
Charles Lamb

Jane Banham had that kind of complexion and figure which is enormously enhanced by clothes and paint and powder. Some were to call it a *beauté de temps*; others had not recognized it as beauty when it was poor or cold or tired or dull. Perhaps one day the knowledge that she had made an effort to look her best would give the girl an additional glow, so that external and internal forces combined to produce a bloom, throwing into shade her rather firm line of jaw and bringing out her deep-set eyes from their shadowed sockets. But her eyes had always been her chief beauty and did not need added colour or crayon or eyebaths to promote themselves. They were of a dark blue with naturally long curly lashes, and round the pupil in the midst of the navy-blue iris was a circle of yellow-gold. In her childhood the hair of her head had been of this gold, but by the time she was twenty it had become a rich golden brown with glancing lights making a sheen over thick tresses which reached down to her knees when she did not loop or braid it. Now that she was in London she knew she ought to conform to fashion and wind it on the crown of her head with a cascade of curls falling from a centre parting and slyly peeping around her ears, but she did not yet care to do that. She was almost, but not quite, unconscious of her own looks; when she was excited or happy she might look in the glass and think, Really I could be quite pretty I suppose!

Mostly, though, she had other things to think about. She knew that she could be a little alluring but this

9

seemed to her to be nothing to do with her features, rather more with her mind and imagination. She discounted charm as being too easily acquired, for she was not vain. At home in the country no one had seemed to remark upon it. She had always known that she could attract people – or at least make them notice her. Here in London there had been glances, some cheeky, some covert, and they had rather astonished her for she did not think of herself as beautiful and rather scorned to try to add to allurements which were not there by right of nature. They must take me as I am, she thought – and then berated herself for arrogance.

On this bright spring morning she sat at a casement window of her uncle's house in Lincoln's Inn Square. The window was open and she sniffed the curious London air which today seemed to have come from the river. She half wished she were back at home in Norfolk, sitting in the apple tree. But that was another life and had to be over; all her hopes must now be set on London with its fantastic crowds and arrays of men and women, some of whom she thought might one day take her in as one of them. She was excited – yet a little apprehensive – before the swell and tide of life that pushed and shoved along the busy streets and even here shouted and hallooed under the windows on the street side of the house, where stood the two coffee houses and Diproses the bookbinders. In the square, the professional men and their ladies and children would take walks, and they fascinated her too. All her own life was, she thought, before her. Her uncle would take her among them and she would claim and be claimed. Any onlooker seeing her at the window would have thought, That is Life I see gazing over the square – young and untried and charming. And Jane Banham thought, This is *my* life. What shall I make of it now?

She was, in truth, rather pleased and satisfied with the course her life had just taken. Rose, her friend back at home in Bedon, had always said something exciting would happen to Jane, something would 'turn up' to change everything. 'You're the sort of person things do happen to,' Rose had said as they lay in the long grass, their stays off, discussing life. At the time Jane had demurred. 'Nothing will ever happen to me,' she remembered saying. It was not long after this that it had.

Her unofficial governess, Miss Sybil Laurentia Snetterton, had always counselled against putting trust in surprises.

'But I want something to happen, Snetters,' Jane had cried.

'Young people spend a quarter of a century wanting something to happen. When you get to my age you are thankful if nothing does,' Snetters had replied, a little sadly, Jane thought. 'You must not expect too much,' Snetters had gone on to say but she had looked at her fondly as she spoke, and smiled. Snetters was a funny old thing but kind, and had taken Jane under her wing at an early age.

Jane remembered how when she was eight years old and Mama had died, Miss Snetterton had come to look after her and teach her in the time she could spare from her duties at the Rectory where she kept house for her papa. Snetters had always had a particular liking for Mama, though two more different women you could not have imagined. Jane recalled the sunny schoolroom and Snetters coming and saying, 'Dear child,' – and then she had known that Mama was gone from them. Mama had been ill for a long time and Jane could not bear it. She had hated herself for not wanting to spend time with Mama, not even wanting to see her pale mother trying to

11

smile – and hated herself for hating the sight. She had loved her mother even though her mama was sometimes 'difficult', with a tendency towards hysteria. Mrs Banham had had enormous and rather appalling charm and her husband had adored her. Jane still tried not to think of her mother, for the memory hurt.

After her death Papa had been very lonely till he had gone away to work for a big landowner. Papa was a land factor and a wonderful manager of other people's money. But he had not been able to take motherless Jane away with him. So she had stayed at the Rectory with Snetters for a time until Papa had remarried. She had tried to like her stepmama, but not succeeded. She would not call her Mama. Only Snetters had understood that she *had* tried, and it was Snetters who had suggested Jane take a little post helping out an old aunt of Papa's, Miss Agnes Sandal, who had been married to the long-since-dead owner of Breckles Hall. Aunt Agnes was very old indeed and lived in her mind in the last century, dressing like the belles of her day with high-piled hair and powdered face. Of course, Snetters had still kept an eye on Jane and still made her go to the Rectory for lessons when she could be spared from listening to the old lady. For Snetters had promised Mama that Jane would be educated in ladylike pursuits. Alas, though Snetters was ladylike, she was not very interested in passing on the gifts ladies apparently needed, being more interested in reading old books and writing her journal. Snetters knew a mighty amount of things – about old plays and poems and people who had circumnavigated the globe and about botany and weather and Greece and Rome. Between Snetters and Aunt Agnes, Jane had picked up a lot of information herself. She had learned French and discovered a talent for reading aloud, and she had learned about the past, for

12

Aunt Agnes lived in English history and sometimes appeared to believe she was herself a dead queen come to life.

'Why did Mama want me to be educated?' Jane had asked once. Snetters's mild face had looked at her in puzzlement.

'Why, because your mama was a lady, dear. She regretted . . .' Snetters had stopped in some embarrassment.

'Regretted what, Snetters?'

'Well,' replied Miss Snetterton reluctantly, 'your mama was a parson's daughter, my dear, like me – you knew that? – and she repented of her folly in leaving her own mama and papa.'

'To marry my papa you mean?'

'No, not that,' answered Snetters after a short silence, which she employed taking off her spectacles and looking earnestly at Jane.

She gathered courage. 'Your mama ran away from her father's house when she was eighteen . . . to be . . . an actress,' she almost whispered.

Jane had felt prickles going down her spine in a strange way.

'Mama was an actress! You mean like the travelling players in Thetford?' It was when Mama was ill and Rose's father had taken them to the market town. Papa had been rather strange about it, she remembered when she reconsidered the matter. He hadn't really wanted her to go but she begged him and it was when he was very worried over Mama, and Jane spent a lot of time at Rose's in any case.

It had all been like a fairy story, she thought – she and Snetters sitting in Aunt Agnes's high-ceilinged faded gilt drawing room talking about Mama. She had so wished she had known all about Mama before she died and that

13

Mama could come back, so she could say to her how marvellous it must have been to be an actress. Yet, as far as she could remember, Mama had never mentioned the boards. Had she ever thought about it when she married Papa and had Jane and then baby Edmund who had died? After the baby's death Mama had seemed to wilt.

'I am only telling you now because you are sixteen,' Snetters had gone on to say and she had put her spectacles back on and continued to look worried. 'Because you ought to know, Jane – and that is why your poor mama's family had nothing more to do with her.'

'But when she married Papa? . . . that made it all right, didn't it?'

'I'm afraid by then it was too late,' replied Snetters, not elaborating at first. Then: 'You see in any case, I'm afraid your mama's family did not think your papa was a gentleman.'

'Well he wasn't an actor,' said Jane. 'Poor Mama – so she had "come down in the world"!'

'He saved her from the stage,' said Snetters solemnly.

Jane was not sure why Mama had needed saving, but she resolved to see Papa in a new light. She had always been rather sorry for him and tried to be pleasant to him, particularly after he had remarried. He was an awkward, silent man who meant to be kind but who had never seemed to know how to talk to her. She had wanted to talk to him about Mama after Snetters's revelations but that lady had asked her not to. It would be too painful for him. All she had to do now was to be a good and dutiful daughter and not get in Stepmama's way.

Papa seemed even more awkward when they were all together, so Jane preferred to stay at Aunt Agnes's where she could sit and read if her tasks were done. There in

14

her little bedroom at the top of the big hall, most of whose rooms were shut up and the furniture shrouded, she could look out of the window and see Papa's house and wonder why, if Mama's family had not thought Papa good enough to have married Mama, and if Mama had enjoyed being an actress, what had made her mother marry her taciturn father and leave the stage? For surely it must have been more fun being an actress – she rolled the word over her tongue – than being married to Papa, even if he had fallen in love with her? He must have been quite a lot older than her. She went on trying to be nice to Papa when she visited him, but it was not any easier to put up with Stepmama who was rather vulgar and fault-finding and never wished to hear Mama discussed.

After that conversation at the hall she had often tried to prise more details about Mama from Snetters, but all she would say was that there was nothing more to be said. It was all in the past and Mama had not deserved to die after little Edmund had died, because *she* had been a good and dutiful wife to her husband – but unfortunately we must accept the will of God.

Snetters had said it to end the conversation, and any like it in the future. Although she was the Rector's daughter, she did not often mention the will of God and Jane felt she had invoked Him to put an end to any further speculation. It was His will, Jane supposed, that she work out her youth fetching and carrying for Aunt Agnes. What, though, if she, Jane, ran away like her unlucky mama? Perhaps she could become famous herself so that Mama's father would recognize her and beg her forgiveness? But although it sometimes seemed a hopeful outcome she was not sure for what she could become famous. She knew she had not the grace or the pretty singing voice of her dead mother, but she loved scribbling stories about the little village and the surrounding countryside. Then the restlessness of youth would come upon her and she would, she supposed, be at Breckles Hall for ever, making possets for the old lady, seeing Snetters for reading and discussion, and talking to Rose in the garden or up in the apple tree, feeling she would never escape and never grow up. Mama must have been awfully brave and awfully rash to have run away from home. But perhaps she had had great talents, or quarrelled with her parents? And she *had* been very beautiful. It was not just because she had been Mama's daughter that she had thought her beautiful. Everyone had said so. Over the next year or two Jane would ponder the mystery of Mama, holding in the palm of her hand the little locket which Mama had left to her, all she had of her now, when even her features and her voice had faded away. The locket was empty; she had not even a miniature of her. Ten, eleven years since Mama had died and however hard she tried she could not call her clearly to mind, except in dreams when she was not trying, when she would see her quite clearly.

She would walk in the village, and in other villages near, and breathe in the air of home and imagine that Mama had returned and they were walking together. It was strange: as a child she had not mourned Mama except in a childish way; she had had to try to forget her in order to survive, but now that she was a young woman and ever since Snetters had told her about Mama being an actress, she had mourned her more than in all the intervening years. She wondered what *she* had made of this sleepy country with its old churches and lanes and fields of corn and windmills. She would pass the little stone cottages with their roofs of thatch or tile and the round-towered, flint-built church where the Reverend Snetterton offici-

16

ated, and wonder whether her mother had ever really felt at home there. To Jane it was the only place she knew as home – and yet there seemed to be some place, somewhere far away, where she might feel even more at home. It puzzled her when she thought this, and she would walk out over the fields and look at the saltwater mere on the way to the next village and wonder how many more villages and fields and churches and meres away would be her final country, if she ever were to go away. Perhaps she would return here as an old lady, to the scenes of her childhood. Or perhaps there was nowhere for her beyond it all, and she would settle down in some rectory or hall, if she were lucky, or in some comfortable Dutch-gabled, red-roofed and tiled house with a walled garden where she would grow flowers and cultivate bees and bring up a large family of children. It was quite a seductive idea, but there was no man in the village or any village near with whom she thought she would want to share such a life. She would go sometimes to the larger town with Snetters to match silks or linger in the old bookshop and exchange gossip and see the coaches which plied between Norwich and London, the mail and the Norwich Flier. How far away London seemed! What would that fat man who had just been helped up into a coach be like when, almost twelve hours later, he arrived in London? When would *she* ever go?

She would wander in the overgrown garden at the hall, sniffing the honeysuckle and the privet, or pinching the leaves of geraniums and she would remember how she had sniffed the flowers and felt the sun on her back when her mother was still alive. It seemed very long ago. She felt that the real Jane was only now about to come out of her chrysalis.

She was waiting for something, but she did not know what. Mama could not come back; her mama's mother and father who (it was said by Snetters) had lived in Hampshire, never wrote to enquire about their grand-daughter. No reverend gentleman arrived on horseback to claim her for his kin. And she felt it was disloyal to Papa to think so much about Mama and her family. He did not seem to want to be reminded of his dead wife and was plunged in his work which took him all over the county with little time even to see his new wife. Jane gave up the effort to get closer to him but would talk about her family to Rose as they sat wreathing garlands of wild flowers at the edge of the common where a flock of sheep roamed round. In the church, where she remembered the Reverend Snetterton had once prayed for victory against Boney, she would dream her way through the service noticing only the little rose carvings at the end of the pew and hoping Aunt Agnes's new cook had not ruined the salt fish with its egg sauce which they ate on Sundays. Or, even further afield, in the dog-cart with Snetters, they would pass a large house to the north of the village with a moat and a rookery and fish ponds with the only sound that of the turtle doves, and again she would wonder whether she had known it earlier and whether Mama had visited there. And she would invent a conversation with Mama as though Mama had not died and was telling her of her life before she had met Papa when she had acted in Swaffham and in Norwich. But it was all her own invention and they would return through the hedges bright with blue periwinkles or with violets and primroses, and come up again to the village gardens and the lane and the old mossy palings of the park that had belonged to the hall, where the briar roses and the woodbine and the ivy entwined, and she would be back in the dark old Eliza-bethan house with Aunt Agnes awaiting her return. She had thought that life would go on like this for ever, in

18

spite of Rose's feeling that she was destined for something grander and more exciting. But it did not, for one day in February when she was already twenty years old, a cold day with no flowers in the hedgerows except the few surviving periwinkles and some coltsfoot, a messenger came from Thetford to say that Papa had died suddenly whilst overseeing some new building for Mr Coke.

After that, time speeded up and she had no more leisure for memories or dreams. Shortly after the funeral her stepmother went away for good, back to her family in Norwich, taking away with her all Papa's old furniture and possessions except a few which Jane had rescued for herself after a terrible argument which she did not care to recall.

One day Snetters came over to the hall rather earlier than usual with news. She would not say what exactly but Jane was to take the coach to Thetford to see a lawyer. Something was about to happen.

The old lawyer in the Thetford notary's shop informed her that under the terms of her father's will he was empowered to communicate with her mother's brother, Mr Henry Stone, and send to him a letter written by the late Mr Banham. This he had done and he had received a reply from Mr Stone saying that he was willing to take over Jane's lodging and her entry into society. He understood she had a small competence from her father. If at any time Miss Banham would consider coming to live with his wife and family in London, he would be happy to offer her hospitality.

Jane sat in the stuffy little office listening to the lawyer and trying to take in this change in her fortunes. She had never heard of Mr Henry Stone and this was the first time she had any confirmation that she might exist in the eyes of her mother's family. It was all a little odd to her but the lawyer seemed to think she was very lucky, for Uncle Henry was evidently, according to his letter, a merchant. This word conjured up immediate visions to Jane's imagination of spices and counting houses and tea and palm trees and faraway places – but most of all it conjured up London. The lawyer hemmed and cleared his throat and took out his eyeglass the better to read the last portion of the letter once more. With a glance at Jane to see if she were listening and a heavy pause, he read: 'If Miss Banham would then care to accept my protection and come to live with my dear wife and myself I should be pleased to comply with her father's wishes and extend the hand of friendship from her late mother's family, the Stones, in greeting and affection as her father suggested I should. Her grandpapa and grandmama are now, alas, deceased but it would be my wish to heal the rift that grew between my late sister and our family that was never by my intent.'

'Why did no one ever tell me about all this?' asked Jane.

'Your father might have lived for many years,' he replied. 'I was to communicate with Mr Stone only on his death.'

After the visit to Thetford and the excited outpouring of it all, first to Snetters and then to Rose, everything seemed to happen at once. Aunt Agnes, who was ninety-four and 'set for a century', took a chill and was laid to rest in Bedon churchyard by the Reverend Snetterton. She was discovered to have left all her property to a long-dead relative, so what was there for Jane to do but to reply to her unknown uncle accepting his generous offer? *London!* Glamour, excitement, young men, the theatre! She was agog for it all. She had had enough of death and grief and a quiet life in the country. It was now or never.

Rose said sadly that she wouldn't want to know them in the village any more. Jane reassured her: 'I shall always love Breckles and Bedon and Snetters and you, you goose, but you do see – I must go?'

Yes, Rose saw.

And in no time at all she was off in the mail coach from Attleborough to London, taking in Newmarket on the way, with Uncle Hal's letter and his banker's name in the City sewn into her under-petticoat lining along with some gold sovereigns, and with Mama's locket around her neck and the memories of twenty years in her head. And with the more recent memory of Snetters's prim, kind face with a suppressed tear at the corner of each eye to accompany her journey. Promises to write, to return if she were not happy, a book pressed into her hand.

She was young. She was the daughter of an actress. She had a rich uncle. She was going to be happy.

And so she found herself to be, a few weeks after this momentous journey, when she sat thinking over her new family and new acquaintance and sniffing the spring air. Norfolk often came back to her mind, of course, and she had written regularly to Snetters and Rose, but she was ready and eager now, the first shock of London being assimilated, to accompany her uncle and aunt wherever they might take her. And tonight they were to take her to Covent Garden.

Henry Stone was a thickset rather florid man of some forty-four years. He was in his dressing room thinking about his dead sister Betsey and her daughter Jane. Now that he knew his niece a little better he found he did not regret the impulse which had led him to extend a helping hand to her. He was looking forward to taking her to the theatre that evening for she so enjoyed herself wherever

21

they took her. He had known his sister Betsey, Jane's mother, only when he was a child, for she had been seven years older than him and had made an abrupt departure from home when she was eighteen. But he had always remembered the beautiful headstrong girl she had been and had always, in spite of all his parents could do, taken her side in the many arguments which had followed her running away. Jane was a little like her – but not in character. He judged his niece to be rather more serious *au fond* than her mother. After his sister had written to tell of her marriage in Norfolk he had replied to her letter but had gone off to make his fortune on the other side of the world, being himself also of an adventurous cast of mind.

Years of travel and of rare visits home to his father's rectory in Hampshire, mainly to see his browbeaten mother, had followed, years when he had determined to be his own man in his own way, to marry and to found a business in the West Indies. It frightened him now a little to look back on his younger self. He *had* married and he *had* succeeded in business but slowly he had realized his wife Edith was homesick for Europe and so he had resigned himself to coming back for good, to manage his trading from London. A smart new office in the City where his expertise was appreciated had followed. His children, born in the West Indies – little James and Thomas and John – had weakened his wife. They were now twelve and ten and eight with a little sister, another Betsey. The three boys needed educating and he was about to place them in a school in London, preparatory, perhaps, to Eton if he could afford it. He did not see why not. Trade was flourishing. If only Edith would flourish too! She seemed drained, a shadow of herself, perpetually with a headache or pains in her joints. He hoped always that the old Edith would return but in his heart he confessed that that was not to be. It was a good thing she had taken to Jane. The girl seemed to have cheered her up . . .

He had not been surprised to find Jane had a good speaking voice and literary taste when she had entertained them in the drawing room with selections from the new poets. But he had been astonished at other evidences of education which he would not have expected from a country girl brought up by that father of hers in the wilds of Norfolk. She seemed to have had a good governess. What had she said? 'Mama wanted me to be a lady.' She had smiled as she said it and it would have been an opportunity to talk about Betsey but he had let it pass. What the girl should have was a good husband and he had searched his acquaintances to find one. He was out of touch with the young, and Edith had not the energy to go husband-hunting. He remembered that he had invited one of the clerks to dinner today because he thought the fellow was clever and of good family. Young people needed young people – that had been his sister's trouble; she had been brought up in such a sheltered way, with their father never allowing her a ball or conversation with a young man. No wonder she had upped and run. Jane would not do that. She needed a father, whereas Betsey had had too much of paternal interference. Manners were changing, though, and he himself was perched uneasily between two ranks of Society. The girl might suit a good professional man, a parson or a lawyer. There were plenty of lawyers around Lincoln's Inn! He must bestir himself, be more sociable. It was good that Jane had come to live with them. Bygones must be bygones and the rift had not been of his choosing. His papa, the Hampshire parson, and his mama, who had suffered from his papa's

23

doctrines, were dead. *He* could give his niece what a family owed to its own.

Carefully he smeared some pomade on his now greying hair and peered into the glass. Jane did not seem to be languishing for lack of male company. She had said yesterday at dinner how much she was looking forward to the play at Covent Garden because it was written by a woman. 'Well, perhaps a *lady*,' she had added, and smiled. Perhaps he ought not to encourage any love she might have for the theatre since it had made her own mother leave home, but Jane had not yet evinced any desire to be an actress like her mama. He would soon have to talk to her about her mother. But what could he say? He remembered her only as an impulsive, rather bewitching girl, beautiful, certainly, and rebellious. Once or twice he had even cleared his throat, preparing himself to say something to Jane, but he had felt strangely reluctant. Edith drove it all out of his head – and the noise the boys made! Jane had seemed quite interested in his work, though, and he had enjoyed telling her about that – how his connections were all spreading and flourishing. She had asked him a few sensible questions about 'Society' too.

He fastened a jewelled pin in his cravat. He was too intelligent and too eccentric, he knew, not to pass muster even as an *arriviste*, and too aware of how other nations in other climates managed their lives to be taken in by systems of rank. Fiddlesticks! he thought. If she were a young man I could give her a tip or two about money. But money was a sensitive subject to her; he had seen that. He was so fearful of appearing to treat her as a poor relation that he pooh-poohed any attempt she had made to thank him for taking her in. After all, she was his sister's daughter and there only because her father had died. There was nothing in all that. No need to resurrect the past. *He* did not care whether Betsey's husband had been a gentleman. Betsey had obviously been happy with him. What he would liked to have talked about with Jane was himself and his old wish to be an explorer! Only the other day at the office in Conduit Court the chief clerk was telling him how some old friend was off to Cathay. If only he were young again! What he could not do now if he were free . . . but he must not think about that. He must find a good husband for his niece, put his boys to school and then take Edith away to Italy to bring back the bloom into her cheeks if that were possible: a bloom that he could not help noticing was always present in Jane's face. Ah Youth!

If the boys *could* be found a suitable school, Jane might be willing to supervise them in their vacation, with the help of the housekeeper, and she might give them a few lessons before they went to school. But he had not offered her a home in order to receive cheap labour. He did wish she could be nicely married before he took Edith away. That way she would have a home his boys could visit. Ah well, he must not think too far ahead. He would have to get round the Ogilvie, of course, in any case. She had been his mother's housekeeper and seemed to have formed no unfavourable opinion of his niece in the short weeks since Jane's arrival. Mrs Ogilvie would hold the fort and Jane could stay on. They called her Mrs Ogilvie, though she had never wed, only been married to the parsonage and the family. She was getting on now and was no longer the bustling little figure of his youth. Yes, surely something could be arranged. Ogilvie could chaperone Jane, if that was what a 'lady' needed now, and Jane could be a family friend to her. He would have to see how it worked out. His sanguine disposition came to his aid and he began to look forward to the play. He would see how Jane got on with his brood. If she were to be left in London it might be a good idea to look round his friends for a protector, someone from the business who could oversee her and the children. He remembered again that he had invited young March to dinner and that bell was probably him arriving. He gave a final smile at his glass, patted his hair and wandered downstairs.

The family of Hal Stone ate their meal at four in the afternoon. They were all sitting in the rather small, dark dining room on the ground floor of the house at the back. The house Hal had rented overlooked Lincoln's Inn Square and was at a mid-distance from the office near St Paul's and the streets of old houses to the north east of the Strand. Jane had come down from her room in her new sprigged muslin dress with a smile on her face and was listening to Edith whilst Mrs Ogilvie was helping the maid receive the dishes on a dumbwaiter which Cook sent up from the kitchen. They had not yet employed a footman, though Hal Stone had plans for the expansion of his domestic staff. It was expected of him, but he did not always do what was expected of him, and in money matters he was shrewd and averse to spending money on show. Enough for him that he had his friends in widely different parts of Society. He was useful to a few members of the aristocracy in placing their money, and had no wish to ape them in their profligate habits. He liked to think he kept a generous and easy-going household although he could have told you exactly how much every item of his household expenditure cost him down to the last penny.

He came in and saw Mrs Ogilvie putting her final touches to the service. Edith was sitting rather listlessly, occasionally clearing her throat in an involuntary manner. The boys had come to this meal though they often ate upstairs. They were a noisy crew and there was a good deal of bickering amongst them which Edith seemed powerless to control. As Jane entered the dining room a servant appeared at the door which gave on to the oak-panelled entrance hall and the flight of steps to the street front. 'Please, ma'am,' she said to Edith, 'there's a young man at the door. Says the master invited him to dinner. Shall I let him in?'

Hal was just entering the room from the other side. 'Why bless me, it will be young March. Of course, Polly. Let him in and bring him in here. Lay another place, Emily. I did tell you, dear,' said Hal to his wife jovially. She sighed.

Jane had been wanting to talk to her uncle about her mother ever since her arrival in London, but the opportunity never seemed to present itself. There were continual interruptions from the noisy boys and Uncle Hal was away so long in the City office. Really, Jimmy and Tommy and Johnny were rather ill-mannered. 'They ran wild abroad,' their mother had said rather apologetically to Jane on her first day. She did not seem to know what to do with them. They were too old for a nursery governess and had no regular tutor. Only Mrs Ogilvie seemed to know what should be done, and soothed and was stern by turns to the ill-regulated brood. Their father was too good-natured towards them. Perhaps he remembered his own strict childhood and wished to make amends. She did not think he acted from any principle. She had explained this to Snetters in one of her letters. How different this noisy house was from the peace and quiet of Aunt Agnes's, but she did not mind. She was grateful to be here.

Jane sat down next to Johnny, the youngest of the boys, and had a good view of the young man who was shortly

27

brought in to dinner by the parlour maid. He was given a
chair opposite her, next to Hal. Hal introduced him to his
wife, who managed a small smile and murmured apologetically that she was afraid he would have to partake of
family noise as well as family food, and then took no
more notice of him. He bowed politely to Jane, and Hal
piled his plate with roast beef which the visitor attacked
with gusto.

Philip March was a medium-built young man with
straight brown hair, an air of interest in his surroundings,
and a capacity for conversation as large as his capacity for
beef.

'I hear you are up from the country,' he said, looking
across at Jane, who had been observing him with interest.

'Yes, I am Mr Stone's niece,' she replied.

'Your uncle told me he had a young lady staying with
his family,' observed Mr March. 'Where are you from?'

'From Norfolk, about twenty miles from Norwich. Do
you know that county?'

'No, I am London born and bred.'

'Mr March is working in my Counting House, Jane,'
said Hal, hearing their conversation and, being assured
that Mrs Ogilvie was attending to his sons, turned to talk
to his young friend.

'Do call me Philip, Miss – er . . .'

'Jane Banham,' said Jane.

'I have taken a great interest in Mr Stone's travels, Miss
Banham,' he went on. 'I should like to travel myself.'

Jane observed that her uncle seemed to have a high
opinion of the youth. He could not be more than about
twenty-four and was enormously self-assured. She was
curious why this clerk rather than any other should be
invited to her uncle's home.

'I am trying to persuade him to stay on with the

Counting House,' said Hal. 'But our young friend has literary aspirations. Hey, March, would you like to see the play with us?'

Philip March was eating away steadily, but replied that he had intended visiting Covent Garden that evening in any case, though he did not hold out very high hopes of the play.

'Do you *write* plays, then?' asked Jane of Philip.

'Not in my line,' he replied. 'I am to be editor of a new magazine. Your uncle' – he bowed to Hal – 'has kindly taken an interest in my extra business activities.'

'I'd wager writing – editing – whatever you call it, is as much a business as any other,' replied the older man shrewdly.

'You are right, sir, but as you know such posts are not very remunerative,' said Philip.

'That is why he has continued to slave away with me,' said Hal with a chuckle. 'Mr March is the son of an old friend of mine from the days before I went to Jamaica,' he explained.

Oh, thought Jane. That is why he is so familiar – if their fathers were good friends. She wondered whether the elder Mr March had known her mama and then wondered why she had wondered.

'Philip's father was at school with me you know, my dear,' said Hal, addressing his remarks to his wife who seemed rather out of the conversation. Edith smiled wanly.

'Do sit up, dear,' she said to her middle son who was marking the white linen tablecloth with a large silver fork. Mrs Ogilvie removed the fork from Master Stone's hands and he kicked his brother under the table.

'I think, my dear, the boys may go, after pudding,' suggested their father.

'Pudding, pudding,' shouted Jimmy. 'What's for pudding?'

'Hush now,' said Edith. 'Ogilvie, dear, would you hurry Cook up?'

In the ensuing bustle and confusion Tommy began an argument with his sister who had sat as good as gold at her mother's side but now began to wail.

'When can *I* go to the theatre?' asked Jimmy.

'When you can behave yourself,' said his father, but with a smile. He was a very patient man, Jane thought.

The nursery maid came for little Betsey and the boys tucked into plum duff as heartily as Philip March who had been silent for a few minutes, affecting not to notice the children's antics. But then he said, 'Have you been much to the theatre, Miss Banham?'

'No, I am afraid I have not,' she replied. 'When I was a child I went to the players in Thetford, but that was a long time ago.'

'Oh, a *very* long time ago,' said Philip. 'It is to be a play by Miss Mitford,' continued the young man carelessly, not knowing that Jane was perfectly aware of this. 'I expect it will please you. I am more interested in the masculine writers myself. Have you read Lamb, Coleridge, Wordsworth, De Quincey?'

'I have heard of them,' said Jane. 'And I *have* read Mr Wordsworth.'

'Aha! – so they read poems in Norfolk, do they?'

'Well I did,' she replied, not sure whether he was teasing her. He had a way of allowing his rather clear, light brown eyes to linger on whoever he was addressing his remarks to.

'Jane will read you something, I expect,' said Hal. 'She is a capital reader of verse.'

'Is that so?' Philip March looked rather keenly at her. 'Have you no aspirations to the boards yourself?'

Jane looked at her uncle – here would be an opportunity to introduce the subject of Mama, but she could not say it, could not say, 'My mama was an actress.' Instead she said: 'Oh no, I am too clumsy and too scatterbrained to make an actress.'

'Then you shall recite in drawing rooms,' said the decisive young man. He seemed to have taken a fancy to her. The awkward moment passed but Jane saw her uncle looking at her rather meditatively. 'You shall meet my sister Henrietta,' went on Philip. 'She has many friends in the world of drawing rooms. We poor writers need encouragement. If nobody reads us, we perish!'

'When do you think your first issue will be at the printers?' asked Hal.

'Ah, sir, that depends upon my subscription list, to which you have been kind enough to add your name.'

'My husband has written of his travels,' said Edith unexpectedly, in a lull in the conversation as second helpings were taken round by Martha. The boys had got down from the table and were heard rampaging somewhere away in the house.

'I must apologize for our lack of ceremony,' she went on. 'But as you will understand – a houseful of children . . .'

'They are not in school, then Ma'am?' asked Philip March, with an effort at appearing interested in the lady's offspring.

A conversation as to the merits of schools – Dr Macdonald's and Dr Tapstick's – ensued and then the party went into the next room where coffee was served.

Jane still wondered why her uncle had invited the young

31

man. Maybe he thought she must meet young men and this was the only one to hand!

She drank her coffee, thinking how strange it was for her to be sitting here in London in the same room as the future editor of a literary review – even if he were yet a clerk in a merchant house.

'Sir, you must let me see your writings,' said the young man. 'My father once told me you were a man of *action*.' Hal smiled but said to his wife: 'The carriage will be ready, my dear. Would you care to accompany us?' he asked Philip. 'If you *are* going to the theatre you might like to join us in our carriage.'

'You are too kind, but I shall walk if you don't mind, sir. I thank you for your hospitality.' He bowed. 'Don't forget, Miss Banham, my sister will send you her card.' He shook hands with his host and was off, bowing once more at the door.

'What an unusual young man,' said Edith when he had gone. 'He is very independent, is he not? How does he manage to do all this work he was talking of? Has he money of his own?'

'If March had left him money, my dear old friend's son would not be spending his time counting out mine,' replied her husband with a laugh. 'But I like to encourage the young, as you know, Edith. He won't be with us long if I'm any judge, and you will be able to say you once knew the famous editor Philip March.' Jane wondered whether her uncle's impulsive nature was joined to any judgement of human beings. She had thought Philip March rather too forward for her tastes, though the lack of shyness and the penetrating glance might just as well have been covers for insecurity as for ambition.

'Are all your clerks like Mr March?' she asked. 'He did seem – rather unusual.'

'Ah, Jane, you have met so few men about Town, God be praised,' said her uncle. 'The boy will go far. Come now, we must all assemble ourselves for our excursion.'

It was the first time that she had been out with her uncle and aunt together. Hal had walked in the City and in nearer parts of London with his niece, she had been out shopping with Edith and Mrs Ogilvie and had walked round the Fields with the children, but she had not yet been in the new carriage. She looked forward with mounting excitement to her first visit to Covent Garden theatre and forgot Mr March and his rather bold manners. Perhaps they would see him there, but she did not really mind. She was far more interested in the play.

The streets round Drury Lane and the Strand were crowded with carriages and horses and pushing multitudes of men and women going in the direction of Covent Garden or disappearing down dark alleys to unknown houses and shops. The din was indescribable. All manners and ranks seemed to be in the same place, but it was as well for respectable families to keep to the broader streets, for not far away were some notorious cellars and coffee houses where a girl could lose her reputation in ten minutes or a man be robbed in broad daylight, though the streets had become safer than a few years before with the institution of the new constables who had replaced the old watchmen. It was not yet dusk and the gas lamps were not lit. The play would begin at seven with many separate turns and acts before the principal drama. Jane felt buoyed up in her new sprigged dress and mantle and with her hair piled up and dressed by Edith's maid. Nearer the theatre there were carriages letting down dandies with overdressed girls, and round the front of the theatre was a street reserved for the nobility's comings and goings.

33

She wondered why the crowds were so thick. They could not all be going to see Miss Mitford's play, surely. Perhaps the King was to visit, or some member of his unlucky family come from the fields of Kensington or the pretty purlieus of Mayfair to the meeting place of royalty and commoner: the theatre.

She looked around her, as she alighted at the corner of a cobbled street after her uncle and aunt, and saw a few grand carriages; some urchins on the far side of the street selling groundsel for canaries; and some flower girls planted by the entrance to the theatre with their wares. Covent Garden Market was close and they were selling lavender, and spring flowers they had haggled for at the Garden. She saw a tall man with a handsome but melancholy face crowned with a curious quiff of dark red hair standing sniffing a bunch of flowers he had bought. Another young man hallooed him across the street and the tall man waved the bunch of flowers in the air. Then her own party turned and made their way into the theatre and to a box which Uncle Hal had ordered. The grand staircase and saloons were most elegant and the lobbies and the corridors were crowded with people of 'ton'. There was a pervasive smell of scent and pomade. The poorer members of the audience were not here, but safely gathered in the pit or above them in the high gallery. Edith was jostled a little and put her hand to her head, but gave a sigh of relief when their box was found for them. The dark red and gold curtain was down and the whole interior of the theatre was painted gilt, yellow and white. It was much bigger than Jane had expected. Had Mama ever acted in a place like this? Mama must have been exceedingly brave if she had. However did you get to know anyone in this pushing mass of Londoners? How did they all earn their livings? It was all so different from

34

what one might have expected from books. She knew how to behave and how to speak from books but the reality was far different. She felt small and unregarded and looked so solemn that Hal leaned over to her. 'The theatre of life, eh?' he said and she smiled. He was determined they should all enjoy themselves.

'They say old Sarah Siddons is in the audience tonight,' said Hal. The legendary Mrs Siddons – why she must be nearly seventy! The vast theatre was filling up with people of all ranks. Perhaps, Jane thought, there was nowhere else in London where this mixture could be effected and this was why Hal liked it, for she had discerned a certain democratic note in her uncle which assorted strangely with his role as a man of business.

Jane wished she had an even smarter gown, for there were many women around her dressed beautifully. Not in the muslins or calicos which she usually wore herself, but in silks and chintzes and materials she could not put a name to. Jane, in her spotted cotton and her cross-over shoes, had felt in the height of fashion but she noticed ladies in tight-waisted gowns – waists tighter than she had ever seen – and some ladies wore dresses with great flounces at the bottom of the hem. She sighed. After all, fashion was fashion and it would be pleasant to be able to afford such dresses. The ladies who did wear them were not, however, always young and beautiful! Still, beautiful clothes could, she supposed, paint the lily. The ladies with poke bonnets had removed them; those ladies in the smartest boxes, ladies who wore waving ostrich plumes with jewelled clasps over their high chignons and curls, had kept their headdresses on. To be sure, some of the men she saw outshone their ladies. Her uncle always, of course, dressed elegantly, if plainly, with his gleaming top hat and careful cravat, but here there were men in

35

pantaloons and hessian boots, with velvet waistcoats of all colours and some embroidered with stars. In the entrance to the theatre she had seen men in green frock coats with large scalloped edges and heavy fastenings, men who surely seemed, even to her unpractised eyes, to have touched their faces with rouge. Some had curled their moustaches and had obviously spent longer on their toilette even than the women they were with. In the great theatre she had seen little groups of such people on the staircases and in the saloons.

'They rent boxes for the Season,' said her uncle and forbore to comment that some of the rentiers were women of the town who had grown rich from their profits in profligacy. She wanted to ask her uncle whether some 'respectable' people did *not* come to the theatre, for she had always heard from her Norfolk friends that there was something rather disreputable about the 'boards'. But Norfolk was full of Evangelicals and Dissenters – and here was an eminently respectable lady, this Miss Mitford, writing for the stage!

She heard some people discussing Macready, an actor, and asked her uncle which actress was to be in the play that evening.

'They say there will be two very pretty young ladies acting,' replied her uncle, 'a Miss Foote and a Miss Lacy.' She decided to be bold and whispered to him: 'Did Mama act here?' He looked at her searchingly in the light of the gas candles which had been lit. 'I believe she *may* have done for a short time,' he replied quietly. 'We must have a little talk about her, Jane, one day.'

Jane then gave herself up to go on observing this fashionable – and in the pit not so fashionable – crowd. It was almost as if a great play were going on around them.

36

In the next box she saw an elegantly dressed man quizzing their party. She pointed him out to Hal.

'Bless me,' he said, glad to get off the subject of her mother, she thought. 'That's Mr Frederick Digby, a good customer of ours.' The man bowed slightly and Hal gave a bow back to him. He seemed to be by himself.

'Will Mr March be coming?' asked Jane.

'I believe he prefers backstage,' said her uncle laughing.

Edith meanwhile was sitting fanning herself with a foreign-looking fan. It was hot and stuffy and the smell from the gas chandeliers was rather overpowering. Jane was now glad she was wearing a simple short-sleeved gown. She did not know how young and fresh and attractive she looked and she was so caught up observing others that she was unselfconscious, which added to her charm. She was impressionable and eager to understand the great world and it showed in her face. For a moment, though, her customary self-confidence had deserted her as she saw the serried ranks of unknown men and women all used to theatres and fashion and London. She looked again for young Philip March but could not see him. But she saw at the front of the house, down below, the tall strange-looking man whom she had glimpsed outside the theatre waving a bunch of flowers, now standing eating oranges.

But thoughts of the audience and the world outside finally faded away when, after many short pieces recited by ladies and gentlemen in front of the curtain and allusions which escaped her but which the audience applauded, the real play began. It was a fervid melodrama in which, as it progressed, she did not believe for one moment, but it seemed to be the vehicle for the actors' feelings of tenderness and despair that had little to do with the plot. There were at first two young ladies, but one of them was acting a youth and when they were together the audience was silent. A castle and a wood and a waterfall appeared and then a handsome man who was applauded when he appeared on stage and spoke his words with great conviction. He was clearly the main actor. He did not 'boom' as the other men did, particularly the villain. Jane found herself wishing the play was *Hamlet* or *Macbeth*, which she knew well, for the chief actor looked a Hamlet. He was often clapped after his speeches but they were clapping him, not the play! Uncle Hal whispered, 'That's Macready.' He was about thirty and she found herself confecting a real-life intrigue between himself and the ladies in the piece. The lady who was a youth was pleasant-looking but her voice was not very strong and her words could not all be heard. Some of the wags in the gallery shouted 'Speak up!' How difficult it must be to take the stage in this way. Had Mama had a loud voice? She could not remember. She thought the women were over-acting in their efforts to show passion: the nuances of their craft went by the board when such efforts were necessary to impress the audience. The plot was somewhat intricate and she was not sure whether she had grasped it. Only the emotions came through. Finally the curtain came down on the first act and the gaslights were turned up again. There was a great stir and buzz as the audience turned once more back to its own concerns. Intervals were rather a pity, though the tired actors probably needed them.

She looked round her at the tier upon tier of row upon row of seats encircling the vast auditorium. Four great circular sweeps, each packed with hundreds of playgoers, though not all the seats were taken, each tier separated by the pillars which supported the division of the two lower circles into boxes like theirs. Gas brackets swung down from each gilded decorated balcony above, except from that of the gallery which was in darkness. The roof was intricately decorated. It seemed higher even than Norwich Cathedral, which was the tallest building she had ever seen. But the 'altar' here was the front stage which swept right into the auditorium on high thin pillars. Down in the pit, almost under the stage, she saw the fiddlers going out for refreshment.

'See the top gallery,' said Uncle Hal. 'There are little holes in the roof – they call them the pigeon lofts – and people used to sit there, but it was said to be dangerous and it was not possible to see properly from them so they are empty.'

'I shouldn't like to go up so high,' she replied. 'How can such a large building be constructed?'

'It was all rebuilt after they had the fire about ten or fifteen years ago.'

'I think theatres are so dangerous,' murmured Edith. 'Just look at the gaslights. They could come crashing down – '

'We'll take a bet they won't tonight,' said her husband comfortably. 'But they do stink!'

Apparently this first long interval could be spent promenading in the lobbies and taking refreshments, if you could afford them, in the various saloons. The gallery frequenters, almost as high up as the pigeon lofts, in their undivided top rows, were already shouting and moving around and an orange came hurtling down into the pit from the heights followed by a cheer. The owners of the most expensive seats had opened the little doors behind them and were chatting with friends. Their own box was shared with another party – four old ladies dressed in the fashions of fifty years before, who nodded and bowed to each other and occasionally waved to what Jane supposed must be imaginary friends. Several dandies with spy-glasses were looking up from the pit at the boxes.

'Drury Lane Theatre is even larger,' Hal was saying.

'Then it must be bigger than the Abbey,' replied Jane.

'We must walk you round the piazzas by day,' said Hal. 'Not the place to come at night, my dear.' He frowned, suddenly aware of the dangers a pretty young niece might run in this area. Here they were safe in the great theatre while, all around, London swarmed in the alleys behind the Strand.

'I should like to go to a coffee house,' said Jane. 'Do ladies go there?'

'There *are* respectable places – and others,' said Hal.

'Oh, my dear,' said Edith, leaning over to speak to Jane. 'Polly must chaperone you if you ever go out alone, but *not* to coffee houses.'

'Come, Edie, it's not as bad as it was when we were young,' replied Hal. 'Don't frighten the girl. There'll be plenty of young sparks who would take her round a little for she must enjoy Town. I was thinking, young March might accompany you, my dear.'

'I wonder if he's here?'

'Tell you what, you and I shall go for a little stroll. What about it, Edie?'

'I shall stay here,' said that lady firmly. 'I might almost fall asleep.'

'No, no, I can't leave you here alone.'

Just then there was a knock on the door of their box and the man who had been pointed out to them before and who had bowed to her uncle came in.

'Stone, I've been wanting to see you about the securities I left last week,' he murmured after glancing at the ladies and making another polite bow. 'May I come Thursday?'

40

'By all means, sir. May I introduce my wife and my niece?' said Hal in his easy, unaffected way. 'Edith, Frederick Digby. Digby, my niece, Jane Banham.'

The man was about thirty-seven or eight and he was not dressed in any dandyish fashion but like a gentleman, Jane noticed.

'Your lady not here tonight?' pursued Hal.

'No, she has gone to her brother abroad for a time. I'm afraid London in the Season tires her. I tell you what, you must bring your family to see my place in Hertfordshire. I'm very quiet down there with Clara away and it would do your lady good to breathe some fresh air. I can't say I miss Town much myself. Were you off for a stroll?'

'I'm afraid my wife is tired,' said Hal. 'I was just going to show Jane around a little.'

'I shall stay and keep your wife company,' said the gentleman gallantly. 'You go and partake of the Covent Garden specials.' Jane wondered what they were. Mr Frederick Digby seemed remarkably *sans façons*. Edith perked up a little at the prospect of a tête-à-tête with a handsome man and Jane followed her uncle out to the corridors behind the boxes and circle, where the promenades were held in earnest and white currant ices and coffee were served in the great saloons.

When they returned Edith was launched on her favourite topic – the boys and their health and their education. Jane was all glowing and excited by her perambulations, the cool ice still sliding down her throat. Frederick bowed to them all once more, and with a 'Thursday, then,' departed.

He looked kind, thought Jane. Her uncle seemed to have such a large circle of friends and this one looked rather aristocratic. It must be through his financial dealings that he knew such a man. Jane was ignorant of business and uncertain about the exact rank of her successful relatives for they did not live extravagantly.

'We shall really have to take on more servants,' Edith was saying. 'How could we ever visit such a man? We could hardly return his hospitality and give him luncheon with the Ogilvie and Emily.' She sighed for a footman and a larger house.

'It's only business, my dear,' said her husband comfortably. 'We saw young March – didn't we, Jane? – footing it with a lady he *said* was his sister.'

'Oh, I'm sure she was his sister,' said Jane, surprised.

Philip March had indeed come up to them in the foyer with a young lady who had rather alarmed Jane. She was about twenty-five but carried a lorgnette and spoke in a breathless and unrestrained fashion.

'How old is Mr Digby?' asked Edith before the curtain rose again.

'He must be nearly forty,' replied Hal. 'What he said about his lady wife – there's more in that than meets the eye. I believe she spends most of her time in Italy.'

'Lucky woman,' sighed Edith.

'But I tell you what: we *shall* go and see his place in Hertfordshire one day. He owes me a debt y'know. I rescued him from a bad move he was about to make – leastways I think it was his lady's idea – anyway, there you are, he feels indebted to me. We'll go and get some roses in your cheeks one of these days. It will do us good to get out of London.'

Jane remembered little of the play afterwards, it was all unsatisfactorily resolved with a murder and two other deaths. She was thinking how pleasant it would have been to have had a brother like Mr March or a father like the gentleman who had come into their box. Their lives,

42

though, did not seem real to her. For a brief moment she thought of Bedon and all she would have to tell Rose, with a suitably edited version for Snetters.

It was a long performance and she was quite glad to emerge at ten o'clock into the chillier air of Bow Street. The nearby piazza had transformed itself into a great seething mass of theatregoers and market sellers and coaches and carriages. The shouts of footmen and watchmen mingled in a phantasmagoria before her eyes. A knot of dandies was twirling away in the direction of a coffee house as the party waited for Hal's carriage to come up.

Philip March had probably gone to a coffee house, though what he would do with his sister was a matter for puzzlement. Jane wished she could suddenly become invisible and follow the fashionable young to their lairs. She would love to listen to them, to say what she herself would like to say about the play and about life in general which was so new and strange and exciting. She supposed Philip March was not actually 'fashionable', though.

As they waited at the corner of the cobbled yard she noticed some rather noisy men in a small gathering across the street, and just as her uncle's carriage came up one of them staggered away from them and almost fell under the wheels, but regained his balance and apologized with a sweep of his arm and a large bow. She saw it was the tall man with the strange auburn hair she had noticed on her way into the theatre hours before, the one who had been eating oranges. He seemed a little tipsy, but she saw in his eyes a sort of terror that moved her in a peculiar fashion. Just for a moment – for then she was being handed into the carriage – he caught her eye, smiled, a little mockingly, paused and said to her: 'She walks in beauty, hey? – ' and was gone. Hal and Edith had ignored

43

him completely. She supposed it was a common enough occurrence, for there was dissolution aplenty in the streets around them. Yet he had looked afraid.

All Edith said was: 'If young men wish to drink they should do it at their clubs,' and Hal said nothing at all. When they reached home the three were served with hot chocolate by Emily.

'We shall have to take you to my mantua-maker,' said Edith to Jane, and to Hal, 'I think we had better advertise for a footman, my dear. Once the boys are settled we can rid ourselves of Mr Dempsey.' The latter was the boys' occasional tutor who had been coming to the house for the past few months to teach them Latin and Globes.

Jane went to her room as soon as she decently could to think over the theatre and the play and the unaccustomed sights and sounds. She found herself wondering whether Philip March would be true to his word and introduce her to his sister's friends. It was true – she missed female company of her own age. Rose was far away and she would have liked to chat with her about everything and nothing. But Rose knew nothing of London life except what Jane told her in her letters and was not a particularly good correspondent. It was true what Rose had said – she would outgrow Bedon. I shall tell her of my meeting with Mr March and Mr Digby, she thought and smiled to herself. To Snetters she would write of the play and the theatre. She fell asleep thinking: At last I am launched upon London. But she dreamed of a tall auburn-haired man who was sitting in a garden with bees swarming round his head.

Edith Stone was as good as her word, and in Hal's long absence at his City office she had a dressmaker call round who was said by her friend Mrs Stacey, a lawyer's widow, to have just the right fashionable touch for young ladies' gowns and frocks. Thus it was that Jane was measured and clucked over, and material bought in a smart shop in Regent Street. The dressmaker was a certain Louisa Collins from St Giles and she inadvertently opened Jane's eyes to the life of the other London, the *unfashionable* one, whose denizens, from the just respectable to the much less than respectable, swarmed in the courts between the Strand and Oxford Street and to the east of that district and north of the City.

Miss Louisa was highly respectable, Jane could see, but she had had a hard life. She counted herself lucky having the magic in her fingers which had pulled her up from ordinary seamstress work to the rank of ladies' private mantua-maker.

As she bent round and over Jane, pins in her mouth and on her person, she would make occasional remarks when they were alone in the room which the girl seized upon eagerly.

'It's easy to tell you ain't a London lady,' she would say, 'Never one word of thanks I gets from them. Why if I was to go back to the village where my old mother came from, I dare say if I told the folks a thing or two about the people I've worked for, they wouldn't believe me.'

'Are all your family in the dressmaking trade, then?' Jane liked to ask such questions, for Miss Louisa Collins liked to talk and it whiled away the tediousness of being fitted.

'Well, Miss, I lodge at present with my sister-in-law and her mother and my brother. It helps them, see, to have me there with them for times are bad, real bad.'

'What does your sister-in-law do, then?' asked Jane with curiosity.

Louisa launched herself into a long description of all

45

her family, and thus it was that Jane began to know all about the family at 363 Ironmongers Row, just as they got to know about her. 'Louisa's families' always kept the pot going at number 363, when a gossip punctuated the busy needles and threads.

'What does your sister-in-law do?' Jane asked her again.

'She's a dolls' dressmaker, Miss. She's ever so neat – dresses the dolls of the nobility as well as for the toy shops.'

'I didn't know there were dolls' dressmakers,' replied Jane, a new facet of this bewildering London presenting itself.

'Oh, yes, she's been doing it for years and she's forty-seven now. Bringing up one of her girls to that trade, too.'

'And your brother – what does he do?'

'He's a street musician, Miss. Plays the hurdy-gurdy and the fiddle. Ever so clever he is. And little Mary, she's going to be a milliner, and the other girl goes down to the Garden and does the bunches.'

'The bunches?'

'Aye – does the flowers and sells them to the nobs.'

'What is *she* called?'

'She's Daisy. Just right for the flowers, ain't it?'

Jane's imagination was soon busy upon Alf, the street musician, and his wife Mary, the dolls' dressmaker, and their children, little Mary the milliner and Kate the one who was to follow her mother with the dolls' dresses and Daisy the flower girl. These sessions with Louisa Collins opened her eyes and her ears to the ordinary lives around her, just a handful from the hundreds and thousands. When Edith had a headache it was pleasant to talk to Louisa and listen and dream.

But eventually the dresses were ready and Jane paraded in them to the delight of little Betsey who sometimes came to the sewing room to watch.

'I wish I could sew like you,' Jane would sigh.

'*You* won't need to work, Miss. These dresses will get you a beau, I'll be bound!'

If Edith could have heard she would not have approved, Jane knew. Somehow the dressmaker made her feel at home in a way even Uncle Hal did not. She supposed it was feminine company, though it was of a rank of Society she was no longer supposed to be acquainted with. At home as a small child she had played with the children of the publican, the shoemaker, the blacksmith, the constable, the collar-maker, the carpenter, the cabinet-maker, the wheelwright and the mason as well as those of the curate!

'Mary's old Ma, she was from a gypsy family they say; she tells fortunes, she does – why even them actors and their girlfriends come to Ma. She has the gift, you know!'

'*My* mother was an actress,' said Jane before she could stop herself.

'Well is that so? Fancy that.' Louisa looked up, surprised, her needle poised.

'Yes, but she married my papa so I didn't know about it.'

'That's a funny life now,' said Louisa. 'Our Ma could tell you a thing or two. It all goes to show – a funny old world we live in and no mistake.'

Jane was not sure why it was such a funny old world but took Louisa to mean that here now was an actress's daughter being brought up a lady in a grand house. But she said nothing else about her mother, feeling that she had perhaps been indiscreet.

47

'I wish I could meet your family, Miss Collins. Perhaps I might call one day on you?'

'Bless you, the carriages don't come down our way!' replied the woman. 'Not that we're not respectable, we are – but it ain't the sort of place you'd want to visit. Tell you what, though. You might see my sister's gal outside the Garden one day if you was ever to go by Henrietta Street. She sells at the corner.'

'Perhaps I will then,' replied Jane. She was really sorry when the dresses were finished.

In the meantime, Philip March had written a short invitation to her:

Mr Philip March, Miss Henrietta March and Miss Charlotte Howard will receive on Sunday at Number Six Temple Gardens Court and beg the pleasure of the company of Miss Banham.

Here was yet another opportunity to meet London and Jane asked Hal if she might go.

'Polly will accompany you and walk you back,' he said.

The evenings were getting lighter now and summer was only just around the corner. Jane experienced a great lift of spirits. Nothing further had come of the invitation from the great Frederick Digby to his country place, though Edith expected one daily.

'You must meet young people,' said Hal. Edith remonstrated that it was not like the Indies or some small town in England. He seemed to forget that Jane was only twenty-one and young ladies of that age needed a chaperone.

'My dear, it is only Phil March! What harm can come to her? He lives with his sister and her friend, I believe. They have a snug little place, I'm told. Tea and whist will be just the thing for Jane,' he said vaguely.

48

Jane had still not had that talk with her uncle and it seemed they never were going to have it. What could he tell her about her mama? Probably Mrs Ogilvie knew more about her than he did. She had said no more to him beyond assuring him that she had no desire to tread the boards. 'Though I should like to write,' she had added. 'If I had any talent.'

She did not think her talent would be up to Mr March's and his sister's and it was with some trepidation that she finally accepted their invitation and set out one warm afternoon after taking a dish of tea with Edith and reading a story to Betsey. There was a slight breeze and she swung along with Polly, who was carrying a basket to pick up some cheese on the way back from the shop at the corner of Tavistock Street. It was the first time Jane had walked any distance in London without her uncle or aunt and it was so pleasant to feel free and to feel she was one of the Londoners who milled around, a Londoner now herself – almost.

Young *men* could go for long walks alone, of course, and indeed did. Young ladies were not so free and even walking accompanied was supposed to tire them. Jane had sighed a great deal over the fact that she was now supposed to be a lady of sorts. She supposed Edith was a lady. How much easier it would be to be a working girl like Louisa Collins's nieces.

Philip March's father had been a barrister and because of this his family went on living in a little corner of the Temple, even though old Mr March had been dead some eight years and had not left much money to them. It was because of this that Philip worked at Hal Stone's Counting House as a clerk. He must hate it, she thought, and wondered how his new literary review was progressing. She had seen that he was very ambitious.

At least she looked her best for a change. She had put on one of her new dresses, an elegant afternoon dress in printed cotton of pale lilac and with a lace frill at the hem which Louisa Collins's nimble fingers had so seemingly effortlessly confected. Over it she wore a light cloak of a darker shade of lilac. She had chosen the colour herself and had never felt so fashionable. She hoped her hostesses would not be in silk. They walked through the Temple Gardens looking at all the undoubtedly elegant company.

She need not have worried about her clothes. Polly deposited her at the door and was off, and the little maid who opened to her knock took her straight up to the first floor of the narrow house which was only part of a much larger chambers. She could hear laughter and a murmur of conversation behind the door at the top of the stairs and the door was suddenly flung open. Here I go, thought Jane. She stepped in a little shyly and looked around the room, as Miss Henrietta March, clad in dark green linen and with a bunch of keys at her waist, came up to her with a careful smile behind her posed lorgnette.

Another young lady was sitting on a narrow sofa at the small window overlooking the gardens and two young men were occupied in smoking long peculiar-looking pipes as they sat by an unlighted grate with their feet on two footstools.

'Ah, Miss Banham!' said one of them and got to his feet. It was Philip March. 'Welcome to the Hatchery,' he said gaily and, pointing to his friend, who also got hurriedly to his feet, 'Meet Christopher Cornwall, our new poet.'

The other young lady turned round and beckoned to Jane to sit beside her. 'I am Charlotte Howard,' she said in a friendly manner. 'Do sit down and Henrietta will call up some tea.'

It was a plain but airy room and Jane felt immediately at home. Charlotte Howard, perhaps, looked a little like Snetters, although of course she was younger – about twenty-eight – and had brown ringlets at each side of her rather long face.

'Philip has told us about you, and that you are interested in his – our – venture.'

Jane gathered herself together. They were being very kind and she hoped she would not disappoint them by some ignorance or inelegant manner of her own. Yet they were very casual in their own manners. At last this was the world of books and plays! Perhaps she could become part of it! She answered with her customary vivacity, hardly knowing the effect a fresh, enthusiastic girl might have upon the rather weary habitués of Temple Court.

'How did you find *Julian*,' Henrietta asked her, coming up and taking a seat near her friend Charlotte. Philip turned his chair towards them and his friend went back to his contemplation of the fireplace.

'I thought it was very fine – well acted I mean – and I enjoyed the tragedy, though I suppose I should not have, but . . .'

'But?' said Henrietta.

'It did not seem to connect with any life I know. Hamlet and Miranda and Imogen I can understand, but these people . . . I wanted to believe in them, but I could not,' she concluded rather lamely.

'Bravo! She has put her finger on the weakness of all attempts to import classical subjects to the English stage,' said Philip. 'Did you know, it came off after only eight performances?'

'Oh, I'm sorry!' replied Jane. 'I thought it was

51

sufficiently interesting to be written by a woman – a lady – and she will be upset, I suppose. What will Mr Macready do?'

'Don't worry about him,' said Henrietta laughing. 'They say he is going over to Drury Lane. You must see him in the Shakespeare you love.'

'I thought he was too good for the play,' said Jane, taking courage from the fact that the others had listened to her opinions seriously. 'He has such a marvellous voice. I suppose it was that – his voice – that excited me, though it was all new for me, Miss March. It is years since I went to a theatre and then it was in a little market town, though my governess told me I saw Edmund Kean, in truth!'

'You must tell us about your county and your life there. Philip is intrigued – he did not know that Mr Stone had a niece,' said Charlotte.

Jane answered a few questions about her life hitherto, which she was sure her interlocutors would find boring, and the talk turned back to the stage and then to Philip March's great new venture, his *New London Review*.

The poet, Christopher Cornwall, roused himself when the dishes of tea were brought in by a little maid. He looked, Jane thought, rather cynical and she was curious as to what he wrote. Never before had she been amongst people of her own age – or not much older – who seemed to know what they wanted and knew how to talk about matters that interested them all. They passed from a discussion of Wordsworth, universally pronouncing him finished and stale, thereby to Coleridge, whom Cornwall had met in the poet's self-imposed isolation in Highgate, and it was Henrietta who mentioned Lord Byron. Where-upon a sanctified silence fell until Philip spoke of the death of the infidel Shelley the summer before, and then

52

how the new poets had been robbed of another great talent who had also died in Italy. They spoke of old critics of whom Jane had never heard and young writers whom she expected to come into the room any moment. Philip outlined his plans for his *New London Review* and spoke of money and offers and printers. Jane was wondering when he would leave her uncle's business and wanted to ask him, but he forestalled her by saying, quite abruptly in the middle of a diatribe against the old *London Magazine*: 'Your uncle has subscribed, of course, but he must have other friends who would sponsor me. I can't keep on asking him at the Counting House.'

'He has many friends,' replied Jane as her cup was filled once more with the delicious amber liquid. 'We met one of them at the theatre.'

'Then he must subscribe, too. We are counting on you, Jane. Whenever you are in society with your uncle and aunt, you can put a good word in for us, *n'est-ce pas*?'

Charlotte Howard said, 'It would help of course.'

'Charlotte has respectable connections,' said Philip. 'They are not, however, willing to aid our project. Money, damn it! – it's the worst thing in the world when you haven't got it.'

'And can be the worst when you have,' said Charlotte quietly.

Jane did not give the name of Frederick Digby to Mr March, but promised that if he were to be entertained in London by her uncle he should be approached for a subscription. 'But you must let me see what they are letting themselves in for,' she smiled, thinking she was not going to be taken for a fool, even if she were useful in milking the cow.

'Philip and his friends have manuscript copies of much

of the projected first number,' said Henrietta. She wore
an abstracted air, Jane thought.

'Do you write, too?' she asked her impulsively.

Henrietta smiled enigmatically. 'My brother and I are
both poets,' she said. 'And Charlotte here does our proof
reading, and Christopher savages everybody.'

'Can you be an editor *and* a poet?' Jane asked Philip.
'I should have thought it needed a rather different form
of talent.' He looked at her rather warily perhaps, thinking the little country cousin was more intelligent than he
had supposed. 'I mean – I am very ignorant of these
matters,' Jane said hurriedly. 'In the country I read a
good deal, but of course it was rather old-fashioned. I
know nothing of editors and poets, you see.'

'It is a question of harnessing the available talent,'
replied Henrietta. 'The time is ripe for change in many
matters, and particularly literary ones. Of course, there
are the established reviews – they say a new review has
just started up in Cambridge – but London is so dull now
for the young. We think many young men and ladies
would like a change. They cannot be reading *Ivanhoe* for
ever.'

'Oh,' breathed Jane. '*That* we did have at home. Have
you read *Kenilworth* and *The Heart of Midlothian* and
*Waverley*?' Here Jane was on safe ground, though Philip
and Christopher groaned.

'It is all *passé*. Granted they will always be popular
among the reading public, but what about our *young*
writers?'

'And our *lady* writers?' interposed Henrietta.

'There are hundreds of writers – better at tragedy than
Miss Mitford, I'll swear, who never get a chance to be
read. That is what we shall do: provide a place for them
to take their first faltering steps in public,' said Philip

54

grandly. 'It has always been my dream, you see – to start up some sort of movement as they do in Paris.'

'Ah, Paris!' murmured his sister.

'Writers need readers,' went on her brother.

'And printers and money,' said Christopher, as from the depths of sleep.

'Come now,' said Charlotte Howard. 'I shall send for more tea. We must not bore Miss Jane. Tell me, Jane, what has most struck you since your arrival in our metropolis?' She seemed to be speaking seriously, and Jane pondered her answer. Was it the noise and the dirt and the crowds of people or the theatre or the confidences of Louisa Collins? It was all such a jumble. She would need years to catch up with these sophisticated new friends. For they did seem friendly. She felt she would know them always, though she was still a little uncertain why they had invited her. Perhaps the girls, if you could call the imposing Henrietta a girl, were pleased to make a new friend. What or who *had* most struck her in the few months since her arrival? Was it the size or the grandeur of London, or even being invited to join these young aspirants themselves? No, curiously enough it was none of these things. What had remained in her mind was the figure of that auburn-haired young man who had shouted out the line of Byron to her on the night of the play. She had never seen him again, but he had affected her strangely.

She replied to the question. 'It is difficult to say. I have seen odd-looking people and many poor people and there is an atmosphere of – I don't know what – menace, perhaps, in the streets which are not fashionable. I did not know that there was so much misery in the world. I don't mean people dragging out their existences in fear – or not quite that – but just some unaccountable moments

55

when there seems to be a mask torn off. I saw a man . . .' she stopped.

'Yes?' encouraged Philip. They were all looking at her. She felt foolish.

'I saw a strange man near Covent Garden. He was rather drunk, I think – in his cups anyway – but he looked at me and I wondered – it was just for a split second – if I had known him before . . .' She trailed away and looked down, feeling foolish for having revealed herself. But the new friends throve on mysteries and unaccountabilities.

'The stuff of art,' breathed Charlotte. 'A strangeness in the air. I know what you mean. It is rare for us to meet a person who can see our London with new eyes. We must appear strange ourselves to others.'

'So many people are strange to us,' said Henrietta. 'We cannot know very much of what goes on in people's lives.'

Philip was silent for a while and then he said: 'We ought to have a fresh young mind sketching her impressions of London today, you know. What about you, Miss Banham? Impressions of a Provincial, eh?'

Jane thought that he might intend to be a trifle rude, but said nothing. It was Henrietta who pursued the idea. 'Sketches of the metropolis – you know, that could be a good idea, Phil – from the point of view of someone new to the place.'

'Why not try, Miss Banham?' said Charlotte. 'If you write as well as you talk.'

'Why not then?' said Philip after another pause and a look at his sister. Then they drank more tea and no more was said.

After Charlotte had played the pianoforte to entertain them and a cake had been demolished, particularly by Mr Cornwall, Polly arrived for Jane and Jane returned to her uncle's in a reflective mood. Why *not* try to write some-

56

thing down? She did it often enough in her letters to Snetters and Rose. Perhaps try to describe the effect of Covent Garden on her, or the feelings she had had of being lost in this great tide of people?

But the next day Edith had one of her headaches and the boys were clamouring to go out.

'I'll take them, Aunt,' said Jane. 'We can go for a walk in the Fields.'

'I want to feed the hansom man's horses,' said the youngest boy, Johnny.

'Then you shall,' said Jane gaily, and went down to the kitchens for a carrot or two. She had plenty to think about as she walked along with the boys. They seemed to obey her quite well, she was surprised to find; perhaps she had the ability to be firm without being angry, though they may have sensed a will of iron under her apparent agreeableness.

'Shall you go to the theatre again?' asked Jimmy, the eldest boy, when she had gathered them together on a bench in the Fields, the cabman's horse having been fed to the satisfaction of them all.

'If anyone asks me,' replied Jane.

'I shall ask you when I am grown up,' said Tommy. 'I want to ride in a circus. Do you think I should need Latin for that?'

'No, you would not,' replied Jane with a smile.

'Was your papa an actor?' asked Jimmy.

'Why no, my papa worked on the land with a big landowner surveying and building.'

'Could I do that?'

'I should think so.'

'Would that need Latin?' asked Johnny.

'Well, my papa did not know any,' she replied truthfully. Fancy them thinking her papa was an actor! It was

57

true, she admitted to herself, that she had wondered whether her 'real' father was an actor – for she was so unlike her papa. But that was impossible. She knew she had been born a year after her mother had married her father in the little village church at Caston. Romantic dreams would not do. She must gather herself together and think about her sketches. It was too hard to concentrate with the boys, who were tireless conversationalists. What they needed was activity. What *she* needed was a little time to herself.

Did she find Philip March attractive? If he had thought he was challenging her, well she would accept the challenge. And if he had not spoken seriously, well – what had she to lose? Perhaps Henrietta March and Miss Howard were wanting to encourage her. She had the idea they were rather 'blue' in their opinions and liked the idea of a woman writing something. Philip was rather intriguing, but she did not think he had taken much notice of her.

Accordingly she sat down over a large quire of paper which Hal had given her and the quills she had brought from home and tried to begin.

But whenever she tried to think of London she found herself thinking of Norfolk instead, of its wide flat fields and the great trees which stood sentinel at their edges or lonely in separate grandeur, waving green in summer and stark black in winter; of the sight of the little cottages in the village with their flint or pebble walls and tiled roofs and of the apple trees in the orchard at the hall. Now that summer was coming she imagined the fields growing green and then yellow with the harvest and the flowers growing in the gardens – the dusky clovers, the tall hollyhocks and the trailing convolvulus major. She remembered the wood where the Babes – a boy and a girl – had been abandoned, according to old legend, by their wicked uncle, a story which had curdled her blood as a child with its unhappy ending of the children found dead, close together, embracing under a tree. And she remembered the gulls coming wailing over the saltwater mere and the lonely sound they made, which had given her strange feelings in childhood. It was all so long ago now, that childhood – or seemed so – yet it was paradoxically nearer to her here in London than it had been for years. She remembered, too, the fields and lanes under the winter snows and the frozen ditches, and how Papa had once taken her sitting in the saddle in front of him with his arm round her on a cold February day. Poor Papa. Had she loved him enough? If she imagined she were back in Norfolk looking at London, it might be easier. She must stop daydreaming and write. She made a great effort and began. And, once she had begun, she found the words flowed easily.

A letter from Snetters arrived for her a few days later in answer to one of her own. It was in Snetters's inimitable style – full of information and injunctions and bits about her reading and even rather involved speculation about religion and the state of England. Snetters was wasted at the Rectory. It should be *she* who was to taste the delights of London and meet people with a taste for words. Snetters was not a country cousin, but a thinker. How lucky she had been to have been educated by her, Jane thought, with a stab of surprise at not quite realizing this before. Without Snetters her style would have been unformed. But Snetters was more interested in ideas than in London.

I should be interested to know (she wrote in her tiny angular writing) what your uncle thinks about the Evangelicals. I gather your grandfather was one such. Or perhaps he is more interested in the new economic theories? You might learn something from him, though I gather visits to the theatre are probably more to your taste. There must be so much going on in Town. My reading has to serve me here for the stimulus of other minds, as you know, is sadly lacking. Is there a radical spirit still in London? Do you go to church regularly? Does your uncle speak of the new 'scientific' inventions at all? I am most interested in all that is afoot. I do hope you are finding time for reading. You said you intended to go to a bookshop nearby and I hope your allowance will stretch to some books of verse, if not to political treatises or philosophical enquiries which are more to my taste than yours! Tell me of what you are reading and thinking, for you know that this county of ours is a backwater as far as the life of the mind is concerned. My brother in Norwich tells me, however, of a Unitarian family who have a brilliant daughter your age who intends to write of Religion.

My uncle from the north arrived yesterday and is full of the new mills which they are building up there. Meanwhile I walk out and see Thomas Tooke's boy scare the crows. Letitia Gooch was delivered of another babe on Saturday – the child is puny – I went to help with the box of Parish swaddlings, but I fear he will not live to grow into them.

The dandies and aristocrats you wrote of seem to have impressed you, my dear. It is a strange world, with one fiftieth of it arrayed in gold lace and the rest scrabbling for a living, is it not? Do not mention my radical sentiments to your uncle or he will think me an unsuitable correspondent. I await a letter from you with great interest and send my deepest affection to you once more in your new life. Do not forget the old one, or your devoted – Sybil Snetterton.

PS Tell me of your scrapings and grazings against life and others. The writers you speak of – particularly Miss March – sound very suitable, but the lives of writers are not, as you write, 'Romantic' dear Jane. That is your imagination. I believe that Scott is of a very sober and businesslike application. Perhaps Miss Mitford's play will be printed and then I can read it and see whether I agree with your estimate. SLS.

Snetters was what they called a 'blue', thought Jane, on rereading this missive. Poetry did not move her, nor novels, as much as theories about life. Well, she would try to reply in an intelligent manner and perhaps look for the works of some lady writers who might interest her old governess, names such as Miss Edgworth and Joanna Baillie and Mrs Barbauld and Mrs Opie. She must save a little money to send on to Norfolk such of these works as Snetters had not read.

But the letter made Jane thoughtful, too. She must try to extend her acquaintance. As for Uncle Hal and church-going, he was not at all like the son of a parson – or perhaps he was! The family attended church only once on a Sunday at Edith's insistence and she had noticed no currents of Evangelical enthusiasm lapping at the doors of the house in Lincoln's Inn Square.

Her second visit to the theatre was rather different from her first. She had been invited to attend by Philip March. Dusk was later now so they were able to go in full daylight to the great pillared and porticoed building in Drury Lane. The dandies were not there in such large numbers as at Covent Garden, or perhaps the evening entertainment, an old-fashioned comedy, was not to their taste. She gathered that Philip was only accompanying the young women in order to stare at Miss Julia Jeffrey who played a minor character. Henrietta appeared not to hold out much hope for her brother's chances with that lady.

In the first interval they had walked in the salon and just for a moment Jane had thought she had glimpsed the tall man who had spoken to her after her visit to Covent Garden. But she could not be sure. There was such a crowd pressing in every direction and she was too small to look over it.

Again, when they came out, she wondered if one of two men lounging against the wall outside the pit entrance could have been him, but he had disappeared when she looked more closely. Perhaps her imagination was over-heated.

Her uncle was to take her next morning to shop near Regent's Street for Edith who was slightly unwell. The post had brought great news for Edith. At last an invitation to spend a few days at Vine House, the residence in Hertfordshire of Mr Frederick Digby, whilst her husband discussed business there with his client. The letter was brief. It also invited Miss Banham, to pay a short visit if she cared to accompany her relations to the country. Jane was less than delighted. She was just beginning to feel ready to explore a little more of London, and Vine House would probably be mortally boring and its manners stiff and starchy. Still, she could not decline the invitation and so went willingly with Uncle Hal to the expensive bow-fronted shops north of the Burlington Arcade to purchase a roll of silk for Edith who must, positively must, have a new dress for the visit to Hertfordshire. How different this was from the village shop in Bedon which sold bread and shoes and tea and cheese and tape and ribbons and bacon, all mixed up! There was a circulating library in a bookshop near the arcade, and Hal was to leave Jane there for half an hour whilst he went to his club, once the silk had been bought. This was riches indeed. She made an effort to choose what would suit her aunt and then, once the parcel was packed for delivery, entered the bookshop where all the latest publications were enticingly laid out for sale or lending. Philip March had told her it was one of the best places to buy books so she was determined to browse there. There did not seem to be any young ladies in the shop, though there were quite a number of middle-aged ones who were either serious-looking and respectable, or of a higher social rank and fashionably dressed, with their footmen standing by outside. She wanted to buy a small book for the March family to show her appreciation of their kindness in taking her to the theatre. It was true Philip March could be very irritating – she smiled when she thought of his obvious infatuation for that young actress Julia Jeffrey; he had spoken of nothing else in the cab – but he seemed kindly disposed to her in the manner of young men with occasionally better things to do.

Perhaps she ought to buy a work of evangelical piety to improve herself? This was not very enticing. She moved to the novels and the slim volumes of poetry and saw that the Scottish baronet and Miss Austen were still the rage. The owner was seated at the back of the shop on a high stool, occasionally conversing with some favoured customer. This would be something else to describe to Rose. There were bound copies of literary reviews stacked at the side of the shop next to the poetry – perhaps one day the *New London Review*, editor Philip March, would be one of them. Henrietta had said last night that Philip would often go into Joy's coffee house after taking his sister and her friend home from the theatre. Why could not girls go to coffee houses if they could write plays and novels? *Some* girls did – but not the sort who wrote plays and novels, on the whole!

She turned over a copy of Lord Byron's *Beppo* dreamily. It had been sitting incongruously between a *Lyrical Ballads* and a *Poems of Coleridge*. She must look for that other Shelley's book – Mrs Shelley's *Frankenstein*. Philip had said it was to be made into a play. She took out the Wordsworth for the moment, having replaced *Beppo*.

'That's a dead bore,' said a voice at her elbow and she looked up, startled. Standing by her, apparently engrossed in another Byron, was – Oh heavens! – a tall man with a quiff of dark auburn hair. Had he spoken to *her* then? Did etiquette demand a reply or that she should ignore him? And which book was he talking about? And to whom? She looked round. There was no one else standing near her. 'I saw you: "She walks in beauty",' he said. 'At Covent Garden. You won't remember. I never forget a face.'

'Yes, I do remember,' she answered before she could stop herself.

He had a bruise under one of his eyes. Perhaps he was drunk. But he did not seem so. 'I am a poet,' he said. 'And I talk too much. I beg your pardon – but you must not read Wordsworth at your age.'

What an extraordinary person. But she found him alluring. Snetters's voice murmured inside her: 'A "Byronic" young man, Jane. Beware!'

'May I not read Wordsworth *and* Byron?' she asked.

He smiled. 'So long as you prefer Byron. The Wicked Lord, eh? Tell me your name, Miss . . .'

'It is Jane Banham.'

'Charles Fitzpercy.' He looked at her with very deep, dark hazel eyes. 'Jane Banham – I shall remember.' Then he bowed with a smile and was gone before she could say anything at all.

She found herself trembling as she put the book back on the shelf. To steady herself she reached for a Miss Edgworth. She must find out more from someone about 'Charles Fitzpercy'. He had intensified the mystery by speaking to her again, and whetted her interest and, it must be admitted, roused her to something more than mere interest. But they were off to Hertfordshire in a day or two. What a pity!

# PART TWO
# On the Threshold

Daisy Collins, Louisa Collins's niece, was sitting talking to her grandmother Rebecca Smith in the back kitchen of the little house in Ironmongers Row. Gran had wanted her to run a few errands for her, and, as the old lady was always well provided with sixpences from the money she had earned telling fortunes, Daisy was pleased to give her flower-selling a miss for the day and let her younger sister take it over. Daisy was seventeen, bonny and black-haired, but her voice was gruff from shouting out her wares and from long exposure to inclement weather. They were discussing the young man who had just left and Daisy was trying to persuade her grandmother to let her into the secret of his fortunes, for Daisy Collins liked the young 'nob' whom she called Mr Fitz.

Outside, the London air was smoky and cloudy. 'He's off to 'ampstead, I s'pose,' said Daisy. 'Wish he'd take me with 'im. Some of them nobs take to girls like me you know, Gran!' She could say anything to her grandmother, whose favourite she was.

'Go on, lass!' replied Rebecca. 'No good comes of mixing with folk like him! Not that he's not handsome, mind, but he's not one for the girls.'

'Lovely velvet weskits he has, though,' mooned Daisy. 'They say he's a lord, down the Market. I know he goes to that nobs' club where they gamble their fortunes away.'

'He hasn't *got* a fortune,' replied Rebecca, stirring some tea in a little flowered pot. Her Gran was always so neat and tidy, thought Daisy. She was a mystery really. A gypsy, she always *said* she was.

'Well, he's not like some of them swells,' she went on. 'Go on, Gran – what's his fortune to be?'

'That's confidential,' said Rebecca.

'Oh, Gran, you can tell *me*. I won't split. Who's he going to marry? Or don't he ask you about that?'

The old woman was a long time before she answered. 'No,' she said finally. 'He don't ask me.'

'What does he ask then? About money and such like? He must have worries or he wouldn't come to you, Gran, would he?' she wheedled.

'I daresay he has his worries, your Mr Fitz. You said he gambles – well he does! You drink your tea and then you can run a message for me to that house on Drury Lane. There's a lady wants advice about her baby.'

'Go on, Gran, what did you tell him? You know a thing or two about him – you always do. See it in their palms, don't you?' she teased. Daisy did not believe her grandmother saw things in the palms of her clients – it wasn't the hands that did it. More likely Grandma was good at summing folks up. She was a shrewd bird even though she was a queer old thing.

'Going to bring him luck, then, are you?' said old Rebecca. 'There's more luck in the cards, girl, than in the hands.' She pointed to a pack of cards of a strange design with pictures Daisy had seen nowhere else. But there was another pack with the ordinary diamonds and hearts, too, on the table near the bird cage. 'Perky's quiet today,' said Rebecca, nodding towards the linnet which seemed to be asleep. 'You know I keep the "knowledge" to myself, so don't go asking me for things I can't tell you.'

'Well, I know he spouts verse because he's spoke to me like as if he were in a play. He comes and goes round the

Garden like a jack-in-the-box. Where does he live, Gran?'

'If you're so clever, find out, girl. We don't discuss that sort of thing.'

'It's my opinion he lives all over the place.'

'Come on, girl, get my taters ready. Then you can go on that errand for me. And your ma would like some thread, I know. They're busy up there.' 'Up there' was the floor above where Daisy's mother and sisters worked at their dolls' dressmaking and their millinery.

'Saw him down Offley's the other day,' Daisy remarked, as she peeled the potatoes for the old woman.

'Did you now?'

'Yer, with some of them dandies – crikey, they look like girls with their waists all pinched in, and walking like this!' She gave a spirited imitation of the dandies prinking along in their padded shoulders, and Rebecca laughed.

'He ain't a dandy, your Mr Fitz,' she said. 'Leastways, I'd say he spent more time in the Harp than Offley's.'

'Oh, so he's "my" Mr Fitz now, is he?' said Daisy, her eyes sparkling. 'D'ye think he'd take me to Highbury tea rooms, then? He ain't no lush, I'm sure. To a nice little garden for tea-drinking with me best boots on and a rose in me hair.' Her grandmother laughed and then idly shuffled her cards.

'Red pavilions, red pavilions, they are the hearts,' she said. 'And diamonds in the dust.'

'What did you say, Gran?' Daisy peered over the table at the woman's little brown hands.

'Hearts and spades are kindred spirits for him,' she muttered. 'That's what I told him if you really want to know, girl. And now run away, and ask your ma for the money for the thread. You can have sixpence if you come straight back.'

'Go on, Gran, what did that mean?'

'What it said. Keep away from the clubs and the diamonds, I said to him.' She looked up at the girl, her eyes narrowed, and for a moment Daisy was almost afraid of her. Rebecca took the little pile of coins which Mr Fitz had left for her and put them into a padded purse she kept in the linnet's cage, having extracted sixpence for Daisy. The purse was of a scarlet material like the curtains of her kitchen, with little pieces stitched together in the shape of hearts and diamonds like patchwork.

'I'm tired,' she said. 'Off with you.'

Reluctantly, the big girl went out, after looking at her grandmother for one long moment.

'Don't go falling for him, dear,' cackled the old woman. 'Nothing would come of that.'

Daisy believed her as she went out. Gran always knew best, whatever she said.


Charles Fitzpercy was already halfway up Camden Road by then. He was thirsty and a little tired but he was still musing over the old woman and what she had said to him. I suppose it's a lot of nonsense, he thought. She probably makes *her* fortune through the cards, but not mine.

On each side of the road now there were patches of wasteland and built-up streets. As he walked up in the direction of Hampstead, he saw half-marooned rows of little houses with scraps of gardens where runner beans were grown and the clothes dried, and round the corners, rows of larger dwellings of the artisan and small trades-men variety. He wondered at their lives. His had been far removed from even minor gentility. Passed between noble ruins and housekeepers' lodges and Mayfair demimonde residences and London tenements, his life had been odd. Still, he had never had to pretend to respectability, and

70

his allowance had come, often late, but still come, from his dead father's attorneys. At least he assumed Percy had been his father, dead now with no explanations. It had been a sort of revenge at first to spend the allowance on gambling. He had worked though, too; he had sung for his supper. Why could he not escape from all this unwanted past, and from his own nature, and become a professional man as surely he had the ability to be?

He decided to call on a friend near Well Walk and tramped across the open Heath now, on a grassy path, and sat for a moment under an elm tree. Great clouds were scudding across a grey-blue sky, the clouds themselves edged with silver. Here, high up, the London smoke had gone away. There was a light westerly wind and in the distance the clouds were piled up like suds in a washerwoman's bowl. He sighed and took out his notebook, which accompanied him wherever he went. He scribbled some lines about the sky and the Heath before getting up and strolling, hands in pockets, to the further edge of the Heath where the land dipped and the houses of the Vale of Health hid themselves. He could talk to Michael. Michael knew him only as a writer – knew nothing of his past or of his inner life. They would sometimes sit for hours in Old Slaughter's Coffee House discussing life and dreams; that was his respectable self and often his happiest. Michael knew no other side of him. Michael did not perhaps *want* to know. He had a wife and children to keep in the small cottage out at Hampstead and newspaper journalism kept him busy. Yet not too busy sometimes to roam the Heath with Charles and come back by Downshire Hill, always looking in one of the gardens of the houses there to see if Mr Constable the painter was still at home. They would stop at an inn nearby and finish the day over beer, or brandy and water, and Charles would walk back to his other life which seemed a fantasy when he was out on the Heath. Which was his real self and why did he have this split in his life? He would have liked a life like Michael's, but it was an impossibility for him. Was it his true nature which he concealed? And if he did, what was the nature he presented to Michael and his family? He would listen to Michael's stories of the young genius who had died in Rome two years ago and who had himself walked the Heath and wonder whether that nature, too, had been divided. Other poets would pass them on long trudges to friends even further away from the Great Wen. And he would think: I shall pack up my bag and leave Town and rent a small room or two and forget, but he never did and once he was back in London the healthy life faded, though it was only a few miles away: and he would be back in the dark alleys and the crowds and the vice, so tempting, so cheap and so easily arranged. Could he be any different? He doubted it. The old woman had not offered much hope with her hearts and love and diamonds and money – and spades and death and clubs and fighting. Today he felt he wanted to settle his spirits after the dark session with her. Daisy's grandmother had disturbed him; it was as if she knew all about him. Yet he had not gambled for weeks, had escaped the attentions of the Wilkins mob and had spoken to that pretty girl in the bookshop. All good things. His senses were filled with mingled depression and excitement which he knew too well presaged either a drinking bout or a hunt through the alleys followed by self-disgust and another attempt to write himself out. It was all the fault of that damned father of his. Only friendship might calm him down and put his life into perspective. Charles Fitzpercy, bastard.

* * *

72

Frederick Digby's house on the borders of Hertfordshire and Buckinghamshire was a lovely Queen Anne building with pleached walks set inside a high wall of mellow brick not far away from a sleepy village. It had Dutch gables with little windows pierced in them and other long Georgian windows added at the end of the previous century. It was, in fact, the Dower House, which his mother had used to occupy. Only forty miles from London, it was yet another world and one which puzzled Jane a little. They were not the only members of the house party, of course; there was a Miss Tovey, a lady of a certain age who, wrapped in many layers of silk, was wont to entertain the company with 'renderings' of Cowper and Goldsmith – and even the Bard. She did not seem to be an actress and Jane wondered if she were a poor relation. Miss Tovey was, in fact, an ancient governess of Digby's sister, taken under the patronage of another family with theatrical connections. There they had discovered she had a talent for the reciting of pieces from the poets and she had been presented at various drawing rooms as a sort of curiosity. This had in no way disconcerted the lady and she was now apt to perform her elocutionary efforts at the drop of a hat. She was tolerated for old times' sake by Frederick, who had a kind heart. The rest of the company was middle-aged and seemed willing to be entertained. There was a baronet, Sir William Dalrymple and his wife Lucy, and an older lady, Miss Theodora Champneys. They all seemed glad to be of the company – the London Season was not to their taste and was, in any case, drawing to a close. Jane guessed they must have been friends of Frederick's father and mother, now alas perished, and whose graves they had been taken to see in the adjoining churchyard.

'I'm afraid it will be dull for you,' Frederick had said to

her on the first evening of their stay. He seemed a little distrait himself. No mention was made of his wife, Clara, after a few perfunctory enquiries from Lady Dalrymple. 'She is well, ma'am,' Frederick had replied and had changed the subject.

Aunt Edith was enchanted with the house and the small park. 'He is a younger son, of course,' she confided to Jane. 'Hal tells me he was meant for the Bar, but he has spent a good deal of time in France. His wife is the daughter of a nobleman, they say. Of course, Mr Digby comes from a very old family, though not a *noble* one.'

At dinner that first evening the talk had been of the neighbouring countryside. Jane was surprised to find that her host did not hunt. He loved the country, but had some mysterious obligations in Town. On certain matters he was very definite. She looked at him as he spoke, comparing his attentive manners with those of Philip March, not exactly to the younger man's advantage. Frederick Digby was easy to talk to. He gave the appearance of actually listening to whatever you had to say. She supposed it must be his breeding. With Uncle Hal he talked Parliamentary reform and with the ladies the education of the young. She supposed he had no children, as none was mentioned. He was a great theatregoer, too, and was well up in all the gossip, though it seemed to Jane that perhaps it bored him slightly. Maybe he felt he must make an effort to take an interest in the world of fashion. He was of medium stature and had a youthful fairness when you would have expected grey. His eyes were slightly hooded at the corners and his mouth was full beneath an aquiline nose. The eyes were grey-blue complementing his fairness, and his hands were those of a practical man. She noticed how his expression would change when he played the fiddle to entertain his guests.

He played rather well and was also a sharp chess player. Then his face would again take on a different look and the hood would come down over his eyes, and a slight frown appear between his fair eyebrows. He drank little and she noticed he treated his servants well. Even so, this paragon had other attributes. She saw he was susceptible to the charm of pretty women and that he found Miss Tovey's 'pieces' a great bore. On the second evening, after he had been closeted all day with Uncle Hal, he came up to talk to Jane as they sat after dinner in the small drawing room.

'I do not know Norfolk,' he began. 'Tell me about Norwich.'

'I did not live in Norwich,' replied Jane. 'I went there only occasionally. My father was a bailiff. We lived in Bedon in Breckland . . .' She hesitated, wondering perhaps whether she should not have mentioned what to this gentleman must seem lowly origins.

'I have visited the county but once, I believe,' he said. 'When I was a lad and some sparks of my acquaintance held a coach race with the mail and the Norwich Flier. It was quite the fashion in those days. Of course, now everything is so much swifter – our old records would be laughed out of court. It took us two or three hours to cover thirty miles. But I do not remember Breckland.'

'Thetford is the nearest town to my home,' replied Jane. 'Though that is not very big. My father moved round the county, but we stayed in Bedon.'

'And your papa is dead? I am sorry. Your mama too?'

'Yes, Mr Digby.'

'May I call you Jane?'

'If you wish,' she said guilelessly.

'Now you come to mention the place, I believe I *did* go

75

once to Thetford Races,' said Frederick Digby. 'It was during my misspent youth. Before Waterloo it was – '

'I was there just after Waterloo!' interrupted Jane. 'I remember Papa took me, and the boys and girls raced and there were donkeys, and a bonfire where they burned the effigy of Napoleon. I remember because my papa told me some boys had been caught stealing handkerchiefs, and I wanted to know why they would steal them – and then Papa would not let me race with the village children. It was a happy day though.' She stopped, aware she had interrupted him, but he did not seem to mind.

'Was your mama from Norfolk then, too?'

'No, Mama was Uncle Hal's sister. She . . .' Jane stopped once more. It was difficult to know where to stop and what to say. She had never spoken to a man like this before. He seemed different from anyone else. 'She married my papa after she left Hampshire,' she concluded lamely.

'And you are happy with your aunt and uncle?' enquired her host.

He was rather surprising, did not seem to follow the *convenances*, but she supposed rich gentlemen could say what they liked. 'I *am* grateful to them for I should never have seen London else,' she said. 'They have taken me to the theatre, as you know, and I have been shopping and viewing the sights. I have made friends, too, through Uncle's Counting House. A young man called Mr March works there – but he is wanting to start a new literary review.' Suddenly she saw her chance. 'I believe you are a great reader, Mr Digby. Uncle has told me of your own writings.'

'That was years ago,' he laughed. 'What is the new review your friend is planning?'

'It is with his friends. I believe they want to rival

Cambridge with a platform for new writers. There are no papers where the young are encouraged,' she added earnestly. 'Of course, they are trying to put up the money first. It must be difficult in such a great city to make one's name.'

She thought she would say no more. It would be too impolite to importune Frederick Digby for a subscription.

'You must ask Miss Tovey,' he said rather maliciously. 'She would recite your editor friend's verses – if he writes verses – wherever she goes. She's quite famous for it, you know.' He looked round before lowering his voice in mock conspiratorial fashion and then said: 'But I wish she would not mangle the Bard.'

'I did not know that ladies did "perform" in this way, although Uncle asked me to read aloud to him,' said Jane. 'I would rather read Shakespeare for myself – even, perhaps, rather than go to a play of his.'

'Some of the best of the Bard is not entirely suitable for the boards, even with the help of Dr Bowdler! Do you know the Sonnets?'

'Why yes – my governess introduced me to them and I often read them.'

'Look in my library tomorrow – browse there – it would be a pleasure to assist you in the cultivation of your mind.' He bowed. 'Take any books you will.'

The conversation had taxed Jane to the utmost, even though he was such a pleasant man. She hoped she had not been found wanting and that he had not thought her forward either. Perhaps she should not have mentioned Mr March, but Frederick had been quite rude about Miss Tovey and seemed to think she would agree with him.

For his part, Frederick went away from Jane's side with feelings which surprised him. She was only a little thing, young and perhaps naïve, but what a refreshment for the spirit! He would be pleased to think he could aid her in her entrée into some sort of Society. And what had she said about that clerk March? She had been animated when discussing her friends and the theatre, animated in a way he had long ceased to feel when all the weight of the weary world was upon him. Perhaps he could change, and learn to be happy again – though he doubted it. He wondered what she had been going to say about her mother and asked Hal when they were alone together, smoking. Hal told him, a little discomfited.

'So I might have seen her mother then? I was a great stage-struck young cove.'

'I doubt it, sir. My sister was, for the most part, working in the provinces.'

'I expect your niece was her best production then?'

Hal laughed. '*She* seems to have got herself involved in some literary venture – at least, she's not involved but interested. It's hard to know what to do with a young woman. I expect I shall find the same problem when my Betsey is twenty.'

'Has she no suitors then?'

'None, or none who has approached me. Of course, she's not been with us long. I don't believe there was anyone in Norfolk she was averse to leaving.'

The two men puffed away and the conversation turned to the gentleman's five per cents and his investments in spices.

After a time, the business talk having been concluded, Frederick left his guest walking in the garden with the baronet and his wife, and went upstairs to his dressing room.

He kept thinking of Jane Banham. She had made a gallant attempt, he thought, to entertain his elderly friends who seemed a little bemused to have such a girl as

78

a fellow guest, so narrow were their apprehensions of the world. When Jane had said she wished she could have gone to the Thetford Free Grammar School and how unfair it was that the education of girls was so neglected, they had looked as though she were a most dangerous radical. And yet he himself in France, and even in London, had heard much stronger sentiments expressed even twenty years ago. Perhaps they were all going backwards and would end in some evangelical canting house frightened of change. The girl Jane was lively without being argumentative and he was amused by her. Hal Stone had saved him quite a lot of money recently and it behoved younger sons of the gentry to take the advice of their financial betters. A bonus if, in addition they had pretty, intelligent nieces. He could not help thinking of his wife, Clara, who was also handsome but of a very different character. Had *she* ever wished for more education? Probably not. Educated to make a marriage, she had found him – and he never ceased to regret it. If only he were twenty again, how differently his life could have turned out. But at twenty he had been at Oxford and it had taken all his willpower to escape the trap his family had set him in the form of reading for the Bar. Instead he had fallen into other traps culminating in his attempt to behave well by marrying Clara Monteith of a poor but aristocratic family. He saw again the face of his little dinner guest trying to look interested in the talk of bank failures and foreign wars – or perhaps she *was* interested? – you never knew with some women nowadays. The ladies of the *demi-monde* were keen on their investments, he knew. Jane Banham was not of that world. He saw her in the world of the Shelleys – he had known Shelley slightly at Eton – and Shelley's relict had written that book about a monster. Women could and did write, even without the

79

benefit of grammar schools. Jane Banham had admitted to having had a governess. He was curious about her. Not for years had anyone so interested or captivated him. He must not let his mind dwell on her, for that way lay danger, but never had he seen a countenance half so alive. He stared in the glass at himself and saw in his mind's eye the light playing through her golden-brown hair like sun on pools of water. And those dark-blue eyes, so deep and soft, the way blue eyes so seldom were. In his youth he had been a connoisseur of eyes. And her creamy-clear skin stretched over her rather high cheek-bones. And the dimple which played round her mouth. And the exuberance, yet tinged with sadness, which pervaded her presence. He must stop. She was only a young girl of not particularly good family. Pshaw! – what did that matter? She was a beauty. No! This was decidedly going too far. He tried to laugh at himself and only succeeded in grimacing. Obviously he needed the refreshment only a woman could bring. His wife had parched him up. Yet he was not a rake. He had had his debaucheries, but that was long ago. With an effort he fixed his mind upon his far-away wife and wondered what she was doing under the Florentine sun. But that, too, was not a particularly pleasant thought. He was a fool, had always been a fool, and perhaps would make a fool of himself once more. No, he would not! He would talk books with the young lady and try to interest himself in that new review she had spoken of. That was the right idea!

The next afternoon Jane was sitting in the library whose door Mr Digby had so kindly unlocked for her. It was a cornucopia of good things and she hardly knew where to start, so she looked for something familiar and found an old brown volume amongst the various books of Shakespeare which were handily disposed near a desk and obviously much read. The little book was, Jane thought, at least from the last century or earlier, for it had the old spelling with its double s's and with delight she saw it was an edition of the Sonnets. She settled down to read on a long sofa which looked out of place in such a room but was comfortable. The sunlight came glancing in through one of the long windows, catching motes of dust in its rays. She hoped the other ladies did not mind that she had absented herself from their company in the sitting room they used when the men were out riding or walking. And they were going back tomorrow, so there was no time to lose. What she would not have given for such a library! It was far more extensive than the one at the Rectory. It even possessed copies of *Blackwood's* and the *Edinburgh Review* and she wondered if her host was a connoisseur of ideas as well as a landowner of sorts. Poor Philip would appreciate it – yet, on the other hand, she found herself wishing that Philip March had the accoutrements of wealth and taste so that his *New London Review* would gain from such a library, where, with time and imagination, something could be drawn up far away from the rigours and expediences of Grub Street and the little house in Temple Gardens. Well, she would do her best for Philip. How slight her own knowledge would appear to Frederick Digby, steeped as he must be in the knowledge of the ages. One part of her would like to live and read and think for ever in such a library. But she had the thought that Shakespeare himself was not the product of a nobleman's library, but had garnered his poems from direct experience of the world. Perhaps all great writers were like that? She might still have hope. She began reading the Sonnets from the beginning and, for the first time, realized that they made a pattern – of love and jealousy and divided loyalties. It all seemed to make a new sort of sense which was speaking directly to her. Yet she could not exactly say what it was. Certainly the poet constantly evoked time and love, love and time, and his obsessions were repeated over and over again. There was a savagery about it which pleased her. But it was mingled with such grief – grief not only about lost love, but about time. Easy tears came to her when she read 'Time will come and take my love away.' She found she was thinking about her mother whom time had stolen away from her. Other sonnets repeated 'how hard true sorrow hits' and she found the tears still in her eyes. How strange that tears she could not shed years ago should be waiting to be called up by these words. She should be weeping for her father who had died such a short time ago, but she could not get him into focus.

She turned back to the verses. No wonder Mr Bowdler had altered them. 'Incapable of more, replete with you.' She felt passion curled in herself, ready to unwind. But for whom? The strange young man, Charles Fitzpercy, came then into her head and seemed to lodge himself there along with the sonnets.

She heard a footstep at the door and a knock and was startled to see by the grandfather clock that she had been reading for well over an hour. Uncle Hal came in.

'I thought you would be here.' He smiled. 'What are you reading, my dear?' He took the book from her and read, '"Thou art thy mother's glass, and she in thee/ Calls back the lovely April of her prime:"' He put the book down and looked at her. 'I never heard that before. Is it Shakespeare?'

'Yes, Uncle, the Sonnets. Mr Digby told me I might come here and read.' She looked at the book he had put back on the table before her. 'There is everything in the world here, Uncle,' she said. 'Not like that play *Julian*.

82

Now I know what was wrong with it. There was no real feeling in it and the words *said* nothing.'

'"Thou art thy mother's glass,"' he repeated. 'Though *she* did not look like *you*, *you* look a little like her. I suppose he means that youth recalls youth?' He cleared his throat, unaccustomed to reading and speaking such things.

'I was just thinking about her when you came in, Uncle. Was she very beautiful? I know I am not beautiful.'

'It is youth which is beautiful, my dear,' said her uncle awkwardly. Now, perhaps, she thought, they could have the 'talk'. But he seemed to have no more to say and there was a silence. 'I am come to fetch you to a dish of tea – ' he was beginning, when there was another tap at the door, which he had only half closed, and their host came in.

'I am glad my library finds such visitors,' he said amiably. 'I hope you found something to your taste, Jane?'

'It is Shakespeare,' she said. 'We were just coming, sir. I am sorry, I forgot the time.'

'And I should have sent a footman to bring you. No, it is seldom I have guests who can amuse themselves.'

'Please may I take the volume up to my room?' asked Jane.

'Of course – if first you will read me what you liked best. Miss Tovey is not here and the tea can wait.'

Uncle Hal looked a little astonished, but hastened to say that Jane read very well and Jane took the book and opened it. She did not want to choose a love poem which might embarrass the men so she read them a sonnet on time – as though she were at the Rectory reading to Snetters. The words seemed to place themselves in her throat and the pauses came at the right moments, almost

83

unconsciously. When she had finished, Frederick said nothing but looked at her and she wondered if she had annoyed him by her choice.

Then, after a pause, he said, 'That was indeed a pleasure,' and they went out to the others. But a little later he came back to get the volume which Jane, in her confusion, had left behind, and he read: 'So thou, thyself outgoing in thy noon,/ Unlook'd on diest, unless thou get a son,' and then shut the book firmly with a grimace and a sigh.

In London the sun which had been gilding Hertfordshire with a pleasant halo of breezy light was casting shadows on the grass of the Temple gardens. Philip and Christopher were walking there, and now and then one of them would stop to make a point whilst the other paused with him before they resumed their slow perambulations.

Philip March had always had a good deal of energy. He had been a precocious youth and had suffered bitterly when his education had been interrupted by the death of his father. Almost immediately after the funeral he had been sent to the City to clerk and now, eight years later, he counted himself lucky to have made the contacts necessary for entry into the literary world. But it was hard. He longed to give in his notice and devote himself heart and soul to his ambitions. They had always been with him, ever since he could remember, and misery and straitened circumstances had only intensified them. With the death of his mother, who had gone to live with his aunt in Surrey, his sister had returned to him, and Henrietta was made of stern stuff. She had governessed, and in the course of her duties had met Charlotte Howard, a runaway from the world of country houses and grand living. The two girls were inseparable and Charlotte had effected some sort of reconciliation with her father on

84

condition she embarrassed them no more at home. She received an allowance which, together with Philip's paltry wages, allowed the three of them to survive in the old chambers which, by some miracle of law, were still in the name of his father, and the rent of which was low. But Philip knew he must strike away soon. The girls would be all right. Henrietta had insinuated herself into some genteel family in Twickenham, and their circle was widening. They even spoke of opening a small boarding establishment for children in Fulham. Now was the time to gather together all his resources and strike out. Plans for his magazine struggled with plans for his own life. Patrons must now be approached and coddled.

There was scarcely time for the needs of the flesh, though they were a burden to him. Women were attracted to him, he knew. His own tastes led to actresses and to the scraps of humanity he picked up in the less salubrious districts of the vast metropolis, milliners and suchlike. They left him feeling triumphant but also disgusted and he was aware that he must curb his sensuality if he were to concentrate all his emotional resources on his other plans. A rich wife would be very well but any other would be a burden he was not prepared to take up.

He had recently met a young spark from Cambridge with an adequate, if not brilliant, income, a man whom he felt would do great things. Perhaps they might do them together? He had talked in coffee houses with many men of this type but he never gave himself wholly to their whims or concerns, preferring to reserve some part of himself on which he could rely if the new friends let him down. He had great hopes of Jane Banham's uncle, too, and others of his rich friends. It was fortunate that Hal had been a friend of the deceased Mr March and had contacts in the world of trade and quickly acquired wealth. He knew that he could be asked to take on more responsibility for his employer, for he was quick and clever, and that could lead to a life of ease. But he wanted the satisfaction of editing his own journal in a different world from that of trade. He was steeped in the literary quarrels and cabales of the century, and had the instinct for acquiring prestige through listening to older men who themselves had money or a little foothold in the literary world. It would soon come to a choice, sooner perhaps than he had imagined. He must adventure forth and give all his time to his projected magazine and say goodbye to his high stool at the Counting House. Old 'Elia' had not yet done it but he, Philip March, was going to prove he could become famous in a few short years without the benefit of parental money or Eton or title – through his native talent alone.

Christopher Cornwall had been on a visit to Cambridge to see his brother and the young man Philip had met earlier, and had brought back news of the review which several undergraduates were preparing.

'We've got to get ours out first,' said Philip after listening to his friend as they strolled round the gardens.

'How can we?' said Christopher mournfully. 'We haven't enough subscriptions promised.'

'Then we take a gamble. The printers won't put their bill in straight away. I shall ask my employer – he's a genial old boy – for a loan or a guarantee as soon as he returns with Jane. And *she* may have found us a patron. I wouldn't put it past her. She can turn those big blue eyes on to some baronets or marquesses, I'm sure.'

'You'd sell your grandmother for a subscription,' grumbled Christopher.

'Yours will go in of course and my own "Prospect for Literature" . . .'

'Are you going to take up Miss Banham on her "Provincial Letters" then? They might be a *succès fou* – something else to ensure sales – even if she has no talent, which I suspect is not the case.'

'I have not yet read any of her productions,' replied Philip stiffly.

The two men betook themselves to Philip's rooms.

'What do you say? Give me a month and the Counting House sees me no more.'

Christopher looked at his friend with narrowed eyes and seemed about to say something, but thought better of it and relapsed into his usual slumberous attitude so that when Charlotte and Henrietta returned from their shopping with the little maid, the men were sitting in their customary postures, Christopher before the empty grate and Philip at a table in front of a mass of manuscripts, writing a letter to be copied and sent to all those whose patronage he had sought.

'Then you take it down to Chapman's in Fleet Street with the guarantees,' Philip was saying. 'And tell them to be quick about it. There's no point waiting. I shall see Hood tonight and his friends. It's July, the end of their damned Season and they'll be gawping for something to take away with them when they leave London. Then we get a mention in the *Literary Review* and before they've recovered, the second issue is ready.'

His enthusiasm even seemed to galvanize the lymphatic Christopher, and the girls were even more excited. At last Philip would burst upon London!

When Jane arrived back in London with her aunt and uncle, she found a letter from Charlotte Howard, who seemed to be the business head of Philip's enterprises. The letter asked whether she had written anything for Philip's new venture, 'as they had discussed it at their last meeting'. Jane went to her room and read through all her attempts at writing her 'Sketches to a Country Cousin' and at dinner that day Hal intimated that Philip March had already touched him for a small guarantee. 'He says you are to appear, Jane, my dear. I had no idea you were a writer.' Jane murmured that perhaps Mr March was being a little premature as he had not yet seen her piece. Privately she thought, He thinks he'll get some money from Uncle by dangling my talents before him. What if he doesn't like what I've written? But at least her first piece would achieve the promise of publication, however bad it was. Once Philip had secured a loan, he might drop her. This annoyed her mightily and she spent all the next day rewriting and polishing up her offering. Let him see how she could write! Charlotte had also enquired in her letter whether Jane had managed to secure any more interest in the project from friends of her uncle, obviously hoping that Jane had secured Mr Digby's name on a list of future subscribers. She felt a little worried about this, for Mr Digby might think he was being used, but resolved not to think about it, and went on with her work. It did occur to her, however, as she wrote, that perhaps Charlotte herself had some interest in Philip and that was why she was so assiduous in carrying out his instructions. Philip was ambitious and Charlotte was ambitious for him.

Hal offered no objections to Jane's appearing in the magazine. If March thought she was good enough he would be delighted, he said. Edith appeared to be a little more surprised, however.

'What do you write about, dear?' she asked next

morning when Jane came down with her neatly copied
out offering to send to the mail.

'It is only my impressions of London, Aunt – just a
trifle. Mr March wanted me to write of my visit to the
theatre, and as I was writing home on that very topic, I
thought I might use my ideas.'

'Hal does encourage him rather. My husband is always
kind to young people. I'm sure you write very well, dear.'
Perhaps the girl was interested in young March or Mr
March interested in Jane? She had better keep her eyes
open.

Jane guessed that these thoughts were going through
Edith's head. It was too absurd. She had no interest in
Philip March beyond his encouragement of her writing –
*she* could use people too! Other women might find him
attractive, she supposed, but she did not. His physique
was not disagreeable to her, but she knew she was not the
sort of girl such a young man might court – unless, of
course, she were an heiress, which she was not. He'll put
in my little piece just to please Uncle Hal, she thought
again. It was rather mortifying and she awaited Charlotte's reaction to her little parcel with some trepidation.
All Hal said, like his wife, was: 'I'm sure you write well,
my dear.'

How could such an easy-going man have made money?
Of course, in large matters of business he was likely to be
not so easy-going.

She had to wait a few days before the reply came and
tortured herself with self-criticism. Would they say that
she had put on a tone of slightly gushing naïveté which
was not her own? It was near enough to her enthusiasm,
so the difference might not be noticed by anyone but
herself.

If only she could write about the one person who had

intrigued her since her arrival in London. She sat in her little room at the top of the house each morning before going down to the family and allowed herself to dream as she looked out at the trees in the square, and wondered where he was, and if she would ever see him again. What was it about him that made her heart beat fast? His manner to her had been familiar – but not frightening. He had teased her – but gently. Yet he was not a gentle person – that much was obvious. If she were Walter Scott she could make him into the hero of a Border romance and describe his quiff of auburn hair and his elongated, rather melancholy face and dress him in doublet and hose and let him nurse a dark secret . . . Was not 'Fitz' an appellation given only to the bastards of kings?

Jane already had some closely written sheaves of paper which she had brought with her from Norfolk and a little book in which she noted impressions and turns of phrase. Something occurred to her almost every day. Perhaps one day they would be the Collected Works of a Country Miss and Charles Fitzpercy would read them and come to see her when she was famous. Even Snetters had never seen her literary productions. When she reread them they filled her with alternate pride and shame. They were written on paper her papa had once given her from unfinished ledger books and they reminded her of the old life, and of Papa too.

On the afternoon of a day which had dawned with a shower of soft, fine rain, and when there had at last been a reply from Charlotte, not Philip, and mentioning a 'surprise', Jane went out with Polly to the Temple Gardens apartments. She had refused Hal's carriage, for she needed the walk to calm herself. It did seem as though they were taking her seriously. She was not quite sure whether they were going to accept the piece, but the letter *had* said: 'Your offering was much appreciated. Do call to discuss it with us and take tea.' Perhaps they wanted her to alter it – or this was just a polite way of rejecting her? But they needed her uncle's money!

Christopher Cornwall opened the door to their knock, and Polly was off before Jane could dismiss her. In the inner upstairs room she saw Henrietta and Charlotte and Philip sitting at a table along with another young man, a Mr Bruce, to whom she was immediately introduced.

'Bruce has come over to the enemy camp,' Philip greeted her. 'May I present Miss Banham, our "country cousin". Jane, this is Edward, fresh from Cambridge.'

The young man was rather dandified and arrogant-looking, she thought. He looked at her, though, with a frankly interested glance and shook her hand before sitting down again and returning to one of a mass of papers spread out before them. He was well-dressed certainly, and in spite of the arrogant appearance, well-mannered, she discovered – better mannered than Philip March. He was a handsome man, too, with an air of melancholy. Afterwards Jane wondered why she was not more attracted to him. Perhaps Charles Fitzpercy had inoculated her against all comers? Bruce had, too, the slightly affected accent which she had noticed in some of the guests at Vine House. It was certainly not like Philip's accent, or her uncle's, not like the actors' either, whose expression was more a matter of placing undue emphasis on unusual words than in the matter of a drawl. But he seemed a pleasant enough fellow, and when he forgot to be shy, spoke in a rhetorical manner with great vitality. He was prone to swift changes of mood, talked 'smartly' and then seemed to jump into gloom. He certainly seemed very young, not much older than herself. Perhaps that was the trouble. She had found very young men – Philip

91

particularly – extremely self-absorbed, never listening to others but waiting to say something themselves. Mr Bruce could dazzle – she could see that – dazzle better than Philip could, and if the fair Julia was not to become entangled with *him*, it would need more than flattering words to her from Philip.

She noticed all this as she observed him. From what she could gather the conversation was moving from his interest in gypsies to his knowledge of High Society. He seemed a little uncertain, as though he really was nursing some despair. Yet it was not like Charles Fitzpercy's despair. *His* seemed to come from the depths of himself while Bruce's, she learned later, came from having been rejected in love – or at least prevented from seeing a lady love of his as a schoolboy. Philip was suitably flattering to Bruce – he name-dropped 'a young barrister friend of mine' and 'as Byron said to a friend of mine many years ago'. She was amused. Apparently the *New London* needed this young Bruce as much as he needed it. When Philip mentioned Byron a shadow seemed to pass over the face of the handsome Bruce and an expression of melancholy seeped into his eyes, which were large and dark. He seemed rather self-sufficient and even a little complacent. She saw that his ambitions matched Philip's. How ambitious young men were! This Mr Bruce would go far – she was sure of that. How interesting it was to meet these young men, but something in her was always ready to judge them. Young ladies were perhaps rather less open to her criticism.

'I shall make tea,' said Charlotte Howard. 'You will not need Henrietta or me.' Jane was longing to ask what was the surprise she had been promised, but held her tongue.

Philip was counting up from a long sheet on which were written the sponsors and willing subscribers. Jane knew

Uncle Hal was amongst them, but Philip's next words astonished her. 'Here's the letter from that Frederick Digby – he underwrites us for fifty pounds. My God, that's generous! Your doing, I suppose, Jane.'

'I did not know,' she exclaimed. 'I mentioned it to him and – about you – and I believe he asked me for your address, but I did not think anything would come of it.'

'You underrate your charms, my dear,' answered Philip, which made Jane feel she ought to blush, but blushing was, unfortunately, something which she had never been able to accomplish. Shock would rather lend a pallor to her cheeks.

'We shall make it, my friends!' shouted Philip, and Christopher sighed noisily.

'It is all down with Chapman – they promise Saturday for the galleys . . .'

'*Your* piece was much appreciated,' said Philip, busily searching under a mass of letters and sealing wax.

'Tell her you are going to use it,' said Henrietta peremptorily. 'Really, Phil, you are very *dégagé*. You don't want your contributors going elsewhere.'

Edward Bruce looked up. 'Indeed not,' he remarked sardonically, 'although there is no reason I can see why a new writer cannot publish his – or should I say her – writing in more than one place at once, provided, of course, it is not the same piece of work.' He smiled at Jane.

Philip looked momentarily ill at ease. 'Come, come, old man, we are sure of *you*, I hope?'

Bruce bowed. 'Unless you want to publish my romance – it's rather long for the *New London* I'm afraid!'

He turned to Jane who was sitting looking from one to the other. 'I read the thoughts of the young lady from the provinces upon our London theatre and thought they were very just – they will add a little *soupçon* of – what shall I say? – mystery, particularly as they are written by a lady. They will think it is Mrs Bowles, I wager.'

'Oh no!' cried Jane. 'I wish I could write like her, but I am only a beginner and know nothing.'

'Except you know how to conceal your art,' said Bruce, who seemed to have taken a fancy to her writing.

'Sometimes,' said Philip in a lordly way, 'it is better to be young and fresh – the mind takes impressions then like wax . . .' Jane thought how he was, surely, not more than a year or two older than herself!

'Are you not going to tell our contributor a little more about her fellow contributors?' asked Henrietta, coming up to the table with Charlotte, who was balancing a tray on which sat a green glazed teapot and some shallow cups.

'Aha!' said Philip. 'Your mysterious stranger. I was sitting last week, as is my wont, at the Slaughter's coffee house when up comes a tall young man – a tall young man with auburn hair. He dumps a great wad of paper at the place of your humble servant with a "I hear you need poems?" and off he goes without another word. I take them home after enquiring from the proprietor who it was. As I had thought, it *was* that Fitzpercy – or so he calls himself – and he looked like the man you described.'

'Oh no!' breathed Jane. She had gone quite pale. 'He does write then – I wondered – ' She stopped, confused. She was not going to tell Philip March about her meeting in the bookshop and indeed wished she had never told him anything about Charles Fitzpercy.

'News passes quickly in the coffee houses. Some friend of a friend, I suppose, tells him I am soliciting manuscripts – I take home a wad and open it sitting over my nightcap which Henrietta so kindly brings me – ' He bowed to his

94

sister. 'And without beating about the bush I can say that the *New London* will be privileged to publish them – not all of them, there are nigh on a hundred sets of verse – extraordinary stuff. It seems he wanders at night in strange places and sees strange sights. It is not quite a *Frankenstein*, my friends, but a *Confessions* to outdo old de Quincey . . .'

Charlotte took the teapot and poured out for each a welcome amber stream.

'We thought it would amuse you. He is intriguing, is he not? They are strange poems, or prose passages if you prefer, but as Philip says, imbued with a sort of Coleridgean "imagination".'

'*We* cannot imagine,' said Henrietta, 'why he has not published before. We are not to use his name – this is between ourselves – but it was writ on the title page, "By the Eagle of Delevinge", and so we are to ascribe the pieces.'

'Charles Fitzpercy,' Edward Bruce was murmuring. 'There is something I know about him – I wish I could call it to mind . . .'

'Beddoes was telling me,' said Philip, 'that he chose that name for himself. Not Charles, but the other. You know they say he is the byblow of one of the northern noblemen of that name, but which of that family I do not know. There is a terrible melancholy in his writing, and a failure to avenge himself, then he denies that and writes of a Gothic castle where deeds lie hidden – but it is not all Mrs Radcliffe. It seems to come quite naturally, as though the poor chap's story is true.'

Jane was listening intently to all this. 'Fitz is the name the King gave to his natural sons, is it not?' she appealed to Henrietta, who looked slightly ill at ease.

'He is not the King's son, I am sure,' said Philip, 'but

95

that is what he calls himself. There is a good deal about his lost high halls and orphan state. It seems his mother died at his birth and the old Earl took him in – at least, I gather from part of the poems that a housekeeper brought him up in a forest lodge. Aye, it is as good as a Walter Scott.'

'Does he not look like Byron?' said Jane.

'Oh, then all the ladies will swoon over him. But seriously, I do not know when I shall see him again – he disappears like shapes on sand. All he left with the proprietor of the coffee house were the words: "If you have a message, tell my friend who sells roses on Henrietta Street."'

'He means the flower girl near Miss Jeffrey's house,' said his sister, teasing him.

Philip flushed slightly. 'How do you know where Miss Jeffrey lives?'

'Oh, stop picking at each other,' said Charlotte sternly. 'Ask the poor creature if she knows Fitzpercy and have done with it. He doesn't want you to know his lodgings, that is all.'

'He does *not* lodge with Julia Jeffrey,' said Bruce, picking at his teeth delicately.

After their little break for the 'cups that cheer', Jane was allowed to help Philip with his accounts and was given a receipt to give to her uncle signed with a flourish by Philip.

'I am leaving the Counting House,' he added as he gave it to her. 'I have written to him. I must commence work for the second issue – for, my friends, I feel that Grub Street is going to pay for once.'

Jane puzzled over the characters of Philip March and his friends as she went home with Polly, who had come to fetch her. It was a new and exciting world and she could not wait to see her own words in print. Henrietta and Charlotte seemed well-disposed to her too, thank goodness. How on earth were *they* going to live, though, if Philip cast his bread upon journalistic waters? The girls must have something up their sleeve, she thought, for she had intercepted a glance from Henrietta to Charlotte when he spoke of leaving the Counting House that did not exactly betoken resignation. But whatever his character as an ambitious man, she still trusted his judgement. When he spoke of his reading it carried the weight of an assured taste. She thought he would succeed in his venture. She knew nothing of the delays of printers and the vagaries of public taste. They had promised her a look at the galleys as soon as they arrived and, more than anything – even more than seeing her own *nom de plume* at the foot of her short piece – she longed to see the poems of Charles Fitzpercy. Philip had not shown any of them the longer poems, which were reserved for the second issue, in spite of their pleas. He liked to keep things to himself. Even Christopher, who had hardly taken part in the conversation, had seemed impressed. He had apparently been vouchsafed a reading and all he had said was: 'Genius or madness – or both, I think.' She did not think Charles Fitzpercy was mad.

Frederick Digby had come again to London and was staying at his house in Bloomsbury. This was told Jane by her uncle, when she informed him of that gentleman's subscription. 'That is generous of him, my dear, but his affairs are now settled,' replied Hal. What was fifty pounds to Frederick, or even to Uncle Hal? They did not live in Grub Street. Jane wished she lived there herself – perhaps she was halfway there? Then perhaps salons would open out to her as to few young women. Philip had

97

spoken of Miss Benger, her parties and soirées, to which he certainly intended to have himself invited one of these days.

The next day Jane went with Polly to shop in Covent Garden for fruit. She had begged to go with her: she was used to bargaining, and to cooking even. Not for her the idle life of the newly rich. Aunt Edith was puzzled, but allowed her to go. She was being troubled once again by feelings of debility and the doctor was a constant visitor at the house in Lincoln's Inn Square. Jane fully intended to pass by Henrietta Street and look for the seller of roses. And she wanted, too, to catch sight of Julia Jeffrey, purely from interest. It was as though she was trying to trace the sort of life her mama had led long ago, maybe on these very streets. Philip March was known, of course, to be making a dead set at Julia, although the lady had many lights of love. Jane had read a criticism of the lady's acting in a copy of *The Times* and had been able to imagine the sort of character a young woman might have who was an undoubted success on the boards. She was playing at Drury Lane along with Miss Foote and Miss Lacy, now that Macready had definitely taken over the new company there, as he had had differences with the management of Covent Garden.

She went down to the Strand with Polly, along the now familiar, noisy crowded streets and they made their way through an alley which gave on to Catherine Street and thence to the market. The costermongers were in full cry: 'Cowcumbers, cool cowcumbers!' and, 'Buy my lovely white sparrowgrass!' they were shouting, and the flower girls were out in scores now that summer had brought its blossoms on carts from the fields of Fulham, Earl's Court and Plumstead to the streets of London.

She managed to lead Polly in the direction of Henrietta

98

Street. If only she could sit down in a coffee house as the young men did, to read the gazette and eye the company. But she knew she was lucky even to be allowed out without a chaperone other than Polly, now that she was on the way to becoming a sort of lady. Writers, however, were not really ladies, she thought. Writers could talk to flower girls. She was unprepared, though, for the conversation which ensued.

At the corner of Henrietta Street, a girl had set up her wares on the cobbles and, as Jane came up in that direction, she noticed another girl was standing by the flowers, too, watering some blooms which had obviously just been fetched up from the market. There were lilies-of-the-valley and violets and some fresh, pink roses.

The older flower girl was a well-built young woman with a lusty voice. Jane hoped that this indeed was the girl who would take messages to Charles Fitzpercy. How to approach her. She felt a little shy of talking to this big, confident-looking working girl, who would regard her as a lady even though she had mixed freely with all the village girls at home when she was little. The only thing to do was to buy a few flowers first and then trust to instinct. She was not doing this for Philip March's convenience, of course, but out of a strong desire to find out more about Fitzpercy. 'Ask the little girl how much the pink roses – the little buttonhole buds – are,' she urged Polly.

'Old blush roses – old blush roses!' sang out the young woman, and the younger girl was holding what Jane recognized as the old pink moss roses that had grown in the Rector's garden and at Breckles Hall. For a moment they brought back the past in a sudden swift gleam, almost as though the London streets had gone away. What were those roses mother used to grow? She had

99

forgotten them till this moment: they had been in the garden under the window of her mama's sitting room when she was very little, a lovely creamy colour with a beautiful scent. They had seemed to go on all summer and she had stroked the petals and held them up against the sun when they fell.

'Blush or moss?' asked the girl when Polly asked the price.

'Have you any white roses?' asked Jane of the older girl.

'Not today, Miss,' the girl replied pleasantly. 'Try next week. There's people nowadays who like white, I know. We gets the pink'uns from Surrey, and they sell white in the market here. But buy them from me – I get the best blooms.'

Jane selected a few pink roses for Aunt's boudoir and impulsively said: 'I have a friend called Rose.' She thought the girl would say nothing as she busily wrapped up the blooms in thin moss to keep them fresh, but she replied: 'My name's Daisy, Miss. Called after the daisies on 'ampstead 'eath I was.'

'Daisy!' repeated Jane. 'Then you must be . . . Have you an aunt who sews – makes dresses? Called Louisa?'

'Why, yes I 'ave,' said the girl, looking up. 'Not been gettin' into no trouble, I 'ope?' with a laugh.

'She made me some lovely gowns,' said Jane. What good luck! Now she could ask about Fitzpercy.

'She's a wonderful seamstress, my auntie,' said the girl and for a moment they looked at each other curiously.

'May I ask you something else? It's not about your aunt – it's for a friend of mine. There is a young man,' she chose her words carefully, 'a young man who writes verse. A friend of mine wants to get in touch with him – to say they want to publish his verse in a – a book.' The girl looked at her rather stony-faced. 'They told him at the coffee house that this man – Mr Fitzpercy I believe he is called – had said you would know where to find him. They only want to tell him they'd like to use his verses . . .'

'I know 'im,' said the girl. 'I don't give no addresses, but I know where he is. You can tell me your name and I'll ask him.'

'Just tell him they want to publish him and give him this address.' Jane had Philip's address at the Temple Gardens ready written. 'Please give him it. We are friends.'

'But what are *you* called?' asked the girl and the other girl – now it was obvious they were sisters – came up. Polly looked from one to the other, mystified.

'My name is Jane,' replied Jane. 'Tell him – the girl in the bookshop.'

'Well I dunno. I don't know when I'll see 'im, but I will tell 'im, Miss. Will they pay 'im for them verses?'

'Oh yes,' said Jane, hoping this was true. 'He gave them to the man whose name is on the paper.'

'Tell you what – you come round here termorrow and I'll tell you if I've seen 'im.'

'Oh, thank you, Daisy.'

'This is Kate,' said Daisy, nodding her head to her sister. 'She's learning the trade along of me.' Kate smiled shyly. She had not yet learned her sister's easy ways.

'You can tell your aunt you saw me,' said Jane. 'But you needn't mention Mr Fitzpercy to her in my connection.'

'Oh, I wouldn't. Don't worry, Miss.'

'Is he a friend of *yours* then?' asked Jane.

'He talks to me – gets his friends to buy my flowers, and I 'elp 'im. You don't know 'im well, Miss, do you?'

101

'No, I've met him – seen him – only twice, but my friend is very impressed with his work. *Tell* him.' The flowers were handed over and paid for and they bade each other farewell.

'You didn't tell her he came over to Gran last night, Daisy,' said Kate after they had gone.

'It ain't nothing to do with her,' replied Daisy. 'Anyway, you know and I know someone had done 'im over. She wouldn't understand. What if I said Gran had cleaned up his bloody nose and put a pad on his black eye?'

'It was you that did that, Daisy!' said her sister.

What a stroke of luck, thought Jane. Now she would be sure to find out Fitzpercy's whereabouts. She was becoming even more attracted in her imagination to this man who befriended flower girls, and kept his address a secret, and wrote poems of a quality which impressed even Philip March.

And Daisy and her sister might lead her to other parts of London. How could she write of London if all she knew were the parts near the Temple and Lincoln's Inn and one or two theatres and the buildings of Mr Nash near the Regent's Street? She wanted to know where the poor lived. Daisy and her sister seemed respectable. How did you manage to keep respectable on the wages of a flower seller? What had Louisa Collins said? That all the children worked at something? She was quiet as she and Polly walked home amid the thronging ragged crowds all of whom were still mysteries to her. Unknowable. Well she must start to try and get to know them. Editors and gentry were well enough, but what about the people? Polly was quiet, too, then she said, 'Take care, Miss. You never know with folk like that.'

'It's all right, Polly. Mr March knows the man we're

looking for, and Miss Collins who came to sew – those girls' aunt – is very respectable.' As a *respectable* servant Polly was on her dignity. She was aware that Jane had more than a passing interest in the whereabouts of that Fitzpercy man. She wasn't born yesterday.

On their return they found the household in great excitement. Uncle Hal had found a school for the boys in Bloomsbury, so James, Thomas and John were to be settled at last.

It occurred to Jane that Daisy also probably knew of the comings and goings of the actors who lived near her pitch. It seemed to be a popular part of town for actors and writers and painters, just a few hundred yards from the insalubrious part of Drury Lane. How strange London was, with genteel districts cheek by jowl with dens of vice. Did Charles Fitzpercy live near there too, and why did he make such a secret of his address?

She was talking of London to her uncle that evening.

'Drury Lane is nothing to Seven Dials, my dear. You must promise me never to go into that part – to the slums near St Giles and Holborn – not even with Polly. Parts of this city are a disgrace to a civilized country.'

Yet Daisy lived *near* there. Perhaps every respectable street was also next to a dangerous one? Even men went to and fro in these parts of London with reluctance, unless for their own private reasons. There were knifings and muggings and no one was safe – particularly rich men, who might be robbed. Girls would suffer a fate worse than being robbed.

'Your aunt has never been anywhere without the carriage,' her uncle went on.

Jane felt the anomaly. Why, in Norfolk she had moved around freely! London could be a prison for a girl.

Jane asked her aunt if she might have the carriage on

103

the morrow to go to Mayfair to purchase some ribbon and some muslin. It was going to be a hot summer, she felt, and she wanted to look her best. Edith was lying down and murmured a tired, 'Yes, my dear, if your uncle approves.'

Then Jane sat down to think things over. It would seem that Charles Fitzpercy was extremely elusive. She dreamed of coming upon him and saving him from some unimaginable danger. She wished she were a flower girl or a milliner with the freedom to roam the town, if freedom it was. At home she would have walked for miles and the only carriage would have been Snetters's gig, which the lady drove herself. Uncle Hal's neat covered carriage with its two horses took her, or the family, shopping to places quite near. She imagined herself hiring a hack-chaise to follow Charles Fitzpercy – where *did* he live? And how did he spend his time when he was not writing verse? She imagined that he gambled. He looked a gambler. But to gamble you had to have money to begin with. He was a puzzle. Her new masculine acquaintances – and she counted Fitzpercy among them, along with Philip March and Edward Bruce and Mr Cornwall and Frederick Digby – were all so different. Still, Daisy Collins and Charlotte Howard were different, too: different from Snetters and different from each other. She toyed with the idea of describing Women about Town, and Men, ironically – including Daisy as a London lady, too – and comparing her life with that of Henrietta and Charlotte. It would be interesting to meet an actress, too, and the Jeffrey woman would do as well as any. Then she would have pen portraits both of women and of men.

She would write that evening when she came back from her shopping. Meanwhile, what if she could persuade the coachman to bring her back by the road that went by St

Giles – or at least near it? She could not, she supposed, ask him to bring her through Seven Dials, as the road would probably be too bad. This time she would ask for only a small divergence and then perhaps he would get used to taking her to different places.

So when she got into the carriage with a list of purchases for Edith and the boys – she must order some lengths of cambric for her aunt and some serge for the boys' winter suits – as well as the sprigged muslin for herself, and the ribbons, she would tell the coachman not to wait outside the various shops but to take himself off for an hour or so and return in the early afternoon and drive her back by Oxford Street and St Giles's Circus, for she was curious to see the Collins's household. The coachman would be glad of an hour to himself and might be willing to do this for her.

'I shall be some time, Aunt. I have much to buy,' she warned Edith. 'Polly will accompany me, and William is ready for our little jaunt.'

'You do not mind going alone, my dear?' sighed Edith.

'I shall enjoy it. Don't worry about me. I would like to *walk*, really – but there will be parcels and packages.'

Edith gave her a few bank notes. Jane was proving most useful and seemed to have no objection to running errands with Polly. When they got a footman, of course, . . . but Edith was beginning to feel that they would not get the footman till the boys were safely away at school and this was a headache. Getting them off and seeing they were settled would take most of the rest of the summer. The doctor had spoken of a holiday then for her; she was suffering a good deal from her chest as well as her head, and Italy had been spoken of. But how could she leave her boys? What if they were not happy at school? For the moment, though, things could be managed and the Collins

105

woman would come in for the sewing. If only she had a better establishment and one which fitted Hal's rising prosperity! And they had planned a house in the country, too; it was only her wretched health which made everything so precarious.

Jane explained her plans to William the coachman, who looked rather sceptical but nodded his head. The young lady had a way with her and he would take the opportunity of calling in on his mother whilst she was making her purchases in Mayfair. Jane wisely said nothing about their return route, reserving that for when William had been given his hour or two off. She and Polly sat looking out of the window at the crowded cobbled streets. Their progress was slow down to Charing Cross and then through St James's and up to the Quadrant and beyond. They passed by squares whose houses – some old, some newly built – were sparkling in the sun, and through the narrower cobbled streets behind the Burlington Arcade. The cobblestones were watered in the little fashionable streets and the orangey-yellow brickwork of the smarter houses, with their grey-blue slate roofs and yellow stucco fronts, were gay and inviting. Some had boxes of flowers in their windows and there were flowers, too, in the squares – red and blue plants which gardeners were tending. The whole district was gleaming and well looked after. The people in the streets were different, too: dandies and a few richly dressed ladies with parasols. She would like to have got down from the carriage and explored it all. But then they were on the ex-Regent's new street again with the great buildings glittering white. It was all so much lighter and airier than the old quarters where Uncle Hal lived – and farther from the City of course. Buildings were still going up in the distance. She sniffed the air when they got out. There were several young ladies shopping or walking the pavements in a leisurely fashion, but she noticed they were always with their mamas.

Jane had some money of her own from her father's frugal bequest to her which had been banked for her by her uncle. It gave her just enough not to feel too dependent upon the latter and able occasionally to make an independent purchase.

Polly was exclaiming at the bales of cloth laid out in the little bow-fronted shop. But Jane wanted to make all her purchases quickly and then run out of the shop and drink in the scene. It was only the third time she had been in this part of London and the shopping had always been done with Edith or Hal before. The bookshop could not be far away. She applied herself to ordering all that Edith wished for and choosing some pale green cotton with a pattern of a darker green flower for herself. She bought Polly a red ribbon for her hair and a green velvet one for herself. There was almost too much in the shop, none of it cheap. The shopkeepers were obsequious and ladies sat around fanning themselves whilst their footmen staggered out with their purchases. Eventually all Jane's goods were paid for and packed up. 'We shall call back in half an hour,' she told the bewhiskered assistant. This would just give her time for a walk before William returned. 'Come, Polly, we shall take the air,' she said. Polly was by now used to Jane's eccentric habits and followed her fairly meekly.

'Do you know St Giles's? It is on our way back if we choose to go that way,' she said.

'Oh, Miss Jane, don't tell him to go down there! There's terrible rookeries there. Carriages don't go through.'

'Yet it's only a mile away,' mused Jane. 'Do you not find it strange, Polly, that depravity should exist hand in

107

hand with' – she gestured to the piles of goods and the fashionable clientèle – 'all this?'

'Well, it's natural,' said Polly, puzzled. 'There's rich and poor, Miss. There's respectable folk and the other kind.'

Jane said no more. She could not imagine that the Collins lived in a – what had Polly called it? – a 'rookery'. There must be some streets which partook of neither vice nor ostentatious wealth. Ironmongers Row was probably on the fringes of the two worlds, for Daisy and her family were all in regular employment. William might go by the street – she could only ask him. In the meantime she would find the bookshop again. She intended to buy each boy a book which would be of use to him at school and had scoured the prospectus for Dr Macdonald's School to ascertain what was needed. Edith never seemed to think of such things.

At first she thought she was lost and it was only after a false move down towards the Quadrant and across the road that she realized the shop had been further towards the top of the Burlington Arcade. What a fool she was, wasting her precious time! She must study a 'carte' of the town or she would be getting lost every day. But they did at last come across the shop and Jane noted a church opposite which she had not noticed before, which would be a future landmark. She kept looking up once they were in the shop in case a tall man with a crooked smile should suddenly enter, but he did not. She looked for and found a recent edition of the Sonnets of Shakespeare in none too good a binding, but tolerably cheap, and then, after paying for it, browsed along the shelves. Perhaps one day her own name would be on one of the volumes: there were plenty written by 'A Lady' and they could not all be the same one! She must tell Philip March to circulate the bookshops with a notice of the *New London Review* if he had not thought of it for himself. It would be a good excuse for her further wanderings if she offered to do it. She wanted to know what she thought of as the 'real' London and who better to go with her than Charlotte or Henrietta? They must know it pretty well themselves. But London was not just this Mecca of novel sights and experiences: it was the place where Charles Fitzpercy lived and had his being. She told herself firmly to stop thinking about him. She did not know him, had only glimpsed him a few times. Why should she feel as she did? She was beginning to seem, even to herself, a lovesick girl and it was ridiculous. But she could not get him out of her head. Surely he would soon come to the Temple Gardens chambers to see his editor? What was she to him? Just a girl whom he had noticed, that was all. He must notice hundreds. There was Daisy for one. What had he said? Read Byron! She looked again at the shelves. Should she buy *Harold in Italy*? Byron was so clever. Had he written any new lyrics? She must ask Philip. Byron had not been encouraged in her schoolroom. Yes, Philip would know. He must be her literary mentor. Polly broke into her reverie.

'Miss, I think William will be waiting.'

With a sigh Jane agreed and they went back to the draper's and mercer's in the sunshine. William was indeed waiting faithfully in front of the shop.

'I am so sorry, William. Did we keep you waiting? I wonder if you would drive back another way. I want to see more of London. Could you go in the direction of the Oxford Road and return by St Giles? Do you know of a little street named Ironmongers Row? It is where our dressmaker lives. I should like to leave a message there,' she improvised rapidly.

William scratched his head. 'I can't go by St Giles, Miss. The carriage wouldn't take it, but the street you mean – I'd say it was not far from there.'

'Well, never mind if you can't find it. I should just like to see it.'

They clambered in. She must not get across William.

Striped awnings changed to dustier thoroughfares and here the crowds were denser, shabbier. The carriage passed by a church and then turned up a side street, and came to a stop after about ten minutes. William got down and knocked at the window. 'It's up there, Miss.' He pointed his whip. She looked across and saw a row of little houses leading off an even dustier street, but it was not dirty. Then she remembered she had forgotten the number.

'Just let me look for a moment,' she said. 'Polly, stay there. I shan't be a minute.' She descended and looked around her. There were children playing on the road and in many other narrow alleys leading off. She crossed the road and looked on the wall. Yes, there it was: Ironmongers Row with, appropriately, a large forge and accompanying shop at the corner and other shops all selling articles of kitchenware as well as stable equipment. She would never find the Collins's – but now she knew where to come. She returned to the carriage and they drove on, and she took particular note of the way home – which was not very far, for once they were in Bloomsbury the wider streets announced the district of the lawyers and professional men. How far were they from the City? She must ask Hal to take her to his work one day. He might agree. What a wonderful, enormous place this London was! She clutched her parcels again, which were tipping up all over their seat with the jolts and bumps of the

110

carriage. All in all it had been a most successful day and she was hungry. Polly smiled.

'Did you find it then, Miss?' she asked in a humouring tone of voice.

'I think so. We *must* get Louisa Collins in to do all the sewing,' replied Jane, her mind far from such matters.

When they arrived home, their purchases were forgotten for a time. Edith had suddenly been taken worse and her maid was bending over her with smelling salts and murmuring, 'We've sent for the Master.'

Mrs Ogilvie said: 'Poor lady, she must get out of London. There is a light meal laid for you, Miss Jane, in the morning room.'

Later in the afternoon Edith seemed slightly better after a visit from the doctor who had prescribed leeches. Hal was there in some distraction.

'What can I do, Uncle?'

'I'm afraid this summer is doing her no good – no good at all. Lawson thinks I must take her away. I think it must be Italy – and soon – when she can stand the journey.'

'I'm sorry, Uncle. She seemed a little better when I went in just now.'

'Oh, I am sure her health *can* be improved, but it is a worry with the boys. They will have to board sooner than I'd planned.'

'Mrs Ogilvie and I could look after them on high days and holidays,' Jane said.

'I thought you might like to come to Italy with us,' replied Hal hesitantly.

Italy! A few weeks ago and this would have been wonderful news indeed – a chance at last to see the world – but now? She realized that she did not want to go, that she must stay in London – for a sight of Charles Fitzpercy and for her own ambitions.

'Oh, Uncle, that would be too much. You and Aunt must go away together till she is well again, and I promise I can repay your kindness by staying here to help keep an eye on the boys – if Mrs Ogilvie would agree – you will not take all your servants with you, will you?'

'Jane, that is a most kind thought. I'm sure Edith would appreciate a member of the family staying here – and you *are* a member of the family now. You seem good with the lads . . . not that they'd be here during the week and, of course, Ogilvie would see to all the practical affairs of their lives. And look after you as well. Still, I don't like it. You're only twenty-one.'

'Why, Uncle, I am so happy here in London! Italy could wait for me, but you must go as soon as you can. If you will speak to Aunt and Mrs Ogilvie and the other servants, I shall be happy to aid you. I have been used to a degree of independence, you know!'

She seemed to convince him, for he went on: 'To cap it all, young March has given in his notice, but I have good clerks in my House and I can't blame the fellow. My business can carry on for a while without the younger fellows, I suppose, so long as the older men stay. I shall have to give power of attorney to a friend.' He sat sunk in thought. 'By the way,' he said suddenly as Jane sat quietly, thinking over the possible changes in his arrangements. 'I had another invitation from Frederick Digby. Shan't be able to go, of course, not with Edith in this state, but I thought *you* might like a little change and he invites you, too. In fact he says something about a party for some writer chaps. I don't know! Everything is happening at once today. Why not reply to him and tell him of your aunt's trouble and accept for yourself? He'd send his coach for you.'

Jane felt she could hardly refuse this invitation after

112

having, ever so firmly, rejected an invitation to go to Italy – though she thought that secretly Hal was relieved about that.

'Digby is a good fellow,' Hal continued. 'He will also keep in touch if we go away. But we must humour him a little: he seems to have taken a fancy to the idea of a little patronage. That young March is dropping everything. I hope he's not too sanguine, though, about his literary prospects. They tell me it's a risky business. I warned him when he spoke of leaving, but he seemed to have something up his sleeve.'

As Jane was sitting drinking her chocolate next day in the morning room with the boys, who were chewing bread and flicking pellets across the room, the maid came in with a letter for her which she had not expected. She had planned to write accepting Frederick Digby's invitation that morning after going in to her aunt and discussing it.

But when she opened it in her own little room at the top of the house, excitement mounted in her. The letter was from Charlotte Howard asking for more of her work. By way of a postscript Charlotte wrote that she and Henrietta were about to open a small establishment themselves in Fulham for the boarding out and instruction of young ladies. What a pity, Jane thought, that my cousins are not girls. That would be ideal for them. Henrietta must have been plotting this for some time. It would be Charlotte's money that enabled them to start up, surely, though they would still be genteelly poor.

Another letter was enclosed with Charlotte's. It had her name, care of Mr Philip March of Temple Garden Buildings, and she opened it curiously, not knowing the writing.

'Dear bookshop browser and Wordsworth reader,' it began.

I am lying low for the present but thank you for your kind enquiries as to my welfare. I did not know you were connected with March until the fair Daisy apprised me. I hear my ravings are to see the light of publication. I am not entirely content – he is sure to choose the worst. My Gothic poetry is my best as you would see if you read it. I expect soon to go north where my inspiration is kindled by sights known since youth. Daisy will be told if I return. The day I met you I had some little luck at the tables but since then, alas, and in spite of long walks for my health on the fair hills of Hampstead I have had a few little setbacks. Do not regard this letter as a precedent – your ways and mine are not along the same paths, dear Miss Banham, but I have been thinking of you.

I was intending to see Macready in *Hamlet* – your favourite play I am sure? – but fate has intervened. Perhaps another day? Please insist that March does *not* have my work signed with the name of – Charles Fitzpercy.

PS He may get in touch with me through Daisy Collins.

She read it through again and again, and found herself in a violent trembling. But he had written to her – he had not forgotten her! There was hope. Even if he was far away in the north, there was hope. She rose excited and impressed, glad that he was not ill and determined to keep in touch with the handsome flower girl in whom he seemed to repose such confidence. Was it unusual that he had communicated with *her* rather than with Philip March? Fitzpercy seemed to have an inordinate secretiveness in his disposition. What could account for it? He clearly wished his verses to see the light of day. 'The Eagle of Delevinge' indeed!

She decided to continue her second 'Letter to a Country Cousin'. If only she could discourse upon her new acquaintances rather than upon the theatre. She knew she had a lively style and just the touch which would go down well with the readers who, she imagined, would like to see themselves as witty and sophisticated and pleased to think they were seen as such in the light of a youthful provincial imagination. There would, of course, be condescension in their attitude towards her impressions – but she would have the last laugh, she determined.

Perhaps her own unjaundiced eye was itself of interest to any neutral observer: irony would be her intended tone at times, but humour *would* come breaking through! Her position was anomalous: neither of the people, not a 'lady', but with enough intelligence to produce a simulacrum of ladylikeness if necessary, and wrap up in it some criticism of manners – particularly of the manners which paid more attention to rank and appearance than genuine talent.

The March ménage and Charles Fitzpercy did not seem to belong to Society either, she was thinking, and yet they were all Londoners. Uncle Hal and his family, too, seemed to be somewhat uneasily perched halfway into the world of 'ton' and it was only money that enabled her uncle to have risen from the ranks of a provincial (though respectable) clergy family.

Money or talent were beginning to take their effect, though they did not touch the High Society of which Frederick Digby was a sort of habitué, and Charles Fitzpercy, perhaps, a tolerated hanger-on. Fitzpercy looked noble, Jane decided, and if the stories were true his blood was pale blue, if not royal blue. Actors were something else, paid to entertain all but the lowest ranks of society. Like writers and poets, she supposed. Would Philip ever attain the salons to which he clearly aspired? She hoped so for his sake. And his sister and her friend? Again, it was scarcely ladylike to have to work at instructing the young. If Henrietta were a man, Jane was sure that she would have been an editor herself. It was tolerated that ladies should write and she herself must use any powers within her ken to discover better how the world worked before she wrote about it; still, you could tell the time even if you did not understand the mechanism of the clock! She dipped her pen in ink and found herself, instead of developing this idea and applying it to the way London and its denizens and its shops and theatres and counting houses worked, actually writing a letter to Charles. I owe him a reply, she thought, and I can always give it to Daisy. I wonder if he has yet departed to the north?

'Dear Mr Fitzpercy,' she began.

I am so very glad that your verses are to be published, but I am sorry you are to leave London for the north of England, for I am sure that Mr March would wish to see you, as he is so delighted with the verses you gave to him. I am longing to read them myself. I have taken your advice and am to read the shorter poems of wicked Lord Byron. I believe there are some magnificent elegies. Oh, I should love to see Macready in *Hamlet* for it is the play above all others of Shakespeare which I venerate – and have done so since I was introduced to it by my governess. I am now engaged upon some writing myself. I am to do the impressions of a provincial girl (I come from Norfolk) in the great metropolis. Mr March liked the piece I wrote for him and all I do is extend the sort of letter I write to my friends at home and add a little pinch of wit when I can – and remove 'myself' from the scene. I do not yet know how I shall sign myself but you are not to say to anyone that you know the author. I am to keep secrets too! How I should love to stride upon Hampstead Heath myself – at times I feel very pent up here with scarce the sight of a tree. I thank you for writing to me and I hope we shall meet again on your return. Yours ever, Jane Banham.

I wonder if he is alone, she thought. He is probably dallying with some light of love. She found the thought painful and surprised herself. How little did she know about him, yet there had been that instant sympathy

116

between them, and she was sure he had felt it too, although it was only chance which had put her in his way that night of her first visit to the theatre. Should she mention these speculations in her 'genuine' letter to Norfolk? Perhaps she might just hint. She would not wish Snetters to be worried about her, and the mention of Charles, as she now found herself calling him to herself, and of Philip, not to mention Frederick Digby, would be sure to arouse speculation in that lady, however unworldly she appeared. She knew Jane had a headstrong nature, although there had been scarcely anyone on whom to expend her feelings in Bedon, save, some years ago, a handsome preacher who had visited at the Rectory but who had disappointed her youthful ardour when he was found to eat his soup with a loud slurp.

Oh, dear, she must stop writing and help Aunt Edith with her preparations for the removal of Johnny and Jimmy and Tommy to school and discuss with her the wardrobe she would need for her journey to Italy. The time was not yet quite fixed. Edith had rallied a little but the flush in her cheeks was a little suspect and Hal was seen to regard her with a very worried expression.

She visited Charlotte once more later that week, hoping to see the proofs from the printers of her 'Letters to a Country Cousin'. The March household was in extreme disarray when she arrived. Both the young ladies were to be seen behind a pile of prospectuses: they were excited at their joint venture. It was surprising that they had kept it a secret – even their brother had not known of their plans. He for his part was eager to hear of his ex-employer's reactions to his suddenly leaving the firm.

'He is not surprised, I think,' she replied to his questions. 'He knew you were always intending to go, and he is so good-natured he does not grudge it.'

117

'Oh, there are plenty of fellows needing work as clerks,' replied Philip airily. 'He will not miss one.'

'I hope you will not regret it,' said Henrietta with a frown on her forehead.

'Christopher is to move into the Chambers here,' said Charlotte to Jane. 'Some money has come from his mama and he is to take over the managing of the printers, leaving Philip to edit and solicit manuscripts.'

'Has Mr Bruce been again?' Jane enquired.

'No, he is gone on a walking tour among the gypsies! I never had much hope of him. I believe he would like to have a journal of his own and it is only to make his name that he is using my brother.'

'Your article will be ready tomorrow,' said Philip. 'It will be sent to you. Now let us have your news.'

She was disappointed not to see her work yet set up, but obliged by recounting the news of Hal and Edith and their projected stay on the Continent.

'Why, everyone is off abroad,' grumbled Philip. 'You will not go with them then?'

'No, I am to stay with the housekeeper and overlook the boys at weekends and holidays.'

The talk passed to the plans Henrietta and Charlotte had made. Jane wondered how long they had been wanting to do something of the sort. ''Tis a pity you won't take boys,' she said. 'My nephews are just off to school. They are taking the little girl to Italy with them.'

'When do they go?'

'As soon as all can be arranged. My aunt is not at all well – she needs a drier climate.'

'Oh, my dear, would you not like to go with them?' cried Henrietta.

'No, no, I am content in London – although I must confess I sometimes miss the country air.' She thought of

118

the real reason for her lack of interest in Italy and wondered where he was. As though divining her thoughts Philip said:

'Charlotte tells me you have been talking to flower girls.'

This made Jane's heart leap up, but she controlled herself and replied:

'The flower girl you spoke of took a message from me to Mr Fitzpercy about the acceptance of his poems – as I told Charlotte. I told the girl to tell him of your pleasure and I had a little note from him – now, where is it? – oh! I must have left it at home. All he said was not to use any name he is known by but to publish anonymously.'

'That's a pity,' said Philip. 'It's bound to come out sooner or later. He's a strange cove.'

'When are you going to show her his poems?' asked Charlotte with a swift look at Jane. Charlotte knew the signs of maidenly interest when she saw them, but was discreet.

'They will come back with the proofs of your own little piece,' replied Philip.

'Then I shall look forward to that,' said Jane coolly, and continued: 'He also said, if I remember aright, that his Gothic pieces were his best.'

'Fiddlesticks!' said Philip. 'Writers can never judge their own work.'

'Still, with *Frankenstein* being so popular, and all the ladies at home read Mrs Radcliffe – '

'My dear, they are quite passé now,' said Henrietta. 'We are to have quite a new form of story. Unless our friend can write narrative verse I fear there will be no call upon his Gothic talents. It was for his satires that my brother liked his work, was it not, Phil?'

119

'Well, I suppose I can have another look,' mused the new editor. 'He will have to trust to my judgement.'

'Will he be paid?' asked Jane. 'I am sure he is a gambler and gamblers always need money.'

'He'll get his tin when we've raised some wind ourselves,' said Philip and with this she had to be content. She had not yet asked for payment for herself and knew she must.

'Where do the Percy family live?' Jane asked Charlotte when Philip had gone out. Henrietta was off, too, to inspect the new apartment and see that the floors had been scrubbed. Their first pupil boarder was to start the next week.

'It used to be Salton Delevinge.'

'Where is that exactly?'

'In Northumberland. A very wild place, I'm told. The new earl is, I believe, a man who is often abroad and has let the old house go completely and is erecting something in the south of England in Classical style, which is more to his taste.'

They fell to discussing Italy. Jane found Charlotte a more sympathetic companion than the other two and it was pleasant to sit drinking tea in the late afternoon. Almost like Bedon. Then the conversation turned to Philip and his plans and Jane was astonished how much Charlotte knew about him and about London life in general.

'He is infiltrating himself into the salons,' said Charlotte. 'One must have patronage. He has met Landor even and Hunt. Landor, of course, is often in Italy, but Hunt is the more famous – ever since his paper, the *Examiner*, was banned by the King when he was Regent and poor old Hunt was thrown into prison. Of course all his friends rallied round, but one still has to be careful.

Not that Phil is interested in politics except so far as they affect himself, of course. He will always put his ambition before his principles, you know.' She said this quite simply, as though it was the most natural thing in the world, but Jane wondered whether she was warning her.

'Where are these salons? I have not heard of all the people they speak of, Philip and his sister. Of course I know of Leigh Hunt and Mr Landor – but it is all a world I do not quite understand.'

Charlotte had added water from the little kettle on the hob to the small green teapot and poured Jane another dish of tea. Jane sipped and looked over the square, over the trees towards the river. The sky was that soft blue of June, and evening was prefigured – though many hours away – by the stillness which came in from the open window.

'Well, there is Miss Benger's for one,' said Charlotte. 'Though I have not met the lady. I believe she lives somewhere in Islington which is become quite fashionable. All the literary ladies go there, I am told, and to Miss Mitford's who also lives near there. But they say old Mrs Barbauld is still active in Newington and Joanna Baillie has her Hampstead parties, and Lady Morgan – both men and women go *there*. But Phil prefers his dining club in Essex Street – he got Bruce to take him there. And Joy's coffee house of course. I believe a good deal of what he calls "business" is conducted there over the champagne punch.' Tea for ladies and punch for the men, thought Jane. But punch could not be a very good drink for writers, since she had been told it gave one headaches.

'They go to the Bedford Head, too, and Phil started by taking in scraps of gossip to the *Globe* offices nearby. I believe the journalists spend a lot of time gossiping over their drinks and concocting news. At least they paid him for his little pieces. So long as he doesn't spend all night at the Cider Cellars on Maiden Lane – ' She sounded rather worried about him and her whole tone was maternal. Jane wondered again if the admirable Charlotte nursed a *tendresse* for her friend's brother. She certainly seemed to know of all his movements. The talk turned to the possible contents of future *New London*s if the first were a success. 'He wanted Knight to publish it, of course,' Charlotte continued. 'But Knight had been nobbled by Bruce's Cambridge friends. Bruce wants a foot in any camp that is set up – he is talented, of course. I believe Phil wants to do something on the lines of Hazlitt who is at present writing of great paintings. He hasn't done Haydon yet and Phil is hopeful of an interview with him. The poor fellow is always in debt and eager to give any interview which will advance his work.'

'I wish I could meet all these people,' sighed Jane. 'But, Charlotte, must one cultivate the artists and writers to get published oneself? After all, Mr March has offered to print my little effusion and I am a nobody.'

'You are a novelty, my dear,' said Charlotte. 'But do not count on his always accepting what you write if he has bigger fish to fry. You write well and, of course, if you become known then others will be after you.'

'I believe I need to write whether published or no,' replied Jane. 'I cannot make sense of this world without the effort to capture it on paper.'

'And because it is all new to you and you have a facility with the pen, dear, you have struck lucky. I do not mean to discourage you – I feel very much for women who wish to write and I wish I had the talent myself. You will be a success at parties, too, I am sure.'

'I don't know if I care about that,' said Jane, thinking of Charles Fitzpercy and his dark hazel eyes. 'Are there no writers who do not need to cultivate social life? Or must one be forever competing and pushing oneself?'

'You are not shy,' said Charlotte. 'But people will resent you if you have easy success. That is the way of the world, I am afraid. Don't worry: I will be your friend, and there are certainly ladies who do not cultivate their publics. Look at Miss Austen – '

'She was, of course, a *genius*,' said Jane simply. 'That is rare, I am sure.'

'Yes, like the painter Constable,' said Charlotte. 'Oh, you *must* see his pictures. I believe he comes from your part of the world.'

'And actors too. I realized that Macready was different from the others on my first visit to Covent Garden.'

'Yes, they say that Macready, though, has a good head for business. I suppose geniuses are human too.'

'I hope he will play Hamlet,' said Jane, thinking of Fitzpercy's mention of that play in his letter.

She fell to thinking of a visit to the theatre with Charles Fitzpercy to hear Macready in *Hamlet*. She would like that almost more than a little success for herself. She wondered if she might ask Charlotte, who seemed to know everything, why such a man should visit a humble family like Daisy's, but decided against it.

'Is there much danger in the streets, Miss Howard? My uncle is always warning me against walking alone. I never thought anything of it at home – of course, I was not brought up with footmen – but what could happen to me?'

'There are street gangs, I know, but they do not usually attack women. If you were walking alone they would think, though, that you were one of the ladies of the night.'

'Oh!' said Jane, distressed. 'But would they not know by my appearance that I was not?'

123

'It is better to be careful, my dear. If your mama were alive you would be far less free.'

'It is because my uncle has lived so long abroad and thinks all men are as kind as himself that he allows me some freedom, but even he is prevailed upon by my aunt to send Polly with me wherever I go.'

'He is right. You must not run risks.'

'But in broad daylight?'

'It is true that pickpockets operate at all times of day and night. The gangs of thieves and procurers are found mainly in the alleys near the Strand and Drury Lane and the worst around St Giles and Seven Dials. The poor do not rob the poor. You are safer in the districts which are well patrolled or in the poorer areas if you are in a respectable poor person's company.'

'Are no women, then, allowed to wander through London and taste it – like men are allowed?'

'Taste it?' Charlotte was amused.

'Yes. When I am out on a sunny day and there are sights and sounds and people all mingling in a sort of play, I feel as though I am a taster of experience. I should like just to stand and watch and immerse myself in the lives going on before my eyes. How can one understand anything if one is continually beset by worry and anxiety that one's simplest actions are injudicious?' She spoke warmly, unconscious of the passion of her tones.

'You must be careful, Jane. I think I understand you – it is akin to the feelings aroused by some of the poets we were discussing the other day. But you are not a man. It is not given to women to be free – for you are talking of freedom, are you not?'

Yes, it was freedom she was thinking of – just to be free to live in the world, to talk to everyone and try to enter into the lives of others. Why should that be dangerous? She felt that Fitzpercy lived like that – but he was a man and so could indulge himself. She felt he must often have been in danger. She shivered. The world was a dangerous place; the danger came not from wild animals or infection, but from other people.

'The critics would blast any *man* who spoke of his true feelings, too,' said Charlotte after a pause. 'Look at the way they have pilloried poor Hazlitt who writes of his love for an innkeeper's daughter – in a very distasteful way, to be sure, making himself appear ridiculous. Phil was talking of nothing else yesterday. Three articles in *John Bull* pouring venom upon him. As though he had not suffered enough from that minx – at least I think she is a minx for she has led him a dreadful dance.'

'I did not know anything about that.'

'It was the book that came out last month. You heard nothing of it? *Liber Amoris* he called it. They say now he is returned to the country, still in love. A *woman* would be even more ridiculous in such a position.'

'I was not thinking of writing about – love,' said Jane. 'Only of being free to feel the world.'

'You are a Romantic,' said Charlotte with a smile.

'Noble ladies seemed to do it,' said Jane. 'At least I read of them.'

'Oh, noble ladies are a law unto themselves – and they usually have their brothers and fathers to protect them. There are, even so, but few who enjoyed such freedom, and one or two who have gone mad or died. They are brought up to listen to the talk of their menfolk and that is no training for the world of freedom.'

'What do such men talk about? What do they choose to spend their time doing? I have met but one noble person – or at least I think he is a *little* noble – Mr Digby, you know. But he talked of Shakespeare.'

'Indeed? Did he also speak of cockfighting and boxing and fencing and claret and blackstrap and riding and racing and pugilism and breeding pollparrots?'

'He talked of nothing like that!'

'Oh, then he is not a *nobleman*,' replied Charlotte smiling. 'Although some gentlemen I have met *do* speak to ladies of painting and rhyming and languages and religions and houses and gardens.'

'I shall indeed be ill-equipped for society,' said Jane with a sigh. 'Unless I meet your paragons. I suppose Frederick Digby may be some sort of a paragon then. I do not understand most men, Charlotte.'

'Well, what do most women converse about? Ribbons and husbands and cooking and furnishing – rather than their music and drawing lessons perhaps?'

Jane was silent, thinking about this.

'Talking of drawing lessons, we are thinking of finding a drawing master, Henrietta and I. Do you know of anyone? It is the one talent which neither of us possesses. I do not suppose you yourself are talented in that line?'

'I'm afraid not, dear Charlotte. My only talent, and I am not sure about that, is for writing – and I am a good *listener* to music. Do you wish to teach them to draw from life or are you hoping to nurture a Constable or a Turner amongst your charges?'

'We cannot run to paints, I fear. When we are very successful perhaps we could employ some embryo young genius who must earn his bread.'

'It is cheaper to write. All you need is a quill and paper. Perhaps that is why so few girls and ladies continue their painting after marriage – the expenditure is too high!'

Just then Polly was heard downstairs and the two friends parted, and Jane returned to her uncle's savouring the evening breezes and entranced to have found a sensible conversationalist in her new friend.

Hal and Edith were to go sooner than had been expected – whilst Edith appeared a little better, in order to undergo the rigours of the journey. Mr Digby was to visit once before their departure and Louisa Collins was a constant visitor, running up clothes for the boys and additional items for Edith's travelling wardrobe, and the beginnings of a winter wardrobe for Jane.

One afternoon when Jane was being fitted for this, she managed a few more words with her.

'I met your niece,' she said, plunging in as was her wont and fiddling with a reel of cotton.

'So I heard, Miss. She has been a naughty girl and could have got us all in trouble.'

'Indeed? How was that?'

Louisa smiled with her lips, not her eyes, a mannerism she had caught from a lady for whom she sewed. 'She has no business to be hobnobbing with the gentry. Even if he is a rascal, he's gentry.' At this Jane's heart missed a beat. 'I'm surprised *you* know him, Miss,' added Louisa.

Jane decided to stand on her dignity. 'I was entrusted with a message for him from his publishers. Your niece was able to tell me she could contact him. I know nothing of anything further.'

Louisa sniffed again. 'Getting respectable people into trouble, I don't doubt. He's a handsome fellow I suppose – at least Daisy thinks so.'

So Daisy was in love with Charles Fitzpercy, was she? Jane's heart sank to her shoes.

'He's been to our home several times, Miss. It's my old mother-in-law he comes to see. We're not supposed to know about it.' Louisa seemed to be suffering under a

127

sense of grievance. What on earth did Charles visit Louisa's mother-in-law for? Then Jane remembered that the old lady was a gypsy – hadn't Louisa said something like that?

'Mr Fitzpercy is only a slight acquaintance of mine,' Jane said with as much dignity as possible. 'I was told that your niece always knew his whereabouts. That's all.'

'She took him in, Miss, when some ruffians had set on him. But it isn't right. Our girls are good girls and don't want to get mixed up with any funny business.'

'No, of course not,' Jane soothed. 'I believe he has gone away, at least I was told so.'

'Then that's a mercy. He'll be back though, I don't doubt. He ain't done nothing wrong, Miss, as far as Daisy goes – it's Mary's mother he comes to see, like I told you.'

This time Jane took the bull by the horns and as Louisa was bent fixing the hem of a paper pattern that was to be the chrysalis for the butterfly of a gown which would eventually emerge from her clever fingers, she said: 'Perhaps the old lady helps him – I believe you told me she was a country woman.'

'Oh, she tells fortunes – actors and even the nobility. It helps us out like. She's always right, with the cards or the hands.'

'Perhaps she told him to go away then,' suggested Jane innocently.

'Very likely – to get him out of Daisy's hair. Daisy hasn't got no call to get herself mixed up in matters that don't concern her.'

'I expect she has a kind heart.'

'And our Kate. Daisy's persuaded her to help with the flowers, 'cos there was no work this season with the dolls – '

'Oh, ask Kate to make me a bonnet,' cried Jane, happy

128

at last to have some positive offering to make. 'Tell her she could send some patterns with you.'

'Thank you, Miss,' said Louisa briefly, and they spoke no more of Charles Fitzpercy.

When Mr Digby came for his final financial chat with her uncle, Jane was called in before he left.

'Mr Digby has promised to keep an eye on you,' said Hal bluffly.

Mr Digby smiled and said he was sure Miss Banham would be quite capable of managing her affairs, but that he would always be there for advice. Hal was clearly pleased that such a pleasant gentleman should offer his services – but of course he himself had done a few good turns to Digby over the past year.

'Next time we go to Italy, Jane shall come with us,' he said.

Jane felt that her uncle sometimes discussed her as though she were a parcel and she saw Mr Digby looking rather keenly at her during this conversation. He also flushed a little when Hal happened to mention Rome. That was where they said his wife was, she remembered.

Frederick turned the subject of conversation swiftly enough. 'Your uncle will have told you that you are invited to come down to my place with a few other young friends?' he enquired.

'Oh yes, sir – Mr Digby.'

'I have invited Mr March and his sister and Miss Howard,' said Frederick.

'Indeed, sir? I did not know you knew them.'

'I asked your uncle,' smiled Frederick. 'I must keep an eye on his protégés!'

Frederick was thinking how easy it was to appear disinterested when all he wanted was to keep his eyes on

Jane Banham with the excuse of overseeing her welfare. He would see her in a week when Hal and his wife and daughter had left England. But I plan no wickedness; there is no reason for me to feel a little guilty when her uncle smiles at me so guilelessly, he thought.

'When we return, we shall launch Jane properly,' Edith said to her husband as they prepared for bed. 'I almost wish we were not going – but I am sure that Italy will revive me completely.'

'Well, it has at least settled our minds about the boys,' replied her husband. 'It was high time, my dear.'

'Oh, I do hope they will not be homesick,' sighed Edith.

'Now, Edith, with Ogilvie and Jane to oversee their weekend leaves and their holidays – by spring they will be grown up, I'll wager – and you won't have any cause to regret our decision.'

'At least I shall have little Betsey,' she murmured.

Ten days later they had gone, after leaving the boys at Dr Macdonald's. Jane sat down with Mrs Ogilvie to their first meal together alone in the dining room. She had promised to write regularly to her uncle with the news and to the boys to keep their spirits up. What with these letters and her letters to Snetters and to Rose and her new article for Philip, she was going to be very busy. And then in a week or two, another visit to Vine House. Polly had consented to accompany her as her personal maid, though Jane thought that was rather ridiculous.

'What's he like then, this Mr Digby?' asked Polly.

'Very kind – very generous – and he knows all sorts of people. You'll like it there, Polly.'

'I'll be glad to have a change. It seems real strange now they've all gone,' replied Polly.

Jane busied herself over the next few days answering a letter from Snetters in Norfolk with the news of riotous assemblies and rick-burnings in that part of the realm. It all seemed far away, though she had forgotten the miserable conditions of some of the villagers. She wrote back asking for more details. 'For my heart is still with you all,' she said. It was a half truth, but would suffice.

London was stuffy and deserted now that the Season was over. Dr Macdonald's establishment went on teaching almost all the summer, and for that they must be thankful at least. She missed the boys at first, but they were noisy and tiring and it was delightful to have a little silence. She would meet – perhaps – Miss Jeffrey – certainly other ladies, at Frederick Digby's; she might, at any moment, perhaps, see Charles Fitzpercy again, should he return to London. Life was not too bad. She returned with a big effort of willpower to her next article for Philip: a description of shopping in the metropolis, adding once more a conscious air of *naïveté* to her descriptions. She had 'come along', she saw it, in her own style.

She did not think a great deal of Philip March – and hardly at all of Frederick Digby. Life was full and interesting enough. She went out little and suffered the final additions to her wardrobe at the hands of Louisa Collins in a calm frame of mind. She would enjoy a little hiatus in her emotional obsession with Charles Fitzpercy. Let fate bring what it would. Soon she would be in the country again among new faces. It was good to be young!

# PART THREE
## 'Those First Feelings'

Mrs Ogilvie was much intrigued by Miss Banham's invitation to stay at Vine House, this time accompanied by no one but Polly.

'I don't know what your uncle could have been thinking of to have given permission for you to go off like this, and you meant to be a lady, to some junketings in the country – *I* don't know.' But there was nothing she could do about it as she was not Jane's guardian and Hal had had every confidence in Frederick Digby's protection for his niece.

It *was* a little unusual, Jane conceded, and fortunately Mrs Ogilvie did not know that Lady Clara was still away abroad.

Even Charlotte had been a little dubious about accepting the invitation which had been worded to include all the editorial staff and the contributors to the *New London Review*. Charlotte, of course, knew what was done and not done, having been brought up in the best society, and it was emphatically not done for a young and unmarried lady to go gallivanting about to house parties without the protection of a father or a mother or a male relative or chaperone. 'But of course, he will be inviting his friends of the *demi-monde* I expect – actresses and writers, for we too are not "respectable".'

'Oh, surely he would not invite anyone whose presence would make a maiden blush?' said Jane with some spirit.

Charlotte looked at her curiously. 'I think you may, my dear Jane, have a slightly rosy view of the world of the scribblers,' she said gently. 'It is all right for men but it is never all right for us. Do you know that Phil has been invited to salons where men never take their wives, never mind their daughters? But there *are* women there!'

'Perhaps Frederick Digby prefers to be unconventional,' suggested Jane. 'Where else can we meet people of our own sort?'

'Oh, they will not be quite of our sort,' replied Henrietta, who had been listening to the conversation. 'We are governesses and Grub Street – they are actresses and novelists.'

In the event Jane was much more at home on this, her second visit, than her first one with Uncle Hal and Aunt Edith. She was invited for several days, and a carriage had been sent to pick them all up in Town so that they need not use the mail or a hack chaise. It was pleasant, once Mrs Ogilvie had been bid farewell, to be seated in a well-upholstered conveyance with Charlotte and Henrietta sitting opposite, and the green countryside jogging past their windows, even though the dust occasionally obscured the trees and the warmth made one feel sleepy.

Philip was not travelling with them because he wanted to make his way alone, said Henrietta. In fact Philip turned up later that evening with Miss Julia Jeffrey, the actress, and Jane was pleased to make her acquaintance at last and amused that Philip had chosen to travel with her.

The later one dined, the higher one's rank, and Frederick Digby, though he might invite the 'raffish' to his table, still adhered to the late hours of Town rather than the more homely dining hour of the country. But he was not as late as the extremest fashion and the ladies were not left alone too long after the men had stayed behind for a drink of port.

'He has shut up his other house,' said another young

lady who it turned out was also an actress, a Miss Frances Kelly.

I *am* among my own kind, thought Jane. It is the sort of company Mama would have liked. As well as the two actresses, who seemed not at all raffish but rather tired and dispirited, and Henrietta and Charlotte and herself, there was a beribboned and lisping young lady whose name Jane did not at first catch. She was very young and dressed to look even younger than her age and was, it seemed, under the respectable protection of one of the older gentlemen now absent in the dining room. Of the men, Jane knew Digby and Philip and Christopher and there were two or three others, more inclining to middle age, who appeared to have some connection with the theatre or literature.

'Where is his other house?' asked Jane of Miss Kelly. 'I did not know he had another.'

'It is in the neighbouring county,' answered Julia Jeffrey. 'But his wife lives there when she is in England.' She did not elaborate further.

The ladies had been asked to produce mottoes for discussion after the gentlemen should return. 'It is a novel way of spending an evening, is it not?' yawned Julia who seemed easily bored. 'Mr Gale shall produce one for me, I declare, for there is nothing in my head at all.'

'Then it will be in Latin,' giggled Miss Kelly. 'All the gentlemen prefer it and then they can wax eloquent on matters we ladies know nothing of.'

Henrietta smiled. 'Ah, but some ladies may know that language,' she said.

'I cannot think of anything either,' said Jane. 'What do we do with our mottoes when we have produced them?'

'We lead a conversation on the subject,' said the beribboned young lady. 'I have chosen mine. It is to be

137

"She is far from the land where her young hero sleeps" –
by Moore,' she added gratuitously.

'But what can you say about that?' asked Charlotte.

'Oh, it would be a wonderful sally to introduce talk of
heroes and women and war and partings, I think.'

I am far from the land where my hero is, thought Jane.
I wonder where he is.

It was a chilly night for August and the fires had been
lit. They were in the small salon with its dark pictures and
hangings. She drew nearer the fire.

'I shall be glad to retire,' said Julia. 'Journeys always
tire me so, and when I am "resting" I cannot abide late
nights.'

'I think we should hint at something in our mottoes to
do with the magazine, don't you?' said Henrietta. 'After
all that is why we are here, I suppose.'

'Oh, Fred is lavish with his hospitality – but by fits and
starts,' said Frances Kelly. 'He will take up some idea and
you are sure it is the greatest thing for him – and then he
will forget it. *We* are here because he is in love with the
stage – or was. Last time there was a young member of
the Commons and the son of an earl, and a young man
aspiring to politics. Very dull.'

'But you liked the young lord,' said Julia, and Frances
blushed.

'It was better than the time he invited Miss Tovey,' said
Frances. 'Are you not going to recite some of your poems,
Miss Landon?' she said to the very young lady, who
simpered: 'I have been told my poems are a little too
"warm" for consumption in public.'

'I declare this will be more like a reading party,' said
Charlotte. 'I thought only young men went in for those.
We are honoured to be able to partake in such revels, I'm
sure.'

138

Jane looked across at her to see if she intended sarcasm, but her face betrayed nothing. Jane thought her friend obviously did not like Miss Landon, who, in spite of her tender age, reviewed for the *Literary Gazette*.

'Tell us of your venture,' said Julia to Henrietta. 'We hear you are to open an academy for young ladies. It will be just the thing for my sister's children.'

But Henrietta was spared any further elucidation of their new venture by the door being flung open by a footman and the return of the gentlemen.

'We were bored with each other's company,' said one of the actors and moved up to the fire to be near Julia.

Another footman arrived with coffee. Jane suddenly decided her motto would be a line from a poem of Charles Fitzpercy. Why not? She had committed it to memory when Philip had let her see the shorter poems Fitzpercy had sent: 'I am ruined by red hair and romance.' Now what could they say about *that*? Philip March was looking across at her, now that Julia seemed to have been reclaimed by her actor friend. Then Frederick Digby came up and made polite enquiries about her uncle and aunt and asked whether the mail from Rome had yet arrived. 'The packets are slow from Italy,' he said. Jane remembered his wife would perhaps write to him from that country, but strove not to appear to know that as she replied.

'Will you read from the new writers?' he asked her, giving her all his attention and seemingly interested in the conversation and her replies.

'I know only a little of our new poets,' she replied. 'But I think I may remember a line or two.'

'Are you a poet yourself, like Miss Landon here?' he enquired.

It was true that Jane did privately scribble verses, but

she replied: 'Oh, I wish I were – but I can write only little essays. I have not the imagination to attempt more.'

'Ah yes, I hear from March that your piece is shortly to appear in the first issue. You must carry on,' he said earnestly. 'The world is jaded – we need something fresh and feminine.'

When all the company were assembled and more coffee poured, a beverage which Jane decided she liked more and more, particularly when it was made as it was at Vine House – hot and pungent and strong – their host began the evening's talk with a motto which he threw negligently to the company with a smile.

'You see – it is in Latin!' cried Miss Kelly.

'I shall translate,' said Frederick. '"Always and everywhere I have so lived, that I might consume the passing light as if it were not to return."'

'Ah,' said the ladies, except for Jane and Henrietta. The latter looked disdainfully out of the window.

'By an under-valued poet,' added their host.

'It is rather dangerous, I think,' said Charlotte, 'and sad, I believe. For if you are perpetually consuming the present you are thinking of the consumption rather than the circumstance.'

'Well said, Miss Howard.' Frederick bowed to her. Charlotte did not seem at all shy in putting forth her opinions. Miss Landon took up an angelic pose.

'I think it is wonderful,' she announced. 'Catch the passing sunbeam, you know – for life passes – ah – how it passes.'

Jane thought, She cannot be above my age. What does she know of the passage of time? And yet, *she* works for a living – and Frances Kelly played Juliet last winter.

The actor, who was called Gale, added a well-turned

little compliment from some comedy he said he had adorned last year and the rest clapped him.

Henrietta went on looking sceptical and Philip added: '"Gather ye rose buds while ye may,"' with a look at Julia who seemed oblivious, but then *she* rose, bowed and uttered, '"Go and catch a falling star,"' and then sat down.

'"Roses and stars and passing lights,"' murmured Christopher Cornwall.

'What does Miss Banham have to say?' asked Frederick.

It was all fantastic, Miss Banham was thinking, these fashionable people with their well-chosen words.

'Miss Banham,' said Philip 'is thinking how she is soon going to punctuate the pretensions of our society where poetry is used as a subject for discussion when we tire of gossip.'

This was rude of Philip and Jane hastened to defend their host. 'Your poet sounds experienced,' she replied with a look at Frederick. 'So he is not a young man – but perhaps he is a greedy one. But why should he think that the light is not to return? Would he not enjoy life more if he were to be a little less self-conscious?'

'Oh no! No! No!' cried Miss Landon, who seemed a little elevated though she had drunk only one glass of wine. 'We must drink to the dregs I do believe, for we are pursued by the passing clouds which may so soon, alas, eclipse life's pleasures.'

This was clapped. Frederick continued to look at Jane and she became rather uncomfortable at his glance. The talk turned to Miss Landon's motto. She had decided against Tom Moore and chosen a verse which was of extreme vapidity and turned out to have been manufactured by herself. Then Frances tossed in a line of Sheridan and the company relaxed. Philip produced the good

141

Doctor's, 'When a man is tired of London he is tired of life,' which raised such a lively conversation that Jane thought she would escape having to produce a line herself. Henrietta said something in French but declined to translate and Charlotte a line or two from *Marmion*.

To this Miss Landon's reaction was excessive, Jane thought. The young lady seemed to think the violence of her feelings a proof that she had a delicate sensibility. Yet on the other hand, was it true that 'what we feel the most we show the least'? She was puzzling over this when she was startled by Frederick's voice once more in her ear.

'Your motto, Jane,' he whispered. Now for it. She must strive to keep the passion out of her voice. She hoped she was not as foolish as Miss Landon.

'Oh, it is just a line from a poet we are publishing,' she murmured, hoping Philip did not mind the royal 'we'. She looked up and said clearly and slowly: 'I am ruined by red hair and romance,' and there was a silence. She looked down.

'By?' asked Frederick Digby.

'It is by an anonymous poet who is contributing to our columns,' said Philip with an angry glance at Jane.

'Go on, more of it,' commanded the actor Gale.

Hardly aware of what she was doing, Jane continued to the end of the verse. Rooks, strands, sunsets, ruins – all passed across her lips and she gave an unconsciously melancholy grace to the lines.

'Ah!' cried Miss Landon once more. The others were silent.

'I am surprised you do not grace the boards,' said Mr Gale most gallantly.

Jane thought, now I have made a fool of myself, but I do not mind. 'I am not graceful enough for the stage,' she replied.

'Oh, but you might make a living reciting in the drawing rooms,' said Julia maliciously.

'Like Miss Tovey!' said Frances Kelly.

'My dear,' said Frederick, 'you are not remotely like Miss Tovey – to that I can swear. But what can we say about your motto? What indeed?'

'Most Gothic,' put in Henrietta.

'It sent shivers down my back,' said Miss Landon.

'But the sentiments are popular,' said Christopher.

'And will sell our little publication,' added Philip.

'And what do *you* think?' pursued Frederick. 'Surely red hair has not ruined you?'

'It was not a personal reaction,' replied Jane, rallying. 'It is about glamour, I think.'

'Oh, Scott again!' groaned Philip.

'I have a feeling the young man who wrote Miss Banham's motto is a little Byronic,' said Julia Jeffrey, with a glance at Jane. She said nothing in reply and Julia continued to regard her meditatively.

The conversation turned to that noble lord and whether he would ever return to his native land. 'Ted Bruce once met the "lady" in question,' said Philip.

'Which one?' asked Miss Kelly, and there was general laughter.

'The aristocratic one, who was Byron's,' said Philip.

'And who is Ted Bruce?' asked Julia.

'A young writer of whom you will hear more,' replied Philip.

'In your *New London* I suppose?' bantered Julia. 'It is going to be quite a collection I can see – Bruce and Miss Banham and your mysterious anonymous poet.'

Philip bowed. 'The present company will all, I hope, subscribe?'

How cosmopolitan they all were, Jane was thinking, yet

143

quite 'respectable', and pleasant, except for Miss Landon who looked as though butter wouldn't melt in her mouth. Julia Jeffrey was especially sophisticated but probably rather conventional. Jane did not dislike her and was amused at the flirtatious glances Philip occasionally threw her. Julia Jeffrey need fear nothing from *her* – whether on account of her male friends or her acting abilities. And Miss Kelly, who had told them she had acted since childhood, seemed a sweet girl whom she could easily see as Juliet. But she was most likely tougher than she looked, for she had joined in with the men in a discussion about money.

The next day, after the company had slept in late and Polly had been in to do Jane's hair and also seen to Charlotte's and Henrietta's, some more friends were to arrive. They were a contrast to the youthful band of the evening before. Two old dandies, who looked as though nothing had happened since Waterloo, arrived in creaking coaches and, with great expressions of affability, were marched up and down the gardens by their host. They contrasted strangely with Grub Street. Did Frederick Digby take some strange delight in thus juxtaposing his acquaintances, or had he just a kind heart? The weather had taken a sudden change for the better. The clouds disappeared and the sun came out to warm the old Queen Anne brickwork and Jane and Charlotte put on their sunbonnets and went out to explore. The bees were at work among the roses whose second flowering was in full swing and there was a mellowness over everything. In the high trees some wood pigeons were moaning their characteristic plangent cries – three short, a long, and two shorts. Jane listened to them in a sort of daze as each time they sang the same, as though the message had to be reiterated since the only reply was like an echo from another high branch. She wandered round the walled garden whose paths were a little overgrown and grassy. Leaning over one russet brick wall was a mulberry tree already dropping its dark red cargo of bunchy berries. She opened a low door in the wall and found herself in parkland where all was still and green, with the beech and oaks hanging their canopies like sunshades over the grass. Then she heard the sound of water and looked for the stream which surely fed the garden on the other side. She felt at home and forgot the competitive conversation of the evening before. Charles Fitzpercy would not be at home here, she knew. There was a little disorder in the garden but no ruins or rooks. Yet she could not help wishing that his tall figure would appear and beckon her under the trees to an assignation. It was pleasant, though, to be alone and to dream of a love which, perhaps, his real presence would disturb. If only for a moment she could make time stop in this hazy dreamy moment when her thoughts could allow themselves to wander to some impossible future and not have to present themselves in a social light.

But that was impossible and Jane soon found herself at the end of the park wall where ivy covered the brick, and bees hummed over from the garden on the other side. She heard the sound of voices then. A man and a woman were walking behind the wall and she paused for a moment, reluctant to be seen. Philip March's rather husky voice seemed to be amusing someone for it was followed by the pleasant trill of ladylike laughter. He must be paying court to Frances Kelly, Julia being out of reach. He seemed to please women when he concentrated his mind upon them. She realized that it would be quite amusing to flirt with Philip March, though it was true he preferred ladies older than himself. But she did not want to flirt with anyone. You could not *flirt* with Charles

145

Fitzpercy – at least she knew *she* could not, in spite of his teasing voice and air of mystery. That was something quite different. Neither could she imagine Charles writing to Julia or to Frances as he had written to her. But perhaps she was wrong. If only she could know him better. If only he would return to London. The voices faded away and she crept back through the low green door hoping to reach the house unnoticed and prepare herself for luncheon. The others would wonder where she had been. She was startled by the voice of Frederick, who suddenly appeared around a privet hedge with a small dog.

'Hello, Miss Banham! You must forgive the weeds and the general air of neglect. That will all disappear when I carry out my plans for improvements.'

'But it is very peaceful and lovely,' she replied.

'You have been for a walk, then? Come, will you sit on my little garden seat in the arbour? Down, Dash, it is only Miss Banham.'

She stroked the little spaniel and followed the man to a shady bench over which arched a thick hedge of clematis and wisteria. There were tulip trees and cedars, parterres of geraniums and an allspice tree in the distance.

'You said you had received but one letter from your uncle?' he said as they sat primly side by side with the dog making circles before them and whining in a plaintive way. 'It is my wife's dog,' he said. 'She misses her mistress, I think, and when she sees a lady she is apt to think her mistress has returned.'

Jane did not know what to say to this. It seemed as though he wanted the conversation somehow to include his absent lady. 'I am sorry, sir,' she ventured, 'that your wife's health does not permit her to be here at home in

146

England. I know how it is with Aunt Edith. We are hoping that Italy will prove a turning point for her.'

'It is not illness which keeps Clara away,' he said after a pause. She felt uncomfortable. The man's gaze seemed fixed on her as though he was expecting her to ask something. 'Are you an only child?' he asked after a pause.

'Yes. Papa and Mama had a little son after me but he died before Mama died.'

'So you are an orphan, Jane? I think we do not need to keep up the *convenances* – please call me Fred.'

She did not really want to call him by his Christian name, although she had no objection to his calling her by hers – he must be at least thirty-seven or eight!

'I liked the lines you read last night,' he said. 'You produced them well. I believe Miss Landon was quite jealous – and Julia Jeffrey may have thought you were thinking of a stage career.'

'Oh, no!' cried Jane, distressed. 'I could not possibly ever be an actress – I am far too clumsy. Reading verse is not the same. I do hope she did not think that.'

'I believe, though, that your uncle told me your own mother was an actress?'

'Yes, Mama ran away from her parents' rectory to go on the boards – but she never told me. I only heard of it later. She was not very happy, I think.'

'And you are?' He looked at her again and she returned his gaze with a frank expression.

'Oh, yes, I am happy. I am lucky to have found such friends as Charlotte – Miss Howard – and Miss March – I never thought I could write for publication. It has all happened so quickly.'

'But you must have scribbled in your schoolroom?'

147

'Yes, yes I did – and I write many letters to my old governess and to my friend.'

'And what will you tell them about this visit, Jane? Tell me – I am curious.'

'I shall say there is a pretty house with a walled garden and a park with wood pigeons and a magnolia tree and it is all greener and more enclosed than our park at home – and that the çompany was very intriguing. That I met two actresses and that our host wanted to know about me,' she said, laughing.

He smiled, seemed to approve of her.

'I shall tell your uncle you are in good spirits,' he said. 'Come, the servants will be hovering with another repast. You must try the claret I laid down three years ago – unless you are of the opinion that young ladies should not drink anything stronger than tea or small beer.' They walked down the path, Frederick stopping now and again to uproot some particularly obnoxious weed with a sigh.

Jane rejoined the other women who had been discussing other parks, other houses. Charlotte seemed the best informed. Miss Landon had departed; her father was ill and could not spare her for more than one night.

'Fred should build a grotto,' Julia was saying.

'First he should see to his gardens,' replied Henrietta. 'They are shamefully neglected.'

'Because he is so much away,' Frances added. 'Have you been to his house in Bloomsbury Square?' she asked Jane.

'No, I met him only recently at my uncle's – I have never been to his town residence. Is it very grand?'

Just then luncheon was announced and Frances never had the opportunity to expatiate upon the 'ton' or lack of it evinced by Frederick Digby's taste.

'He is an unusual man, is he not?' Jane remarked to

148

Charlotte afterwards when they were sitting on the little terrace looking out over the 'landscape' and the tufted trees. The men were occupied in some manly pursuit.

'He does not own much land,' replied her friend. 'I believe he is one of the new style gentry who have to use their brains – of which I am sure he possesses many.'

Frances Kelly overheard them. 'He likes nothing better than to sit in his library. Julia and I met him two or three years ago – that is how these little parties started. He was lonely when Clara went to Italy and instead of dissipating his time in Town he had retired here. The house was terribly neglected. Then, when he got to know Macready and became interested in putting some of his money into a theatrical venture or two, we were introduced to him. I suppose he is tired now of the theatre and wants to be seen as an encourager of literature.' She spoke rather sharply.

'Oh, that's not quite true, my dear,' said Julia. 'He is sincere in all he does – it is only that he was lonely and having no heir or any daughters even, he surrounded himself with us "children".'

'But he is not very old,' said Charlotte. 'Surely he could marry again?'

'He does not want to divorce. I am sure he is always hoping his wife will give up her travels and return to him.'

'A complaisant husband indeed,' said Henrietta. After a short pause Charlotte said: 'It has all been very pleasant.' Then, 'Philip tells me Digby has underwritten the first issue for us – perhaps his money from the West Indies has arrived.'

Jane, to whom all this talk of money was a mystery, was silent. How did people manage to find money for houses – even neglected ones – and literary reviews? Her own papa had worked so hard for his living, yet they had never become rich. And people like Louisa Collins and her family slaved away for days and received a pittance.

'I believe he is a friend of emancipation,' remarked Charlotte. 'I was told by Philip that Digby has friends among the radical Whigs.'

'That would be unusual, indeed,' said Henrietta. 'Digby should be content to be a Tory Squire and *cultiver son jardin*.'

'I think he is kind – though I should not like to be criticized by him,' Jane offered. 'Last night when he was talking to Christopher I thought he was being rather icy about religion. I did not understand all they were saying.'

'They are matters meant to be too deep for us poor females,' sighed Miss Kelly.

But, thought Jane, Charlotte and Henrietta and the two women actresses were very intelligent people. If Henrietta had been born male, she could have been a better editor than her brother. It was unusual to find such women unmarried. They were spared further discussion of Digby's pecuniary position and his political and religious sympathies by the advent of the two oldish gentlemen who had been at luncheon. They had been Regency bucks and even then were not in the first flush of youth and Jane was amazed – and had been amazed all through luncheon – at their dandified appearance and their drawling accents. What could Frederick Digby have in common with them? They had ignored the ladies except to quiz them occasionally through their monocles and had kept up a conversation of almost perpetual denigration of everyone and everything. Frederick must once have belonged to this world of theirs though he had clearly left it long ago, the world of 'ton' and 'High Life'.

She decided that he was a 'new' man and wanted the company of the young to ally himself with the new world and the new thinking that was creeping upon them. It only needed an evangelical clergyman and a Whig grandee and perhaps, she thought, a philosopher like Mr Godwin, and the whole of human life would have been there!

Philip March paid a little more attention to her that evening. She felt it was because Frederick Digby seemed to approve of her, because Julia was not interested in him and Fanny Kelly had been rather cool toward him since their walk in the garden. Frances Kelly might find him attractive but she knew on which side her bread was buttered, thought Jane – and it was not with a penniless scribbler.

'We are an incongruous collection, are we not?' said Philip flippantly.

They were once more in the drawing room which opened out into the little salon next to the library and another pleasant dinner had been consumed. Then there had been much toing and froing with horses and carriages in the stable yards, for the two old dandies had decided they had urgent business in town.

'Digby has been generous,' continued Philip. 'But I shall need the entrée to something a little more influential – the Penman's Club or Joanna Baillie's evenings – we cannot make a stir if only actors and minor gentlemen and poets as penurious as ourselves read us. I shall hope to go and buy Lady Morgan another green fan and sit at her feet!'

'How do Hunt and Campbell pay their contributors?' asked Jane. 'I do not know many journalists, but they cannot all belong to the world you speak of.'

'No, it is true most writers are not rich – some are very poor. Some make their name, others make money, and some do both.'

'The best are not rich,' said Jane. 'I should not want to be rich. Surely if you have a success with this first issue it will bring enough money to bring out another, and employ

151

a variety of writers? I suppose I must expect to be paid myself for my contribution?'

'A *succès d'estime* is enough for you, Jane,' said Philip. 'Your uncle is rich and you do not need money.'

She was a little annoyed. 'Uncle is not *so* rich. He is only beginning to feel secure – and *I* am not rich.' She could see he did not believe her. 'A guinea or two would be riches indeed had I earned it myself. Of course, if *you* are successful and they like what *I* write, I think I should be paid.' She stopped, discomfited. She had not known she thought that. 'There are ladies who keep their families on their writings,' she added.

'You mean Miss Mitford and the married ladies? Most of it is paltry stuff – fashionable and worthless.'

'All praise to Miss Mitford,' she replied. 'She writes prose well. Why should other "worthless" writing be so lucrative?'

'There is no accounting for public taste, my dear,' said Philip in an avuncular fashion.

Jane puzzled over it all. The ladies she had been thinking of kept husbands and children by dint of their pens – because they had to. *She* was writing for her own satisfaction and felt ashamed. If she could earn a living with it, why, she could be free and need not ever marry! Philip broke in to her thoughts again.

'Of course, you will marry – that is what girls like you always do. Then you will have a brood of children and never write another word.'

She was silent. Whom would she ever wish to marry? The only person she had ever thought of in that connection, she hardly knew. Oh she would slave away to keep *him*! Was Charles Fitzpercy rich or poor? Poor, she thought – rich husbands were not for her. It did not occur to her to consider Philip March as a candidate for her charitable efforts. He, she was sure, would one day be comfortably circumstanced himself – he had literary ideals but was shrewd enough to import them into the market-place though he would not descend to a Miss Landon. In this she misjudged Philip, for he was genuinely devoted to literature and it was not money but fame among his equals that he desired most – and even perhaps to be first among equals on some distant day.

Jane was later to modify her idea of Frederick Digby's parties as gatherings of the last word in elegant unconventionality and sophisticated unrespectability. There were far more raffish radicals and cosmopolitan roués in the world outside Vine House, though perhaps nowhere else where old dandies and young actresses, aspiring editors and bluestocking ladies who lived on a pittance could meet on equal terms.

Whilst the men played billiards or vingt et un and Charlotte and Julia were riding around the estate on Frederick's two mild mares, she drank green tea in the library with Henrietta or listened to Frances playing the old harp. It was all most agreeable. There was lacking only a centre to her life. She perhaps confused her longing for a lover with a longing for appreciation of herself. She felt stupid and raw in the midst of elegance, too abstracted to talk of fans and gloves with the ladies and with little taste for cards. Yet she was an unconsciously amusing conversationalist and when Frederick Digby was tired of his game of chess with Philip he would seat himself down and continue the chat he had begun in the garden. What did they talk about? Jane asked him to play chess with her – Snetters had once taught her but she was out of practice. He promised he would one day when she should visit again.

'For you will visit again, Jane, I hope,' he said

153

earnestly. 'Take what you want from the library – I have the new Scott. Only just arrived from my bookseller. *Quentin Durward* – that should keep you happy for many a long day!'

It was curious, she felt, he treated her not quite like an indulgent father and yet this very fact brought her own father back into her mind. If only she could have spoken to *him* about chess and novels. Frederick even mentioned her mother once again – he was sure he had seen her at Drury Lane in his schoolboy days. Jane did not want to talk about her mother with him; she did not know why. Perhaps her mama now seemed so far removed from this world of Vine House; perhaps she did not want to know of a mother who had had a life long before she herself came on the scene; perhaps she wanted to remember the mother she had known, not the one she had never known. It seemed somehow, in a strange way, a sort of disloyalty to her papa to abolish her mother's domestic life and think of her only as a young woman. And it made her feel, too, that she would herself, however pleasant her little success with these people, one day marry and become just a mama herself. And yet, at first, she had thought that Vine House would have been just the place for her young Mama!

Frederick Digby was sensitive and did not press her when he saw her reluctance to speak of her mother; instead he turned the subject to politics, just as though she were a young man, and she was surprised to find the depths of his convictions.

'Just because the revolution of France ended so dismally, it does not mean we do not need reform,' he said quite sharply. 'All this harking back to the good old days before the Terror is unhealthy.' She was wondering how he would justify his own rather pleasant way of life and,

154

although she said nothing, he said: 'I would be prepared to give up some of my own possessions if a juster society would emerge.' And he talked of the New World and the settlers there and of how he had himself once considered leaving England for America. Philip came into the library then and paused on the threshold. 'I must not monopolize you,' said their host pleasantly, and rose. Jane was disappointed. She had enjoyed their talk. She excused herself to them both and said she must dress for dinner.

Polly was waiting for her in her dressing room. The tapestry was rather faded and the gilt a little tarnished, but only a little, and the place had its own beauty. Polly had found the servants' quarters rather dull. But there had been gossip and she passed on to Jane what she had heard.

'They say his lady went off to Italy with another gentleman!' she announced round-eyed, as she brushed Jane's hair rather inexpertly.

'Let me do it,' said Jane rather impatiently. 'I'm sure it was not Mr Digby's fault, Polly – he is an honourable man, I believe.'

'And handsome too,' added the irrepressible Polly.

Jane had not really considered this aspect. She was too wrapped up in the thought of Fitzpercy to notice other men's external appearance. She sighed. She must try to find out more from Julia about Charles Fitzpercy. She was sure there was more to know. And who were the 'Georgian gangs' Julia had been talking about?

But at dinner on the last night of their stay the talk was all of Miss Edgeworth and she could not find a way of leading Julia off to another subject. After dinner they all played cards, which Jane found a 'dead bore' – as the dandies would have said. She was amused at Philip's name-dropping. He seemed to wish to compete in worldly

155

knowledge with the actresses. Jane suspected, from something Polly had said, that his lack of success with them had led him to a little sortie the night before to the quarters of the domestics where there were two or three buxom country girls. She pushed the thought away. Philip, in spite of his ambition or perhaps because of it, still competed with other men for success in other fields of endeavour – for women, for example. It had been quite an exhausting stay and she would be glad to have a few quiet days alone when she did not feel she was on parade, so to speak. She hardly dare hope there might be a letter from Charles Fitzpercy on her return to Lincoln's Inn Square, but the hope sustained her.

The last morning of her stay Jane felt her host's manner somewhat changed. He seemed rather cold and abstracted at first – not only to her but to all his guests. Perhaps he would be glad to be left alone when they had all gone. Later on in the morning he seemed to cheer up, but this was evidenced by a rather ostentatious silliness, she thought – a sequence of quips which would have better graced the lips of one of his old dandified friends. She was puzzled, and all her estimate of his character turned upside down. She wondered if he were acting a part, though why he should feel he had to act a part was a mystery. He tossed a monocle in his eye and grimaced and said: 'Ha!' to Philip whenever the latter ventured upon an observation.

Once Julia and Frances were in his stylish but comfortable carriage and Jane and Polly were about to be handed in after them, he came up to Jane, this time neither cold nor frivolous in manner.

She was thanking him politely and sincerely for her stay when he interrrupted her: 'You *will* come again – promise, Jane Banham. You *will* come?'

'Why, sir, I . . .'

Then he said – and took her hand as he spoke – 'You can rely on me, you know.'

'Why, yes – I shall tell Uncle Hal what an interesting time I have had.'

'You can rely on me,' he repeated quietly. 'Trust me.' Then he let drop her hand and turned away as she climbed into the large vehicle.

He had said it so strangely that she was puzzled.

The girls were, however, in no doubt about him.

'Take care,' said Julia. 'The old rake has his eye upon young flesh.' The girls had lapsed into the more careless speech of the theatre.

Jane was amused rather than horrified. 'Don't be ridiculous,' she said. They were all packed together in the carriage – she and Frances and Charlotte facing Julia and Henrietta and Polly. The men were coming back in Frederick's tandem. In spite of the slight discomfort, the conversation was lively. Jane was relieved when they stopped discussing their erstwhile host. She studied Julia and Frances, the better to have something to say in her projected 'Letter on the London Players'. There was talk of a Mr Elliston and a Mr Knight, two of their fellow Thespians who had also once visited Vine House along with Mr Gale and who were both to play the next season's *Hamlet* and *Macbeth*, and then Fanny fell to discussing fashion. 'Blue shoes are now *démodé* my dear,' she pronounced. Charlotte was looking at them shrewdly and Henrietta, bored, was trying to see out of the window when the conversation turned to the 'new' dandies.

'They are quite different from those two old fossils at Fred's,' said Julia. 'They paint and rhyme and cook and fence – and although their French, I am told, leaves much to be desired, who wants to talk like a lover of Marie

157

Antoinette's? Of course, they are all addicted to champagne and snuff and divide their time between the Park and Almack's when they are not in our Green Rooms – but I adore them.'

'I have never met a *young* dandy,' remarked Jane.

'Ah, be careful then. If you want to know London you must be acquainted with the Fashion – but if you write about them you had better take care. They eat up little girls,' said Julia.

'Perhaps your famous anonymous poet is one of them,' mused Fanny.

'Mr – ' She checked herself in time.

'If that Byronic fellow is who I think he is – a tall, witty dissolute creature – I've often seen him in their company. The Georgian gangs hate the dandies, you know,' said Julia.

'But who are the "Georgian gangs"?' enquired Jane, satisfied at last to have brought the conversation round to her preoccupation.

'Oh, they eat up little girls, too – and little boys.'

'Descendants of the old Drury Lane mob,' added Fanny.

'There is no cause for any law-abiding citizen to be "eaten up",' said Henrietta, suddenly but firmly.

'Provided they don't go out at night,' replied Julia.

'But they have to go out at night if they go to see *you*,' objected Jane.

'In carriages, yes – not on foot. You must have your wits about you, my dear,' replied Fanny quite kindly.

'That is why you must have a gentleman protector, you see,' said Julia. Charlotte sniffed. The conversation was not to her taste.

'I have often thought how unfair it is that ladies cannot go to the coffee houses,' said Jane.

'You should have been born a man, Miss. There *are* respectable places, though, where I am sure your brother' – she bowed to Henrietta – 'could take you.'

'All the literary world meets in coffee houses and drinking dens,' pursued Jane.

'*Fraser's* and *Blackwood's* and the *New Monthly* and the *Examiner* are not all hatched in dens of vice,' said Charlotte gently.

'Oh, when they have *arrived* – then they are hatched in the Clubs,' replied Julia. 'It is the difference between the Regent's Street or St James's and the Strand: as much vice, I dare say, but more expensive!'

'You will not find the dandies in the cheap places.'

'So, to be a dandy you must be rich?'

'Of course. One costume would launch a periodical!'

The talk passed to whether Jane had been to Bullock's museum or seen the Panorama to which she had to reply in the negative.

'There is so much for you to see then.'

'Yes – I am very ignorant.'

'But you are not silent in company, Miss Banham.'

'Surely to speak, within the limits of one's ignorance, is one's duty in society – and say what one *feels* in any case?'

'If you are a gentleman you may – otherwise you had better write tragedies for us which bear little relation to life as it is lived now in Town.'

'Like Miss Mitford,' added Julia.

Jane was silent and the rest of the journey, with its change of horses at Barnet, was accomplished with no further verbal skirmishes. Jane got down with Polly near Lincoln's Inn and Julia opened her eyes sufficiently to bid her farewell with a sharp and condescending: 'Take care, my dear.'

All Polly said as they pulled the bell of number

159

seventeen was: 'She is a very high and mighty young lady, Miss, that one.' But Jane was still thinking of Julia's words: 'A tall, witty, dissolute creature.' They made her shiver rather. In what way was Charles dissolute? Did he gamble or drink over much? Was that all?

Mrs Ogilvie greeted Jane with a polite, but rather suspicious, look which was saying, Jane always thought: You know and I know that you are not quite a lady. But beyond remarking that her visit to Dr Macdonald's had passed off well on the Sunday and that the boys seemed to be settling down and full of stories about their new friends, though Johnny was a little pale, she said nothing. I must see them next Sunday, Jane was thinking. I must not neglect them, or Mrs Ogilvie will be able to criticize me for other things. The house was very quiet and she went up to her room at the top which looked out over the leafy square. She would write to her aunt and uncle immediately after her solitary meal.

The next morning she was just sealing up her letter before asking Polly to take it to the point where mail for the Continent was collected, when she heard the postboy's bell. That could mean only that there were letters for the household. She had better hold her missive back in case there was another letter from Italy.

But the letter was for herself – and bore the seal of Charles Fitzpercy. Her heart beat faster and she went back up into her room to read it. It was dated two days before and written from S – House, a large mansion in Middlesex. 'My dear girl,' it said.

I am but yesterday returned to the South of England and hasten to thank you for the letter you wrote before I left London. I had to go away – . If I told you I had enemies it would shock and

160

frighten you, would it not? But at the moment all is quiet and I am released for a time from my own daemon of melancholy. I write from near the family seat of my cousins – or they would be my cousins if I had been acknowledged as my father's child. One of them takes pity on me now and then. Our other family seat is at Salton Delevinge where I have been to soothe my spirit. The verses whose publication you so kindly arranged were written under the influence of that place. I long for a little fresh air and the company of someone young and green, yours in fact. Will you walk with me at Hampstead? It is a fancy I have taken – that I should introduce you to a good friend of mine – also a writer. He would be glad to know I had a friend such as you. Will you come? You could leave your maid at the house of my friend who is perfectly respectable – Mr Farquharson. You can get a coach to Camden Town, and then a hack chaise. Tell Daisy if you can come, and meet me at two of the clock on Wednesday at the Well Walk Cottages, number seven.

Your friend, Charles Fitzpercy.

To say that Jane was astonished would be an understatement; she was puzzled, excited, worried, and incredulously happy. Charles Fitzpercy felt a little for her! Sufficiently to want to walk with her, to talk with her. It was amazing. Yet it was a strange letter. She read it over and over again. Why had he had to leave London? Why could he not ask her to write to the address from which he wrote? Who were these enemies about whom he seemed to want to warn her? Hastily she went down with the letter she had written to her uncle and took Polly out with her to Covent Garden. She found Daisy there, who promised to deliver the message. She seemed a little shy, a little abrupt, and they did not linger in conversation.

Why could Charles not meet her himself? Why such obfuscations? Did he think he was living in a novel by Mrs Radcliffe? Was he a Hamlet or a Lord Byron, or just a disappointed man?

161

On her return she dined with Mrs Ogilvie who talked about little Johnny being homesick. Poor little boy, she thought, with his mama and papa away. Had little Charles Fitzpercy missed a mama and a papa when he was small? Not for the first time she found herself feeling a strange maternal sort of feeling for the grown man – wished she could look after him and cherish him. How strange. He *was* a grown man, not a child! She wondered what sort of child he had been. Had he been a victim of bullying? She knew how cruel children could be. Yet he was tall and looked strong enough. His queer way of speaking though – as though humour was a defence against himself – for it could not be a defence against her the few times she had spoken to him, surely? Well, she would find out.

She could scarcely sleep for thinking about the morrow; long speeches wound in and out of her head and her brain seemed to be excited. She tried to calm herself by breathing slowly and deeply.

'I shall be out with Polly this afternoon, doing an errand in Hampstead for Charlotte Howard,' she said glibly to Mrs Ogilvie next morning. 'I have to collect some copy for our paper,' she added unnecessarily and before Ogilvie could say: However are you to get to Hampstead? she was out of the house. She chafed at the fact of Ogilvie's presence but did not wish to worry the good lady, and, after all, she was of age and had a perfect right to take a drive to Hampstead, had she not? If she were not yet a 'lady', well, she might as well enjoy the privileges of not being one.

She forgot about Mrs Ogilvie and about everything else when, after the journey had been successfully accomplished, they finally arrived in Hampstead, and took directions to Well Walk. Only six miles from Lincoln's Inn and it was a different world. The sun shone and the Heath was glinting under it. Several families were walking

162

near the village. She had imagined a deserted heath, but this was a pretty little place with a spa spring. They made their way down to number seven and a fresh, cheerful-looking girl opened the door of a little cottage.

'There, Polly, I shall leave you here,' she was saying just as the maid retreated, and then there appeared a shadow on the path behind them and, as she turned, she saw it was indeed Charles. Polly looked at him curiously as she followed the other maid into the cottage. For a moment Jane felt she could not move. Her excitement had ended in paralysing her!

'Come,' he said, without more ado. 'It is a delightful afternoon for a walk.' He turned back and shouted through the still open door: 'We are to take the air, Mrs Farquharson,' and then he turned to Jane, smiling. She made an effort and smiled at him. She had never had the time to look at him closely for long and wished to feast her eyes on him, but felt she must not. Her feet finally obeyed her will and she followed him meekly.

'It was good of you to come all this way,' he said as he led her across a little lane to a stile and helped her over it. She said nothing till they were over the stile and walking towards a pond where several boys were fishing. He looked different today, not tortured or brooding, but just a young man out for a walk. 'Let us sit down,' he said with a half-look at her. There was a bench not far from the pond and they sat down, the sunshine beaming down upon them. She wanted to say: Why are you so mysterious? but did not want to spoil his mood.

'I wish it were easier for ladies to walk alone in London,' she ventured instead. 'It is such an affair to get out – and then I must take Polly. It would be easier in Bedon, but then people would talk I suppose.'

'You mean if you were walking out with me?'

163

'Well, with any man. People have no thoughts in their head but gossiping about one's doings – it is easy for men. You can go where you want, do what you want . . .'

'You would rather be a man, Jane Banham?'

'I think so – except, of course, I believe women are a superior race.'

He laughed. 'You may be right about that – but tell me, are you not afraid to make an assignation with a man you have met only twice?'

'We have written to each other,' she replied stiffly – and then, 'No I am not afraid. I could never be afraid of *you* – though you do write strange things.'

'Did you read more Byron?' he asked after a pause.

'Oh, yes – and Philip says some more cantos of "Don Juan" are just arrived from the poet and all London is talking of them.'

'And did they talk about Byron when you went to Hertfordshire? I gather the whole March coterie was at Frederick Digby's.'

'How did you know that?'

'Ha – I have my spies,' he replied.

Jane was silent, thinking how she had recited that verse of his. Would he be angry if she told him? 'Did you go to Salton Delevinge?' she asked instead.

'Yes, I told you – and then to my family's other house.'

'Charles,' she said. 'Who was your father?'

'A nobleman.'

'And who your mother?'

'I believe she was a servant of my father's – she died when I was born. Tell me about yourself, Jane Banham.'

'Why do you want to know?'

'Why do *you* want to know about *me*?'

'Because I – I like you,' she answered and looked up at him. 'Will you send Philip some more of your verses?' she

164

asked after another pause. 'You must put your name to them.'

'You may invent a name for me. I have no real name – the Fitzpercy was a fancy of mine when I was seventeen or so.'

'Why not Percy Charles?'

'Why not indeed! Thank you – that sounds well.'

She looked up at him and he seemed to flinch a little. 'Are you very unhappy?'

'Not today. Tell me about your doings – your uncle and your host of last week – and Philip March.'

As she spoke she realized that he paid attention to all she said. Should she try to discover more, or would that annoy him? She felt she knew him in all the essential ways. What did it matter what other people said? Why should she spoil the first – or perhaps the only – time she would ever be alone with him, in gossip? He was there. She was with him and she felt comfortable, as though she had known him all her life.

'You have not told me which of these accomplished young men you are going to marry,' he said when she had finished describing Vine House and the dandies and Frederick Digby, with Philip March thrown in for good measure. She found herself speaking rather sharply of Philip without any intention of belittling him but his question took her by surprise.

'I am not going to marry any of them,' she replied.

'No, I think you will be a bluestocking girl and end up like those spinster ladies who write for Drury Lane and tend their aged parents.'

'I have no aged parents to tend,' she said. 'But I admire those ladies. I'm sure I could never be so unselfish.' (Except on your behalf, she thought.)

Then she told him about Miss Landon, which made him

165

laugh. When he laughed, his mouth revealed slightly crooked teeth. Then he turned away again and she regarded his profile. He was certainly handsome, she thought, although his nose was rather big. His eyes were deep yet clear and his smile lit up his face, making it the face of a youth, not someone who must be about ten years older than herself. When his face changed and brooded he looked older.

They talked on and each moment was precious to her. Yet he seemed to want to say more than he had so far revealed about himself, though she could not say how she knew that.

'You have the advantage over me,' she said at last. 'For you know more about me than I do about you.'

'Perhaps there is just more of the same,' he said. 'As I have the advantage of age over you, I have some years' experience which you will never catch up. I thought when I first saw you that I had known you, and in the bookshop – and then what someone said – I don't know. I am not mad, you know, and you need not be frightened of me. I would do you no harm. I felt I should like a friend like you, some girl who was young and unspoilt and yet intelligent – am I presuming too much? It is not what you think. I am not out to seduce you – '

'Oh, but you do seduce me,' she replied, 'by your way of talking to me and by your poems, and because you are so mysterious, and I think you are – wayward – though you make me laugh. I expect you gamble and drink like all men seem to – well, most men – yet I . . . I did not know you before and perhaps I do not know you now, but I feel I do.'

'Perhaps we are twin souls,' he said with a smile. Then his face changed and he said: 'I do not bring luck to my friends – it might be better if we had not met – but I

166

wanted to talk to you. I talk to Daisy, you know, but Daisy does not understand. She likes you. She thought you were "funny" – I think she meant not like most young ladies, and you are not.'

And you are not like any man I have ever met before, she thought. And I would like to give my heart away to you – but I don't think that is what you want. Not my heart, or my body . . . something else, I don't know what. Perhaps it *is* my soul?

'Now we know each other a little better,' he said, 'I can introduce you to my friends over there. Come – let us go – I think Mrs Farquharson will expect me to take you into her parlour for one of her cups of green tea. They live on it, except when he drinks beer with me. They will not think it odd that I should have a girl for a friend – do not worry about that. You are a good girl, Jane: *will* you be that friend?'

Oh, yes, she would! She would be anything he wanted. But all she could say, still unsure of what one could say to a young man whom one did not really know, although at another level one felt one knew profoundly, was, I wish we could meet more often. Then she added, 'Of course, I understand you would not wish to come to my uncle's house.'

'No, I do not belong there,' he said shortly.

Charles was not unmindful of the fact that Jane was not free to return home at all hours as he was himself, and knew she would worry about finding her way in a chaise back to London, for he said: 'I know we cannot stay all day talking. It was kind of you to come all this way to see me.'

'I can see you in London whenever you want,' she answered boldly, looking up to him with her dark blue eyes and wishing she could drink him like a draught of potent wine. He smiled but then he turned away.

'Where is your home now?' she asked him, after a silence.

'Ah, do not ask me where I lay my head,' he said. 'Everywhere, nowhere.'

'But where do you feel most at home?'

'Oh, at Salton in the north. It is so wild – and it *was* my home.'

For a time he said no more and she stole a look at him and thought he looked haunted. She wanted to take his hand, somehow to comfort him. But they began to drift slowly back across the Heath to the stile in the direction of the Vale. When they got to the stile where the sandy path joined the lane to the little cottages in the dip and up to the walk, she leaned against it. She had taken her bonnet off and its ribbons trailed over her hands. She felt sad – and yet she was by his side. She looked up into the sky before turning to steal another glance at him.

'Stay for a moment like that,' he said. 'The sight of you does my soul good, I believe.' Then she turned her face full on to his and it was as if they both involuntarily shivered, as though a ghost had passed over their graves or some wandering wind had touched them both.

She is not just a pretty little girl, he was thinking. And yet why should I feel my destiny is interwoven with hers? He had always been chary of revealing anything of himself to another, but he remembered the words of Rebecca the last time she looked over his hands and cast the cards when she had said something about a 'Jennet' bringing him luck. So he said lightly: 'Did they ever call you Jennet – for "little Jane", I mean – when you were a child?'

She looked puzzled for a moment for she was aware that he was thinking strange thoughts. 'Papa may have called me so,' she replied, considering for a moment. 'But I do not really remember. 'Why, Charles?' Then she stopped in some confusion. 'I am sorry – I should say Mr Fitzpercy, should I not? – or Mr Fitz, perhaps, as your friend Daisy calls you.'

'No, you must call me Charles,' he said firmly. He laid his hand over her pale brown one and appeared to study her other hand which he took in his as though he were a palmist himself. 'It baffles me. There is a sort of recognition I feel. Forgive me if I speak wildly. It was that night when I nearly stumbled under your carriage – and I felt it then, for no reason that I know of . . .' He did not add: that is why I followed you into the bookshop.

'Yes,' she said simply. 'I feel it, too.'

'A sudden intimation that we should be friends – if that is possible between men and women.' Then he added, trying to sound less serious, 'Come, I must introduce you to Mrs Farquharson – and to Michael, too, if he is returned from London. We must take our dish of tea.'

As they walked slowly across the lane with the great clouds sweeping over them, but not obscuring the golden light from the sun, she had the curious feeling of having somehow been there before; that moment and its complex of feelings seemed to arouse something felt long ago. It puzzled her and went on puzzling her, even up to the door of the cottage which they had to stoop low to enter. Then it faded and she said nothing of it to him but gathered up her social sense. The spell was broken, in any case. Other people seemed to accept her as Charles's friend quite naturally and she had no more opportunity to speak of her own feelings. It was enough to have had their object before her, with her hand in his. She did not feel at all shy in his company or in the company of Michael Farquharson and his young wife, who was nursing

169

a baby and had another at her skirts. But her heart could not help singing: I love you, I love you, and wishing, in spite of common sense, that she could stay with him for ever and share his life and his thoughts and his bed.

In spite, too, of the general sense of ordinariness brought about by the cottage and its inhabitants and the tea-drinking and the quiet conversation, when she had to bid them all 'farewell and return to the chaise with Polly, her heart was still singing. But to leave him was like a pain and as he handed her into the carriage on the dusty road, she briefly took his hand herself and said: 'Please let me know you are well – do not forget.'

She was silent all the way back to Town and Polly stole a glance at her now and then and remained silent herself, out of respect for her mistress's mood. Lincoln's Inn Square seemed to have nothing to do with her and her real life when they returned. She went up to her room and sat thinking about him till the night fell.

She had to pull herself together, of course. Jane had plenty of common sense and she was also determined that her love for Charles Fitzpercy should never reach the ears of anyone but Polly. In the meantime she must continue her self-imposed task of writing her sketches. But she often found herself hearing his voice as though he were there in the room with her. What did he really want from her? She wanted, and yet did not want, to talk about him to someone else, to talk of his charm and his wayward-ness, to think of his brooding good looks – for surely anyone must agree he was handsome? To think of his character, to recall their conversation, to read his verse. I was in love with him before I even knew him, she thought – and now I *do* know him. I should like to follow him to the end of the world, to be with him at that place in the north. She dreamed that he cried: 'Save me, save me,

Jane!' but she kept all this to herself except that her private book of poems began to fill with verses of her own.

His name did come up some time later, though she had heard no more from him. She was at Charlotte's and Henrietta's new house where they had now moved and had already received two girls for boarding. The *New London* was to burst upon the world in a few days and Jane had been summoned to receive her copy. Jane had already told Philip that Charles wished to sign himself in future 'Percy Charles'. Julia Jeffrey was there and Miss Kelly and the talk was of the *Hamlet* shortly to be staged. No men were present which made the conversation more unbuttoned. Frances Kelly, and even Julia, seemed a little more ordinary in the cruel light of London and both rattled on exclusively about their roles in the next Macready production. Frances had hoped to play Ophelia, but her voice was not now strong enough even for the whisper of a mad girl, a whisper which had to be projected over the vast auditorium. Julia was not cast at all in the *Hamlet*, but was sure she would be taken on for *Macbeth*. The plans for that play were still unformulated, except in Macready's mind, according to them. He himself would be Hamlet, of course. Jane did not take much part in the conversation at first, but listened carefully. How she would like to go to *Hamlet*! She hoped someone would produce tickets. The talk passed to the opera, about which she was even more ignorant, and then to the difficulties Charlotte and her friend were experiencing in filling their little academy. Charlotte had now been to a soirée at Miss Benger's, the literary lady of great fame, and was hopeful that some contacts she had made there would produce some infant daughters to be consigned to their care.

171

'I'm sure Mr Bruce would help,' said Henrietta. 'He moves in just the right circles. Has he yet returned from his walking tour?'

'A little bird told me,' said Julia, 'that your "Mr Bruce" is busy in the country with a lady.'

'Bruce is not his real name, of course,' said Charlotte. 'His mama would not like his real name known. Up till now he has used Bruce for his *nom de plume*. I hear that he comes from a very wealthy family.'

'And was slighted in love if you remember, but not by the present lady,' said Julia. She seemed to know all the gossip. Jane wondered if she had anything more to say on the subject of Fitzpercy, but was determined not to introduce his name.

But Julia was off on another subject – Fred Digby. 'That silly rake', she called him.

'Oh, Miss Jeffrey. I am sure he is not,' protested Jane.

'No? Now, my dear, we know what we know,' said Julia provokingly. 'Not as rakish, perhaps, as that poet whose verse you quoted, but still a rake.' They were going on to discuss dandies, of whom both girls seemed to know a good many. Jane wondered, if they so disapproved of their men friends, why they put up with their company. But at least the conversation was not very 'ladylike'. The girls were only on the fringes of smart society, of course – they had not yet been invited to Almack's. But their friends Miss Foote and Miss Stevens had their sights set on young lords who preferred actresses to the insipid seventeen-year-olds cast up by the Season.

The conversation was waning and the ladies making gestures preparatory to leaving, when the little maid who had moved with them from Temple Gardens, showed up Philip and Christopher.

They were bearing bundles of magazines and trailing

brown paper behind them. 'See!' – Philip was almost dancing with glee – 'Here we are – first edition. We brought them straight along. We're *out*!' Jane caught her breath. She was not thinking of her own small contribution, but of the verse of Charles's which she had not yet seen, since Philip had shown her only what he was not using.

Julia grabbed a copy and began to study it intently. '"Remarks on Elia" . . . "the case for a National Portrait Gallery" . . . "A Gothic story" by E. Bruce – "Two Ladies" – the writings of Mrs Baillie and Miss Edgeworth – "A Soul in Vauxhall" . . . "Round the Clubs" by Socrates. Who is that? You, Phil? "Death of a young Poet" – Shelley or someone else? . . . "Letter to a Country Cousin – From a Friend" . . .' Jane's heart began to beat so strongly she was sure they could see it jumping up and down behind her bodice. Julia went on. '"The Sunset over the Sea", lyrics by P. C. – aha that's Jane's stranger.' Philip rescued a copy of the journal, which was printed on flimsy paper, and tossed it to Jane.

'There you are. It's not too bad, is it? Cockburn is to do the distribution – '

Julia interrupted him. 'I should say it has something for all tastes, Mr March.'

Charlotte and Henrietta were sharing the pages eagerly. Christopher had taken up his usual stance, supporting his head on his hand and looking reflectively into the empty grate.

Jane finally saw her little piece tucked away at the end of the magazine. It did not seem to have anything to do with her. It was strange – had she really written that?

'It's quite good, Miss,' said Frances Kelly observing her.

173

'Why, it's all very good – and will soon be followed by our next special issue,' said Philip taking the opportunity to sit down next to Julia who now ignored him.

'I suppose we are filling a gap between the *Examiner* and the *London Magazine*, but I wish we had not called ours the *new* London,' said Henrietta.

'We really must go,' said Julia.

'I'll get you a hackney carriage, if you must,' said Philip, disappointed. 'See – you may have a free copy for your friends at Drury Lane. Make sure they read it.'

The ladies retired downstairs with many protestations of affection to Charlotte. When only Charlotte and Henrietta were left in the room – Christopher seemed asleep – Jane turned to 'The Sunset over the Sea'. It was a very strange poem, full of turbulent rhymes and garish colours, almost nightmarish in its intensity. She wondered if he took opium – it had that hectic quality – but as she read on the colours dissolved into the picture of a calm sea and strand, a pale and ghostly moon changed into a new sunrise. What sort of man could write like that? It was powerful stuff. She turned back again to the beginning: 'For there a lady walks with hair distraught/ And casts her form into the boiling sea./ Returning to the water all her grief/ To join her tears to all eternity . . ./ And nevermore shall Halls cast pools of light/ Nor birds be drawn into the house of life/ But wandering evermore they'll plough the sea . . .' He must be writing of the place that he said haunted him. She looked up and saw Charlotte observing her.

'Are you not going to look at your own work?' she asked. 'I thought it read very well – just the right touch of the provinces, but cleverly done.'

'I wish I could write verse,' sighed Jane.

'Oh, few people read the verse – they want only to read

of themselves,' said Henrietta. 'Philip is pleased, is he not?'

'Will it make his name? Will it fall on the right ears?' mused Charlotte. 'For the general taste, and yet with enough of literary value to keep the reviewers busy?'

'We can only wait and see,' replied Philip's sister. 'For my part I feel ready to get on with our own plans – we must write the rest of the letters, my dear. Perhaps Jane would help?'

So Jane spent the rest of the afternoon copying the letter of introduction of the 'New Fulham Boarding Academy for the Daughters of Gentlemen' to various parents. They had had three more little girls promised for the next week and from now on their time would be fully employed teaching and nurturing the young charges who arrived in Fulham. There was a great deal to do and Charlotte, for one, was glad to have it to do.

Jane and Polly returned in a hansom, Jane clutching her precious copy of the *New London* and wondering how it would be received by Charles and by its sponsor, Fred Digby, and by all the men who accounted themselves readers.

There were two letters awaiting her on her return. Letters were one of her chief delights and she still enjoyed writing them, so long as she could live in delicious anticipation of replies. One was from her aunt, the other was from Frederick Digby, whom she had thought to be in Hertfordshire. She scanned it rapidly. It was written in a small, neat and beautifully flowing hand. An invitation to *Hamlet* the Tuesday of the next week – when he was making up a party. He signed himself 'Ever yours'.

She wondered whether what Julia had said was true, that he was 'rakish'. Julia talks a lot of nonsense, she thought. She remembered his 'Trust me' on the occasion

175

of her leaving Vine House for the second time and was sure he had been sincere.

She replied to her aunt and uncle, reassuring them as to the health and happiness of their boys who were to come home soon for a Saturday and Sunday, and then decided to accept Frederick Digby's invitation. Perhaps Mr Digby had a *faiblesse* for her: it was not unknown for married men whose wives were absent to take a fancy to a girl. But he was honourable – not that it would have stopped Jane if he had not been and if she had nursed a spark in her heart for the elegant Fred. But the spark she nursed was for the outcast Charles. She supposed women should always have their wits about them, even so.

She was to be in a party along with Fred's sister at the theatre, which seemed excessively respectable. The theatre was always an attraction; this would be her third visit. She knew Charles would never take her to the theatre. It would be a waste to go to the theatre with *him*, for she would be looking at him rather than the stage. She could not see herself in any company with Charles Fitzpercy. He did sometimes go to theatres like anyone else, she knew, but he did not belong to a shared social world. Or perhaps to any social world. Fred, though, was a perfect companion for the theatre – better than Philip, more worldly wise and more amusing.

In the event she forgot all her scruples when she entered the theatre with Frederick Digby's party. His sister was a quiet and dignified woman some years older than himself; and there were two young men of about Philip March's age who also seemed to have something to do with writing, a girl cousin of his who was almost tongue-tied, and a handsome young lady who apparently adored one of the young men. The men were addressed as Hood and Ainsworth and it was only later that she realized the elder

176

of the two had worked on the original *London Magazine*. He was a dark, slight, young man who talked a good deal of engraving, nothing of poetry. He was most amusing company and most solicitous to the young lady who adored him. The younger man was scarcely more than a boy, but excessively handsome and seemed to be some connection of Fred Digby's solicitor. He spoke with a strong northern accent and discussed opera with Fred with great aplomb. It was a most successful party, all of whose members had something to say for themselves with the exception of the girl cousin who kept twisting her fan in her fingers till Jane thought it must take flight from such prolonged mangling. But Fred's sister took charge of her and spoke in a kindly fashion, so that by the interval the girl was almost human. Jane gave herself up to her favourite tragedy and forgot the company whilst Macready's mellifluous tones and the Bard's wonderful language transported her to the other world of imagination. She did not think of making words about it, wanted only to submit herself to the art. There would be time enough to think about it later. So many times she had read the play, but never seen it, and she was quite surprised when, in the second interval, the two young men discussed the 'production' not the play. What other way was there of 'producing' such a play than to have England's finest young actor speak England's finest words? Fred noticed that she was quiet and came up to her in the salon where the party had repaired to eat the usual delicious confections.

'You say little. Do you agree, then, with Tom Hood that Macready is stealing the thunder from Ophelia and making solemn what should be a whimsical madness?'

'I could not think of the "production" I am afraid – I was listening to the words. How else could they be said? He is

177

perfect – and yet there is so much to think about in the words themselves. I should like to see it a thousand times.'

Fred gave his delighted smile and his sharp eyes looked into hers a little disconcertingly, yet with a good deal of interest. 'Are we to expect that the Country Cousin's Correspondent will deliver herself of her verdict very soon?'

'Oh, please – don't mention that. I'm sure Mr March thinks I was lucky to get those rather artless paragraphs printed and now he will be looking for another sort of critic.'

'But that is what the readers want. You tell them what they probably think themselves, but are too worldly to dare to say.'

'Mr Digby,' began Jane. 'Tell me truly – am I *very* naïve? I thought I was playing at being so – but perhaps it is my natural foolishness.' She was aware as she spoke that she was flirting a little with him but he took her seriously and said:

'But I saw March the other day and he was full of your praise – and my sister, too, has read you.'

'Mr March – Philip – praised me?'

'Why, yes – he has not seen you? He thought you would be soon ready with another of your sketches.'

'He has said nothing to me – but, of course, he was too busy and excited to say anything very much. Well I shall be ready with another piece when he asks me.'

'And how are you managing? You should have been to Vine House this week with the wonderful weather. It was a pity we had only one good day when you came. Did you like my house?'

'I loved it,' replied Jane simply. 'I should like to describe your garden one day – it made me a little homesick for Norfolk.'

'Will you write of it for the *New London* then? If you are a horticultural enthusiast, I shall send you lists of all my plants so you don't get them wrong.'

'Oh, I should never write of it for the *New London*. I could not be "amusing" about a place like that.'

He was silent, regarding her. 'You always mean what you say and say what you mean, Jane. It is a rare talent.'

She was a little discomfited but did not drop her eyes when he continued to look at her. She thought he had rather a sorrowful expression. But he had a command not unlike Charles's. He was his own man. His sister came up and Fred led the talk back to journalism. The young cousin gaped at Jane till Jane took her arm and said: 'Are you enjoying the play? I expect you have seen it many times?'

'Oh, no, Miss. I am staying with my aunt at Uncle Fred's and it is the first time I have been out with them. At home Papa and Mama are too busy with their hunting and their gardens and their children – my sisters and brothers – to take me to the theatre. I have been to the Assembly Rooms, though,' she added proudly.

Jane saw she was not above seventeen and a pretty girl. Perhaps she had been brought along for Mr Ainsworth, but he was paying her no attention, being wrapped up in a discussion with Mr Hood, productive of occasional loud guffaws.

After the theatre they were to eat supper at Fred Digby's town house. It was not in fashionable Mayfair nor Belgravia, but tucked away in a part of Bloomsbury in a leafy square of old houses with a Dutch look. 'They are going to build around us,' sighed Fred when the party were at last sitting round his oval dining table and cold meats had been brought in. His sister, Clarissa, was doing the honours as hostess.

179

'Alas,' said Clarissa. 'All will soon be changed in our old London – and not only here, but I believe in parts of lower Belgravia. There is money for every sort of speculation.'

The conversation passed to a criticism of Mr Nash's style and thence to the doings at Court and the Wars and back to the state of England and once more to *Hamlet* and thence – to please the young cousin and Mr Ainsworth – to the novels of the age. The older couple were always ready to hear the opinions of the younger members of the party. They fell to criticizing the 'new' vocabulary with its 'pseudos and antis and ultras', the sort of words Philip March was wont to use.

It was an unusual combination, thought Jane. Not many middle-aged people would put themselves about to invite the young. Mr Hood, whose nickname seemed to be Theodore, told a story or two with a keenly adjusted sense of humour and many puns appropriate to a fairly refined, mixed party and kept glancing at the young lady who adored him, a Miss Reynolds.

'I have to be a lively Hood to earn my livelihood,' he said at one point with a lingering look at his beloved.

'I shall take Theodore to Norfolk in summer,' said she and the conversation turned to Jane's home county where, apparently, Miss Reynolds had relatives. Miss Reynolds knew of Frances Kelly, too, and had known the poet John Keats. Then Mr Ainsworth spoke of English history and told a few anecdotes in his strong northern voice and, all in all, when the party broke up, and they were waiting for the carriages, it was a merry and harmonious assembly who bade each other farewell. Jane was thinking of the library she had seen adjoining the room where they had supped and was plucking up courage to ask if she might

180

borrow a book from it one day when Fred came up to her.

'You may bring Hal's boys on a Sunday,' he said. 'They would like a walk and I am not averse to the company of children. My sister will be here for a few weeks, so do come. Then I can tell my old friend how his charges are getting along. I shall write to him of you – of course. Young people keep us young, you know.'

'Too many little boys might age one, I think,' replied Jane. 'They are very fine in small doses but tiring to have at home all the time.'

'I was thinking more of you – and Hood here – and Ainsworth,' he answered. 'I think of you as young. I hope all will go well with you – apart from the scribbling, of course.'

He was such a kind man, she thought, and genuine in his protestations. 'I should indeed like to visit with the children – and perhaps I might look at your town library? I so enjoyed browsing in the one at Vine House.'

'Of course you may, but do bring them before the month is out. I may visit abroad myself in winter – and see your uncle in person.'

Perhaps he was going to rejoin his wife?

'Goodbye, Jane, and thank you for gracing *Hamlet* and my table,' he said as she was thanking him once more for the evening. His hand lingered for a moment in hers before he turned at the portico of the narrow house and went indoors with his sister.

Jane had plenty of time during the rest of the week to think about *Hamlet* and went back to her old copy of Shakespeare once more. She wondered if the infamous Byron had, in part, modelled himself on that hero, just as she was sure both Bruce and even her dear Charles

181

Fitzpercy had perhaps unknowingly been influenced by the Bad Lord. Who was there on whom girls could model themselves? Scarcely Ophelia. Beatrice might be more appropriate. *She* was a little like Miss Austen's Elizabeth Bennett, both of them with a ready wit and great feelings carefully concealed. Both of them, too, got their lovers in the end. She herself felt more like *Hamlet* – it did not seem to matter that he was a man!

When Sunday came, it brought the boys with it and she made a special effort to talk to them and listen to their tales. At first they were very quiet, adjusting themselves to their old home and the absence of their papa and mama. Then, little by little, they became more confiding and made a good dinner. In the afternoon little Johnny crept close to her and she petted him. He seemed quite happy to sit near her and was more subdued than he had been at the school. The other two boys became boisterous, but she sat on with Johnny and talked about Italy and how his parents would soon be back.

'I think you are like a big sister,' said Johnny. 'Did you ever have a brother?'

'No, dear. I did have a little boy brother – but he died when he was a baby.' She did not believe in mincing matters to children. 'He was only very small,' she added, 'and so I never knew him like I know you.' Then she added, in case the child should become morbid: 'Of course, he was rather weak – not like you and Jimmy and Tom who are all big strong boys.'

'Oh, I am very strong,' replied the little boy, 'only it is nice to be at home.'

She thought he was not unhappy at Dr Macdonald's, if a little homesick.

Before they left she gave them each some sweetmeats and asked Jimmy to take special care of his brothers.

182

'And mind, if anyone worries you – or you are not satisfied with things – you must tell me or Mrs Ogilvie. Promise? Then I shall write again to your mama to tell her of all your adventures.'

They were borne away once more and she felt a little sad. She *would* have liked a brother, or a sister, of her own age.

On the Monday following she received a letter from the offices of the *New London* enclosing a note for one guinea signed by the Editor, Philip March, with a flourishing signature that she could scarcely have deciphered if she had not known it. He had changed his mind then and was taking her work as worthy of payment? There was a scrawl around it on a piece of flimsy paper written in a great hurry. The gist was that several people had commented on her little piece and he would be happy to receive another. She was watering the indoor garden which she had promised her aunt to nurture when the post-boy arrived again, his bell tinkling before him. At this rate she would have to earn another guinea to pay her franks!

It was from the fair Julia herself – an invitation to a small assembly at her house on Henrietta Street. Charlotte and Henrietta would no longer be able to attend such a function, being immersed in their little academy, but she and Fanny would be pleased if Jane would take a dish of tea with them at four o'clock on Wednesday. Heigh-ho, she supposed she had 'arrived' if she were to be invited by such persons in her own right and not as a friend of so-and-so. Philip would be there and it might be amusing. William would, she hoped, take her in the carriage since Uncle Hal had left instructions she might use it. She wanted to arrive in a little style. It was only for tea and perhaps there would only be ladies there, since

183

gentlemen avoided tea and did not usually visit at such hours. Except, of course, for men like Philip who were free at all hours.

In fact, when she did arrive at Julia's that afternoon, she was amazed at the number of carriages outside the rather shabby house. She had forgotten that actors were often free before going on to the theatre and always free when they had no engagements. The party was crowded up the stairs and into a small courtyard at the back and she felt happily inconspicuous until a voice hailed her.

'My dear Jane!' It was Philip dressed in a new suit of serge with a noble cravat and a general air of casual elegance. He was continually greeted by other men who were trooping up and down the stairs.

Jane did not think she would get her dish of tea, but stuck to Philip as Julia and Fanny were not visible. Apparently it was *de rigueur* to pass through the little salon at the top of the stairs, greet the hostesses, and pass down again. A little like the crowd for the guillotine, she thought. Finally they arrived at the top of the stairs. Julia was pouring tea, decked out in a robe of vaguely Indian provenance and wearing a turban.

'My dear! Do stay behind when the crowd has gone – too, too wearing – and Philip!' She appeared to almost swoon with joy. There were several other young men drifting around in attendance and Fanny, dressed in pink silk, sat on a high chair decked with ribbons. Somehow Jane was separated from Philip for a time and managed to balance her tea on a high window-sill and listen to the conversation around her.

'Oh, he'll not get Julia,' someone said.

'An ambitious cove,' someone else replied.

And a female voice: 'My dear, it was a *grande passion*.'

'What has love to do with anything?' asked another

184

voice. 'Laurence has his little milliners and servants. Actresses are all very well, but chaps need heiresses.'

'Don't be naughty, Martin – here comes a beauty.'

She wondered if Philip had been the subject of part of their conversation, but was never to know, for Philip appeared again and introduced her to a portly old man. 'Here is our Country Cousin's correspondent,' were his words and Jane strove to interest the portly man, who stared at her rather rudely. Her first contact with her unknown public!

Later, she managed to elude him and was on the point of going out when, the crush now having lessened, she was intercepted by Fanny, who had got down from her throne. 'Come – there is another room and we can talk. Do tell us all the gossip! I hear you have been to *Hamlet* – did you see me? Was I good?' Fanny had had a minor part as serving maid to Ophelia, but Jane was able to tell her she had been truly magnificent.

'And how is Mr Digby? I hear he is still in London.'

'I believe he goes abroad for the winter.'

'Ah, that will be to Italy to see his wife.' She sighed. 'Such a pity, that marriage. It was Clara's money that kept Vine House going, you know.' No, Jane did not know. 'And have you seen your mysterious man – the poet? I read him in Phil's magazine – ah, my dear, it was splendid stuff.' She rattled on and Jane found herself in an antechamber where Julia was holding court.

Philip was now lounging against the chair in which she sat dispensing her favours and seemed not displeased to be seen in the company of his goddess. Fanny led Jane to another chair, and various young men circled round the room before finally disposing themselves to take a seat.

They all seemed excessively agreeable and were

185

obviously of Julia's 'inner circle', for the crowd had begun to thin and at last one could hear oneself speak.

'They will all go on to Miss Lacy's,' said Fanny. 'Julia will disappear too, I think, for she has been invited. I can't go as I am on stage in an hour or two. It is a great nuisance when everyone will have their at home days on the same afternoon.'

This was not anything like any at home day Jane had ever before attended, but she drank her tea with every appearance of enjoyment. Some time later, Julia arose from her seat and bowed to everyone, including Philip, before disappearing with a young actor. Jane smiled at Philip, left stranded in the middle of the room. He came up to her, a little cross.

'How did you find Campbell, then?'

'Campbell?'

'Yes, the old gent I introduced you to.'

'Oh dear, I'm afraid he stared at me rather and I managed to elude him – is he important?'

'Only another editor,' said Philip. 'Never mind – we don't want you going over to *him*. When will your next *pièce de résistance* be ready? Have you chosen your subjects? I want you to write me several and then I can choose which will go best with the contents of the second number.'

'Thank you for the guinea,' said Jane after a pause. 'I believe I shall write of *Hamlet*. I shall pretend to discuss it but discuss the costumes – and the *production*,' she added. 'That is what they were all talking about when I went.'

'Don't you think you could leave the theatre and write of the streets – say a posy or garland of beauties – something like that – for our lady readers?'

'Now you are being malicious, Philip. Maybe I can't be

a dramatic critic, but I have no wish just to lighten the tone so that *ladies* will buy our review.'

'Well, you must do as you wish. Perhaps you could write of the contrasts between ladies in the country and here.'

'Yes, I might do that. I could write of the comparative restrictions placed upon us in Town.'

'You feel unduly restricted then? I thought we had introduced you to all the unrespectable in Grub Street.'

'You know you have not.'

Philip seemed inclined today to listen to her. Probably because Julia had gone, he was making the best of it. It amused Jane and she was a little sorry for him.

The time came, though, when she felt she would be overstaying her welcome to accept any more refreshment and she resolved to see if Polly had arrived to accompany her back to Lincoln's Inn Fields. She had not wanted the carriage to wait. Philip decided to leave, too, and they both assured Fanny how much they had enjoyed themselves. Polly was waiting on the stairs and they all came out into the sunshine and blue sky over the arcades of Covent Garden. They were just crossing the street to walk in a northerly direction, when Jane heard 'Miss!' and a whistle and saw Daisy Collins amongst her bright flowers. Daisy waved and then turned away to serve a customer and by the time Jane came up with Philip and Polly she was pretending not to see them.

'Wait a moment,' said Jane. 'She will want to see me alone, perhaps.' She asked the mystified Philip to walk on a few paces. 'Hello, Daisy. Did you whistle me?'

'Well I did – but seeing you was with another gentleman thought perhaps I'd better not.'

'You don't need to worry about Mr March. He is the editor of the magazine I told you about. Is it a message from Charles – from Mr Fitzpercy?'

'I thought you ought to know like, he's been ter see my grandma again, drat 'er. I told my auntie to tell you when she came to you for the sewing yesterday, but she wouldn't.'

'But *why* does he visit your grandmother, Daisy? Or why does your aunt think *I* ought not to know that he does?'

'It's just that he's back in London, Miss, and I knew you'd like to know he was well. He comes to Gran for the cards, you see. He says to me the other night – pitch black it was and I didn't know what was on our doorstep coming out when I came in and it was Fitz all excited and – "Tell Jane," he says, "I'll be writing to her. I'm staying in Mayfair – she might be wondering what has happened to me," he says.'

'Yes, I was – so you think he will write to me?'

'Course he will if he says so – some might think you couldn't trust Mr Fitz, but I know different.'

'Thank you for telling me, Daisy. Can I buy one of your little bunches?'

'I've got some lovely purple daisies this week. Mr Fitz, he said, "You're a purple daisy yourself, Daisy," 'cos I was wearing my purple shawl, see, that night, and he stands me in the doorway and he brings a candle and he says, "Here's a purple daisy." He's a funny one – here you are, Miss.' She thrust a generous bunch of the Michaelmas daisies into Jane's hand in return for a few pence.

'If you see him, tell him I'll await his letter. I must go now. Tell him, Daisy – and thank you.' She ran to where Philip and Polly were waiting, each ignoring the other.

'I'm sorry, Philip, a message about my dressmaker,' she said glibly.

'Isn't that the girl who knew where Charles Fitzpercy

lodged?' he asked, turning back and staring at Daisy who was busy bunching up some more flowers.

'Oh, she sees everyone round here. She is like an unofficial post-boy, with flowers instead of a lanthorn,' said Jane lightly. No more was said, but Philip looked at her curiously once or twice as they walked along in silence before he parted from them at the top of the Strand.

'Don't forget,' he said as he bowed his goodbye, 'I shall expect a handful of sketches this time.'

'You shall have them, sir,' replied Jane and was glad when he had gone so she could think about Charles again. In Mayfair! With whom?

She did not have long to wait to find out. Louisa Collins was already ensconced in the sewing room the next morning with no more than a tight-lipped good morning and a sniff for Jane when she came in, and shortly afterwards Jane found a sealed paper waiting for her where the parlour maid had put the mail offerings. She read it over her coffee.

'Dear Jane – I am in Bruton Street – the house with the green door after the opening to the Mews – I have something to tell you – or perhaps ask you. Can you come any afternoon this week to see me?'

Her heart beat faster at the sight of his writing and his strange, almost illegible, signature. There was a post-script: 'Choose your day and write care of Archie Colquo-houn at number twenty-six.'

Why could he not be more explicit – or at least more ordinary? Must there always be this attempt at mystery? Was he afraid of something or someone that he usually kept his whereabouts a secret? Or did he just prefer to be mysterious? She could not believe the latter, and yet of whom could he be afraid? According to him his parents

189

were dead, but he knew members of his father's family, even so – and what could they have against him, since he did not claim to be legitimate? Why should he be persecuted or did he imagine it? Perhaps he *was* a little mad. But she did not believe that.

On the afternoon of Jane's expedition to Bruton Street, Charles Fitzpercy was sitting on a rather uncomfortable, but highly fashionable, sofa in the house of his highly fashionable friend, Archie Colquohoun, the slim young man with whom he had sometimes been seen in Town. The apartment in which they sat was also highly fashionable, hung with rich dark damask, with mirrors on each wall reflecting each other and the damask beyond. One small room was hardly more than a cupboard, leading off the large drawing room and containing a piece of Louis Quinze furniture used as a bookshelf. Another room, leading likewise off the first but on the opposite side, was furnished in a fantastic mixture of mother-of-pearl and beaten silver; chandeliers and looking-glasses were silver, too, and bordered with mother-of-pearl and this was repeated on the door handles. There were pictures on the walls of the drawing room which might, to an unpractised eye, have appeared copies of something vaguely famous, but which the connoisseur would realize were masterpieces bought from one of the impoverished noblemen who had made the collection in the first place in the eighteenth century and been forced to sell his smaller pieces to pay gambling debts. Archie was sitting in his robe on a chair looking out of the window and picking his teeth, which were small, white and even.

'Devil take it, Percy – I don't know why you want me here. What are you going to tell this girl, anyway?'

'I don't know,' sighed Charles. 'Now I wish I hadn't

190

written to her. She is a good girl and I wouldn't want her to come to any harm.'

'Why should she come to any harm? The Miss is probably quite capable of looking after herself – they all are nowadays, are they not? And in any case, she is not smart or even in Society, so what she thinks can be of little account.'

Charles flushed. 'Perhaps you had better go and just come in after half an hour or so. I should have gone to Middlesex and not stayed here. She will be out of place in your rooms.'

'Then I shall go and dress,' said Archie with a sigh. 'You can ring for tea whilst I get Morton to lace me up. Do you think your little friend would take fright at a well-padded gentleman?'

'My dear, she will see that you live for effect,' replied Charles. 'Of course,' he added, 'girls like dashing and elegant young men and you are certainly that!'

Archie went out nonchalantly and met Jane on the stairs, being shown up by his footman. He said nothing but gestured to the door out of which he had come and disappeared to a higher floor.

She was announced by the footman and Charles ordered a tray of coffee for two. For a moment, as he saw her, he felt a slight shock of recognition – but why should he not recognize Jane since she was here on his invitation? She came into the salon and stared at its heavy opulence with the light touches of French taste in the girandoles and mirrors.

He drew the blinds up, which had been half closed against the afternoon light, and turned to look at her. She stood in the middle of the floor looking, in her turn, at him. He thought he had never seen a face so beautiful and yet the beauty touched him as the beauty of tone of the paintings in Archie's room touched him, touched his eye not his heart, for it was not for her beauty that he liked Jane. She was wearing her hair down her back and had put on a light green cloak. Her long-lashed eyes seemed to look at him as from the depths of some dream and she seemed all light and glowing, shyer than she had been when they walked on the Heath, but still with a clear regard.

'It was good of you to visit,' he said.

'You invited me,' she answered, looking up at him wonderingly. He seemed different. Perhaps it was the grand house.

'Do sit down,' said Charles and seemed as nervous as she herself.

Jane sat down and could not forbear to comment upon the surroundings. 'It is a beautiful room – is it Mr Colquohoun's house?'

'Yes, Archie lives here when in town – and I stay here sometimes.'

She was thinking how different it was from Frederick Digby's house in Bloomsbury. Fred's house was furnished with old-looking things, whereas *this* – she had the impression of silver surfaces and pearl handles and a sort of gliding light over everything. It did not seem to go with Charles. She waited for him to say something, but he sat apparently deep in thought and silent until the footman arrived with a tray on which sat a very ordinary-looking coffee pot and cups.

Then Charles appeared to rouse himself. She thought he must tell her why he wanted to see her, what he had to tell her as promised in his letter, but all he said was: 'I shall pour the coffee, as you are my guest.'

It was all rather odd, yet she determined to absorb as much as possible from the visit if Charles were not in a

192

talkative mood. What did it matter? It was enough to be sitting in the same room as him and to be sipping coffee. The room was scented and smelt like spring jonquils.

Finally she asked: 'Has Daisy ever been here?'

'The fair flower girl? No – why do you ask?'

'She seems to know more about you than I do. She said you had visited her grandmother again.'

At this he raised his head and looked rather angry. Then his face softened and he said: 'It was perhaps a little in connection with her that I wanted to see you.' He seemed nervous, ill-at-ease.

'Please, Charles, don't look so far away. It is only me. I don't want to pry into your movements, but you must admit you are mysterious, and I asked Daisy if she knew your whereabouts. She tells me now and again if she's seen you.'

He was silent.

She went on: 'They were talking about your poems the other day at Julia Jeffrey's at home. I listened to many conversations and took the local colour so to speak.'

'I am sure that was interesting. What did they say about me?'

'They thought your poems were "fascinating", and there was speculation as to who you were. I heard something else about you – not about your verse. They were talking about "Fitzpercy" and some great house.'

He turned his face away.

'Perhaps I shouldn't have mentioned it? They made no connection between the author of the "Sunset" lyrics and the Fitzpercy they said "haunted Salton" because it should have been his – or he said it should have been, they said. A lot of gossip, but I couldn't help hearing especially when *your* name was mentioned!'

'Jane – you don't imagine that I have ever thought I

193

would inherit Salton? How could I, since I am a bastard? It's the property of my father's cousin's son.'

'Then your father had no legitimate children? Sons of course – or perhaps even a daughter he could entail it to in the female line?'

'No – and your gossiping creatures are ill-informed. I do not care for "owning" things. But it surprises me that people gossip about me – it's – disturbing.' He *looked* disturbed and a little flushed. 'I loved Salton,' he added in a different tone of voice. 'But Salton is a ruin, and no-one can own the sea.'

She said nothing, feeling she must tread carefully. After a moment he took up his coffee cup. 'I was living there as a child in my father's lifetime but have only recently begun to visit it again. London society is merciless. I cannot escape my connections with the family. Foolishly I took the name of Fitzpercy for myself. I wish I had denied it and then I could escape their tongues.'

'They made no connection between you and the poet,' she said again, seeing that he was inordinately sensitive about his lack of a name, whatever he said.

'And it is the poet who interests you Jane – is that not true?'

'I do not care who your father was,' she answered. 'But I do care for your genius – and,' she added quietly, not looking at him, 'for you.'

He tried to lighten the atmosphere, but looked wretched. 'Do not care for me, Jane. I told you I am unlucky and bring nought but ill luck to others. I wanted to tell you – '. He stopped again and then cleared his throat. 'Tell me of your own writings – were they well received?'

'Oh, moderately I believe. Philip wants more from me – but I am not ambitious to spend my days in literary

194

salons, you know – it is enough that I am taken a *little* seriously.'

'You are like Michael,' he said. 'Now there's a good fellow – cares nothing for fame so long as he is among books. Barely keeps his wife and children. His wife's parents want to help him out, but he won't let them.'

'I doubt *I* could earn my living with my pen like Mrs Opie or Mrs Baillie – I admire them,' replied Jane.

'Necessity is the mother of invention,' he replied.

'I like meeting all these London men and women – but I do not think I should want to be among them for ever. Perhaps in the end I shall go back to Bedon and tend the garden.'

'Oh, you will marry some successful man,' he said lightly.

Oh, no, she wanted to say, and wanted it so much that she was almost fearful of having spoken it aloud – I do not want to marry anyone but you.

After a pause he said: 'I am not like Michael, or like you. I don't want to belong to the flock – I am not a marrying man – and yet . . .'

She waited.

'Were you not afraid to visit the house of a ne'er-do-well alone, without a female attendant? It is not the conduct of a lady, Jane.'

'Do not speak of such things,' she cried in distress. 'I would never be afraid of *you*. That is what you said when I came to see you in Hampstead.'

'Oh, you might be afraid of Archie,' he said. 'Never mind – tell me – I asked you before – have you remembered if they ever called you Jennet?'

'Yes, I remember you asked, and I told you Papa *may* have called me it once – I can't remember exactly.'

'It is to do with Daisy's grandmother. I cannot tell you

195

the whole story, but she asked me again when I saw her a few days ago. She is a witch, I think. "Trust Jennet, she will bring you luck," she said after a long rigmarole of spades and hearts and diamonds. Why should she keep saying that name? You never knew her before, did you – before you came to London?'

'Why, I met Louisa Collins only when Aunt got her in to sew – and then, of course, met Daisy – but I've never seen her grandmother. What do you think she means?'

'I do not know – it disturbs me. If she said "Sophia" or "Lucy" it would not have stayed in my mind – but it is always Jennet.'

'Ask her if Jane will do,' smiled Jane. 'Why do you go to her, Charles? There is so much I do not understand about you. Do you live here always when you are in London, then?' She looked around her again at the sumptuous furnishings and the general appearance of riches. 'It is not like you, this room,' she said. Then: 'Am I to meet your friend Archie?'

'Always straight and true and to the point,' replied Charles. 'He may look in – I think he is rather shy. Of course,' he went on, 'unlike myself he is a true gentleman – has travelled widely, is graceful in society, but likes his beagles and his fishing.'

'Oh, the "true gentlemen",' said Jane. 'I have not met many such – I think they must all be in the country improving their tenantry and attending church regularly, and with an enormous brood of children – '

'You do not regard Mr Frederick Digby as a gentleman, then?'

'Why, I suppose he is – but I think he is too intelligent to be a member of a species.'

'And you prefer the *demi-monde*. How is your Philip

196

March? – Apart from urging you to further literary endeavours?'

'He is trying to spend a good deal of his time with Miss Jeffrey the actress, but I don't think she thinks he will ever be rich enough to keep her in the way she has been accustomed.'

'She will marry a real lord,' said Charles. 'Those actresses manage to carry off quite a number of such coups.'

'Then she will be able to buy any number of pairs of pink shoes and have a house with French windows,' replied Jane, laughing.

'And go to Brighton in the Season and have excessively dull children.'

They were both laughing and Jane was pouring another cup of the strong coffee for Charles when there was a tap at the door and they both looked up. Archie Colquohoun stood regarding them, twiddling the mother-of-pearl door handle in his elegant hand. A look passed between the two men and Charles seemed to drop his light-heartedness, but he said: 'Jane, this is Mr Colquohoun – Archie – the owner of this splendid house.'

Jane inclined her head as she had seen well-born ladies incline their heads and Archie advanced his hand and then sat in one gracefully feline movement against the eau de nil cushions of the sofa.

'I must be going,' said Jane hastily. 'No – I really must – it was most kind of you to ask me here, but Polly will be waiting for me.' She thought, Mr Colquohoun is very elegant. I suppose he must belong to 'high life'. He looks more at home here than Charles does.

Archie was wearing a very dandyish jacket, nipped in at the waist and with broad shoulders, and there was an indefinable aura of another perfume which had wafted in with him. 'Oh, do not go on my account,' he said. 'It is rare for us to entertain young ladies. Will you take a drink of French peppermint with me?' he asked Jane in a lazy voice.

'No – truly – I must go,' she replied.

He was very polite. 'I hear you have had some success with a little writing,' he said. 'Charles told me – it is not often we meet literary ladies. And as our mutual friend – ' he bowed towards Charles – 'will, I gather, soon be off again on his peregrinations. It is pleasant to take the opportunity of drinking coffee *en famille*, as it were.'

Jane looked at Charles to see how he was taking this rather waspish humour, but he was not looking at either of them. Then he turned to Jane. 'Thank you for compromising your reputation and visiting me – if you *must* go, Watson will show you out.'

The light from the westward-facing window fell on his face as he spoke and she thought how she would like to draw down the blind and banish Archie of the elegant boots and stay talking for ever to Charles in this strange room. She did not want to go, but she knew she must – Charles wanted her to go now, she saw. So she rose and the slim young man rose with her and shook hands and she felt heartsick and could not resist saying as she moved towards the door: 'Please write to me if there is anything I can do for you whilst you are away – you know where to find me.'

'Perhaps on my return we may walk again in Hampstead,' he said. Archie had gone back to the centre of the enormous room and then disappeared into the writing cabinet after a bow. At the door, Charles took her hand. 'Thank you for coming,' he murmured.

'I wish I knew what you wanted of me,' she murmured back and then forced herself to turn and follow the

198

hovering footman down the stairs to the outer door. Charles remained silhouetted at the top of the stairs and she saw him, tall and enigmatic, as her feet took her down the stairs. Charles went back into the room, sighing, and drank the coffee Jane had poured. After a time Archie joined him, sipping a green liquor and humming a ditty under his breath.

'Did you tell her?' he asked idly.

'How could I?' answered Charles.

'Your old lady said "Tell Jennet" and you have not. I'm surprised at you, Charley boy.'

'Cut it out Archie,' said Charles. 'She wanted to come and we had a nice conversation till you came in.'

'Perhaps she was frightened of me,' said Archie.

'I don't think so – she is just tactful, I believe,' said his friend.

Meanwhile Jane was on her way home with the faithful Polly. She was baffled by Charles. Perhaps he had had some kind of wager with his friend that a young lady would visit without a chaperone. But it seemed stupid. He knew she would not care about that. She was a little sick at heart when she arrived home in the house which seemed so plain and ordinary after the glories of Bruton Street. Maybe, after all, that was where Charles belonged. She would leave the next move to him. There was something he had wanted to say to her, but he had not said it, that she understood.

That night she had a strange dream. She was on a dark, cold shore and behind her, as though it were part of a cliff, was a high, roofless ruin. The sea was coming in and she must climb the path behind her to the ruin or drown. She turned and began the ascent, feeling giddy, and every now and then her feet slipping on mud and sliding pebbles. Then just as she was despairing of ever reaching the top and frightened to look behind in case she fell into the waters which were now boiling beneath her, she saw a figure climbing up before her. Yet however quickly she climbed now, no longer afraid, the figure kept just the same distance between them. She knew it was Charles, though he was wearing an old-fashioned coat which she glimpsed when the moon came from behind a cloud.

'Wait for me! Wait for me!' she shouted, but her voice was carried away on the wind and the figure went steadily plodding upwards. Then he disappeared and as she herself came up to the sheer wall of the ruin, she looked up and saw two figures now leaning from a high window. 'Take care,' she screamed. 'Don't lean out or you will fall.' She heard a laugh which was part of the wind and then the figures disappeared into the ruin behind and she found herself, once more, back on the shore with no memory of having climbed down. This time the sea had gone out and the moon had disappeared and she was alone walking on the lower cliff path and everything was ordinary again. Ordinary and lifeless.

PART FOUR

# Flesh and Spirit

Jane heard no more from Charles and could only surmise where he had gone. It was easier said than done to leave the next move to him. Neither did she hear for some time from Fred Digby and it was well into autumn after his return from Vine House when a card came from him inviting her, with the boys, to visit his sister and himself at their house in Bloomsbury. Only the leaves of the plane trees had not yet fallen and the London autumn, a new experience for her, seemed chilly and sad. She struggled on trying to put down on paper some of her further impressions and reading all she could lay her hands on. It seemed to help her sad feelings about Charles. Sometimes she felt she would never see him again, that he had called her to Bruton Street only to say goodbye. Her dream haunted her, though she did not dream the same one again.

The only visitor apart from Louisa Collins, who preserved a pinched silence about her family's concerns, was Philip March. He too was downcast. The lovely Julia had gone to Brighton to play before the King. It was a small part – her role in *Macbeth* had apparently not materialized. Jane was pleased to see Philip and pleased when he accepted her next two pieces, chosen from several she had laid before him. He seemed rather more interested in her than previously – perhaps her success with others had led him to reconsider her from the point of view of usefulness. Still, it was he who had published her and she was grateful. When she was not reading or writing, her time was mostly spent chatting to Mrs Ogilvie and helping with some of the tasks of the household, which she certainly did not consider beneath her. Polly was a good friend, too, and she learned a lot about London from her.

Fred entertained her and the boys one afternoon but was shortly to go abroad. Winter would soon be upon them once all the plane tree leaves in the square had gone from their branches. For a time everything seemed to be holding its breath, waiting for winter and gathering resources before the cold and ice should descend.

She felt rather lonely. Time seemed to have come to a stop. And yet it passed – it passed as she sat with her paper and pen and conjured up the feelings of her nine months in London. Mrs Ogilvie, too, seemed a little dispirited and suffered 'from her chest'. The only good news was that from Italy – Edith was rallying and feeling much stronger and the attacks of weakness were now not so frequent. Two or three weeks after seeing Frederick Digby Jane received a letter from him, written, apparently, *en route* to the Continent. In it he said he would be seeing his wife in Rome. He also wrote that Jane was constantly in his thoughts – a somewhat surprising admission from a married man who had formally seemed to regard himself as her adviser and parent *in absentia*. But she still did not forget his 'Trust me' and the pressure of his hand as she left Vine House that day. She knew that it was as far as he dared to go, that it was like a declaration of love and she remembered Julia's 'silly rake'. But he did not write like a silly rake. It sounded as though, if he were free, his intentions towards her would not have been dishonourable, that he felt some true affection towards her. But he was not free and he was going to his wife. It made her a little uneasy, but she determined not to think about it – he would be gone till spring at least.

She tried, too, not to think about Charles, but that was more difficult. She dreamed often of him; the dreams had fled when she awoke, yet she knew she had been dreaming of him because she awoke with the feelings of mingled happiness and sadness which only he aroused in her.

As time went by she began to want to visit the old lady, Rebecca Smith, to find out just a little more about him, but had she enough courage to dare to do this? Louisa had now finished her sewing for the year. She could always ask Daisy about Charles but whenever she had walked by Covent Garden lately she had not seen the cheerful figure amongst its bunches of flowers. Of course, the flowers would be gone – that would be the reason – unless Daisy could buy from hothouses. What could she sell in winter?

Thoughts of Charles and a complete absence of him went on tormenting her as November slid into December, a cold, misty season with the gas flares lit earlier in town and a sulphurous smell in the air. One afternoon, she took her courage in both hands and asked William to take her to Ironmongers Row. She had now ascertained the number.

'I am going to buy some ribbon I saw in Regent's Street,' she told the housekeeper. 'Polly will accompany me – we need a little drive.'

Mrs Ogilvie acknowledged her expedition without suspicions and soon they were off through the cobbled streets, across to Bloomsbury and then stopping and turning south before they reached Oxford Street.

'We can walk the rest on foot,' she told William. 'I shall be visiting my dressmaker at number 363. Meet us here in two hours.' William gave her a long look, but she smiled and said: 'Come, Polly – it is not very far.'

They skirted an area of dingy alleys which led off St

Giles and made their way easily to Ironmongers Row whose whereabouts Jane remembered from her last attempt to find it. The shop at the corner gave her her bearings and they progressed to number 363 with nothing worse than a few urchins shouting rude words after them.

The street was long and the houses low, abutting straight on to cobbled pavements. There seemed to be no lamps around and she was glad they had not ventured out at night. But her heart was beating like a sledgehammer when they stood in front of number 363. There was no sign of life behind the window which was small and had its curtain drawn. Louisa, she guessed, would be out, but did not Daisy's mother work at home? Then she heard a step which sounded as though it were coming down some uncarpeted stairs and then proceeding to the door. The door opened only a crack and a woman's face, a pretty, careworn face, poked round it.

'I've come to see Mrs Smith,' said Jane in a polite but firm voice. She had rehearsed her words. 'I know Miss Louisa Collins and Daisy,' she added.

The woman opened the door, then: 'Mother's at the back,' she said. 'You were lucky – we was working upstairs. Who shall I say?' She seemed unsurprised to see a visitor for her mother. 'They usually comes at night. You'd better wait and I'll see if she's up.'

'I'm sorry not to have written first,' said Jane as they were ushered into a tiny passage which went straight through to a door at the back.

'Ma, it's a lady for you!' she shouted. She turned round and said: 'Who shall I say?'

'Tell her "Jennet",' said Jane plucking up more courage. Polly looked at her curiously and seemed a little embarrassed.

The woman went through the door and for a few

206

moments there was silence, except for the murmur of voices from upstairs, young girls' voices. The door on the right was half open and Jane glimpsed a hurdy-gurdy on a stand blocking the entrance. How did a family of seven manage to live in such a small house?

'Polly, will you wait for me here?' she whispered. 'The old lady may not want to see two people.'

'You can have your secrets,' said Polly virtuously.

Then the pretty woman came back and pointed to the door at the back. 'She'll see you,' she stated.

'Could my maid wait here?' asked Jane.

'I suppose so.'

Jane followed the woman down the passage. Then she was alone behind the door in a back kitchen which was yet not a kitchen. There was a fire and a table with a green cover and the curtains were drawn and there was a sweetish scent in the room and a linnet silent in a cage. She did not see anyone at first, but then saw two eyes regarding her in a head balanced on a shawl which belonged to a body sitting in a high-backed chair at the far side of the table.

'I apologize for coming without warning,' she said nervously. 'But I thought you might know if Mr Fitzpercy is well. It is so long since I heard from him.'

'And why should you worry?' said a crackly voice and the old woman shifted her weight and fished inside the pockets of a voluminous apron for a pipe which she placed on the table before her.

'I know you tell fortunes, Mrs Smith. Your grand-daughter, Daisy, told me – and that Mr Fitzpercy comes here. I don't want my fortune told, but I will pay what is your usual – price – charge.' She sought for the word. 'Just to know he is safe.'

'Who are you, girl?' asked the old lady, putting the pipe in her mouth.

'I think I am a Jennet,' said Jane, feeling rather foolish.

'You think you are a Jennet. What is your name then?'

'Jane Banham.' She was trying to place the accent of the old woman. It was a country accent. Though her voice crackled with age, she spoke briskly. Her eyes were black and her hands brown and wrinkled.

'You are not frightened of me, then? So many are,' said the old woman. 'They come for my hand-reading or for my cards. You have not come for them, but to enquire about your friend?'

'Yes, that is it! I am worried about him and have no way of finding him. I believe he may have gone north.'

'Sit down then.' The old woman gestured to a seat before the fire. 'And let me see your face.' Jane sat down and looked at her steadily. After a long pause the woman said: 'It's a pretty face!' and then was silent again.

She was not obsequious like gypsies Jane had met at home, but commanding.

Jane waited.

'And you want to know about Fitz, then. Why?'

'Because I love him,' said Jane with no hesitation as though she were mesmerized, and added, 'And you told him a Jennet would bring him luck.'

'Did I now. And you think you are that Jennet?'

'Yes.'

'Listen girl, don't try to find him – he's not for you.'

Jane felt tears come into her eyes. Perhaps the old woman was just a fraud and knew nothing about Charles, just took his money and invented things to make the money go on rolling in. But the next thing she said arrested that thought.

'He's gone away again because he had to – he has

enemies,' she said. '*You* can't save him, "Jennet", my darling.'

'I don't want him for myself, but for his sake,' she said stumblingly.

'They all say that. But partings must be – that's written down for you – I can tell without the ball or the cards. Show me your hands if you will.'

For a moment Jane hesitated and then got up from her chair and stood in front of the old woman. Mrs Smith took her left hand and turned it over. She felt it and ran her finger down the knuckles. 'You work with this,' she said. 'Ladies do not work.'

'Then perhaps I am not a lady,' replied Jane. 'But I do work with it – I write and I am left-handed.'

'Oh, there's a lot of time to pass here – oh, aye – you've a strong mind, lass, but your heart will be torn. Don't try to find him – he'll ask you for help if he needs it. He's to lose himself before he finds himself.'

'Is he ill?' Jane persisted. 'Please tell me. Maybe he doesn't want me, but I feel I have to look after him somehow. We met only by chance, and he wanted to make my acquaintance, he *did*.'

'Nothing is by chance,' replied Rebecca Smith. She looked up at her and released Jane's hand. 'I can't tell another's secrets, lass. You *will* see him again, that I promise. Go home and look for someone else to bind up your life. You're a pretty lass – don't try to get hold of him – leave it to him. You can't be his. You can come to me again, "Jennet". And how old are you?'

'Twenty-one, Mrs Smith.'

'Twenty-one and eating your heart out. Don't worry, there'll be something for you out there in the world. You'll have to sacrifice but you'll manage. You know our Daisy?' she added in a different voice.

'Yes, I talk to her at the Garden, but I haven't seen her for a long time.'

'She's over in the Borough with a friend,' said Mrs Smith matter-of-factly.

The visit seemed to be at an end. 'Give me five shillings – I've helped you, haven't I?'

'You have,' said Jane.

'And remember: don't try to find him – it will all be explained one day, that I do know. I can't say more.'

Jane handed over five silver shillings and said: 'Thank you – I am grateful – at least I know he is alive.'

'Aye,' said the old lady, and then: 'Goodbye girl. Take care of yourself.' She smiled and bent her head and just raised her hand when Jane went out. But she sat long at the table before taking out her cards and sighing deeply.

Jane, for her part, returned to the passage where Polly was leaning against the wall.

'Tell your fortune then, Miss?' she asked.

'No, no, not really.'

Polly looked sceptical but said good-humouredly, 'Wish she'd tell me mine. Come on, Miss, William'll be waiting and he won't want them little lads gathering round the carriage.'

They let themselves out as no one seemed to be coming from the upstairs room.

As they turned to walk back to the main street, Jane saw a curtain twitch in the first-floor window. 'Gives you the creeps, don't it?' said Polly as they walked along.

William was waiting for them, looking grim-faced, and Jane had to bribe him with another shilling to make up for his wait.

She was thoughtful all the way home, going over and over the old lady's talk in her mind.

\* \* \*

210

After the visit to Rebecca Smith, Jane made another effort to stop thinking about Charles. If he didn't want her to know where he was or to see her, she must abide by his decision. She would try to think of other things and to meet other people. Yet the longing for him was something which she thought she would never have believed she could feel, almost as if a part of herself was drifting somewhere and looking for a home. She must do something, feel something other than this dull longing which could so easily turn to misery. She thought of going to Hampstead, to walk where they had walked together, but the old lady had told her not to brood and not to try to find him. She thought he must be away from London. Wherever he was, her longing for him would never be satisfied. What had Mrs Smith said? – that she was strong. She must try to be so.

The next week was a week of changed weather. Suddenly the sun came out again and people began to think of Advent and the turning of the year. Mrs Ogilvie's health recovered and there was a letter from Hal to say he had met Frederick Digby and was glad that all was going so well. He had also heard from his children once more and was grateful for Jane's regular visits to them.

Then Mrs Ogilvie herself received a letter from a friend of her brother's in Scotland with news of that brother's death, and in no time at all she was off, bonneted and distressed, to Edinburgh, with many apologies and a promise to return within the week. So Jane was left alone with the servants to amuse herself as best she could. At first she was glad. Now she could muse all day long and dream about her love. Then after a day or two she wrote a long letter to Snetters wishing she could tell her more of what was in her mind, but asking whether she *had* been called Jennet as a child. This still puzzled her.

211

When Philip March called one afternoon, she was sitting before a fire in Edith's room. She was now using this room since her bedroom was too cold. She woke as from a long period of blight and decided to be as friendly as possible.

But Philip did not seem to want to talk business and, after he had discussed his sister's school and they had exchanged news, he was silent.

She looked into the fire wishing, as she usually did, that it was Charles Fitzpercy who was in the room with her. Philip was the one person with whom she did *not* want to talk about Charles. With an effort she began to speak of Frederick Digby and his sojourn in Italy. She tried again when this brought forth nothing but, 'Don't suppose we shall get any more money out of *him*,' and asked Philip's honest opinion of her talents. She was surprised when Philip answered her tentative remark with, 'You could be quite good, Jane. Why don't you write a romance – not for the *New London*, of course, but for wider consumption?'

'I think I need a little more experience of the world,' she replied, 'before I could harness any talent I have to the construction of imaginary people.'

He looked at her with frank appraisal and she was uncomfortable under his gaze. It struck her that Philip was quite personable. The success of his journal had filled him out physically but he seemed a little less full of himself, since others had obviously seen fit to agree with his own self-appraisal and he need not be continually pouring the wine of self-regard into his throat.

He coughed slightly. 'How is Julia?' she asked innocently.

'Enjoying herself, I expect,' he answered, rather

grimly. 'You know, Jane, I should have taken my sister's advice and paid a little more attention to *you*.'

She was astounded. 'Paid *me* more attention?'

'Henrietta and Charlotte, I believe, have a high opinion of you – now I think I see what they meant.' She knew that Charlotte was hardly likely to have sung her praises, since she herself had a 'penchant' for Philip, in spite of his faults, so she discounted this. 'One day I shall have a good income,' he began again.

Oh heavens! Was *he* about to make a proposal to her? She thought she had better put him right immediately. 'I am poor myself,' she said. 'Uncle has four children to bring up. I must live by my wits if I am not to remain a poor relation for the rest of my life.'

'Oh, yes, of course,' he said, disconcerted. 'I expect your uncle will find you a rich husband.'

'I do not want a rich husband,' she replied. 'I do not know that I want a husband at all!'

'You know you are very attractive? Attractive girls must take care to appear virtuous.'

She said nothing and he added: 'People do not assume that pretty women are virtuous – it is easier if you are plain.'

'Surely true virtue does not reside in being conventional?' she said.

For answer, he rose and took her hand and kissed it and was out of the room before she could recover her breath. It was astonishing. Was she to be courted by every man she knew or liked, except the only man she wanted? Yet Philip had not really seemed insincere. What was she to think about him? What would happen if he did not think her 'virtuous'? Men had a very narrow definition of that word!

\* \* \*

Jane was sitting at the casement window, looking out over the field of snow which had transformed Lincoln's Inn Square into a white counterpane. Snow had arrived early in December after a week of sunny weather and caught them all unawares. The tall house was cold, in blue shadows during the day but candlelit and firelit in the evening. It was a good thing they had ordered several loads of coal in the autumn, as Mrs Ogilvie, now back from Scotland, kept reiterating to Jane and to the servants. The servants were, of course, resigned to feeling cold, and Jane, too, was used to it. This snow here fell more thinly on the ground than over the fields in Bedon, but it inconvenienced the London folk more than she had noticed in Norfolk where winter was winter and even springs could be windy and cold. Snow had always pleased her and drawn her back to childhood though she knew it made a great deal of work for the servants and stopped the farm labourers in the country from getting on with their seasonal work. What must it be like in Northumberland though? She shivered.

Jane had changed in appearance during the past year: she had grown slimmer and her hair was now always worn up, though nothing could persuade her to spend too long in the arrangement of kiss-curls and ringlets. The cold was pinching all their faces that winter, but Jane's youth still glowed out.

'She's not really a beauty,' Mrs Ogilvie had confided to her family up in Scotland, 'but sometimes she *seems* to be. She's got something her mother had, yet – I don't know – she's not really like her mother as I remember her.'

Mrs Ogilvie's chest was playing her up again. Jane implored her to stay in bed when she had been coughing

214

in the night but Ogilvie was reluctant to loosen her control over the household.

'What a mercy your aunt's in a nice warm place,' she kept saying.

They were to have Jimmy and Tommy and Johnny home for Christmas. They were only allowed a few days and many boys were not going to be able to take advantage of the break. Jane was looking forward to the change their noise would bring to the house.

She was thinking of all this as she looked out at the snow and breathed a space on the windowpane, the better to see out. That morning Jack Frost had been and the glass of the window had had a fantastic whorled pattern on every pane, each one different. Jane closed her eyes for a moment. Norfolk did seem far away. It would be the first Christmas she had spent away from Snetters and she was wishing that just for a moment she might be transported back to Bedon. Mrs Ogilvie had even offered to send her in the mail to spend a few days there, but when it came to deciding, Jane was loth to go. Snetters *would* be pleased to see her but her home was now London – and Charles would be even further away from her, she thought, if she were in a place where he had never been. She had heard nothing more from him since the visit to Bruton Street, but she was not a girl to give up easily and had decided to trust old Rebecca Smith in the matter of seeing him again. Philip March had not visited again since his peculiar behaviour, but had invited her to a gathering at his sister's in the New Year. She did not often think of Philip.

The snow was beginning to fall again. It was late afternoon and the sun about to set. Perhaps it would be only a light shower. A few children were trying to scoop up balls of snow, and sliding on the pathways. A few

215

years ago and she would have been one of them. The adults were all comfortably behind their shutters and soon the curtains would be drawn and backgammon or piquet would while away the evening. In the poor quarters the gin shops would be full – not far away, by the hansom stand, the flares had been lit and there was a crowd of men and women continually passing in and out of one with their jugs.

If Charles returned to town from wherever he was, he might pass a message to Daisy and she knew that Daisy was reliable. Had Rebecca said anything to her grand-daughter? she wondered. She doubted it, though Mrs Collins must have mentioned Jane's visit to her daughter. Yet Daisy might not have connected the lady visitor with Jane. Many people must consult Rebecca and exchange comfort or a warning for a handful of shillings.

For the hundredth time Jane went over the old lady's talk. It all seemed remote as she stood there in the gathering dusk, safe behind glass from weather and from the wide world of love. But Charles – was he cold tonight? Or was he still comfortable in that fancy house in Mayfair? Somehow she thought he was now in London. She wondered what it was like up in Hampstead in the snow. If it held, there would perhaps be skating on the ponds there. She sighed and went to the fire and took her book and listened to the wind rise as night fell and the sun went down and the eerie light still came in from the window. She must draw the curtains and send for toast and tea and try to concentrate on her reading, and work out a piece – perhaps on London in winter – for the consumption of the readers of the *New London*. She had had a letter that morning from Charlotte Howard and she decided to reread it. Poor Charlotte – what a waste of her feelings to care still so clearly for Philip. Yet perhaps people would

216

say that she herself was wasting her youth dreaming of Charles Fitzpercy. Were all women the same? Perhaps it was only the tug of the flesh disguised under these powerful yearnings for the soul of another. She thought about this. Why were girls not supposed to think about such things? Perhaps other girls did not – she had no idea of the depth of feelings Charlotte had for Philip. Perhaps every person loved differently and it was only by finding someone who loved as you did that you would be happy. Charles did not desire her – she knew he did not; he felt something but it was not the love *she* felt. But if he did love anyone, it would be in the same way she loved. They were the same sort of people. It would never be a mutual shared love, between him and her, she knew that. Yet that did not stop her feeling as she did; perhaps it only intensified her love. How had her father loved her mother? At first, before they married? How had Fred Digby loved his Clara? Perhaps no one had anything in common with anyone else and we knew nothing about each other. Thinking of Fred Digby she turned her other side to the fire and toasted it. If life were easy and love drew out love, who would claim her – and whom would she claim? It would not work out. People would not be allowed more than one love – for she might then force Charles to love her, and Fred Digby or even Philip would both require her to 'love' them. Maybe things were not shared out properly ever and there were some souls who never found love, others who were adored and worshipped by many.

She was sorry for Fred, but she guessed that neither Fred nor Philip would want anyone feeling sorry for them. They were both proud. Was Charles proud? How little she knew of him in reality. Yet she would not wish to exchange the dull, painful feeling of absence of feeling for

217

the piercing sword that seemed to go through her when she allowed herself to think of him. If he had never existed, or if she had never made his acquaintance, her life would be bearable, but something would be missing from it. She hardly knew him – and yet she felt she had 'known' him all her life.

She sat on in the dusk, now turning dark, remembering how she had used to sit like this at Breckles Hall in the drawing room with her old aunt upstairs and the curtains open on the moonlit garden and how she had thought that a change in her life would be like suddenly lighting a candle in a dark room. That everything would be illuminated and exciting. And now she was sitting alone again, preferring the dark, and her thoughts, to the world outside. If Charles loved her he would soon have her out in the world. But Charles did not love her and the world was still there, the world she mocked a little in her sketches for Philip but which she felt she did not truly understand. Perhaps all the worlds of different people were different; perhaps Fred's world was unknowable, and Philip's – Charles's – even more so. Men were so different from women. People did not expect girls to get up and go out and conquer the world outside. What if they were right, and everyone would be much happier if women stayed at home? If Charles stayed 'at home', *he* would not be in danger. She still had the feeling that he was in danger. She had too much imagination. Perhaps it was her imagination which allowed herself to be pierced through by thoughts of Charles when a sensible girl would have encouraged a sensible young man.

Mrs Ogilvie came in at that moment and started: 'Why Miss Jane, sitting in the dark? I've brought up your toast as Polly and the other girl were busy.'

'Mrs Ogilvie, you mustn't do that – I would have come for it myself – there – I'll light a candle.'

'Your mother used to like sitting while it was dark,' said Ogilvie. 'She used to look in the fire and see pictures.'

'Oh, I do that too. I expect Mama taught me. Was she superstitious, Mrs Ogilvie?'

'I think she was,' said Ogilvie putting a silver tray on a table by the fireplace. 'She used to sit in the dark, though, because your grandpapa was mean with his candles. I shouldn't comment upon it, I suppose, but my late mistress, your own grandmother, was always one for saving the candles, too. Of course, it's different in the country – none of that gas light there either, of course. I don't know, such changes I've seen!' What a noisy place this is, too. There were crowds out there just now, singing.' She seemed to want to chat.

'Waits? But it is not yet Christmas.'

'Oh, no, some other sort of singing. I never liked crowds – '

'I know, crowds can be frightening, even at home when the men got together over the farmers' prices – and now my governess tells me there has been more frame-breaking.'

'How is it all going to end? Though I don't blame them – nasty machines taking bread out of folks' mouths.'

'Yes, I expect you have seen many changes,' replied Jane, waiting to eat her toast.

'That I have, even at church, Miss. Psalms aren't good enough for folks now, they must have those new-fangled hymns. And the things in the market! I don't know the new names – calico and fustian and muslin I *do* know – but chintz and those French silks with fancy names, I'll never get used to them. And the things folk eat now! It's all too much for a body to take in. I got used to Hampshire

219

– after all I went there when I was only a young lass – but London! Too many folk if you ask me. I'll *never* get used to it and that's a fact. Aye, well, I mustn't stay gossiping. There's a new girl to instruct. I wanted to have her ready for when Mrs Stone comes home, though she'll want to take on a footman then. Well, all very well, the Master'll change *his* ways I expect.' She went out when Jane said no more and closed the door, none too softly. She was a good old body, even though she fussed about Jane's going out with Polly on foot. She did not try to stop her, but confined herself to grumbling. Tomorrow Jane intended venturing out in the snow and passing by Covent Garden.

She wanted to go to Booksellers Row near Charing Cross to buy something for Snetters. The circulating library in Norwich, where Snetters could go in any case but once a month, was very old-fashioned and the *new* books were what Snetters wanted. And perhaps some tinsel pictures for Polly, to mark her appreciation for her companionship. She found it hard to think of Polly as a servant – she was more like the village girls who had been her friends in Bedon.

But the next morning brought a letter from Italy, from Fred Digby. It was full of witty comments about the English emigrés there and those he had met in France on his way to Rome, who did not always give a very good impression of themselves, complaining about food which was, Fred said, much better cooked than anything they had eaten at home in England. He was to go back to Florence where he would see Hal and Edith once more after Christmas. Only at the end of his letter did he write of anything personal. 'I am glad the writing is going well – I like to think of you sitting by the fire thinking about your next piece. I hope March has paid you? I met one of his contributors – Mr "Bruce", doing a sort of modified grand tour and looking very "Wertherish". Blessings on you all at Christmas – your devoted Fred Digby.'

Jane thought about this letter as she was trudging through the snow the next day to Charing Cross. One snowball had narrowly missed her, and Polly had cleverly sent one back in the right direction and the small boy had fled. The boys would soon be home – she must buy them a little New Year box, too, not something improving; she thought they might prefer sweetmeats.

It was a hard walk back to Covent Garden, slipping and sliding in the rutted streets.

She was not sure whether Daisy would be there at her pitch for there were no flowers at this time of year. She would be selling chestnuts and Kentish cobs, if anything, today. People would be laying in stores for Christmas, and Jane decided to buy some for the boys from her. At first she saw no one on the corner of Henrietta Street and then looked across the road to a small fire burning in an iron cauldron on legs. A girl was standing with a little shovel, stamping her feet to keep warm. It was Daisy.

'Oh, Miss Jane,' she exclaimed as they came up. 'I ain't seen you for so long – ain't seen no one. It is cold though!'

'I'll take some chestnuts,' replied Jane, looking at Daisy with concern. It was a day fit to freeze off your finger ends. 'Have you seen Mr Fitz?' she asked quietly as Daisy stirred the glowing chestnuts and then scrabbled in the mass for the ones which were done through.

'Gone away,' she said. 'Not a whisker of him have I seen. Oh, Miss Jane, it was you that came, wasn't it, to Gran's?'

'Yes, I did,' replied Jane, seeing no point in prevaricating.

'Thought so. Mum said a young lady with lovely 'air.'

'I was worried about him. Daisy, you don't know anyone called "Jennet", do you?'

'Why Miss, that's a name for Jane, ain't it?'

'I suppose so. Your grandmother told Mr Fitzpercy something about a Jennet – '

'Then she must 'ave meant you, Miss. Gran knows everything.'

'How could she know me, Daisy? I've only met you and your Aunt Louisa – '

'Well maybe she heard Aunt Lu talking about you.'

Yes, that must be the most likely explanation. 'I'll take some cobs for the boys at Christmas,' she said.

'They're ever so dear. Still – it's for Christmas,' said Daisy, bringing out a sack from under her stand. 'And if you go to that there theatre, I'll sell you some oranges. They're going to let me. It's hard to get the go-ahead – some of the costers are jealous when the women sell oranges.'

Another customer came up then and Jane said her farewells to Daisy and she and Polly went slipping and sliding back home.


Jane invited Henrietta and Charlotte to Lincoln's Inn Square for Christmas Eve, but only Henrietta could be spared as several of their young charges were staying in Fulham for Christmas.

'Philip sends you his greetings,' said Henrietta when she had finally unpeeled herself from layers of mantle, scarves, gloves and extra tippet. 'He sends you a book, I believe.' She handed a small package over.

'I'll open it as a New Year gift,' said Jane. 'Now, boys, Miss March is not a dispenser of gifts to all and sundry,' she said as they came up to see if there was anything for

222

them. They had arrived home the night before and Jane had had her hands full with them. They were to return to Dr Macdonald's on the day after Boxing Day.

'Oh, yes, I have something,' said Henrietta and presented them each with a small book.

'Oranges tomorrow, and nuts,' said Jane. 'And now go up to the old schoolroom.'

'Children are a great deal of work,' sighed Henrietta. 'I thought girls would be easier, but they are not. I thought I should know about children from having a younger brother, but I don't believe Philip was ever quite like other children. He always had his nose in a book – or was writing things to sell among friends. Papa used to have to buy from him! He was indulged, of course. We girls were not – at least I know I was not – though I believe Charlotte had a rather easy childhood.' She talked on, seeming less affected than she had been when Jane first knew her. She still had the eyeglass on a cord, however, and spoke of the old 'blues' and how few of them there were left. 'Alas, I feel we women are entering upon a hard time. We shall be expected to be saints and angels and not bother our pretty little heads with thinking. Ah, the good old days!'

'Mrs Barbauld and Mrs More are still with us, are they not?' replied Jane. 'My own governess had a grandmother who knew the old bluestocking circle.'

'They are both very old and who will follow them? I wish we could establish salons just for women,' sighed her friend. 'I know the men would mock us and call us mincing little boarding school misses. Life is hard for women, particularly if they are not rich and are looked down upon by the fashionable. Women are only supposed to be fitted for cards and children.' Henrietta seemed gloomy. 'If they are rich they are full of their plans for a cottage *orné*, and if they are poor they are too busy filling

223

their infants with Daffy's elixir to think of higher things. I suppose it is better to be trying to do what Charlotte and I are doing.'

'Do you not wish to marry, then?' asked Jane, a little timidly, but Henrietta seemed, for once, to be inviting confidences.

'No – that is not for Charlotte or for me,' she replied. 'You, of course, will marry, dear Jane.' Jane felt uncomfortable and hoped the conversation would not turn back to Philip.

'I think I would rather be in love than marry,' she replied. 'And the two do not go together, do they?'

'Ah, if you are a loving kind of woman, then you will marry. Love is only a trap,' said Henrietta.

'It is not just "love" – it is feeling – you know – about *life* – I should not like that to pass me by.'

'Then you must take care. Men are pleased to find passionate girls, but they very rarely marry them, my dear.'

'Would you not like to have children, Henrietta?' she asked after a pause.

'Me? No, indeed, and neither would Charlotte I imagine. She would have made a good wife, but she has lost her chances by moving out of Society. You know she was very grand?'

'She is a most unusual person,' Jane agreed.

'Marriage *without* children would be unusual, I suppose?' mused Henrietta further.

'I cannot see *that* at all,' said Jane.

'Then you will marry and have a brood. I wonder whether you will go on with your writing? There are many women who do – I admire them; writing for a living is the hardest life – and if it is added to the trials and tribulations of husbands and sick children! No, no, I could not do it!'

'Are there, then, no men worthy of us?' smiled Jane.

'None,' said Henrietta decisively.

'What is your brother's opinion of the married state – and women?' asked Jane boldly.

'Oh, Phil likes women – but I cannot see he will marry until he is old, unless – if I may speak frankly – a rich heiress comes upon the scene.'

'Might he not fall in love?'

'He will love a pretty face for a week or two and protest eternal passion, but it will not last. Few men are capable of self-sacrifice.'

'So you believe love is self-sacrifice.'

'Why, of course – by women on behalf of men.'

'Yet I have seen men who seemed to love a girl and who might marry their love.' She was thinking of that dark young Mr Hood and his one who adored him.

'Oh, I daresay there are some, but I have not met any – whereas I have known many, many girls who have sacrificed everything for their lovers.'

Jane thought she was perhaps warning her – but surely not off Philip whom she must know Jane did not love.

'It is natural for women to slave and sacrifice and protect – it is their way of love, is it not? Because they are mothers, I suppose.'

'So you think all men are babes? Take care, Jane, that way lies a good deal of sorrow. Grown men are quite capable of looking after themselves. Of course, you may also wish to be looked after. Many women yearn for protection.'

'But I think it is the women who, for the most part, do the protecting.'

'You are right there. Men will rove – they may return – but they will rove, whilst we women stay and wait – at

225

least *I* do not, but I can see *you* might. How is your Mr Fitzpercy?' she asked.

Jane was loth to lead the conversation to him. Henrietta was shrewd enough to know Jane's true feelings for that man. 'I believe he is away from London – I have not seen him,' she answered stiffly.

'And all *my* philosophy will not be proof against a pair of flashing eyes, my girl. Don't deny it – I know it is true. Well, I wish you well. Phil says he will put some more of Fitzpercy's Gothic pieces into the next number – if there is a next number.'

Jane was glad to lead the conversation back to the *New London*.

Later, she opened the parcel from Philip. It was Mrs Baillie's *Poems and Lays*. How kind.

They went to church, Jane and Mrs Ogilvie and the boys, and all the servants, on Christmas Day. The weather had suddenly turned mild again, but by Boxing Day the wind had come back and then the day after there was another fall of snow. Jimmy and Tommy and Johnny leapt around enjoying their last hours of freedom, being spoilt in the kitchen and indulged by all the household.

'Shall you like a mouse?' Johnny had asked Jane, feeling that he must somehow reciprocate the little New Year boxes she had given them.

'It is a kind thought,' said Jane, 'but I'd perhaps not find a pet mouse very convenient. Maybe you could all buy a canary in summer.'

She was going to take the boys back in the carriage that afternoon and all was ready for William to come round for them, when she heard the sound of the post-boy's bell. Perhaps there would be a letter for the boys from their parents. But no, it was for her, addressed in an

226

unknown hand. She went up to her room to open it, somehow filled with foreboding. The note was short and signed 'Michael Farquharson':

Mr Charles Fitzpercy is ill at my house. He thinks life not worth living. We have done our best. He mentioned your name, and we took the liberty of writing to you. Will you come to see us on the twenty-eighth or the twenty-ninth? I think we can keep him here till then. Perhaps you could persuade him to seek medical advice. Yours faithfully. MF.

Gracious heavens! She would have to go! How, though, to persuade Mrs Ogilvie of the necessity of her going out to Hampstead in such inclement weather? She would have to do it somehow. Perhaps a contributor to the magazine was ill? Something like that. Or an invitation from Mrs Farquharson? Yes, that would be better.

She wrote a quick note to take to the mail collection, asking Mr Farquharson to send a note from his wife inviting her to take tea with them. 'Please do – she wrote – and then I can leave. Be assured I will, however, come in any case to Charles. But this would make it easier.'

If she were a man and had a horse she could go out with impunity, and would not need a servant to accompany her wherever she went. But she was determined not to let her sex stand in the way of her freedom.

Fortunately her note must have reached Hampstead during the evening, for by eleven o'clock next morning there was a letter from Maggie Farquharson asking her to take tea with them.

'Mrs Ogilvie, I am asked by a friend of Henrietta's to take tea in Hampstead,' she said casually, hoping the small lie would do. 'It is a little warmer, I believe, and Polly and I can take the mail coach and then a hackney or a public chaise. Mrs Farquharson,' she added, 'is married

227

to a journalist in Fleet Street and has something important to tell me.'

'You could ask William if you are determined to go,' replied Mrs Ogilvie, with a look at Jane and a sigh.

'No, no – we managed before with the public conveyances.'

'Why can't they see you in Town?' asked the housekeeper.

'I don't know. I believe there has been illness in the family,' Jane invented rapidly. 'Nothing catching, of course.'

Jane had pondered and pondered all night as to what could be wrong with Charles.

'Life not worth living' – it sounded dreadful. And he must have spoken of her to Michael and his wife – or had they decided themselves that she was the only person who might help? He must have spoken highly of her to them in that case and that sent a glow through her. And what sort of medical advice did you give to someone who did not think life worth living? She was frightened. What should she tell Polly?

The coach had to stop several times in the snow and the pull up the hill to the village in the chaise was only just possible. 'Thank goodness I told Ogilvie we might have to stay the night,' Jane remarked to Polly. Polly had been told a friend was ill, but appeared to think their visit a wild goose chase. I am mad, thought Jane. But perhaps Mr and Mrs Farquharson are mad too if they think I can do anything for that wonderful, terrible man. What would she find when she arrived at the little cottage by the Heath? She strove to banish dreadful visions of his lying there dead by his own hand. Why should such a gifted man not want to live? It must be something to do with

228

where he had spent his time since Bruton Street. Surely he could not have been holed up in Hampstead all those weeks? He had probably gone there at Christmas.

The Heath was white and ghostly when the chaise from Camden finally deposited them at the top of the hill. She looked round for a moment, uncertain of the way. It all looked so different from the peaceful green scene of summer. But she took Polly's hand and let her feet guide her as though there were some cord that linked her to the little cottage by the old spa.

Scarcely had the two young women entered the door, which was opened to them by Mrs Farquharson with tears in her eyes and a baby on her shoulder, than her husband came in from the back room.

'Please tell me what is the matter with him? I've come as soon as I could.'

'He says he will see no one,' said Michael Farquharson, looking extremely anxious.

'Tell him I am not no one,' said Jane. 'And I shall return straight away to Town in any case. I only brought him his New Year present.' In truth she had bought a little book for Charles at Booksellers Row at Christmas, some poems of Shelley's, which she knew would please him. 'But if it is any trouble,' she added, 'I shall leave the book and go – for I am sure that if he is ill the book will speak better than I can.'

Michael Farquharson went into the back room again and his wife motioned Jane to sit by the fire.

'It was so good of you to come – we could think of no-one else. He came here on Christmas Day – not well at all – though *I* do not know what the matter is. Since then he has hardly eaten and all he says is "I am better left alone."'

Jane was feeling steadily more alarmed herself, but tried to stay composed.

Michael was a good ten minutes out of the room and then came in, closing the inner door softly behind him. 'He will see you – but only because you have come so far on such a wretched day. I am sorry to have made you come – *I* do not understand what the trouble is. He is safe with us though – do not worry. He will probably be as right as rain in a few days. We'll always have room for him.' This could not be true, Jane thought, for there was little enough room at the cottage.

'He will not let us send for the apothecary. He says he is "sick in his soul". Maggie – my wife – told him he ought to be with his folks, but he always says he has no "folks", and then he says he does not wish to live and if we would only turn him out he would die quite happily on the road. What ought we to do?' Jane could not ask him how well he knew his friend and he must be wondering himself how well his guest knew Jane and what was their relationship. 'He told us where to find you – he said *yesterday* that he would see you. *Now* he seems to have changed his mind.'

'You go through to him, dear,' said Maggie Farquharson.

Jane thought they probably imagined there had been some lovers' tiff. If only there had!

He was sitting, fully dressed, in the little back room and did not look up at first when she came in. Then she said softly: 'Charles.' He still did not answer or look up. Perhaps he would be angry that she had come. 'You asked me to come,' she said firmly.

He looked up then and she was pained at the thinness of his face and the dark shadows under his eyes. He said nothing for a long time. He seemed to have become mute.

'You can do nothing,' he said finally, as though it hurt him to speak.

'But I *am* here and you can talk to me even if I can *do* nothing.'

'I was raving. Why should a girl like you come and visit an old reprobate?' he said. 'I am a nuisance to Michael – I know – I don't deny it – but there was nowhere else to go – when – when I came to London at Christmas. I thought I had caught a chill.' He was silent then, for the effort of speaking seemed to have drained him.

'Perhaps you *have* caught a chill – you don't look as though you have eaten for days,' said Jane.

'No – it is my mind – I don't want to do anything – do you understand? Not even write – what is the point?'

'They promise to print some more of your Gothic poems,' she said after a few minutes. She had moved to the window and saw his eyes follow her there. Then there was a long silence. The snow lay under a heavy sky, and a few birds were perched on the crest of a snowdrift. The shadows of the snow were everywhere.

'Go away, Jane,' he said softly. 'I shall go too, soon, I am sorry – but no one can do anything. I have to fight it myself. If only my limbs did not feel so heavy – '

At least he was *speaking* to her!

'You are melancholy,' she said. 'I understand – '

'No, no, you do not understand – it is more than melancholy. Sometimes it is a mental pain to move or to speak.'

'Yet you are not feverish – you have no chill?'

'No, the fever is in my head – or it was. Now there is just an empty space. Go away, Jane,' he said again. 'I thank you for coming. You are very good to me – but you can do nothing for me.'

231

'If you won't say what is the matter – I mean apart from the melancholy. Is there no cause?'

'No cause,' he repeated dully, yet bitterly.

'There must be! Have you fought someone, lost a wager, hurt yourself somehow?' She realized she was speaking to him as though he were a child she loved. Oh, she did love him. If only he would need her.

'I often don't want to go on living,' he said after a pause. 'How could *you* understand that when you are like life itself: good, strong life? I have not been gambling or drinking or fighting,' he said when she said nothing.

'I love you,' she said, as though her words came from far away and were formed on her lips without volition. Then she turned away and looked out of the window again. The snow silence was heavy and everything but her own heart seemed muffled. She could feel her own heart beating under her clothes and hear it in her ears. Yet she did not regret her words. They hung around in the air of the little room and the snow seemed to lift them up.

Finally, he said slowly: 'I don't believe in "love".'

'I do,' she said.

'I can never love *you*, Jane, never,' he added. 'Not in the way you want.'

She waited, was sure there was more to come. It was enough that she had acknowledged her feelings for him. 'I can still help you, though,' she said then, when he had turned away in his chair and was tracing the blue flowers on the wallpaper of the little room with a long finger.

'I am not to fight a duel – or be transported – do not let that imagination of yours run on matters like that. I might be killed – but I shan't mind.'

'Do not say such things, Charles. I shall mind.'

He looked up at her. 'Why should you care for me?

232

You don't know me, Jane Banham – you think you do, but you do not.'

'Why shall you not mind?' she asked steadily. 'Why let someone else do what you are doing to yourself. Killing yourself – that is what you are doing.'

'How perceptive you are,' he mocked, but then said more gently, not looking at her, 'I can't love women, Jane.'

'Why should you want to die because of that? There are many men, I believe, who cannot love,' she answered.

'You don't understand. I have passions – oh yes, I have passions.'

After a moment she said, hesitantly now, 'I think I *do* understand.'

'Now you will find me repugnant. All good women – and honest, upright men – will find me repugnant. A repugnance for all that makes my own life worth living.'

'How can love be wrong? Wherever it is directed?'

'Oh – *love*. I would not call it that. Madness, lust – oh yes! Do I frighten you now?'

She was silent.

'My "crime" is not spoken of in polite society – or in any other society. It is against God, you see. Of course, that does not stop it being committed in polite society – oh especially there! It is still a sin – a sin that will be punished.'

'I do not believe you are a bad man,' she said. 'Whatever you say – and if it is a sin, why, I think we should blame the God of whom you spoke for putting it in your head!' She was still not quite sure what he was talking about, but began to have a vague idea of unlawful and perverted pleasures.

He echoed her thoughts. 'For people who do not care

233

about virtue it is a thoughtless pleasure. But for me it is a compelling urge. All my life is a lie, Jane.'

'Then, if it hurts you so, why do you give in to it?'

'Why do *you* love me, Jane Banham? You do not want to stop loving me – am I not right? I understand human feelings you know – too well!'

'If my loving you were a sin, then I should still love you,' she answered.

'Ah, there speaks the spirit of Shelley, and in a woman's body, too.'

'Even if you sin in the eyes of the world, why should you be so melancholy? Is it that you want to be liked by the world?'

'I am pursued by demons. They lead me to men, and then they lead me to one man – and he does not want me – and so I have others. I speak rudely – I ought not to speak to you of these things – yet I *am* telling you. I have not spoken of such things to a woman. That is a sin, too, is it not?'

She looked at him and she did not pity him, but she was angry that such a man should be made so unhappy – or make himself so.

She went up to him and took his hand. Let her be punished too, if necessary. What else could she do but take his hand – and then try to forget?

'Oh, I wish I could love a girl like you,' he said, with a sigh. 'But, of course, I should not be a good person for women, even if I were like other men. But, yes, I wish I could love you. Yet I can never love you. You must go away and pray for me if that is what you do. I expect *this* time I shall survive my self-hatred.'

Jane was thinking, irrelevantly almost, that Fred Digby might understand this man. He would be tolerant even if he had no fellow feeling for the man's nature.

234

'They call it being "so-so" or "the other way inclined",' said Charles. 'Most of us glory in it, you know, but other men hate us – especially the gangs. You must not speak of this to anyone, Jane, not ever.' He added, 'Yes, men hate us – the pious men – but women do not always hate us.'

'Could we not, even so, be friends?' she asked. 'I wish *I* were a man – that I might protect you!'

He smiled at her spirit, but he replied: 'I do not think it is my unfortunate propensities alone that make me melancholy, for I do not think I am wrong in that. It is deeper than that. Perhaps I feel doomed for other reasons that I cannot understand. It is not just the whips and scorpions of "Society" that push me to a doom I half dread, half invite – no, it is something I see only in dreams.'

'If you were an ordinary man . . .' she began and then stopped.

'If?'

'Then a woman would be able to love you in the way you wanted, but you would not be a happy man, would you? Is that what you mean?'

'Did you not know? I told you I am a bastard – think of that – added to all my wickedness. I am also born of sin.'

'There have always been bastards,' she said. 'And why must they always pay for the sins of their parents? The God I was told to love always proffers forgiveness.'

'Oh, it is kind of Him, is it not?' he said with a flash in his eye. She saw that whatever else she had done she had roused him from his lethargy. But what is wrong with *me* that I should love him? she was thinking.

He seemed to take a deep breath. 'You have lightened my burden just a little,' he whispered, and she saw there were tears in his eyes. 'Now, go away and never see me again. Go to a man who will love you – I am sure there must be many. I shall go north again, and try to stay away from temptation.'

'Why do you go to Rebecca Smith?' she asked then, turning towards him as he sat, head bent, as though the sins of the world were upon him even though he said the burden had been lightened.

He looked up, surprised. 'How do you know her?'

'I do not know her. I went to see her. I was worried about you – I had not heard from you or seen you for so long. She called me "Jennet".'

'She did?'

'Yes, and yet I do not remember Papa ever called it me. Perhaps long ago . . . I told her I was a Jennet myself,' she added, trying to to be truthful.

'Are you superstitious, Jennet?'

His calling her that was strange and painful in a way she could not understand. 'No – I don't know – there are things we do not understand. I liked Mrs Smith and yet I was a little afraid of her.'

'I expect it is all nonsense,' he said.

'Oh, Charles, if you ever need me – if there is anything, anything at all – you *will* call out for me? I shall come.'

'I shall not change. You must go away and you must promise to banish these thoughts of me and to look to a natural happiness. Jane, you must promise me. I know I am right.'

She loved him then even more, but it was despairing love.

'There is the whole world outside,' he said pointing through the casement. 'You will keep my secret?'

The loss of him, the *loss*, she was thinking. When *he* is the man above all in the world I should like to comfort

236

and succour and protect and love and yes, even worship! She who had always thought of an equal love and some happiness of a calm sort, whatever the initial trials and tribulations. *Why* must she leave him?

'Come here,' he said, and he seemed the old Charles, for he tried to smile. 'Whatever they say about me, do not forget. But we must not meet again. You have your own reputation to consider. You – a young woman – beautiful – for yes, you are beautiful – and good – I know you are good – but you must not try to see me again. Please, Jane, for my sake, seek out a passion that can reply to yours.'

She saw years and years of parting and loss, loss, loss.

'But if you ever want to see me, if you need me . . . you might – '

'I shall not change. I should not have mentioned your name to Michael, but it is true you have heartened me a little.'

She thought, Why could we not live together as friends? Why should I lose him for ever?

As though to underline her thoughts he said: 'We are spiritual kin, you and I, Jane, I know it. But it is worse for a woman in this world. However bad the world is for men like me, it can be worse for women. You must know that and you must not take risks. Your nature is a *little* like mine under your sunny features, I can see it.'

'But promise me if you ever need me, you will write to me and I will come wherever you are. I cannot lose you for ever.'

'When I first saw you I began to like you, Jane, more than I usually like women. But it is to do with your soul, not your body.'

'Sometimes I think that bodies are all we have,' said Jane. 'But they must go hand in hand with our minds.'

237

'That they do not is my fate. I hope it will not be yours – it need not be.' He got up from the chair and turned towards the window. 'Something more than anything we have spoken of – something that makes me write – is that God-given? And which God?' He spoke as though she were not in the room. Then he turned and said fiercely: 'Perhaps I should not have spoken at all. And now I am weary. I shall sleep.'

'Promise me, promise me,' she cried, 'that you will not do away with yourself. You are not a wicked man. I do not understand all your feelings, but I will be there for you if you need me.'

'You have been good – and now you must go and you must not try to see me again – I can and will survive my ordinary melancholy, glut it on the salt sea-wave, aye, but you have done all you can ever do. Go now, Jane.'

'Charles, I shall not try to see you. So long as I know you are alive, I shall bear it.'

'Now you are crying,' he said wonderingly. 'I don't think I ever made a woman cry. Go now. Tell Michael I shall soon be well. Yes, tell him.'

She went up to him at the window and took his hand and kissed it and wiped her tears on the kerchief round her neck and said: 'How can I go back to that empty world out there? But you *will* be well again and then the world will be full for you, too. And then I shall be happy.'

'Try to forget,' he said and turned again to the window.

She took a great hold on herself and went out to the other room where a fire was burning cheerfully. She took a deep breath and said to Michael, who was sitting with a child on his knee, 'I think he will be all right now. Please look after him for a little while and then he will go home.' But where *was* that home?

Maggie came out of the kitchen with Polly and the baby. Jane hoped they did not see she had been crying.

'Then he is better?' she asked.

'I think so. Come, Polly, we must go. There will be a chaise down from the village to Camden.'

I shall never see him again, this is the end. It went round and round her head, but she had to greet the ordinary world, compose herself, fulfil her ordinary obligations. She managed to refuse a cup of tea, to say her farewells, to trudge up to the snow-covered village and to wait for a chaise with every appearance of normality.

'You should have had a cup of tea,' was all Polly said.

'*I* did, *and* I played with the baby.'

A little later, when they were in the conveyance, Polly stole a look at her. 'I shouldn't worry, Miss, if I were you. Mrs Farquharson was telling me all them literary gents are the same, 'cept her husband. He's very steady. Nice people, they are.'

'Yes, Polly. Do not say anything to Mrs Ogilvie – will you? – about Mr Fitzpercy.'

'Shouldn't dream of it,' replied Polly. 'We've all got our lives to lead, without others gossiping.'

In spite of his asking her not to remember him and the sadness with which his words had filled her, Jane had, paradoxically, never felt closer to Charles. If this closeness could be achieved only by withdrawing – if he wanted her to withdraw – well, withdraw she must, but only apparently. There was something in the bridge made between her feelings and his which she could not abolish. He knew she loved him – and that was enough, would have to be enough. She had felt, though, a sense of the withdrawal of his own physical person, even as she had kissed his hand, and only when she was home and sitting by the evening fire with snowflakes once more swirling

239

outside the uncurtained window, did she try to understand that. The least important fact which Charles had presented her with was that of his 'love for men'. Yet it was – or ought to be – the most important. Could she ever, she wondered, be able to live a life of ordinary sensual passion and yet keep Charles in her heart inviolable? Part of her wanted to embody the idea of a masculine lover in a masculine person. The other part wished to enjoy the feelings aroused in her by Charles in solitude. She wanted to make a world for her feelings to live in. But she doubted her ability to withdraw for ever from the other world. Her feelings must find expression – yet she did not see how that could be with anyone but Charles. She was melancholy, but not despairing. She wanted to be a *person* for Charles Fitzpercy if she could not be a lover. She knew she could love him for ever, but she was determined that it would not be just her own feelings she loved. He was a real person in his own world. If he chose for the normal intercourse between men and women to be suspended in her case, she could not fight that.

For the next few days the snow continued to fall and she veered from grief to exaltation. She did not want to change, but was aware that to go on living she must change. Alone, she could not effect that change. There was no one to talk to who might understand. Not even Snetters would understand, or Charlotte. She sat every evening by the fire and saw that she was at a turning point in her life. Loving was so much less simple than she had supposed. She tried to reverse the roles they had taken, tried to imagine how *she* would feel if some man had fallen in love with her soul and yet wanted her body too, which she did not, or could not, give. The reversal was impossible. She had been taught that love called out love for mutual feelings to be expressed – and usually it was men who made the first move. If Charles had 'loved women' she knew that he would have loved *her*, his love drawn out by hers. And that would still have been strange since it was for women to be courted and wooed, not do the wooing. Was the whole world in a conspiracy to believe this – or was it true? Perhaps it was true that 'good' women waited and suffered and achieved their ends through passivity? She could not do that. If she were a man she would have fallen in love many times with women. Why could not women have just one love which they declared first? No one might ever love her in the way Charles was beloved by her and the very thought made her feel her world was at an end. There must be parting and loss – that much was sure. But she could not forget – that was sure, too. Something of him was anchored in her, and she could not pull up the anchor. Was it possible that life was a series of partings and losses for some unfortunate people?

Then she would wake in the night in her little bed in the room at the top of the house with the night skies cruising slowly past her window and the moon falling over her carpet in silvery beams, and she would think: I must *try* to forget him even if I cannot. Where was he now? Where would he ever be? It was not the end of her or of him, even if she never saw him again. She longed for him, not to take her in his arms, but only to be there to be appreciated and loved by her. She often thought how much easier life would be if she had never met him. How much longer then it would have taken her to personify the feelings she surely must have had before she met him. Perhaps they would never have crystallized and she would have never known of what she was capable. But as she sat up in bed hugging her knees and trying to recall his face before slipping back down again to the warmth of her feather mattress, she knew that was not true and thought she was destined for some irregular adoration, some impossible worship. Even in the midst of that recognition, she told herself not to indulge in the pleasures of grief. She had been taught stoicism as a child and even if it warred with her nature, which was self-indulgent and impetuous, she knew she must be stern with herself and try to keep Charles apart from other feelings which might, at any moment, crowd in on her. At present she felt no other feelings were possible, did not want them, but dreamed of a soft enfolding, some person who loved her and who had no face, unless it was his.

A week or two later, she had escaped to walk in the City, trying to interest herself in the life all around her, to grow up and come to some conclusions about herself and the world. The snow had now almost gone and the streets were filthy and yellow with mud and a few frozen rivulets of ice over which horses slipped and slithered. Then, across the street, she saw Michael Farquharson coming out of a newspaper office. He had not seen her, but was crossing the road in her direction. She waited until he was bound to pass her. He was walking with an abstracted air, a large bundle of copy under one arm. His hands were red and cold. He looked up as he passed her and his face spread into welcome.

'Why, Miss Banham! What are you doing here? It's foul weather – even snow would be better.'

'How do you do, Mr Farquharson. What news have you of Mr Fitzpercy?' she said, trying to keep her feelings out of her voice.

He shifted his bundle and drew back on to the pavement, where she followed him under the arch of an old building. 'He's gone away. I believe he will be better

242

now,' he said. 'I can't thank you enough for coming to our aid – Maggie was very worried. It was her idea to send for you. She forced him to give us your address.'

'Has he gone north?' she asked.

'I believe he may have done. He said we must not worry any more about him – he would be all right. It was a miracle, what you did. We thought he would be sitting in our little bedroom all winter and he had not eaten, you know. But he went off happy as a lark a few days after you saw him. Aye, he's a strange fellow. You must come and see us on a better day. Hampstead in spring is delightful – we should be pleased to see you. We both thank you,' he added. 'I was going to write to you in any case.'

'Thank you, Mr Farquharson.' And after a few more commonplaces about the baby and his own health and that of his wife, they parted and moved on.

She went back home pensive. Glad that Charles seemed to have recovered his appetite for life. Sad that there seemed no more place for her now in that life. Charles would not worry his head about her – it probably embarrassed him to feel he had needed her ministrations. She must learn to walk alone in this great bustling place: literally alone, so that Polly need not always accompany her wherever she went, and figuratively alone. All around her were men walking alone, or in groups of other men. Their wives and servants and women friends would all be at home awaiting their return. That was the way of the world. She would have accepted it if Charles could have been her companion. She must not weep, she told herself sternly, the warm tears splashing down her cheeks in an unexpected torrent. She pretended that the wind had made her eyes water and rubbed them with her knuckle, then walked back slowly past the tall houses and the little houses, and the shops and the dogs and the streetsellers and the clerks and the boy with his iron hoop in the gardens and the trudging horses and the occasional maid-servant and returned to her room and her duties with a little knot of grief behind her throat.

The days and the weeks passed and the letters from Rome spoke of improvement in Edith's health and then a little setback and then some more improvement. Frederick Digby had visited them twice; his lady was in Florence. Every weekend Jane went to see the boys on Hunter Street. It kept her busy.

Charlotte and Henrietta were to give the reception postponed from the New Year in March and Philip had taken her piece on 'London in Winter', one of three which she had submitted to him. The next was to be on City churches. She had visited several with Polly and sat through innumerable sermons. When she thought of her own conduct, and even more her own desires, she knew she ought not to be sitting in churches, even if she did not take Communion. The churches were full of the middle classes; no poor people visited them. She amused herself wondering what these guardians of morality would think of her, if they knew her innermost thoughts. Charles's secret she kept to herself, of course, having a sure instinct for what was sayable and what was not.

She knew that the best part of her was laid up with Charles and would remain lodged there whatever he did, whoever he loved, wherever he went.

Sometimes she tired of the struggle to keep up a façade of polite young lady. The only refuge then was satire, to treat with irony her bafflement at the ways of the world. She did not abjure her childish God, but felt He ought to understand, better than His representatives on earth, the impulses which acted upon Charles Fitzpercy and upon herself. She often thought that it would be so pleasant to have feelings approved of by everyone, pleasant but impossible, regarding herself as probably more of a pariah than any of her actions had, as yet, made her.

One day temptation was to come from a very different quarter. For so long she had been thinking of nothing but her love for Charles and the absence of Charles. Three months of wrestling with loneliness and sadness, with no word from him and probably no word from him ever again, had made her shrink from other men and even feel quite sick when they took an interest in her. Girls, of course, were not supposed, in any case, to think of passion, even if their flirtations and marriage plans and gossip were all posited on the possibility of losing their 'virtue' one day – if only to a husband who would set the seal on that virtue by acting like the men they were! Men, of course, were not expected to be virtuous in this way, but to afford protection so that women might remain so.

She examined her conscience and realized that she was not able to interest herself in others because she did not truly believe that whatever the strange, tenuous relationship she had had with Charles had been, it was over. Something was being worked out. But Charles did not need her, she needed Charles: that was the truth. She needed him to need her and he did not. Yet how could she wrench her feelings on to another track without doing violence to her best self? After all, a year ago and she had not known of his existence. Something in her said, it was not an accident. And he noticed you, sought you out even, so there must be something. She told herself she must have been mistaken.

In all this, her writing was her greatest solace and she even began to plan a story about self-deception. But the feelings were too raw, too near, for her to make them live in words.

The continual feeling of wanting something to happen, wanting to live in a different way from this regular and habit-ridden routine of walks with Polly, chats with Mrs Ogilvie, letters to her friends in Norfolk and visits to the boys at Dr Macdonald's stayed with her. She was waiting for something, but she did not know what. It could not be what she wanted since she would never be loved by Charles Fitzpercy. Reason did not come into it. One did not choose whom one loved, and neither could one 'choose' whom to be loved by.

Her stoicism often gave way to impatience and a sense of waste. She knew she was wilful and headstrong and needed strong feelings to give her ballast. She tried to interest herself in the world, in ideas and politics. She read the newspaper and the journals when she could afford them. Hal's city clerk brought *The Times* round to the house for her every evening. She tried to read, too, idle romances which seemed shadowy compared with her own feelings. She reread Charles's poems – those she had read in the first issue of the *New London*, and managed to borrow from Charlotte the copies of the other poems and 'Gothic' pieces which Charlotte herself was copying for Philip's next issue.

Perhaps it was given to women only to wait and be discovered, not to ride out on a charger of love and longing. But perhaps she had saved his life by going to him. Charles needed a strong person to succour him, whom he could rely on. She dreamed of coming upon him and all being made well. She placed her daydreams in a 'romantic' place: Vauxhall Gardens in the moonlight, and Charles with his face lit up by green and gold fireworks in the sky; Charles in a church or in the ruined house he had spoken of on the northern coast. She thought of him again in that silvery drawing room in Bruton Street, and in the fashionable crowd at Drury Lane. She even imagined coming across him in Italy in the shadow of fountains and myrtle bushes. She dreamed of persuading old Mrs Smith that she was the girl for him next time she read his fortune in the cards. But she knew that none of it would ever come to pass. She had lost him as a future lover and must wait patiently as a friend in case he ever needed her.

What else could she do?

Here Mother Nature, or perhaps her wicked fairy, took over.

It was the night of Charlotte's and Henrietta's party in Fulham, a cold, clear night in late March.

Let it be said – and Jane often said it – that she was never in love with, could never be in love with Philip March. And that Philip March, if love was to be the name of the feelings Jane Banham had for her Charles, was never in love with, and could never be in love with her. All that Jane needed, all that she imagined to be necessary for the perfect love, was in Charles Fitzpercy. And Philip March? His projects and projections were towards high and mighty young ladies, possibly with fortunes, whom he would rouse to passion, or towards pretty, but rather stupid and also libidinous girls of the lower classes, who aroused his lust and gave him a sensation of power. Jane needed to be needed; Philip liked to make conquests and move on. He lived in the present, whereas Jane, like Charles, lived in a mixture of past and future where some ancestral longings tinged a paradise of imagined perfection.

She had determined not to stay too long at the party, to chat pleasantly to her women friends and return home at a decent hour. She had been given the key to her uncle's house since Polly and Mrs Ogilvie retired early.

247

She had no wish to stay over in Fulham till the following morning, for she liked to get up early and write.

She had even been half minded to send a message to plead indisposition, except that her cold was now departed and she knew that her disinclination proceeded from laziness and boredom as much as from her leaden feelings of gloom. Gloom over Charles, gloom over her own work which seemed to her vacuous and lacking in imagination, and gloom over her own wretchedness. Whenever she felt that she had overcome her sadness for Charles and that she would arise anew, grown up and ready to stand alone, the sudden thought of him – of his hair with its coppery tinges, of his long nose and mellow voice, of the despair in his eyes – would assail her anew till she groaned to be rid of the vision. It was painful to feel, and she wished she need not feel it.

At ten o'clock, Jane, who had been drinking claret and talking rather warmly to the several young men present – including Mr Bruce who had returned from his mysterious visit abroad and was to survive another term in Cambridge – was prevailed upon to return home in a hackney carriage with Philip. 'I can drop you at your uncle's – do come with me. I find parties rather boring and have work to do at Temple Gardens,' he had said.

Jane had quite enjoyed herself and the claret had, for a moment, lifted her mind off its accustomed dreary treadmill. She was, in truth, a little 'elevated'. She would go with Philip in spite of her knowledge that he had been eyeing her with the same look she had surprised on his face at Christmas. She took the conscious decision to be tempted by him in order to alleviate the misery of thoughts of Charles. Why could she not at least be ordinary and allow a young man to flirt with her if she were not allowed to be extraordinary? She needed experience.

And it turned out that Philip, whom she knew to have been rejected by Julia Jeffrey, was initially not at all averse to pleading his case. She thought that he would be quite willing to take advantage of the situation, although he had not been drinking very much and would be amazed if she agreed to be taken advantage of. First he held her hand in the carriage and she allowed it to be held. It did not make her happy, but it did not make her unhappy either. He was not exactly paying court to her – she could tell that, neither was he in love with her – although for a moment he might feel she was interesting enough to conquer. She knew exactly what she was doing – that was the pity of it and she knew how it could end and she did not mind. If this were temptation, well she would go to meet it halfway. When he suggested that she come into the Chambers for a nightcap – 'And then I can accompany you home' – she did not demur. He did seem a little surprised, it was true, but she was past caring.

When they finally arrived at Temple Gardens and she had followed him up to the little room where she had first met him, but which was now rather bare since the girls' possessions were absent, she decided to take action. He was not going to seduce her – but she would flirt with him, and then perhaps the pain of Charles would be lessened. She would balance Charles's Archie Colquohoun with an affair of her own. She knew she was doing wrong, but she tried not to think about it. She implied to him as they sat together on the long sofa with a dying fire in the grate, that she knew very well that marriageable ladies should not have tête-à-tête conversations with young men at night.

'Ah, marriage!' said Phil, with a worldly look. '*You* are

too intelligent for that, Jane. I did not realize at first, but your pieces have impressed me. Even Bruce and others have said you could earn your living by writing, but you need more experience of the world and of men. You are not like my sister and the others – you should travel and acquire experience and love.'

So she was no longer among the marriageable, it appeared. Yet all she had done was to agree to take a cup of coffee with him and allow him to take her hand! She was a little amused that he should seek to win her through flattery. She seemed to be looking at him and at herself as though they were behind glass and she gritted her teeth to see if she were real. So this was how young men approached girls they desired. But what if she were to say: No, I am a virtuous girl – I need my reputation. At one stroke you will deprive me of my virtue – I must go. If it had been anyone but Philip she would have got up then and there, but she was curious to see what he would do next. What he did was to get down on his knees and tell her how adorable she was. It was a farce – if Philip 'loved' her, as *he* understood the word to apply to the relations between young men and 'good' girls, he would take her home immediately. Philip had decided that she was not a 'good' girl, as he defined the term. How ridiculous. What difference did it make? Why should she be judged differently from a man? Centuries of advice, of the common sense of ages, the morals of several hundred years, all the Church's teaching, were on the side of her 'virtue'. Why should she not cast it away? She was tempted, although she was no longer a trifle elevated, but quite clear-headed and she replied:

'Do get up, Phil. I don't think I shall ever marry – you are quite right. But men and women are meant to enjoy each other, are they not?' She was quite willing for him to take advantage of her: she would prove she was a woman, but she would do what *she* wanted – like a man. Why should she not take him as a lover – just as much as he her? She could not be more unhappy if she stayed in his arms and he had his will with her. She locked her mind up with Charles inside it, and waited to see how Phil would proceed.

But Philip, who had shown every appearance of impending passion and who had fallen back on the sofa with his arms around her and given her the strange sensation of being so close to him that she might as well be naked in his arms, suddenly drew away. He knew that she was saying: Take me as a lover, and, strangely enough, it cooled his ardour.

'You are shameless, Jane. You do not struggle – and yet I could overpower you in a moment.'

'I still would not marry you,' she said, a little surprised.

'I have not asked you,' he said. 'You are a very pretty and naughty child – but – ' He kissed her temples quite tenderly. 'I could not do it.'

She groaned. 'If you make love to me, you will not "love" me – and you will forget me by tomorrow! If you don't, you will remember me – I suppose that is the truth.'

'Do not say such things,' he cried. 'It is not womanly.'

She knew now that she must either lure him to make love to her or stop and keep him as a rather uneasy friend.

'In any case,' he said rather maliciously, 'if anyone knows you have been here with me alone at night your reputation will already be gone.'

'Then why not make it worthwhile?' something led her to say and she leaned forward and put his hand on her heart. How dare he speak of her reputation! She would show him she was as warm-blooded as he.

251

'Stop!' he shouted. 'You are a devil – I shall take you home.'

He rose and turned away, and poured himself a glass of brandy. His ardour had evaporated. His flush had turned to pallor.

The game seemed to be over and she closed her eyes. Mother Nature had seemingly been defeated and there was no more to be done. Was she 'ruined' now? she wondered, as he took her home in silence.

When she thought over her conduct the next day, she at first shuddered with embarrassment and then was angry. Not angry that Philip had not seduced her or even with herself for making it clear that he could have done, but angry with the code they all lived by – that 'good' women never had impure thoughts, that it was men, not women, who must make the advances and do the rejecting – and most of all that, in the eyes of the world, whatever had or had not taken place that night in Temple Gardens Chambers, she *would* actually, if the fact were known that she consented to go with a young man alone to his chambers, be ruined. She did not care that she had been made to look a fool, but she did care that the conventions could not be overturned without a young man losing his manly powers. There was clearly no equality in matters of the flesh, just as there was none in matters of the spirit. What if they had both wanted the same thing at the same time? Should she have simpered and refused and played a game in order to get her man? It was all stupid – but unfortunately not the sort of thing she could write about for the *New London*! Not that Philip would probably ever want any more copy from her, she thought, as she sat the next morning sipping a very late breakfast of chocolate, having arrived home well past midnight.

But in this she was wrong. Philip March wrote to her a short note apologizing for the 'misunderstanding' and hoping that she would soon be ready with her piece on City churches which she had been working on for many days. Obviously he needed her contribution in a hurry!

The episode continued to embarrass her but his rejection did not. Some men were evidently delicately balanced and complicated creatures. She supposed that he was congratulating himself on his self-control and that was how he would look back on the episode. She would hold her tongue, too, and not allude to it. If her adventure ever came to the ears of others it would not be by her doing. She knew that claret and boredom and sensuality could surely act upon a woman as it did thousands of times upon men. She thought no more and no less of Philip – he, too, was a child of convention; only she wished that, like Charles Fitzpercy, she might have the courage to be a *true* outlaw, if that was ever possible for a weak woman. But Philip March was neither intelligent enough nor strong enough for her.

Her blood ran cold when she realized that if Philip had taken advantage of her she could have ended up with child – just from a chance whim of curiosity bred by despair at her unrequited love for Charles, and lust and ennui. There must be many claret children. What would she have done then? The answer came easily – gone to Rebecca Smith or someone like her. They said there were women who knew about doing away with unwanted children before they were born, long before they were born, and she knew she might have done that. Philip March had saved her from herself. But a child of Charles – oh, that would be different – *that* she could love.

The weather turned warmer and the trees began to put out leaves – not yet the plane trees, the last always to welcome spring, but there was a balm in the air after the cold March winds, and the rain when it came was warm. Why not visit Rebecca again? Surely she would have news of Charles, might know at least if he were alive, if not where he laid his head.

She had had a busy week, visiting the boys twice as Johnny had not been well, and helping Mrs Ogilvie to clean the silver from the cellar where it lay in soft rags till its mistress and master returned. This time she would not take Polly. She would go alone, now that she knew London better and Mrs Ogilvie had become accustomed to her comings and goings. And she must also go later on foot to the City to look at more churches for her article. That would be a pleasure. She loved the City where people were too busy to notice a girl alone and where she could sit out of the rain, looking at the monuments and tombs of the countless, often neglected, little buildings tucked away in corners and behind graveyards and at the ends of streets.

But first to Mrs Smith. She put on her new bonnet and took her basket like a servant so that she might be about to buy fruit and flowers on her way and set off one morning in early April.

It was a beautiful spring morning and even London appeared freshly watered. Soon it would be summer and the dew would lie on the grasses of Lincoln's Inn Fields and there would be the smell of sun in the air.

Should she try to speak to Daisy first? Perhaps better not – she was sure that if Daisy had known of Charles's whereabouts, or if he had been to visit her grandmother recently, the girl would have found some means of telling her – if she knew of the visit, of course. As she went through Bloomsbury nobody appeared to notice her. She

254

must just be brave when she came to the edges of the poorer district near Ironmongers Row. She ought not to have put on her new bonnet, and for a moment she contemplated taking it off and putting on a kerchief or a servant's white frilly cap, but why should she disguise herself in a free country? It *was* a little frightening to be without Polly, though, and on foot, and she tried not to look at people. It took her about twenty minutes of brisk walking to reach the road she remembered from before.

She had passed Bloomsbury Square and Frederick's house. He must be still in Italy; the blinds were drawn. There was a sense of quiet in that square which contrasted with the alleys further south and west.

She walked by streets of little houses with smoke curling out of their chimneys. It was not very far from Seven Dials and St Giles, and people eyed her curiously as she walked along looking for number 363. All the houses looked the same. She was on the right side of the road and there were children playing and running up and down and screaming everywhere. Some doors were open but she walked along without looking in, though she would have liked to know how others lived. Then she recognized the shop at the corner and walked along briskly. The air was not so sweet here and there were no trees. For how long had Londoners lived in this street? It looked very old. She passed a house with 'Rooms to Let' on a dirty card in the window and now number 363 was approaching. It was a little cleaner than its next-door neighbours, she noticed. When she arrived at the door she was almost out of breath and her heart was thumping. A simple walk through my own city, she reflected, and I am as nervous as a cat. A year ago I should have been less wary. Still, she had managed to arrive on her own two feet. What if old Mrs Smith were not in? She knocked a little timidly and no one answered at first. A bolder knock and the door was opened by a child of about eleven. This must be Mary, Daisy's sister.

'Muvver says she ain't at home,' the girl said.

'It's your grandma I want to see,' said Jane with a smile. 'Could you ask her if she could spare me just two minutes? Tell her it's Jennet.'

'Jennet's a funny name, Miss!'

'Miss Banham,' said Jane after a pause. 'Tell her Miss Banham.'

The girl shut the door and went tramping off. She wore rather large boys' boots. Oh Lord! Now she would have to wait, and she looked around hastily in case any passer-by were about to rob her. But of course they wouldn't rob her – this was not an area of vice or depravity, just an ordinary street of people in work. Yet it was so shabby: how hard did you have to work to live here?

After a long wait the door was opened by the child. 'She says you can come in, but she ain't very well today.'

Jane wondered whether to give the girl a penny, but decided she would wait till she was let out. She followed her down the familiar passage and a cat brushed against her skirts. A young woman, whom she had not seen before, came out of the room at the end. She must have been a client, for she averted her eyes as she passed her. She looked as though she had been weeping. What fortune or advice had old Rebecca been giving her? The child appeared again and said: 'Wait until she calls you,' and was off upstairs.

Jane opened her cloak and put down her basket and prepared to wait. What would Philip March think of her coming to a place like this? He had probably decided that she was mad, so it did not matter. What mattered was news of Charles. But she had better be honest with the

256

old lady; in truth, she was not exactly sure why she had felt impelled to come again, and her visit might not be welcome. She would tell Rebecca Smith that Charles did not love her but that she continued to be haunted by him.

Hadn't Charles talked about haunting that day on the Heath? It seemed long, long ago. *He* was haunted, but not by a person. *She* was haunted now. Mrs Smith could not take away his ghost, but she might have something for her, advice if not news.

She wondered again why the young lady she had passed on her way to the room had been to see Rebecca. Not to tell the future – but to receive practical advice, she was sure. A love child, or worse. She shuddered: it might very well have been her own fate, and her own fault.

The woman was a long time before calling 'Come in' and Jane had almost decided to go away, but just as she was turning irresolutely on her heel, the cracked, gruff voice did call and she opened the door once more to the little room with its drawn curtains and fire and the linnet in its cage. The woman was sitting by the fire this time, her shawl drawn closely around her. She looked up and looked long at Jane and said: 'Sit down, then. Take your cloak off. I keep it warm in here.' Jane took off her cloak and the woman got up, gave the fire a poke saying, 'Come and sit near me, near my fire. I reckon it's not the cards or the hands you've come for?'

'No, Mrs Smith. I don't want my fortune told – it's just – just – that I don't know where he is – and he made me promise not to look for him or go after him – and I've tried to forget him – but I can't.' To her dismay she found she was almost ready to cry. She swallowed and took hold of her dignity. 'I thought you might have some news – or even some advice for me.'

'I told you not to count on him, didn't I?' asked the

257

woman after another long pause, during which she was scrutinizing her visitor with those coal-black eyes.

'Yes, I know, and I will not expect anything from him – on my own account. But I went to see him after Christmas – he had been ill – some strange sorrow I did not understand. His friends were worried and so I went. He did not want to see me at first, and then I persuaded him that – that life was worth living, I suppose, and then he told me . . . told me – ' She searched for the right words, but the old woman interrupted her.

'That he was "that way inclined", is what they say, I believe – meaning girls are not for him, my dear.'

'Yes – how did you know? That *is* what he said.'

'And it broke your pretty heart, and now you want an old woman to tell you it's not true?'

'No – I mean – I know it's true – how did *you* know, Mrs Smith?'

'There's not much I don't know about him,' she replied. 'Nutty about him still, are you?'

The slang word startled Jane. The old woman had seemed to live in some past age so that a word that was going the theatrical rounds seemed incongruous on her lips.

'Aye, he's fortune's bastard all right,' she went on. 'Jack of Hearts, and Queen of Hearts . . . Do you want to know if he came to me again? Do you want to know where he is?'

'Yes.' She felt nervous again. The woman was not exactly menacing, but she seemed to have a slightly bantering tone.

'You'll have to pay for it,' said Mrs Smith, shrewdly.

'Yes. I brought you this.' Jane had taken off her shawl so that her belt, with its little purse in which she had hidden a golden guinea was easy to twist round and open.

258

As she did so and bent to unfasten the purse, her locket swung out from under her collar and Rebecca Smith said quickly, 'That's a pretty locket – can I see?' Was she going to take her locket – surely a guinea was enough? But the woman seemed interested in its workmanship for she said: 'Let me look at that.'

Jane took it off from round her neck – usually it reposed under her gown, for it was, she thought, a private jewel and not one for public gaze. 'It was Mama's,' she said. 'Mama left it to me – she had not many pieces of jewellery, but this was to be mine. I believe it used to have a picture in it, a miniature, but Papa took it when she died and it was lost. It is a pretty locket.'

'Ayc,' said the woman, turning it over and over in her palm. 'It is gold and the workmanship is fine.'

For a moment Jane thought she was going to ask for it in payment and she could not possibly give it to her. 'It is all I have of Mama,' she said. The woman gave it back to her with a long look as though some inner debate were going on behind those eyes of coal.

Jane handed the guinea over then and sat waiting, after putting her locket back around her neck and tucking it under her gown.

'So you want news of Mr Fitzpercy,' said Rebecca, pocketing the guinea nonchalantly.

'Yes, please.'

'You know he is not for you. Why should you still want to know of him? You must forget him, girl. There are other young men in the world.'

'That is the trouble,' replied Jane. 'I feel I *was* meant for him – how can I explain it? I feel I have to know, even if it makes me unhappy.'

'He is not in London – he is far away,' said Rebecca. 'Where he thinks he belongs. No place for you, Miss.'

'Then did he come to you? May I ask you – *did* he mention me?'

'I believe he did now, but he was concerned with his other problems. I told him to go away. What could I do? I always knew he was different.' Then she spoke in a sort of croon. 'Shouldn't have been born, shouldn't have been born – but there he is – and we can't question that, can we, Miss? . . . Oh, yes,' she went on when Jane did not answer. 'Gone where he belongs. Said he'd stay there, too.'

'Mrs Smith, is he in Salton Delevinge?' Jane asked. The woman looked up at her and then turned once more to the fire. 'Please – is he there?'

'Oh, aye, I expect so. There's nothing you can do about that.'

'Is he alone?'

'That I can't say. I expect not. He'll go on looking for a friend I expect – or for God.' She said the last word quite naturally as though God were another possible friend.

'Is he safe enough from his enemies, there?'

'As safe as anywhere. How did *you* come to hear of that place?'

'People told me that he had been brought up there and lived there sometimes and he said so himself. I can see him there, far away. I can feel the summer wind blowing round him, a salty wind combing the trees . . .'

'You know it's a ruin,' interrupted the old woman, staring at her. '"Ruin to ruins", he said to me.'

'Mrs Smith – why is he so? Is there nothing I can do? Whatever he says, I dream of him. I cannot love anyone else. Sometimes I think it must be some sort of curse laid on me. That I can see him there and feel him there and I can hear the sound of the surf – and when I try to look at his face, I can't see it.'

260

'A young lady like you knows nothing about curses,' said Rebecca. 'Take my advice, my dear. I told you to forget him. I say it again. For this guinea I could look in the cards or the ball for you, but they'd tell me the same – '

'Then why did you tell him a Jennet might bring him luck?' Jane asked boldly.

'But you are *Jane* not Jennet, aren't you?' said Rebecca slyly.

'I could have been called that when I was little. My governess says my papa and mama called me many little names when I was a baby girl. And how did *you* know about a Jennet? Was it in his cards?'

'Don't ask me the secrets of my trade,' said Rebecca in quite an ordinary voice. 'If Mr Fitzpercy comes here again, which I doubt, for he said he was off to that ruin of his – not that he'll stay there for ever, young men like him are restless – well if he comes again I shall only tell him what I see, and that's a secret. It's not your business, or really mine.'

'But, Mrs Smith, what can I do? I know I can't make him love me. I know that now, but how can I forget – how can I think of anyone else?'

'I haven't the powers to make you fall in love with anyone else that's for sure,' replied Rebecca. 'If it's your fate to love him, then love him you will, but you can keep it in your heart, little lady, and the years will go along and you'll take him out and dust him now and then and life will slip by and there'll be other fates for you. How old are you?' she asked abruptly. 'You did tell me but I forgot.'

'I shall be twenty-two very soon.'

'Come, sit at the table. I owe you a fortune,' said Rebecca and, rather stiffly, got up and sat at the table as

261

she had done before. 'I'll take your hand. Ah, what a slim little hand! I remember it, hands are all different. I may be wrong – no, your fate hasn't changed. Still writing, my dear?' she added as she felt Jane's left hand once more.

'Yes, I suppose that is my fate, if I am lucky.'

'Like I told him, you've got a bit in common with him. Make something of your life through your eyes and hands, maybe writing, maybe fashioning something . . . oh, not a thing like Louisa and the others do, but still it's making something – that's what I see.'

'Should I write about Mr Fitzpercy, then?' asked Jane.

'Not yet, not yet – later perhaps. You must be patient, Miss, that's your weakness, impatience. But you've good spirits, not like him. Use your dreams, Miss, use your dreams. I can't see it clearly.' She shut her eyes, continuing to hold Jane's hand in her own dry palm. 'There is something,' she said finally. 'I don't know what it is – you're an independent creature, like our Louisa. Good can come of it, but there's a long path to tread . . . a long path.'

She let the hand drop and opened her eyes.

'Did you lose your mama and papa then?' she asked conversationally.

'Yes – Mama died when I was eight and Papa later when I was sixteen.'

The old woman looked long in her eyes before she turned away. 'Go now – don't bother me no more, I can't help you more.'

'But if he should come to you again, please, Mrs Smith, will you tell him to call for me if he needs help, a place of safety, or money, or anything? Will you tell your grand-daughter, tell Daisy – *please*.'

'I can't promise anything. You're a rum lass, got a bit of the gypsy in you, too, I dare say, a long way back.'

With that Jane had to be content and she gathered up

262

her mantle and her basket and crept out. But the old woman returned to the fire and sat long before it thinking. Perhaps she was asleep or half asleep, but she muttered now and again. Jane's visit had tired her and also worried her. She said a brief prayer to the God of her fathers before calling up to her daughter to come and make her a pan of broth. The golden guinea was put in her box with her other treasures, and locked, and placed in the linnet's cage.

Jane's mind was in a turmoil as she returned home. Scarcely did she notice the passers-by this time as she turned up High Holborn in the direction of Bloomsbury. On her left there were crowds watching the workmen who were busy with the foundations of what they said was to become the Great British Museum and she passed through the little streets opposite and on and on, wishing somehow that she could find a church or a quiet place where she could take a rest and think. Once she was home she knew the dailiness of life would close, once more, around her. She did not even feel hungry, although she had had nothing since her morning chocolate. She was glad she had been to Mrs Smith's, glad that she had unburdened herself even if there was nothing for her comfort in that woman's remarks. Rebecca Smith did seem to understand her. She was an intelligent woman who must know the secrets of many women's and men's hearts. It was too cruel of Charles to have been so friendly and so mentally accessible and then to have thrown it all away in his 'confession'. She wondered how many men there were like him in the whole of London. That dandy Colquohoun must have been laughing up his sleeve – yet Charles had never laughed at *her*.

Once she arrived home, she arranged to go out again

263

the following day if it were fine, to walk in the City and explore some more forgotten corners of churches there. Perhaps there would be some balm for her soul in those beautiful, dusty buildings where thousands must have worshipped and taken their worries and heartaches over many, many years. She determined to occupy herself writing something worthy of Charles and which would also make Philip March realize he was dealing with no genteel miss.

All that evening she tried to think about her plans for writing, but found that Mrs Smith's voice kept insinuating itself into her ears. Still, the golden guinea had been well spent. Charles was alive, even if far away!

In bed that night the old woman's voice still pursued her. Was she no longer the 'Jennet' named by Rebecca, Charles's Jennet? She heard that voice say 'Jennet'. A sort of answer came in her dreams, which pursued her all night. She awoke from one – only to be drawn into another, remembering in the intervals of consciousness that Rebecca Smith had told her to listen to her dreams. The old lady's voice had gone now, but was the old woman somehow directing her dreams for her?

The dreams began with a bird in a cage, a sweet bird, which was looking at her, head on one side as though she were about to speak. I am Jennet and she is Linnet, she thought in the dream, and smiled. But the bird suddenly flew away through an opening in the opposite side of the cage and she found herself in a great room with a glassless window stretching almost the whole length of one side of the room which she knew was an upper chamber. She looked round for the door, but there was none. Only the great open space of window where glass once had been. How could she get out of it except by climbing down? She leaned out of the window and saw far below, a garden –

264

and beyond that garden a line of sand and a sea stretching to the horizon. As she looked at it it seemed to come nearer and when she looked back in the room, giddy and fearful, she saw she was now in a large hall with rafters and beams and a fire in an open chimney-piece. There was a birdcage there, too, a large cage hanging from a rafter in front of tapestry, and inside the cage, not a linnet, but a great eagle staring at her, his claws splayed over a piece of bark. There was menace in the eye of this great bird and she saw his cage was open and that at any moment he might take flight and pursue her. Again she looked around — no door, only the chimney. She looked up it and saw the sky at the top. Then she turned and the tapestries seemed to crumble away and as she looked at them they changed into walls of grey stone where there was again no window, nor any opening, but a large dungeon-like door, studded with nails. She looked up once more at this new room and saw, at the top of the high stone walls, a tiny bird, not a linnet, nor an eagle, but a sparrow with a beady eye. As she watched him he flitted across the roof and disappeared through a tiny, small chink. Now she was lost indeed. At least in the other room she could have climbed over the sill and shouted for help, but there was no window. She began to scream and found she was shouting: 'Charles! Charles!'

The sound of her own voice seemed to echo, and, by degrees, it faded away as she half awoke. Then she shut her eyes again and willed herself to make an opening in the wall of the dungeon as the dream merged again with her waking consciousness. And she succeeded, for she found herself now in a wild garden with the door of the lower room shut behind her and she looked around and began to walk in the direction of the ocean, which she sensed was there. A figure came then towards her. The sunlight was suddenly around her and the sound of water. She knew it must be Charles – surely it was Charles, and she ran towards him, but he turned on his heel and, as she tried to follow him, grass of a bright green, enamelled like a painting, grew up around her feet. A small stream meandered through it and she took off her shoes and waded into its shallows and followed it. The sea must be in that direction. There was no sight of the figure now, but she seemed to hear a voice, singing, a beautiful voice that comforted. The voice promised balm and honey and peace, but it led her away from the sea back into the garden. Everything else melted away and the voice changed into the sound of a bird. And, once more, the linnet was in her cage and the musical voice was the linnet's and the other sounds and all the rooms and the fears and the grass and the sun had gone and she was alone once more, staring at the bird who was now in a cage with no door, a cage of gold, intricately worked.

She woke again, this time to full consciousness, with tears streaming down her face. She held all the dream in her mind, but even as she held it, parts of it faded and she was left only with the halo of feelings that had passed over her, and the sun of early April was coming in at her window over the square, and the sounds were of London.

She was aware of this long skein of dreams all the day that followed, not wanting to lose their thread and astonished that she should have dreamed in this way immediately Rebecca Smith had mentioned dreaming. She had always dreamed a great deal, but this was one of the most impressive dreams she had ever had. What could it mean? There seemed no sense to it and she did not truly look for some simple interpretation. Something in herself had done the dreaming for her and maybe it was the feelings behind the objects in the dream that were the most important parts of the whole affair. There had been fear – of the high, open window and of the eagle, and yet there had also been the little sparrow and the linnet and the feel of her bare feet in the brook which ran through the bright green grass. Charles had been there, without a doubt, though he had turned his back on her. That was, she thought sadly, to be expected. Her heart had realized he was not for her. But the voice, so soothing and happy, remained with her. She was to puzzle over it for many long days to come and to dream other dreams, but the very next day there arrived a letter from Philip March, which almost broke the mixture of dread and melancholy and sweetness the dreams had left with her.

The letter stated quite simply that he would be away for a time as a prospect of gathering work from some expatriate writers had presented itself. Where, he did not say. In the meantime, Christopher and Mr Bruce would receive contributions in London. He added:

I do not expect to see you for some time. I *had* imagined you virtuous. Your ruin will not be caused by me. We shall not refer to these affairs in future and I hope that you will continue to see my sister and Charlotte. I cannot say you have charmed me, but you have left some anxiety in my mind I cannot quite account for. Still, I wish you well and Christopher will await your contribution on City churches. Yours P. March.

'Thought her virtuous', indeed! Was that why he had been laying siege to her? He had wanted a conquest and the intended victim had laid down her arms and invited him to take her. So now she was no longer 'virtuous' – at least *that* must be true. One law for men and another for women. Jane put down the letter and brushed her hair fiercely. She had been rash and 'unwomanly', but she had not been wrong. Would she never learn to conform?

267

Perhaps some girls were just not meant to be ladies. Perhaps she was just as much a misfit as Charles.

But these were just day-time thoughts. At night she went on imagining Charles so vividly that her imaginings seemed to merge with her dreams and she was not quite sure what she had imagined, what dreamed. She 'saw' a great ruin and a grand park and plantations of oak trees. She saw sunsets and rainbows and heard storms as though she was in the place and Charles was with her. Sometimes Charles was in danger and she rescued him. Often she tried to wean her mind away from these detailed land-scapes and adventures of her imagination but still they came in dreams to her. She tried to use common sense and to find out all she could about the Percy estates in the north from Charlotte or from books, but it did not help. She was imprisoned in the glamour that seemed to surround the man who had rejected her love. Eagles and owls came to her in the night and just occasionally Charles himself.

If she could have seen Charles Fitzpercy as he really was, up in the north, alone but not always lonely, Jane would have felt no differently about him. If she had been able to be invisible and to observe him as he wandered over the old estate, she would have discovered nothing she was not already able to imagine. For Salton was much as she imagined it with its lodge where Charles had spent many of his early years, and its mausoleum and its crumbling west wing on whose ground floor logs were burned in a great open hall. The splendid apartments and the hunting parties and the guests had gone long ago. Only occasionally an artist would ask permission to sketch there and one painter had made a great landscape painting of 'The Rainbow at Salton' which now hung in the hall of S – House in Middlesex. Jane would have walked over

268

the woods and fields of Salton as once she had walked over the fields of Bedon where the gulls came inland and screeched and where the skies, too, were often of pewter grey, swathed in great clouds like smoky shawls. But Jane was left to her dreams and Charles alone walked there, buffeted by the winds, and Charles heard the night owls hooting in the ivy-covered barns, and hoped that the rough magic of Salton would work upon him and bring him some peace. Charles alone contemplated the grey sea over the cornfields of the nearby farm and let his gaze rest on the clumps of alder in the valley bottoms and heard the country folk with their Norse-sounding voices return at night to the village. Charles alone looked at the symphony of green and grey and the line of grey-blue sea over the distant sands and wished the sea could absolve him from his lusts and his miseries.

But they both turned to writing when their dreams and hopes failed them, and writing soothed them both. When Charles returned to London it was with a vow to study more sensibly and to some better purpose. He took his notebooks with him, filled with his irregular, backward-sloping handwriting, a little released, a little humbled, and ready to try once more to live in the real world even if he, like his old home, was a ruin. And Jane went on thinking of him, though by and by she dreamed of him a little less often, for she was exhausted by her own imagination. She determined that something good should come out of it all and that one day if she could not have him, she could fix him for ever in her memory by writing of him and of the sights and sounds that had accompanied her dreams of him.

# PART FIVE
# Summer 1824

Jane's second summer in London arrived on a certain day in June when the weather was, for once, living up to its seasonal promise. The trees were all out and Mr Nash's buildings were gleaming in the Regent's street. All over the greener parts of London there lay that veil of summer, that warm stillness in the air which presages a hot day but not a parched or dry day; a blue, blue sky with no hint of late thunder. For once London smelt fresh. Early morning dew had spangled the grasses in the public parks, and in the gardens of Mayfair squares. Roses had begun to bloom in private gardens and Covent Garden Market itself was filled with the flowers and fruit brought up from the suburbs, from the fields near Earl's Court, and from Lewisham and Plumstead. On such a beautiful summer morning human sorrows seemed impossibly far away. People were smiling at each other as they passed in the street and even maidservants on the sides of terraces as yet untouched by sun sniffed the air and felt a little less tired. Awnings were up over the pavements and women lingered to look in shop windows, catching reflections of themselves in the glass which showed off their summer dresses and the glow of their skin. The sun had begun to shine even on Ironmongers Row, and the few straggling plants in the gardens of the houses on Camden Road and the many streets on each side of it had turned their leaves up to the sun. On such a day the interior of theatres looked tawdry and artificial. The great salons and staircases of Drury Lane Theatre and Covent Garden were

273

hushed. Sunlight crept through the blinds drawn against the light, and later perhaps the theatres would be a refuge against the heat, as were the churches of London and the City where an occasional sunbeam would alight on some forgotten cherubim or some marble memorial to the dead of other summers. In the new St Pancras Church the rector had already celebrated two weddings by nine o'clock and his words echoed round the great nave with its dead light and followed the wedding guests as they came blinking out into the sun.

In the Vale of Health in Hampstead and in Well Walk the sun had brought out the hollyhocks in the cottage gardens; and in the gentlemen's clubs of St James's some all-night gamblers had staggered blearily out on to the sunny street rubbing their eyes and wondering why they had not gone to bed the night before. Horses were pawing the air and neighing friskily in the light and general cheerfulness, before the streets turned dusty again and they trotted more slowly in the heat of the afternoon. In the new houses of Hackney, Streatham, Stoke Newington and Canonbury and in the villas of Footscray and Ealing and Hayes and the larger residences of Chiswick and Strawberry Hill and Sion and Osterley, women were getting ready to drive out or to walk in their own gardens and later sit in the shade afforded by their beeches and cedars. From Richmond Hill in the west by way of Chelsea and Millbank and Westminster, over to Blooms-bury, Holborn and Finsbury and the busy crowded City of London, the millions who made up London and called themselves Londoners, or who were still in Town before the Season ended, gave thanks for this day of days and felt life was a good thing. Even the boys at Dr Macdon-ald's in Hunter Street were less fractious and willing to sit quietly and take their books in the garden behind the tall

274

house, whilst the little girls of the New Fulham Boarding Academy for the Daughters of Gentlemen took their sewing and went to sit by the river a mile or so away, accompanied by their teachers who themselves could not bear to miss a summer day like this.

In the kitchens, cold meals were the order of the day and many were the white currant ices which melted in the sun and the icy-misty bottles of hock cooling in cellars. Poorer folk sat out in their yards and put off the endless tasks of poverty. If they had a few pence they slaked their thirst as the day went on with beer or lemonade; if not they drank the dirty London water when they could find it, for there were long lines of people at every public fountain.

Lincoln's Inn Street had a pump at each end. Most of the houses in the square had piped water. The servants in these houses were larking about in basements and hoping their employers would take naps in the afternoon so they might rest their own weary feet. Much the same behaviour was going on in Bruton Street whose houses mostly stood with blinds drawn. The blinds had been drawn for some time, too, in one of the houses of Bloomsbury Square whose owner was still abroad, for Frederick Digby was not at home to taste the first day of a London summer. Temple Gardens, too, had lost one of its habitués when Philip March crossed to France for the first time in his life. Julia Jeffrey was not missing him for she was in Brighton accompanying the scion of a noble family on decorous walks to the sea-front to take the air. Sometimes she wished she were walking back in the Burlington Arcade, but a girl had to grasp at respectability if it were offered.

In Covent Garden, Daisy Collins was hard at work selling her marguerites and mignonettes. Today, it being

275

so fine, she might make ten times as much tin as usual. The sun made people buy and the flowers were at their best; she had sweet-scented stocks too, and her little sister was sitting winding up roses into buttonholes and watching the strolling crowds the while. It was funny how the sun changed folks for the better – unless they got too hot. There was no pleasing some of them. For the present it was just right and she was doing good business. A few military were around from the barracks and they were always noisy and generous, except when they had been in the beer houses. Little sister Kate was enjoying her work with Daisy and was glad she had left the sewing.

Jane Banham was thinking of other things. The death of Lord Byron had been announced the month previously and people were saying he would be buried in England. Now he was gone perhaps people would see his death as the end of an era. First Shelley, then him – and of course that John Keats, whose poems she had heard quoted in the New Year. How long ago *that* seemed. She had not seen Charles again, yet all her thoughts seemed somehow to end with him still.

She felt that so long as she could still think of him he was alive. And there had been no further message from Rebecca Smith, though Jane had seen Daisy several times selling her flowers. Today would be a good day for Daisy. Everyone but herself seemed busy – she had hardly seen Charlotte and Henrietta since Philip had gone to Italy, though they did write to her. Life seemed, once more, to be confined to Mrs Ogilvie and the visits to the boys. She had been to the theatre, it was true, with a ticket from Mr Hood who had been given her address from Fred Digby, and she had finished her piece on the churches and sent it to Christopher who was planning some move to an office on Waterloo Place, though she doubted how they could

276

afford it. She had seen Mr Leigh Hunt in the distance, pointed out by handsome Mr Ainsworth who had called once and taken her for a stroll in the park. It had been pleasant, but she found him rather overbearing and he only wanted to talk about himself and his literary productions. It seemed he was writing a novel. She had written to Frederick and, as yet, received no reply. Her uncle and his wife had gone on to Florence and were taking a house in the hills during the heat of the summer and hoping to return in autumn to London. She was lonely but not unhappy, except when she thought of Charles. She occupied all her leisure time in reading. Somehow, though, life seemed to have come to a full stop. At least Philip did not seem to have told anyone of her 'wicked' conduct and she was grateful. What could she have been thinking of? Her senses were lying dormant now, she felt.

Perhaps there would be a letter from Frederick soon. He had written very amusingly to her, never mentioning his wife, and she found herself thinking of things to tell him. She was still trying to educate herself through the reading of newspapers. London was beautiful today and, after reading for a time, she felt a little of the old restlessness and then wondered where Charles was and what he was doing and thinking. He seemed to have been swallowed up. Perhaps he was still at Salton. She went on to the little balcony over her uncle's room to look at the square and decide whether she wished to go out. It might be pleasant to go with Polly to buy some grapes. Polly would like a change. Or if it were too hot she had Mrs Shelley's *Frankenstein* to reread.

Maybe when the boys' parents returned she ought to ask about going to help Henrietta and Charlotte with their school. They had offered her a post and she was tempted to earn a little more money to repay Uncle Hal his kindness. But her secret wish was to write, to write of her own dreams in a dream landscape and make, if not a fortune, a little money that way. She sighed. However lovely such a summer day could be in London, the sun made her wish to return to the country. How beautiful Vine House and its gardens would be today. There would be the smell of elder flowers and sweet briars, and the nightingales would be singing at dusk in the wood nearby. She doubted whether there would be any nightingales at Salton. Nor in Norfolk either. She thought of Bedon and of all the old friends there and wondered when she would see them again. Snetters still wrote regularly, but Rose appeared to be courting a young farmer and her letters had become less regular.

For a moment she shut her eyes against the London sun and tried to see the old garden at home and the hedgerows outside the gate and the path that led to the church where her papa was buried. Snetters was keeping his grave tidy. She, Jane, should have been doing that. She had not been a very dutiful daughter, but he had wanted her to go away – otherwise he would not have arranged things as he did. And now there would have been two summers when the May flowers had bloomed in the churchyard with no daughter to mourn him. Why should she suddenly think of Papa?

Papa had been proud of his tiger lilies and his geraniums – and he had known all about timber and trees and woods; when she was little he had shown her the different leaves – ash and oak and elm – they were easy to recognize – but also hazel and birch and holly and hawthorn and in the autumn the long brambles which snapped at your fingers. He had not cared so much for wild flowers. How stupid she was, sitting on a lovely summer day thinking of childhood flowers and village life. Of course, she *should* think of Papa – but it still made her regretful that she had not been able to get nearer to him when he was alive. As a tiny girl she had been close to him – perhaps it was he who had called her Jennet? But after her mother's death he had been morose and silent until he had remarried, and even that had not made him happy. Worse, in fact. Ah well, she must go out and chase these demons of memory away. Perhaps, after all, she was not really suited to this London life. She was not exactly homesick, but sad with a sort of happy sadness – that so much could never return and that she would never be a child again.

She looked over the square again, but it was sleeping in the noonday sun. Really it was too hot to go fetch fruit – perhaps Polly would go for her. She had better draw the sun-blinds and concentrate on *Frankenstein*.

It was an hour or so later, when almost dozing over her book, that the post-boy's bell was heard in the square and she leaned out to look and see if he were on his way to her. Yes – he was walking towards their doorstep, and soon Polly came in for the money for the franks. How she looked forward to mail! It must be the dullness of her present life and she upbraided herself as she waited impatiently for Polly to bring up the letter.

There were two: one from Italy and one from London. The one from Italy was from Frederick Digby and the other – she glanced at it quickly – just in case. No. It was not from Charles – it seemed to be in the hand of Christopher Cornwall and she was, once more, disappointed, although she had not truly thought it could be from Charles. It was just that every time the post-boy came, there was the anticipation she could not forgo, a sort of grim pleasure, soon to be dissipated.

Christopher's letter first. Perhaps he wanted another

279

article quickly. She read it sitting at her writing table and, at first, could not quite grasp what he was saying.

We think that the *Review* will need in future more weighty criticism if we are to compete with our rivals and have therefore decided that we shall not have space for the sort of light pieces with which you have so skilfully provided us. This is, of course, not to cast doubts on your own capacities. Mr Bruce has taken his writing elsewhere and we suggest you contact him if you would wish to place your vignettes before a different public . . .

So that was it. They had rejected her. Well, it was to be expected. She had never really imagined she could go on for ever writing for Philip March. She bit her lip with disappointment, though. Could it have anything to do with Philip? Had he instructed Christopher to deal the blow – or had Christopher decided for himself, now that he was acting editor, that they would change tack? How could she find out? She remained thoughtful for a moment, then carefully folded the letter and put it away to answer when she felt calmer. But she would not give up. She would thank the *Review* for the interest they had shown in her work which had given her confidence to carry on. It was true – they had. But how could it have lasted? Six pieces in all she had done for them and they had seemed to be going from strength to strength. And so would she. They would not want Charles's verse either, she supposed – 'sub-Byronic' an unkind critic had called it – but he had seen only a few of the poems, and not the best. She sighed and turned to the other letter, hoping there was no more bad news about Aunt Edith, who might have seen Mr Digby.

She broke the seal and read Frederick's neat penmanship. A long letter. He wrote well and pungently, giving an impersonal pleasure to the recipient.

I saw Mr March in Rome (he wrote). My wife is still there; there are many English people in Rome at present – indeed it would seem that all ranks of society but the lowest have transported themselves to Italy. You come across them at every turn. My business in Rome concluded (she wondered – did he mean his wife?) I have come along to Florence where I heard your aunt and uncle were residing till last week. They have now migrated to a Tuscany villa with the arrival of the heat and I shall visit in a day or two. It is indeed warm and I would prefer the gentler English summer – except of course when it rains, which is too often. I think of you constantly and wonder how goes your literary work. Are you able to get out of London, I wonder? I think of you bustling along Hunter Street with sweetmeats for the boys or walking with your maid on those paths forbidden to young ladies. Do take care of yourself, my dear Jane. I look forward to seeing you again and noting the bright enthusiasm in your eye. Mr March said something odd to me. (Jane's heart gave a slight lurch.) He seemed to think you should be married, and I confess I did hope that he was not considering you in the light of a future wife, for I believe him to be a rather immature young man who needs a lady of advanced years to reduce him of his puppy fat! I speak metaphorically . . . My affairs have all been in confusion because of the state of affairs in Portugal and the new import and export laws which you probably have not bothered your head with. Your uncle's advice will be sought as soon as I can drive over to see him. I hope to be in London within two or three weeks. I have done all I can for Clara. (The last eight words were underlined.) Please accept my affection and my continuing interest in your welfare and forgive my avuncular tone. I do not always feel like someone's uncle. Yours ever, Frederick.


Well, that was a puzzling letter. What on earth had Philip been saying to him? She hoped whatever it was that it had not come to the ears of her aunt and uncle. She shook her head. Really, it was too bad. One man wanted her married; another – Christopher – dismissed her from her gainful employment. But Fred was a good man and true, and she was touched. Things must have come to a pretty pass between Clara and him. She looked at his letter again – 'I think of you constantly' and 'I do not always feel like someone's uncle' – and she felt the sincerity of his words, remembering his 'Trust me' and the way he had clasped her hand. Yet it was surely impossible that Frederick Digby thought of her in any way other than that of a forty-year-old man who appreciated a young woman for the qualities of mind he imagined in her? Yet – 'constantly'? Poor Frederick – he must sometimes tire of being married to an absent wife. She wished she knew the whole of that story.

It was the middle of June now and the weather was still holding; skies of a perpetual cloudless blue looked down upon dusty, yet still green, London. The good weather was welcomed in the western part of the great city, but was less of a boon for the hundreds of thousands who toiled in the docks and the wharves and in the crowded streets of the eastern side of the vast metropolis.

Four young women were sitting in a first-floor drawing room of a rented house in Fulham whilst the infant charges of two of them were supervised by the young maid who had brought in tea. The children were on the ground floor and one of the two women would occasionally descend to that level to see that all was going well. It was rarely that Charlotte Howard was free to take a dish of tea with friends and she had, even now on a chair by her side, an assortment of calico which was being hemstitched and then embroidered by the young girls who were at present practising the piano or writing letters home or copying a passage of French.

Her friend, Henrietta, was restless and showed it by continually getting up and walking to and fro in a most unladylike manner. Her two guests sat each on the side of

282

the fireplace whose unlit grate was screened by a pretty poker-work stand.

Charlotte Howard seemed rather upset.

'I am sure Philip cannot have known that Christopher would dismiss you in such a peremptory fashion,' she was saying to Jane who was sitting by the screen, dressed in a gown of pale lemon cotton which assorted well with her brown-gold hair. Jane's attempts to remain unaffected by the rejection of her writing by Christopher Cornwall had made her rather on the defensive and her annoyance showed through.

'I have written to Mr Bruce – we shall have to see – I can understand Christopher wants to "raise the tone" of his contributors somewhat. I am not dissatisfied with what *I* wrote, but perhaps the *New London* is no longer the place for it? You must not worry, Charlotte. Christopher is more interested in the poetical contributions. Philip may have told him before he left England that my work was no longer quite what they wanted.'

'You are putting a brave face on it,' said Henrietta March. 'Your work was well received – you know that – Philip sees himself as the new Hunt and wants to involve the *New London* in more political writing.'

'Country Cousins do not want to hear of politics,' replied Jane.

The fourth member of the party spoke up. Julia Jeffrey had come over to her friends with great news and it seemed they were more interested in the problems of a scribbling miss. After a genuine, but not too extended manner of congratulation to her on her recent engagement to the son of Lord H – , the others had retreated into silence before the subject of Jane Banham's banishment had turned up. 'I think you may have overdone the naïveté,' she said.

283

'Perhaps I poked too much fun at the fashionable crowd – I did not like all I saw in London,' Jane offered. 'But please don't let's say any more about it – I was lucky to be taken on and I shall just wait to see if there is a market anywhere else for what I wrote. How are the girls?' she asked, turning to Henrietta, who was at that moment wondering whether there was anything – or had been anything – between her brother and Jane. Enough to make him decide against her work? She had thought he rather admired her and would have been pleased to be the instrument of her advancement – and it was he who had given her the chance of publication, after all. There had been the business of the subscribers, of course, and Jane had been very helpful there – but perhaps what she wrote was a little too pleasant and amusing, not weighty enough for a journal of opinion.

Julia Jeffrey, however, still seemed to be of another opinion entirely.

'You always wrote what you wanted, Miss,' said she, 'and said what you thought, didn't you? People don't always like it and that's a fact. We can't all do what we want – and it isn't the job of young ladies up from the country to think that a few little sly paragraphs will change the minds of Society – not that Society of course reads the *New London*.' Then she recollected that perhaps this was not very tactful, with the sister of the editor sitting there, so she added: 'I mean – you have to understand the theatre and make your way in it before you can criticize.'

'I'm sure, Ma'am, that I put forward only my own initial impression,' replied Jane with a spark in her eye. They could criticize *her* as much as they wanted, but it was another thing to criticize her style.

'Jane wrote what a girl unused to London might feel –

and dressed it up very well, I thought,' said Charlotte, springing to her defence.

Jane and Mrs Ogilvie were sitting together a few days later over the work-box. The silks from it were laid over the table and they were choosing colours for the embroidery and tapestry work which the old lady so loved doing. Jane had not been tempted to assist, knowing herself to have no talents in that line.

'Your poor mother was a very good needlewoman,' said Ogilvie.

'I'm afraid I didn't inherit her abilities,' said Jane. 'Tell me,' she began, as Mrs Ogilvie sorted out some pale buff thread with which to embroider the handkerchiefs . . . She was capable of the tiniest, most intricate stitching and Jane marvelled the old eyes could see so well. But Mrs Ogilvie was rather deaf and was saying: 'They say the ladies at Court used to put their sewing work in their handkerchiefs in the old Queen's time – the Ladies-in-Waiting had to have something to do as they chatted, so they took their work into the drawing rooms. You can always tell a lady by her drawn-thread work.'

Jane sighed. After a silence, she ventured again: 'Tell me, Mrs Ogilvie: do you remember Mama having this locket when she was young?' She took off the exquisite little gold piece and laid it on the table next to the silks.

'That's a lovely piece. I hope you don't wear it outside your gown when you go out with Polly? That would be asking for trouble in this wicked place.'

'No, Mrs Ogilvie, I always wear it under my shift except indoors. Mama gave it to me. I just wondered if it were a piece she had worn when you knew her – perhaps my grandmama gave it to her.'

Mrs Ogilvie took the locket between her small, nimble fingers and felt it on her palm. 'No, I can't remember your mother ever wore it. Probably your father gave it to her when she married. People used to exchange baubles instead of rings sometimes.' She clicked it open. 'You had no picture of your mama in it then?'

'I think Papa must have taken it away when she died.'

'Oh, well, poor man, he probably had no other picture of her.'

'I suppose not. Do you think it valuable then, Mrs Ogilvie?'

'Very valuable I should think, my dear. Your father must have thought the world of her. Aye, it all ended well – she found a good man who didn't mind she'd been on the boards.'

'But some of the actresses are very respectable. One I know – Miss Jeffrey, you remember she went to Vine House? – she is engaged to be married to the son of Lord H – . Society is angry, they say – she hasn't a bean – but she is very attractive.'

'Lucky lass,' said Ogilvie shortly. 'Though I expect it will take some settling down after all her excitements. Was she an actress long, then?'

'Oh, yes, I believe for some years – but she doesn't suit the new manager. She was hoping to be Lady Macbeth, but the new management didn't choose her and I expect she has cut her losses and concentrated on finding a husband.'

'You are getting cynical, Miss Jane!'

'No, I am not – it is just what seems to happen to all women.'

'It didn't to me,' replied Ogilvie. 'Never had time. First with your grandma, and then I nursed my own mother

286

and then Mr Hal wanted me back for Edith. No, I never got time.'

'Well, marriage isn't everything.'

'It is *not* – though rich ladies seem to think so. And other women think themselves lucky to find a husband.'

'I should like to have written something good – had some success before I marry,' said Jane.

'You've got your little pieces printed,' said Ogilvie comfortably. 'And that's more than most ladies do. Your mama would be proud of you, and your papa.'

Jane had never thought of it in this light. 'Yes, I suppose they would – but all geese are swans to their mamas and papas, are they not?'

'There's truth in that. If it were not so some children would have a hard time of it!'

Jane put her precious locket back round her neck and they fell to discussing Hal's boys and deciding what to take them to eat on the Sunday. Jane fingered her locket thinking again of Jennet and whether she was that girl.

She wished she could have shown Rebecca a picture of her mother for she was sure that, somehow, many, many years ago, when Rebecca Smith would have been a dark-eyed beauty of about forty, she would have known actresses and perhaps even befriended them.

Frederick Digby returned to England early in July.

Jane knew that he had returned when she received a letter from him written in Bloomsbury the night before, saying he had much news to impart to her. He had spent several days with Hal and Edith in the Tuscany hills where Hal had rented a beautiful little Palladian villa. Would she care to take luncheon with him at the end of the week so he could tell her more? She accepted his invitation gladly and on the Friday set off in the carriage with

287

William. She had tried to overcome the dailiness of life and the vacancy left in her heart by Charles's words – oh, how she had tried. She had nothing to reproach herself with except her own estimate of herself. She looked out of the carriage window and saw the people carrying on just as usual, too busy to waste time in speculation over morality or love. Why had she ever come to London? She might have been more content in the end to have her little circle of friends from Bedon and the villages nearby, with a trip each month to Norwich. How did Snetters manage? And how had her own mother managed? She, of course, had had Jane and little Edmund to tend. She remembered her mother's sad face whenever little Edmund was mentioned after he had died when he was still in long clothes. She could recall it well for Mama had been in an agony of grief and she had crept on her lap and tried to comfort her, even though she was only a child herself. Somehow the thought of Mama seemed everywhere she looked in her own heart. Mama seemed to be of more importance here than she had been for all those years since her death in Bedon. She supposed it was because a mama would have seen to her happiness, would have guided her in affairs of the heart, chided her and comforted her. She shook her head. Silly to be needing a mama when she had managed so far so well alone.

She was shown into Frederick's house by a footman. The house was shrouded, quiet, and she stood still for a moment, steadying herself, before following the footman upstairs. There was no evidence of Fred's sister, but a large portmanteau on the entresol, as yet unpacked, which she passed on her way up, bore the evidence of Fred's travels.

The footman opened a door to a light and airy room she had not seen before. When the door closed behind

288

her she looked for Fred. A heap of books on a chaise-longue attested to his occupation of the room. She stood irresolutely for a moment and then a door at the other end of the room was opened and a leaner, browner Fred was there putting the last touches to his neck-tie. He advanced towards her. She was beginning, 'I am sorry, I am too early,' but his beaming face cut her short.

'I decided – yellow for today,' he said, pointing to the cravat; he seemed lighter, younger and even a little nervous. 'Sit down and I shall get you a glass of Madeira. It was good of you to come. I hope I did not interrupt your work.'

'Oh, no – it's such a lovely morning – the summer has been delightful – I was wanting to go out all week and was so pleased to get your letter.'

He poured her a topaz-coloured drink from a decanter and one for himself and sat down facing her. He gestured to the books. 'I am out of touch with England so sent out for the latest publications. *Now* I am to send their heartiest and most affectionate greetings – your uncle is a wonder! He has travelled all over to see the sights, and your aunt is looking so much better. She has even accompanied him once or twice. They adore Italy, though Hal is occasionally restless and must see the English papers and rush to the mail coach for his financial news – but they are well, very well. I think you may expect them back in November, if not before. They are guilty they left you in England. Edith is sure you must be dying of boredom.'

'And you – did you enjoy Italy?' she asked after a few more items of news had been delivered.

She had written to him telling him of her 'dismissal' from the *New London*, and she knew he would get on to the subject of that and Philip, and wished to put it off for as long as possible.

'Italy is beautiful. The climate would assure that if nothing else. I am glad I went – you know I went to see my wife in Rome?' It was rare for him to allude to her and Jane murmured faintly, 'You said you had seen her. You found her well?'

But Fred seemed determined not to be embarrassed, for he said: 'She will not return again to England. I went to see if she would *ever* return.'

She remembered: 'I have done all I can for Clara' and was silent.

He went on. 'I should not wish to live in Italy all the year round and, in any case, my activities preclude it. My wife has not wished to live in England for many years.' He looked at her keenly, but seemed resolved to say nothing more on that score. Instead he offered: 'I hope you have found another review suited to your talents? I was angry when I heard they had dropped you.'

'Oh, it happens all the time – I was lucky at first, that was all. I've written to Mr Bruce and I am waiting for a reply.'

'Then you will continue to write. You have not become downcast over the rejection?'

'Well, I didn't like it – but I won't let it depress me,' she replied.

'I can't imagine what *would* depress you,' he said thoughtfully. 'I can guess what would make you sad, but not what would depress you.' He continued, now, to regard her steadfastly, till she was almost put out by the sheer brilliance of his eyes, but she rallied and said: 'I was glad of your letter. I have been thinking about my life, and it was kind of you to find time to show me you did

290

care about me. You bothered to write and I am truly grateful.'

'You have no need to feel grateful – it was my pleasure,' he replied. He seemed to want to say more, but turned the subject back. 'You wrote in your letter that you went to visit an old lady. Tell me about her. Why did you go?'

Jane thought rapidly. She did not want to mention Charles. 'Our sewing woman has a niece in Covent Garden Market to whom I talk now and again – I hate moving only amongst the genteel classes – and they both mentioned that the girl's grandmother is a gypsy – or was – I suppose you are always a gypsy if you are born one? And she tells fortunes. It was at a time I was rather bothered about my work, and so I went for a "lark", for an adventure, with Polly, because I had the impression that this old lady, I don't know why, except Louisa said she used to know actresses long ago, that this old lady – she's called Rebecca Smith, by the way – might know something about my mother. You know my Mama was an actress, long before she married Papa? I told you, or Uncle Hal did? Anyway I did go, as I said in my letter. And she kept talking about someone called Jennet. And then she was rather interested in a locket which I wear that was my mother's. Gypsies always like bright things, don't they? She looked at it and she seemed interested in me.'

'Well, well – she was honest, I hope? And did she tell you your fortune?'

'In a way. She seems to know about people.'

'I must go and see her myself,' he said. 'Perhaps she would tell me mine.'

Jane was congratulating herself on not mentioning Charles or Philip and was glad to turn the conversation.

291

But then he said, 'Is it also something to do with that young poet you know?'

'Oh, she knows him as a Mr Entwhistle. She once told his fortune and said a "Jennet" would bring him luck. And of course I am a "Jane".'

'I expect that, just by looking at you and talking to you, she would know something about you.'

'She knew I wrote. Writers, too, have to observe people very closely.'

'And what would you, as a writer of course, what would you say about me?' he asked. 'Come, you can tell me over lunch.'

Jane found she was enjoying herself as she had not done for a long time. It was pleasant to talk to a man who was intelligent and to whom one did not have to pretend anything, and who actually seemed to take an interest in oneself. But she was determined to lead the conversation back to him, so as soon as they sat down to a little luncheon – consommé, chicken and grapes with a light wine from Alsace, she said: 'The old lady thought *I* might have gypsy blood, so I should, of course, tell you your fortune.'

'I expect I can guess it,' he said. 'You can put two and two together and make three – or five, as well as the next woman. It would be harder for me to tell yours.'

'I do not know much about you,' she replied, taking a sip of the delicious liquid which tasted of flowers. 'But I think you have a great capacity for friendship and that you have had sorrows in your life, but who has not? You are kind and you are generous with your time. I think you like women. You are not a Lord Byron who loves and leaves them.' She stopped, aware that she had perhaps gone too far, but Fred said: 'Go on.' 'Perhaps you are a

292

bit like my papa,' she said ingenuously. 'He was not a gentleman like you, of course, but he was kind, I think.'

Fred, groaning inwardly, was thinking that his feelings towards this young woman were not at all fatherly.

'And you are unconventional,' Jane continued. 'Or you would not ask me to luncheon to talk to you. Yet I like that, for I do not feel uneasy.'

'I am not a paragon of manly virtues, Jane.'

'Oh, I hope not, if virtue is what they say it is. I mean conventional virtue. Or is it only women who have to have that?'

'You sound bitter.'

'Well, yes – I made rather a fool of myself with Mr March over that.' The wine was making her tongue flow, but she knew it and left it alone for a time. In vino veritas.

'I guessed something of the kind – he was rather cool about you.'

'Well, he is right, I suppose – it was only a silly misunderstanding. I can't really tell you about it – it would not be seemly.'

'He pursued you. You found him quite attractive. You shut your eyes and decided to plunge and then the young puppy became mindful of the sort of girl you were supposed to be and remembered just in time that one cannot – or must not, according to his code – seduce a "serious" girl. So he was angry with you for "leading him on"?'

'Well, not quite, nearly that. How did you know?'

'You forget – I am a gypsy, too,' said Fred.

'It was the double standard. I was foolish to think I could ever have experience and not pay for it, but I was angry that it was because I was not "coy" that his ardour cooled.'

293

Fred sat looking at her very seriously. 'You must be careful – or you will be your own executioner.'

'Because I am a woman.'

'Not only that. Because you have a passionate temperament. I am glad he did not take advantage of it. But, of course, now he feels hard done by.'

'But he did not really like me, or no more than any girl – I was just there – and being quite a success – and he *did* give me the chance to be that – and he would not believe that I was not rich. Why could one not just give in to the urge of the moment? Men do without being ruined.'

'I do not think you are "ruined", Jane Banham.'

'If I am not, it is not from any virtue of mine,' she countered.

'You never loved him? – Philip March?' he asked, after offering her the bunch of grapes.

'No.'

'And there is someone you love?'

She was silent.

'No, I have no right to ask you,' he said. Then, 'It is only that I can guess that, too.'

'And your wife?' she asked boldly.

'Ah – Clara. I think it is time I said a few things to you. I didn't know whether I should. Come, let us go for a short stroll round the square. It will clear our heads.'

Now he seemed sad, but he handed her into her cloak and they went out into the balmy air. Perhaps there would be a storm later that day. For the moment it was still. There was a little garden in the square and in it a seat for the residents. Some children were bowling their hoops along the paths and there was a fountain playing in the centre.

'Quite like Italy,' he remarked. 'Do you mind if I smoke?'

He lit a thin cigar and seemed to be regarding the treetops.

'I have a weakness,' he began, 'for beautiful girls. My wife was a beautiful girl and I married her very young. She did not love me. Her family had no dowry to offer and I was a good 'parti' at the time. I suppose we both tried our best to keep our marriage alive, but unfortunately it did not work. I was a faithful husband for ten years and I did not neglect her. Then she became restless and wanted to go abroad, enjoy herself. She had none of my own interests, but plenty of her own. She fell in love with some rake – it does not matter who. I did not want to let her go. She ran away, I followed her. Then I realized I could not force her to stay with me – better to act the complaisant husband than hold a woman captive – it must happen to many men. So I let her go – we had no children – yet she was jealous of any interest I had, even more, I think, of my intellectual life, than of any woman I might perhaps fancy. She did understand me – I am not blaming her – I was the wrong man for her, although I thought for many years that she was right for me. For the last five years we have lived apart – she has been over to England only seldom and then she has not stayed at Vine House. We are what the world calls separated, but we are still married.'

'I am sorry,' said Jane finally. It seemed such a waste of a man and he did not appear self-pitying. Most men in his position would have had a string of mistresses, she supposed, but Fred seemed to have become more of a hermit.

'I tell you this, Jane Banham, because I know you do not love me – but since I met you I believe a little spark has ignited into a flame – and it is impossible. You are young and lovely and I am a married man – I have no

295

right to tell you, but I thought I must. You do love someone else, do you not? It is not Philip March.'

'You have told me, so I can tell you,' she said, screwing up her courage. It suddenly seemed very important that he know. 'I did fall in love – I don't know even if that is what it would be called. He caught my imagination. I never thought of marriage, or really of his loving me. I wanted to look after him like a mother almost. Then he told me, that he did not love women and never could. All that part of him was inaccessible, yet I still love him – I shall always love him. I think it is some enchantment, like a fairy spell, and that I shall never be released. He went away in January and I have not seen him since. But I know I shall see him again.'

'Poor Jane,' he said. 'Have we spoken of him already?'

'We may have done.'

'You quoted his verse too!' said Fred. 'I remember. Then we are equal. *I* love *you* and I cannot pay court to you. And *you* love a man who says he cannot love you. We are a fine couple.' He *loved* her! She could not believe it, but she felt close to him then.

'I am glad I've told someone – I thought I should go mad with longing – it is terrible,' she said, choosing to speak of herself.

'I know,' he replied, and they looked at each other.

'I am sorry if I have distressed you,' she said timidly.

'I am not distressed – *I* have had my chance, Jane, but *you* have not. We will talk of other things, but promise me, if I can be of assistance to you you will call on me? Promise. You can always live under my protection, you know. I should not ask anything of you.' He took her hand and kissed it and she let it lie for a moment in his. 'My wife will never return to me, but you can trust me,' he said.

'I don't think I could ever marry,' said Jane. 'It is too much of a leap in the dark – I like solitude.'

'My dear child – no, you are not a child – sorry! – you will, I am sure, find happiness one day. It is hard for women. I know that.'

He said no more and they walked back to the house in quite a companionable fashion. Jane left him finally with much to think over and Fred sat long and alone before his empty hearth, as the promised thunder came and spattered the square where they had walked, with long slanting drops of rain. What a pity it all was.

How could any man, loved by Jane Banham, refuse that love? Perhaps he ought not to have spoken. But he could not help his thoughts. Damn this beautiful poet – he imagined he *must* be beautiful. By making himself inaccessible to Jane he had probably increased her love. She was young and romantic and, like all women, would think she could save a soul in torment. He himself might be in torment, too – but he resolved to say no more about that and to let things take their course. It would not do to be too insistent – at this rate he would be consulting gypsies himself! But he was not superstitious. He turned to his copy of *Blackwood's Magazine* and the *London* and read the poet Wordsworth's opinions of Canning and the Holy Alliance and a piece on the claims of new nations and the new attitude of non-interference in their internal policies, and then turned to the fiscal and commercial reforms. Even more interesting for a closet radical were the new Combination Acts. He sighed – he was better at theory than practice. Jane's uncle would have to advise him about his financial affairs in the new climate. A pity his loving seemed to him to be 'in theory' too.

His mind kept running on the theme of maidenly modesty. He was glad Jane was not a shrinking violet, though he thought she was both maidenly and modest. In fact he'd be damned before she'd 'ruin' herself!

There was a stink over London which the thunder of the days before had not cleared. It rose from Smithfield where the livestock were sold, from the fish at Billingsgate, the fruit and vegetables at Covent Garden and the tanning factories and chicken slaughterers of Southwark. In the West End the goldsmiths and silversmiths were soon to close their shops at the end of the Season, but the ice-makers were doing a roaring trade in the sticky weather. The lunatics in Bedlam were quiet – it was windy weather that roused their sick fancies and made them restless. The brothels in the alleys behind the Strand found their trade quite lively – the heat always turned men's minds to lustful thoughts, though the old days had been far livelier. Newgate was, as usual, full, though there was no one that week for execution. The swarming poor of St Giles and Whitechapel and parts of Southwark found their conditions even more unbearable than usual and sallied forth on the streets for air and perhaps for the purpose of theft. Their targets were unwary foreigners who had come to see all the dazzling spectacles of the largest city in the world, and who were to pay rather heavily for the privilege.

Lord Byron's body had almost arrived at its destination in England. His friends were hoping for it to be buried in Poets' Corner and had got up a petition to that effect. Those who had known Byron well were sceptical of its being received.

Fred wished he could be off sooner to Vine House for a few days. London was already beginning to feel oppressive, or perhaps it was that the days before had been so cloudless, so beautiful, and had, if they had not given him

298

hope, calmed him. But he had a few affairs to settle in London once the unpacking had taken place. Later he must go to see what was happening to his garden. He wrote a short letter to Jane, after tearing up many previous efforts. What he wanted to say was, 'Do not waste your life on a man who does not want you,' but of course, he could not say this. He was not her parent and had no rights in the matter. Any idea of becoming a heavy 'guardian' was repugnant, too.

What could he say? He knew nothing of the gentleman in question, though he would make it his business to find out. If he were a lush or a gambler or a fighter, so much the better. If he were handsome and talented, so much the worse. Jane loved him and Jane was a girl who held on to people and ideas – he could see that.

He simply sent her his respects and sincere good wishes and hoped he would see her again before too long. Vine House was always open to her if she would care to visit, alone or with a woman friend. He asked a footman to see if he could find out anything about a woman called Rebecca Smith who was reputed to live on the borders of Bloomsbury and to tell fortunes and be acquainted with theatricals. But he did not have much hope of discovering anything. There was no more he could do.

On the fifth of July the body of Lord Byron had arrived in London and it lay in state at a private house in Westminster on the ninth and tenth of that month, permission having been refused for its burial in Westminster Abbey. Byron's half-sister, Augusta Leigh, had spent long hours by it, but she and Byron's old crony Hobhouse had finally decided that it should be buried in the family vault in Nottinghamshire. There had been crowds around the house in Great George Street where the body lay in state, but only ticket-holders had been allowed in. Most of the literary set kept away from what they regarded as a peepshow. Jane had read all about it in the *The Times*, still faithfully brought to her by one of Hal's clerks each evening, and she had sat wistfully wishing that she could go and pay her respects to the dead hero. Who was she, though, to go and gawp at the remains of a great man? Yet she felt that Byron was connected with Charles Fitzpercy and that in some strange way Charles's body might lie there instead of the great poet's. She determined to go out and watch the funeral procession on the Monday following.

There were many women thinking of Byron that week and perhaps thinking, too, of their dead youth and of the days not so long past before Byron had left the shores of Albion for good. The fading courtesan, Harriette Wilson, was to sit at her window in Mayfair to watch the funeral procession go by and a few miles away in Highgate the beautiful Mary Shelley would wait and watch, too, for Byron had truly appreciated her dead husband. And, further away, in Hertfordshire, not far from Vine House, another woman who had known him and been ruined by her feeling for him, if not by him, was on the route the cortège would take.

Jane had gone out with Polly to wait for the hearse, sure that Charles would also make it his business to be there. The hearse and its procession would pass from Westminster Abbey up Whitehall to the Haymarket and round the top of Oxford Street to the Tottenham Court Road. Early in the morning the crowds were already lining the route and Polly and Jane were waiting on Tottenham Court Road, Jane searching everywhere for a glimpse of Charles. She did so wish that he would be there and that she could see him, even if he did not see

300

her. The common crowds were walking up and down but they were not disorderly, strangely muted in fact. They had liked the dead lord and rather gloried in the reported scandals of his private life.

The procession took almost an hour to reach the spot where Jane was standing, for its progress was slow. Then she glimpsed the outriders – the High Constable and two mutes on horseback followed by pages, and a horse bearing black plumes with six more attendants on horseback too. The crowds pushed and swayed as there then followed the caparisoned state horse and a bareheaded rider, led by two pages all in black. The rider was bearing an enormous crimson velvet cushion with Lord Byron's coronet placed upon it and he was closely followed by the hearse itself, the coffin draped in a black velvet pall and a tall plume motionless in the still air. Four other young pages walked by its side and then six horses came into view drawing the mourning coach. Jane glimpsed an urn covered with a black pall placed in the carriage, and she remembered from her reading of the arrangements for the funeral that it must contain Lord Byron's heart. Her throat went tight as there passed this black object. It was as though Byron's heart and his body were for ever separated. There were others, too, in the crowd who recognized its significance and were pointing to it. Several women were in tears and Jane herself blinked tears away and saw the rest of the mourning coaches – each drawn by six horses with pages walking beside them – through a wavering mist. The crowds remained silent and the men took off their hats whilst the long black procession moved slowly over the cobblestones. It *was* the end of an era.

But when she looked more closely she saw that the other coaches of the nobility following upon the mourning coaches were mostly empty or filled with servants. It seemed that though Byron had been a nobleman and his rank must be respected, it had been too much too hope that there would be many personal mourners of the same rank as himself. Byron had been dangerous. He had misbehaved and cocked a snook at English public and private life – and, what was worse, gone to live abroad and never- returned – so the acknowledgement was abstract. Ceremonial took the place of aristocratic grief. The *convenances* had been observed; the thirty-five carriages of the nobility, for the most part empty, had followed the hearse like ghosts of themselves. It was both sad and ridiculous. Just so might society regard Charles Fitzpercy if he ever grew to fame.

The last of the procession disappeared on its way to the North Road by Pancras Church where the carriages of the nobility were to turn back to London, and only the hearse and the mourning carriages would trundle over the Turnpike Road and up to Highgate and through Hertfordshire, winding their way gloomily on and on. On and on by the grounds of Brocket Hall where Lady Caroline Lamb, who had been ill, was out for a drive, and on and on again to the midland counties. Four days of roads lined with the populace, crowds following for miles and a young sailor who had served with the noble lord on his tour of the Isles of Greece, walking alongside the hearse, bareheaded, mile after weary mile. And many poets travelled to rest their hands on his coffin as it passed, in order to be able to say: 'On a summer day in the year 1824 I touched the pall of Lord Byron.' The poets were honouring the writer; the crowds were honouring the man. But on that day in London, as the cortège passed and as ladies hastened to write in their diaries that they had that day seen Byron's funeral procession, and as *The Times* reporter tried to write a tactful piece, one man did weep for the man as much as for the writer – though unlike the author of *Frankenstein*, he had never known him. Unlike Mary Shelley, too, and unlike all the silent crowds, he felt some need to compose a poem from the feelings stirred in him. He had seemed to see his own funeral cortège and it had struck terror in his heart. He had no memories as had Lady Caroline Lamb, or as had the ladies of the *demi-monde*, who had honoured Byron with their locks of hair and their tears. But his imagination made the link, and he was sure that Byron had felt as he had felt, though Byron had loved and dallied with countless *women*, too. This one man did weep, but it may be he was weeping for himself as he turned his face away amd melted into an alley near St Giles, thinking to seek solace in a bottle or two or the touch of another human being. For Charles had seen Jane standing across the road next to Polly, though she had not seen him. He had seen her bow her head as the coffin passed, and he had known she was thinking of him.

He would not seek her out; he could not speak to her, for what could he offer her but more sorrow, more despair? His writing was going well, but other things had not gone well with him since his return to London. Where could he go? For weeks he had been in a state of indecision about his affairs. There was something he must do, someone he must see before he disappeared once more and sought, in debauchery, some strong sensation to reassure himself he was truly alive and not a corpse like the noble lord. He must go to Rebecca. He could put it off no longer. His hands closed round an object in his coat pocket, something he had brought all the way from Salton, feeling that Rebecca must see it and she would know what to do. He made his mind up and, instead of turning down the street that led to St Giles, he crossed and went into the road that led to Ironmongers Row and was lost in the crowd.

Rebecca Smith sat still and thoughtful for long after Charles Fitzpercy had left her that evening. Although it was summer, she had drawn the scarlet curtains over the little window of her back kitchen and, from habit, sat by the fireplace, which today was empty of warmth and had a screen of red and silver in an intricate pattern of roses and lilies on the side facing the room. She had turned and turned in her old hands the small piece of jewellery which he had given her, remembering and remembering. Had he spoken the truth? She thought so. Why should he invent or lie? She saw him again, slumped wearily in the high-backed chair at her table, staring and staring at her with his hazel coloured eyes. Such beautiful eyes. The same colour eyes as had looked out from the tiny painting that he had taken away with him, but lighter and more melancholy.

She sighed again and wondered what to do. It was easy to advise him, but he did not always take her advice, she knew. And now she must act herself before it was too late, for she feared for him.

'You spoke of hearts and diamonds and of clubs leading to spades – a jack of spades and a queen of hearts – and you said they might be the same,' he had murmured, almost whispered, his face averted then. And then he had turned his face to her again and said: 'What use are your fortunes when it is all past?' She had not replied, waited for him to go on. 'I knew I had hidden it somewhere – years ago – and that if I found it you would tell me what to do – I was sure you had known her – you did, didn't you? That is why you could tell me those things about myself – you didn't guess – you knew.'

'I didn't know – I was not sure,' she said in reply, with a certain indignation in her tone. 'And, in any case, young man, you do not do as I tell you. You want old Rebecca to save you – that is not my work. I am only an old gypsy, not God.' She did not say, And if I had advised otherwise long, long ago, you would not be sitting before me now. Perhaps she had advised wrongly. It seemed so. This young man – not so young now – was still filled with the poison of self-disgust which seemed to run as strongly as that of perversity in his blood.

But she had other matters to worry her. Perhaps in the end he could be saved. 'You are sure you found it at Salton?'

'Yes, of course – I do not lie to you.' She believed him again. 'So you *will* tell me all about her? It cannot hurt her now. Think hard, old woman, I cannot pay you with gold but you may have that empty thing for it's no use to me now and I expect you will want some payment for your services.'

'Listen, Mr Fitz, or Mr Entwhistle as you say they called you, go away and let me think it out. I shan't keep your jewel. I shall give it you back but there is something only I can do. I have to be certain, you see.' She had spoken in tones unlike her usual, rather decided and heavily allusive, ones, and he looked at her inquiringly.

'Tell me – what do you have to do and why are you looking at me like that?'

'Listen, tomorrow I promise Daisy will come with a message to you at seven in the evening, if you'll tell me now where to find you. Don't go rushing off north again and don't get into any scrapes. Where are you staying – Bruton Street? Or Hampstead?'

'If you know so much about me, why not tell me what all this is about? If you know the secret of my birth, tell

305

me and I shall have done with it. I came to you because you are the only person who might know it.'

'Wait till tomorrow and Daisy will come with the message. Now tell me where you are staying – I may have a great deal to tell you.'

'I am staying in Charlotte Street,' he said after a pause. 'A friend has lent me his room whilst he is away. I didn't intend to stay on after his return.'

'That is a new address,' she remarked.

'Yes, I was resolved to turn over a new leaf. I have been writing in that room for the past ten days. I only went out today to watch poor old Byron return home, and I plan to return north soon myself.'

She took the number of the house and the name of the landlady. 'Go now – Charlie – ' she said, and he looked at her in surprise. 'Be in at seven tomorrow evening and Daisy will be there.'

'Very well,' he replied. 'Though I can't see why you can't tell me what you have to tell me now.'

'I promise there will be more,' she said. 'At least I promise as far as I'd stake my craft on it. You be there, will you?'

Charles had gone off to his garishly *nouveau* lodgings, all chintz and gilt-framed convex mirrors and a blend of red and green carpet, and had soon plunged himself, once more, in his work.

But Rebecca was still sitting on and the summer night darkened before she roused herself. She walked slowly to her inner door and shouted: 'Daisy! Daisy girl! Are you home?'

Daisy yelled back, 'Coming,' from the next floor. She was just finishing a late supper. The crowds had been good tonight – lots of provincials come to Town to see the poet's funeral and she'd made a tidy bit of profit. She swallowed the last of her pigs' trotters and came down to see what the old lady wanted.

'Listen, girl, I want you to ask your auntie the way to where Miss Banham lives. You know, near Lincoln's Inn, but make sure from Louisa. Go early tomorrow and, *early* mind, before you goes to the market. I want you to knock at Miss Banham's door. The servant will answer, but ask to see Miss Jane and tell her to come to me at noon, just like she did before, just as she always is, tell her that. There'll be a bit of money for you if you do as I say.'

'It was *him*, wasn't it?' asked Daisy, wiping her mouth on her wrist. 'I know it was him – what do you want with Jane, then?'

'Never you mind, just do as I say – right?'

'That's all right, Gran – I will. You're not goin' in for dressmakin' yourself, then?'

'Get along with you and don't be cheeky,' replied Rebecca and she slapped the girl on the backside affectionately.

'What's it all about, then?'

'Wait and see – you'll soon know.'

Daisy went up to bed whistling and the old woman undressed in her little room by moonlight, having opened her curtains. But she hardly slept.

Jane, too, had a restless night. The funeral procession had led her thoughts to Charles once more. So she was not really surprised when, before breakfast the next morning, Polly came in saying there was that young girl from the Garden on the doorstep and she wanted to see her. Mrs Ogilvie was busy giving orders to Cook in the basement and Jane went straight down to the front hall with Polly.

Daisy was looking rather shy, unused to paying visits in

307

this part of the town. 'My Gran says, please will you come to see her at twelve noon today,' she said in a rush.

'What is it? Is anything wrong?' Jane's thoughts had never left Charles and Daisy knew this.

'*He* was with her yesterday – but it's not 'im, it's Gran. She says come just as you were.' She enunciated this carefully.

'Just as I was?'

'Yes – that's what she said.'

'Thank you, Daisy. Have you had any breakfast?'

'Oh yes, Miss Jane. I've to get to work – ' and she was off quickly with a little wave. She had not had any breakfast, but she was too shy to go in.

Polly was standing gaping at her and Jane shut the door. 'I have to go to Ironmongers Row later – you don't need to accompany me. Will you ask William to bring the carriage round at half past eleven – no, I think it would be better if I walked.'

What could have happened? But Charles was alive! Charles had seen Rebecca Smith yesterday and she felt a great wave of relief. Perhaps he wanted to see her and was using Mrs Smith as an intermediary – perhaps he had decided he had been wrong and . . .

She stopped this line of thought as quickly as it came into her mind, but it kept recurring all morning. She vividly remembered her last visit to Mrs Smith and what she had been wearing. That was what the woman meant for sure, her gown and shoes and her hat and her gloves and the ribbon in her hair, and, of course, the locket. It was round her neck – it always was. Could Charles be in any danger, if he had been to see Rebecca the night before? Could he perhaps be in a danger only the old woman understood? Did she want Jane to guard him, watch over him? What was it all about? She set out, feeling slightly sick in the pit of her stomach and stopped to take two or three deep breaths, but hurried on when she saw people staring at this nicely dressed girl, stock-still on the pavement. Well, she would soon know.

When Jane stood before number 363 Ironmongers Row, the door was opened immediately this time. They had been waiting for her. Daisy's mother gestured her in with a, 'She's in her back room, Miss,' before melting away upstairs. Rebecca Smith's door was ajar and, when Jane knocked, there was a quick, 'Is it Miss Banham? – come in, my dear.'

Jane stepped in and saw the curtains once more drawn and the linnet busy fluttering round its little cage. But there was a teapot and two reddish-gold cups on the table. She was a welcome guest.

'I came when you asked me to,' she was saying as they heard noon strike in a church at St Giles's or St George's, its peal heard clearly in the summer stillness.

'You will take a cup of char with me?' said the old woman, sitting behind her teapot like some tutelary deity.

'Please, Mrs Smith, you must tell me – is he all right? Mr Fitzpercy?' Jane felt she must know before she as much as sat down.

'He was perfectly all right yesterday – sat here where you are going to sit, and looked at me just as you are doing,' replied Rebecca. The water had already been poured into the pot – evidently she had expected Jane to be punctual.

Jane sat down with relief. 'It was kind of Daisy to fetch me – I knew it must be something important.'

The old woman said nothing until she had finished pouring the strong-looking brew and handed a cup over to the girl with great ceremony. 'Drink your tea and listen to me. I'll not keep you long.'

309

If it were not about Charles, then what could Rebecca have to say? Surely she would not bring her just to say she had noticed some ill fortune or good fortune in her hand which she had forgotten to acquaint her with? Yet Charles had been here, in this very room, so it must be something to do with him. Jane tried to steady her nerves, but her teacup rattled a little on its saucer. The warm drink did, however, calm her a little.

'I've got something to show you,' said the woman, drinking her own tea with every appearance of enjoyment. 'But first I see you've come dressed as you were – did you, by any chance, put on that little locket you showed me?'

'Oh, yes – I always wear it under my gown!' Surely she had not been decoyed for the gypsy to take it from her? This was an ignoble thought – Mrs Smith was honest. It was only the way Jane had been brought up, with its distrust of the odd or unconventional and its fear of the poor, which had given her that instinctive lack of faith. She drew out the locket on its thin chain and laid it down on the table.

'Open it,' commanded Rebecca.

'I told you – there was nothing inside it when it was given to me – perhaps Papa wanted the picture of Mama for himself and took it when Mama died before giving me the locket.' But she opened it and saw the space for the tiny miniature, an empty space.

Rebecca now felt under the cloth on her table and brought out a tiny bag. She fished in the bag and seemed to be involved in some sort of conjuring act, for there on the table now was another locket. Jane caught her breath. 'Mr Fitz had it, along with one or two other things,' remarked Rebecca conversationally. 'Go on, take it – lay it by yours.' Jane looked at the two pieces of intricate gold. They were identical with the same whorls and fancy scroll design on the front. 'His was not empty,' said Rebecca. 'A pity yours is.'

'Mrs Smith – what are you trying to say? If Charles has a piece of jewellery like mine, where did his come from? Why didn't you ask him to come here today? What is it all about?'

'I'm not sure. I wanted to see them together,' replied Rebecca, turning the lockets round and peering at them again. 'Would you know yours apart?' she asked. 'If I took one away – would you know?'

'No, I don't suppose so – except mine would be warmer as it's always round my neck. It may have been rubbed a little, too, but why did Charles bring the other one to you?'

Rebecca poured Jane another cup of tea. 'He had had it for years, lost it, couldn't be bothered with it, found it again when he was up at Salton – found it where he'd put it years ago in some angry mood, I expect. He's an angry man, but he thought I would help him over his own problems – nothing to do with you, or perhaps it is, perhaps it isn't.'

Jane's mind was in a whirl.

'Now, young lady. I want you to go home and wait till tomorrow evening. I promise you'll have a visitor, let's say about nine o'clock. You'll be at home?'

'Yes, of course.'

'When I tell him to pay a visit on you, he will pay it. It's not really my business – I can't interfere beyond that – but you'll have a visitor, I'm sure – when he's had a day to think it over.'

'You mean Mr Fitzpercy – *Charles* will come to see me?' Jane was overjoyed. 'Are you sure? Oh, I'll wait for him, of course – I'd wait all my life.'

311

'Come, come, girl – it's a Mr Entwhistle who'll come to see you – no, no, don't ask me more.'

'Where is Charles? I must see him.' Jane rose as if to go, but Rebecca gestured her down again.

'None of that – I can't tell you where he is. He doesn't like it known and it's up to him, remember, up to him.'

Jane sank down again and buried her face in her hands.

'I don't know what he'll have to say – it's his business. Now, have you finished your tea? Then you can go. Take your locket and give me back the other.'

Jane touched the other locket with the tips of her fingers before giving it back to Rebecca.

'Go – "Jennet" – forget all about this till you see Mr Entwhistle.' The old woman got up stiffly and filled her kettle from a large stoup of water on the hearth and placed the kettle on a low fire. 'There's nothing you can do,' she said more kindly. 'Go now. Tomorrow at nine in the evening in your uncle's house.'

Jane stood and put her own locket back round her neck and twitched together her clothes and took up her light summer cloak. There was a little wind whirling the dust in the alley when she went out of the house. Even the sky seemed different, colder. She walked along in a daze and found herself home, as though someone else had walked back.

'Daisy'll go to tell him . . . I'm convinced, *now*,' muttered Rebecca to herself. 'So long as he keeps out of mischief till tomorrow. Suppose I should have given him a bit longer to make up his mind, but tomorrow will do.'

She took out her cards to amuse herself and played a game of patience. The days were long now that she was old. But as she played, she thought back on her long life and relived certain scenes. She had never, till now, known whether she had given one person in the past good advice

312

or no; only time would tell, as they always said, and they were right.

For her part Jane was restless. She wondered whether to see if Frederick had returned, but stopped herself. She wished she could tell someone about her extraordinary morning but there was no one but Fred who would be interested or to whom she might care to unburden herself. What did it amount to anyway? Yet her imagination took wing and went over and over her conversation with Rebecca Smith, adding bits and taking bits away. As she sat, her chin cupped on one hand, she felt for her locket with the other.

In the meantime Daisy fulfilled Rebecca's second errand and knocked upon the Charlotte Street door that evening at seven. A voice shouted from upstairs, 'If it's for Mrs White, she's away,' and a frowsty maid leaned out of the upper floor.

'It's for Mr Entwhistle,' called Daisy lustily.

'First floor at the back,' said the maid. 'Door's open.'

Daisy pushed at the door which led into a passage where several closed doors presented sullen brown faces, but unexpectedly polished knockers. Steps led to the next floor where there were similar doors. Obviously these two floors were let out to separate tenants. She knocked at the door at the back and waited patiently till a voice said: 'Who is it?'

'It's Daisy,' she replied. 'I've brought back your property.'

The door was opened suddenly and Charles stood there. His clothes were dishevelled and his fingers inky. Daisy looked through to the room beyond and saw a garishly coloured carpet and wallpaper with bluebirds,

313

chintz cushions and lots of brasswork. She thought it looked lovely.

'I am writing, Daisy. What does the old woman want, then?'

'Don't you speak so disrespectful about my Gran – she sent you this.' Daisy handed over a small parcel. 'And she says please will you go to Miss Banham's at number seventeen Lincoln's Inn Square with this parcel and your little picture you showed her. Look she's writ it down, though I can't read it – it's something she got a neighbour to help her write – you're to go at nine o'clock *tomorrow* evening, right? Number seventeen Lincoln's Inn Square. Do you know where that is, Mr Fitz?'

'Yes, I know. I know Miss Banham's address.' He opened the letter and placed the parcel on a little table.

'She says you're to read it when I'm gone, but will you *promise* to go tomorrow? She said that special. "It's his business, not mine," she says. "It's up to him."'

'But why should I see Miss *Banham*?' asked Charles, perplexed.

'It's all writ down. "A piece of news for him," she says – that'll maybe "mend him" and another bit of news, too – all writ down.'

'Thank you, Daisy.'

'I have to go now, Mr Fitz,' said Daisy wistfully. 'So this is where you hang out now? Very smart, I must say – you'll soon be getting too good for talking to flower girls, I reckon.'

'Come here, Daisy. You're a good girl. There's a silver shilling for you.'

'I don't want it,' replied Daisy, with spirit. 'But you can give me a kiss if you like.'

He took her hand and bent over it elaborately and kissed it. 'There, will that do?'

314

'Goodbye, Mr Fitz,' was her only answer, but there were tears in her eyes as she retraced her steps downstairs. Some men could break your heart – yet she held the hand he had kissed to her cheek for a little time before her natural spirits reasserted themselves and she went along a short cut, whistling. I wonder what it was all about, she was thinking. Gran's a secretive old devil, but she seemed a bit queer today.

When Charles Fitzpercy had slowly deciphered the letter, or rather the short message which Rebecca's neighbour, the ironmonger who owed her a good turn had helped her compose, a look of amazement came over his face and he let it drop from his hand and sat, stunned, for a good half-hour before recollecting himself. He had just been about to eat when Daisy had knocked at his door but now he did not feel hungry. What he needed was a stiff drink. He must go to Lincoln's Inn Square at nine tomorrow evening when Jane Banham would be expecting him. Jane – whom he had thought, for her own good, never to see again – except perhaps glimpsed in a crowd once or twice in a lifetime. She had touched his heart, had Jane. And now? Incredible!

Finally Charles knew he could write nothing more that night. He decided to go out for a glass or two of brandy and water. He looked for a moment at his face in the glass and then went back for the little parcel and put it in his waistcoat pocket, blew out his candle and after grimacing at the furnishings of his lodgings, sallied forth. He might pay another surprise visit on old Mrs Smith, too. There was plenty to ask her.

The next day Jane sat in a turmoil of contradictory hopes and fears. She had told Mrs Ogilvie she would have a visitor 'from the magazine' in the late evening and asked the old lady's permission to offer him a glass of wine. Mrs Ogilvie, now accustomed to Jane's unconventionalities of behaviour had pursed her lips but agreed.

The afternoon crawled by. Why had Charles gone to Rebecca with a locket? Charles had never seen her own locket, as far as she knew. And men didn't notice such things, in any case. And why should Rebecca Smith know anything about him, except what he told her? And what did Rebecca Smith know about *her*, to call her Jennet and even tell Charles of a girl of this name?

To steady her mind, she picked up a book of poems which was but recently printed, and which she had seen on Booksellers Row and bought for herself. The poems spoke of 'man's forgotten pageantries', a phrase which attracted her, and of the waves forever following one upon the other, each departing for ever, like moments of time – but 'still flows on the eternal river'. This last phrase caught her imagination – the unchanging waters underneath, with the waves breaking on top of them. What of *her* time would be left to her when succeeding waves had crashed on the shore? What – or where – was the eternal river? Perhaps it was just the endlessness of the years as they moved on with oneself, just a tiny ripple, on the surface. It did not quite make her sad, but made her reflective. How feeble were her own attempts to arrest time in words. They would soon be forgotten, as she herself would be forgotten. Better, then, be like Philip and gather the rosebuds whilst she could? No, she was not like Philip – she must have something other than herself to live for, other than fame or gratification. But what? Her thoughts came back of course to Charles – she was sure the poem would have appealed to *him*.

Charles, Charles – what mystery was to be revealed to her about him? And why to her? There was nothing mysterious about herself, that she knew – even if Papa had called her Jennet when she was a baby as Snetters had seemed to remember. She closed her eyes and half dozed for a few moments, worn out with the effort over the past months to forget Charles, and with the effort to make a place for herself in life. She seemed to see the face of Charles coming and going all afternoon as the summer day darkened. There was no rain, but still the feeling of wind far away, and the sound of birds, as though they expected thunder. All still. Well, she would know at nine o'clock. She thought of Fred who had said 'Trust me', and 'If ever I can be of any use' – hadn't he.

She dined early and after the meal had been cleared she sat in the front sitting room with Polly, feeling sick in her stomach with excitement. Not that she had been able to eat very much. She kept looking at the pretty carriage clock of Edith's which Edith had placed on the high chimney piece. Still only eight o'clock.

She took off her locket for a moment and held it in her hand. Then she put it back round her neck where it had been ever since her mother's death years and years ago. Would nine o'clock ever come?

She could not read or settle to anything and got up several times and walked to the windows and looked out past the balcony to the square. Finally the little clock gave a faint tinkly strike. He should be here soon. She looked at her face in the glass again.

'If Mr Fitzpercy comes to the front door, let him in immediately, Polly.'

'Yes, Miss, you've told me,' said Polly. She should be in the kitchen but Miss Jane had asked her to stay for a minute or two. What a to do. Her young mistress looked so strange. But that Mr Fitzpercy wasn't coming to ask her hand in marriage, she was sure. It couldn't be that.

317

Not from anything Miss Jane had told her, but from the way he acted. You could see he wasn't interested in young ladies. A curiosity *he* was, but ever so handsome. She went back to the kitchen to sit with Emily and be handier for the front door.

Jane was wondering whether she ought to say anything more about her visitor to Mrs Ogilvie. But she didn't want to worry her. She would think her as madcap as her mother, visiting fortune-tellers and all. Not for the first time Jane longed for a house of her own where she could invite friends freely without being a burden to her uncle's servants.

Surely Charles would come soon?

She went to the window again, but there was no one to be seen. The greenery of the square gardens seemed of an intense emerald and the sky was still light, a paler shade of green, and pink. Night would soon fall, if only the short night of summer. She turned back to stand again by the empty hearth. She was convinced something had gone wrong. Then suddenly she heard a commotion downstairs in the entrance hall. Surely Charles would not come in at the servants' entrance? There were two voices and presently Polly came in without knocking.

'It's that Daisy again. She's in a state. Shall I send her up?'

'No, I shall come down,' cried Jane and rushed downstairs. The door to the square was open and Daisy was standing in the fading light.

'Oh, Miss Jane, oh Miss,' was all she could get out.

'Daisy! Come in and sit down.' Jane brought a chair forward and Polly closed the door.

'Miss – there's not a minute to lose – it's Mr Fitz – '

'He was to come at nine – we're waiting – '

'Oh, Miss,' gulped Daisy, 'I've run all the way – my

318

friend at the Middlesex told me – all last night he must 'ave been out – she came for me 'cos he kept asking them – he's hurt, Miss – he's hurt. And he kept saying, "Tell Daisy Collins to get Jane, seventeen Lincoln's Inn Square" over and over, she said.'

A cold dull worm of fear began to travel up from Jane's stomach to her lungs but she took a hold on herself. 'Daisy, what do you mean the "Middlesex"?'

'She means the hospital,' said Polly, looking frightened.

'He wants *you*, he wants *you*,' wailed Daisy. 'They found him last night or early morning, near Exchange Court – near a drinking place – thought he was drunk – moved him and then saw – he . . . the girl I know told me some men brought him in. I'd heard this morning at the Garden, Miss, that there'd been a knifing . . . When Dolly came to Gran's I came straight out. Dolly works at the Middlesex, you see, but she knows me. He's there, Miss – he wants you – straight away. Oh, please Miss – no time to be lost.'

'Polly, run to Mr Digby's in Bloomsbury. He may be back from the country by now – you know where he lives. Tell him to come to the Middlesex Hospital straight away – I'll be there – I must ask William to take me now – is he downstairs?'

Mrs Ogilvie, although she was deaf, had sensed some commotion and was at the head of the stairs calling down: 'Miss Jane – whatever is it?'

'An accident to a friend,' said Jane, running halfway up the stairs. 'I must go to the Middlesex Hospital. Will you please tell William to get the carriage out – it's a fair walk – *please*, Mrs Ogilvie.'

Daisy was sobbing: 'It's a matter of life and death,' she shouted. Mrs Ogilvie took one look at them and went down to do Jane's bidding.

319

'I'll go to Mr Digby's, Miss,' said Polly, and was off through the door on wings.

'Is it very bad, then?' asked Jane as she put on her light mantle and took her purse. She heard nothing more from Daisy who was a dreadful sight with the tears running down her cheeks making grimy little pathways. The carriage horse was harnessed to the small carriage and Jane pressed Mrs Ogilvie's hand. 'Thank you – don't worry about me – I'll send a message if I have to stay.' Then they were out in the street and the two of them, she and Daisy, were driven off.

It was almost dark now. The carriage turned up Tottenham Court Road, drew to the left and drove into the courtyard of the great barrack-like building. The entrance porch was lit by gas, but the softer light of oil lamps shone through the myriad windows, row upon row of them. As soon as the carriage stopped, Jane opened the doors, not waiting for William to get down from his perch.

'Wait for us, William,' she flung behind her, and ran to the large entrance, Daisy following close behind.

The nightwatchman was in his cubby-hole, but he came out. 'Will he be Charles Fitzpercy or Mr Entwhistle?' she whispered to Daisy, but before they needed to say anything at all, the man caught sight of Daisy.

'You the friend of Dolly? You're expected – take 'em in then.'

A hospital orderly in a long smock came out of the shadows. 'For the young gentleman? Right, Miss. I'll take you along. Follow me. We'll need some details. He's awake, but he's weak, very weak.'

'Please – if Mr Frederick Digby arrives, will you send him to me? I've asked him to come and I'm sure he'll be here soon if he's in London.'

They entered a long, low room with an oil lamp in each

320

alcove where there were truckle beds. Candles stood on a table in the middle, taken now and again by men whom Jane supposed to be doctors, who approached some of the beds, held their candles aloft, for the lamplight did not reach into all the crannies of the room, and peered at their patients. A bed at the end on the left had a screen round it, but the window above was uncurtained and the dark night sky could be seen through it.

'He's picked up a little,' muttered a young doctor. 'He keeps asking for "Jane" – is that you, Miss?'

'Yes – I'm Jane,' she whispered.

'You go to him then.'

There was a white sheeted sofa standing against the wall and Daisy sat down on it. Jane went up to the flimsy screen, parted it and looked down at the bed – and at Charles Fitzpercy's face. He lay, his face turned to the side, his arms lying motionless over the sheet which she saw was bloodstained. Oh, who had done this to him?

She knelt by his side and, after a moment, he opened his eyes. 'Charles. It's Jane. I was waiting for you. I knew you would come if you could. Can you hear me?'

A faint whisper answered her. 'Jane Banham. See what they've done? No time to be lost.' He made an effort to speak more clearly. She saw he was in great pain. His eyes flickered as though a little flame was being guarded there, blown by a mortal wind. She put her hand over his, hoping she did not hurt him, and touching his flesh as lightly as possible. 'Jane,' he murmured. 'In my jacket – find it – over there – in the pocket . . .'

She looked round and saw a bloodstained jacket on the chair at the foot of the bed. There was a gash in the material and all around it a clotted mass of blood. But she knew what he wanted. Whoever had attacked him had not done it for gain. She felt inside the inner lining. There

321

was a little packet and she drew it out and brought it back to him. Then he smiled. 'Open it,' he said. 'I was going to – bring it – to you – tonight.' His voice was a little stronger now. She saw in the lamplight that his left side was stiff and she tried not to look closely. She was trembling so that she could hardly open the packet, but for Charles's sake she mastered her shaking and drew out the little locket. 'Take yours off, too,' he said hoarsely. She put her hands round her neck and, once more, undid the clasp of her own locket. 'Open mine,' he whispered. She took it in her hands and pressed a little catch at the side. 'Look, look at it,' he went on. She had it open now and was staring at a face, a tiny miniature face, fitted into one side of the locket. She stared and stared and then she took a candle that was on the window-sill and looked again and then she looked at Charles Fitzpercy. He was smiling at her in all his pain, smiling and smiling. She went up to him and knelt down again. 'It is my mother,' she whispered.

'And mine,' he answered. Hot tears filled her eyes and she brushed them away with her cuff and took his hand again. 'You are my brother?'

Light filled his eyes as she looked at him, liquid light from his own tears.

'A sister – too late,' he said, and everything fell into place in her head and she put her arms round him as he lay with the life draining out of him and kissed him on the forehead and on the cheeks and on the lips and then on his hands. 'She left it me,' he whispered, and then: 'Mrs Smith knows it all. Pray for me, Jane,' he said and closed his eyes. She thought he was dying then and was about to go for help, but he was breathing still, lightly and slowly.

'God help you! God help you! I love you. Love you, dearest, dearest Charles,' she said and then she put the locket with her mother's, his mother's, likeness into his hand and on the hand that lay stiff, she put her own hand again and stayed there, motionless, until he should wake.

'Kiss me,' he said. And she kissed his forehead. A brother and a sister. Babes in the wood. Together at last, together for ever. There was nothing she could do – her feelings that had run hither and thither questioning, wondering, gathered themselves together – a lover lost – a brother found – a brother gained. Never had she been so close to a living man, the one man she had truly loved and longed for, and he was a brother, her own flesh and blood. Cruel, cruel not to have known it earlier. And now? He seemed to drift off to sleep. She knelt by his side, keeping vigil.

Fred Digby had been out when Polly rushed round to him in Bloomsbury Square. But she had waited until his return and he had gone straight to the hospital. Jane was still kneeling at Charles Fitzpercy's side when he arrived. Her arm was spread round Charles's neck and one hand holding Charles's. Jane living and breathing and her half-brother, Charles Fitzpercy, smiling in death.

The doctor had followed Frederick to the bed and together they helped Jane to loosen her clutch on Charles's hand. Her dress was all bloodstained and her face stiff, as though *she* had died. Gently they placed her on a chair and she sat unresistingly. Then the doctor went to Charles again and closed his eyes and took a little locket he had in his hand and gave it to Fred. As he did so, there was the tinkle of another locket falling on the floor. 'Yours, Miss?' asked the man and Jane raised her head then and said: 'They are both mine,' and swooned away.

She came to in Fred's carriage. Daisy had gone.

She cried: 'Where is he? Where is he? What happened?'

323

'Hush – you can do nothing now,' came Fred's voice. 'I sent a message to your housekeeper by Polly *and* told that girl I'd like to see her grandmother.' He was looking away, not at her until she said clearly, if shakily, 'He was my brother.'

Fred stared at her, and a weight lifted from his heart.

'He is dead,' she whispered. 'He was my brother,' wonderingly. Then: 'Take me to your house – where are the lockets?' she said, quite firmly.

Fred gave them into her hand, asking no questions. All that could wait. He wanted to put his arm round her but dared not, awed by her revelation.

The sun had risen and the early dawn light had changed to a bright sun which was now flooding over London.

'It was like a candle going out,' she said in a small voice.

Soon they arrived at Fred's house and then Jane was taken upstairs and placed on a little bed and bidden to rest. Before Fred left her to try to sleep she said: 'You know, I think Daisy loved him, too.' But she did not cry, not then. A little shutter came down for an hour in her mind and she slept, worn out with shock and sorrow.

Early the next morning Fred sent his servant to enquire at the Middlesex the circumstances of Charles's being taken there. When the man had gone he sat sunk in thought and roused himself only to drink a little coffee. *Jane had sent for him*, he was thinking, *Jane had sent for him*. Never would he forget the dim candlelight and that girl Daisy sitting on the white sofa and Jane bent over the figure on the bed. He was curious as to the whole story, but that could wait a little and depended on Jane.

No more summer, no more days, ever, for that poor fellow – Jane's brother – he could not believe he was that, and yet she had seemed completely convinced. He must see that woman Rebecca Smith. She alone must be able to clear up all the mystery. But how had he died? A pickpocket does not usually kill – unless he is mad – and the jewel had still been in Charles's pocket. The two lockets were at present clutched in Jane's hand. When he went into the room where she was now asleep, he saw her closed hands on the pillow and her hair spread out all around her like a mermaid. Poor Jane – she must not drown now. She would need all her courage. He resolved to say nothing to her that might show any lack of tact, yet thanked God that Fitzpercy had not fallen in love with the girl. A sister and a brother, to be brought together like that – the ways of Providence were strange indeed – and now she would have to mourn a real brother, not an unrequited passion. And they would have to see the man was decently buried. What had that officious doctor said to him? Something about, 'He said he must be buried in Salton – Seaton – we couldn't quite catch the words – he knew he was a gonner, poor chap.' Salton – that was the place Jane had spoken of, wasn't it?

It was the *blood* that Fred could not get out of his head. There had been blood all over Jane's overdress, which his housekeeper had taken off before laying the girl down. And Jane's hands were still smeared with it. That poor man's life had ebbed away like the tide going out – it was too horrible to contemplate. Thank God he had come at her bidding. At last he could try to do something for her.

He looked, once more, at the sleeping girl. How beautiful she was. And how bravely she had kept her vigil over her brother. Fred went downstairs to drink a cup of coffee and ordered soup to be taken up to Jane when she should wake. His housekeeper was wide-eyed and concerned. Perhaps soon his servant would return – and then the old gypsy woman, and he could find out more. Would it be better not to wake Jane, though? He was spared the question after his solitary breakfast, for his housekeeper came in to say that the young lady had woken and was asking for him and was not hungry.

He went, upstairs again, taking a moistened cloth to wipe her hands for her. She was lying fully awake now and stared at him as he came in.

'You must send for Mrs Smith – 363 Ironmongers Row,' she said, and sat up. She was pale but composed. 'I had such a strange dream, about Mama – and a little boy,' she said.

'Do rest, Jane, you will be exhausted.'

'I must talk to you,' she said.

'There'll be time later for explanation,' he replied.

'If I could find whoever did it to him I'd – ' She turned her face away, clenching her fists.

'Give me your hands.' Fred took one palm and opened it and then the other and wiped the traces of Charles's blood from them. 'Mrs Wilson will come to help you dress. I sent the boot-boy with another message to your housekeeper telling her you are to stay here for the moment and Polly has brought you clothes.'

He went out and gave Mrs Wilson the clothes to clean and then went downstairs once more, having asked Jane to come down as soon as she was ready. He was sure Rebecca Smith would not be long in arriving.

Jane, for her part, in all the confusion and disorder of her thoughts, and all the anguish for Charles and the manner of his dying, had a most curious feeling that seemed connected with what she had been half dreaming. It was a shape, a sensation rather than a thought and she could not describe it to herself, except it was as though she had given birth to something. Something or someone was lying there when she closed her eyes, a kind of bodily abstraction that had passed from her. She did not want to chase the shape away, nor did she, or could she, turn her mind away from the scenes of the night.

She felt a little dizzy, too, and her thoughts were whirling ahead of her – but there was still the 'shape' lying at the back of them. She picked up the lockets which Fred had laid on the table when he wiped her hands and put down her own locket again. Steadfastly she opened the locket Charles had had with him and looked, once more, at the face of the young, pretty, auburn-haired woman who was undoubtedly her mother – and his. She did not look above twenty-one or two, but Jane saw that face change into the mother she had known as a child, no longer so auburn-haired, thinner, but the same person. Mama must have been Lord Percy's mistress then. She shivered. Ten years or so before her daughter was born to her as a respectably married woman – at the same age she herself was now, her Mama had had a son! Had Papa ever known? Why had she given Charles away? She thought, with another stab of recognition, that Uncle Hal would once have been auburn-haired – and little Johnny, too, had that colour of hair. Yet she had never seen any connection. Her mother, dead so long ago now, seemed to be taking shape. That was the shape she had given birth to, – a new mama – Charles's mama – a new person, and another shape, a brother.

If only Charles had not gone out the night before; if only she had known. Why had Mrs Smith not told *her*? But she supposed it had been up to Charles to tell her. All that passion she had felt for him, wanting to cherish him, almost like a mother, she thought – and she *would* have done – the ideal would have turned into a real person! And he was dead.

\* \* \*

327

Rebecca made her way slowly, alone, to the house on Bloomsbury Square, after saying goodbye to Daisy, who had wanted to go with her. She was wearing her black mantle that she had had for forty years and her bonnet with the satin ribbon. She had done nothing to be ashamed of. If those bullies who had beaten him up had not finished him, Jane would have had her brother and Charlie his sister – and any love nonsense on the girl's part would have been nipped in the bud. Charlie needed family – that was his trouble. He had paid for his parents' sins all right. She would have done them both a good turn. That was what she had planned. But she wasn't God and Charles had paid for his tastes with his life. Still, it was clever of her to have worked it all out, she thought.

She tugged on the large bell-pull and stood there, a strange diminutive, dark figure who looked as though she rightly belonged to another age. Mrs Wilson had been hovering around the entrance hall. Mr Digby had asked her to let the woman in. There had been that many comings and goings. Harrison had returned from the hospital and was closeted in with the Master, and Miss Jane was sitting as pale as alabaster in the small sitting-room where a fire had been lit in spite of summer, for she kept shivering.

Mrs Wilson let the new visitor in with a haughty air. The woman looked like a gypsy, but orders were orders.

Rebecca Smith was standing in the hall waiting for someone to take her in when a pleasant-looking man came downstairs and gave a slight bow. He was well-bred, you could see that. She looked around for a lady, a wife, but there was only the housekeeper. Fred motioned Rebecca into the room where Jane was sitting by the fire. The man poured Rebecca a drink of brandy, which she didn't refuse, and then he sat down in one of the armchairs and pulled up another for her. It didn't look as though there would be any trouble.

Away from her kitchen and her linnet and her curtains, Rebecca seemed to Jane an old woman with no special powers. But the woman's eyes were on *her* and she asked: 'Please tell us all you know. It can't matter now that Charles – ' Her voice thickened, but she carried on bravely. 'How did you know he was my brother? It *is* a picture of Mama in his locket.'

'I didn't *know*, Miss. I guessed.'

'It is better we know the whole story,' said Fred. 'Miss Banham has had two terrible shocks, but she says she wants the whole story.'

'Yes,' said Jane in a firmer voice.

'He came to me a year or two ago,' Rebecca began in her gruff voice. 'Said he wanted advice. I could see he was unhappy – wished he'd never been born – he told me his story bit by bit like they always do. Called himself Mr Entwhistle. That didn't mean anything to me, of course. But then after a bit he told me his mama was dead and his father and she hadn't been married. Brought up by a woman at the lodge of a great ruined place – went abroad – gambled – wrote verses, he said. I was troubled at first by him. My cards didn't tell me anything about him – it was the eyes . . . and I thought, I think I knew your mother, young man.' Jane looked up. 'It was about thirty years ago when I lived near Drury Lane and the actresses used to visit me. I'd been a dresser when I was young – I had a way with clothes and the girls used to call round and ask for their fortunes. I always knew things about them – it's in my blood – but I never told them anything bad. Times was hard then – harder than today and the girls were lucky if they saw twenty-five sometimes, traipsing round the country playing in the theatres. They'd catch colds –

329

and worse – and if they found a protector, well, who would blame them? Some of the girls were from families that had been on the boards for generations – some were girls of good family, run away from home after a tiff. Well, there was one girl – she'd run off with some actor, in Winchester I think it was, and she was a well brought up girl, looking bolder than she really was. He'd ditched her, of course, but she'd found work and was doing well – called herself Betsey Diamond then. Not her real name, she said, but didn't want to bring disgrace on her family. She'd been up north and someone had taken a fancy to her. A nobleman he was. "Advise me, Rebecca," she said to me. "He says he loves me – he's got an old wife who won't last long and we can be wed." Some of the nobility did wed these girls, you know – not often, but it did happen – and Miss Betsey was a good girl. She'd never gone with the men after her first chap left her and before she'd taken up with this nobleman. She'd a good friend – Sophia, I think was her name, and she says to me: "Sophia says I shouldn't say yes – but I'm tired, Rebecca, and he's mad for me." Saving your honour,' said Rebecca, recollecting herself and bowing towards Fred.

'Go on.'

'Well, she came round not long after that and said she was going to have his baby. I remember it was the time all those Frenchies were coming over, when they were cutting people's heads off. And she said, "If it's a girl I'm going to call her Jennet – little Jane, after my mother – but if it's a boy, *he* says lie low – his wife isn't long for this world and he'll marry me and we can say the child is younger than he is and he'll be the heir." The gentleman had no children, you see. I saw her once after the baby was born and she called in to say she was off north. "He wants to bring him up," she said. "Don't worry, Becky,"

330

she said, "it's all going to be all right. Her Ladyship's not got long for this world." And I saw the little, wee creature, with his red hair and she was right fond of him, but in a funny way, as though she thought she ought not to love him and he ought to be his dad's – she was only very young, you know – '

'About my age,' said Jane.

'Well, I saw no more of her till just once, years later. She'd never married that man. She didn't love him, but he said he loved the child and no child of his was going to be carried in a basket with his mother, an actress. He'd have him brought up right. So the laddie stayed with his father and Betsey waited for the old lady to die. But she didn't die, and Betsey still felt the baby should have a home, so she'd gone. And for seven years she hadn't seen him. When I saw her I said, "Miss Betsey, you must take your little boy back." "Oh, I can't now," she says. "He won't know me and Percy has promised he'll recognize him. And I've met a good man who wants to marry me," she says. "But I want to know if I should tell him about my little boy." I advised against it, God forgive me. I thought she'd better leave things as they were and not risk it again. "I'm off to Norwich," she says – I can hear her now. I never knew what became of her and that's the truth. Then, as I told you, years and years later, there comes this tall young man. "My friends tell me you do fortunes, old woman," he says, not rudely, but with a joke in his voice. "Tell me mine," he says. And it didn't take me long to put two and two together.' She paused for a moment and Fred offered her more brandy.

'Well, Miss Jane – there's not much more to tell you won't have guessed. You comes to me with this tale of a young man who says a Jennet will do him a power of good. I'd said it to him as a joke like – thinking he would

331

have been Jane if he hadn't turned out a boy – and then and there he meets you! "Something drew me to her," he says. "But I'm not a man who wants girls." And I get thinking – you said your mother was an actress and then I see your locket, the very image of the one I remember Miss Betsey wearing – I remember it because she showed me a picture of the nobleman in it and she says, "He's got my likeness in his." And then this spring, when Mr Charles is up in that old place he visits where he was brought up, he takes a fancy to looking through his desk when he's nothing better to do and he finds his locket where he'd put it years ago in a temper, because he thought his mother never loved him and abandoned him and he can't bear to see her face even though he thinks she died long since. It's still there at the back of the drawer. And in London he shows it to me, out of interest. "That's my mother," he says. Of course, I knew *her*, but I'd seen the other one on you and there you were – a Jane – and you say you come from Norfolk – and you got feelings for this young man you've met – so what can I do but ask him to tell you if he wants to? I wrote it down for him and Daisy took the letter to him. I knew he'd be glad – ever so glad. He came round to see me again that very night. "I've got a sister," he says. "*You* tell her. I've told her to expect you tomorrow," I say. "I *shall* go," he says. "It's the best thing that ever happened to me," he says. And he goes off and – well he must have gone for another drink down St Giles way – and then down near the Strand – he never took fright of the people – but there was a nasty crew who were paying back some old debt, I imagine. They're not averse to a bit of blackmail and people like Mr Charles have to be careful. They probably threatened him, or they picked a fight for no reason. He wouldn't go getting himself into trouble when he'd got that piece of news for you. Daisy's often warned him. She hears the bullies round the Garden and there's a nasty set who call themselves "cleansers" – they don't like men like him, though he done them no wrong. I can't tell you the ins and outs. But, Miss Jane,' – She turned towards Jane, who was staring wide-eyed. ' – I never meant any harm. I wasn't *sure* till I saw the two lockets together. Perhaps I should have kept my mouth shut. It wasn't my place to tell you, though. I wanted it to be Mr Fitz.'

'No, Mrs Smith – you were not to blame,' Jane said. 'My poor mother – no wonder she was so upset when my younger brother died. She seemed to take it as a punishment. I can't understand how she could have left Charles – her little boy. I haven't had the sort of life that would help me understand, but I know my father loved her.'

'Like you loved Mr Charles,' said Rebecca. 'But that wasn't no good, you see.'

'No, it wasn't any good,' said Jane. 'I always wanted a brother.' She bit her lip and Fred went over and put his arm round her.

'We are grateful, Mrs Smith. Tell me, what was the name you said he called himself by first?'

'Mr Entwhistle, Sir. The name of the woman who brought him up, I believe. But she's dead – he told me that.'

'I shall make enquiries. Mr Fitzpercy told the doctor he wanted to be buried in Salton.'

Jane raised her head. 'I thought he could be buried by Mama,' she said. 'But if Charles wanted – '

'He said *he* was like that place – often, to me,' said Rebecca. 'He was there in the winter, said he'd written a long poem about bones, or something. I didn't like him talking of it, though I saw Stones and a lost Diamond –

that would be his inheritance – and he was the Jack of Hearts. Death by Clubs and a wicked Jack of Spades . . .' She stopped, aware that she was speaking her thoughts aloud. 'I must go, Sir,' she said, in her ordinary voice. 'Your mother did want to go home,' she said, turning to Jane. 'You are your mother's daughter, and I hope you will find a home the way she did. There's no more I can tell you.'

Fred looked at Jane who said, 'Thank you,' in a low voice to Mrs Smith.

'She thought she was acting for the best,' said Rebecca as she went out. 'Don't blame her. Life is hard for young women – you don't need me to tell you that.'

If only Percy had adopted the lad and given him a true name after his wife's death, Fred was thinking. He would have grown up less bitter. Even if he thought his mother hadn't cared for him. And they had told him his mother was dead. If he had discovered she had married someone else, that would have been a blow which even the knowledge of a sister might not have softened. That must have occurred to him when he went out for a drink to think it over.

Jane was still sitting by the fire when he returned into the room. She turned a pale face up to him.

'It is all extraordinary. I am so sorry, Jane. We must arrange to follow your brother's wishes and bury him in Salton. I shall send a messenger up there to see if there are any family of this Entwhistle person.'

'I shall come with you, then,' she said.

'Leave it all to me. You have had enough heartache.'

'I shall see him laid to rest and lay the ghost of my mother, too,' she said. 'I was just beginning to know him, you see. I never really knew him, but there was always something, Fred. Always something.'

334

He had been everything, she wanted to say – the man of her dreams. But it was no dream that he was dead and no dream that he was her brother. It would take some time for her mind to struggle towards believing that he was dead and that he was her brother. She knew it, but she scarcely believed it. Only time might aid her and there was no time to be lost, for Charles Fitzpercy, Charles Entwhistle – Charles *Stone* – would soon have to be buried.

# PART SIX
# Rebuildings

Charles was to be buried by the mausoleum of his natural father and a cleric had agreed to officiate. Fred Digby was taxed to the utmost to see that all was done respectfully and with taste, and even more concerned that Jane Banham should be enabled to face and absorb her grief. She had written to her uncle, as Fred had advised, and he wondered how the news of Hal's unknown nephew would be received in Italy. Fred shuddered a little at the ghoulish journey ahead of them, but showed the utmost tact to Jane. 'Afterwards you can stay at Vine House or even go home to Norfolk,' he said, but did not press either idea. He hoped she might need him when time had led her to full acceptance of the tragedy. At present she had no thoughts of anyone but Charles and her mother – even a letter from Mr Hood offering to consider her work for his own review had not roused her to any joy or even seemed to have registered with her. Fred knew that he must wait, but intended that one day he would suggest she write an appreciation of Charles's verse.

They had found a trunk stuffed with papers in his lodgings and Fred had put them under lock and key, knowing that Jane would want to see them later. One of the verses which he had quickly scanned, had a few lines interpolated with 'Bury me in Salton' written after some intimation he seemed to have had there of his own mortality. Altogether they were a strange collection of writings, thought Fred. He himself was longing for the funeral to be over. Funerals were necessary to finish off

339

the chapter of a life for the mourners. It was they who must know there had been a conclusion fitting to a human being, a person who had lived on the same earth as the living and was to be returned to it.

Fred would then bide his time. *He* had had no news from Italy and avoided thinking of the disaster of his own marriage. He could not help drawing a dreadful parallel between the old Lord Percy and himself. Both with a wife, and both in love with a young woman. He prayed he would treat her in a better manner than Percy had her mother. For the moment he concentrated on being useful and, indeed, Jane was grateful for all he did. He knew she would speak of her love for Charles when she was ready. The peculiar Mrs Smith had, he thought, probably told as much of the truth as she knew. All that his servants had been able to extract from the hospital workers who had been in attendance when Charles was brought in dying had tended to make them believe he had been knifed by someone who had attacked him before; who had perhaps followed him as he skirted the alley between the Strand and Maiden Lane on his way back to his lodgings. There had been only one deep wound, but it had been aimed at his heart. There was bruising and injury to his right hand, but his face was unmarked. A tragic and horrible business. Unlikely, too, that his attacker would ever be caught. Perhaps Daisy knew him or would have recognized him. She said it was not the first time he had been victimized. Men who found other men attractive were harshly treated – by villains, by rivals or by moral crusaders: the end result was the same.

Fred had arranged for a closed hearse to convey Charles Fitzpercy's body to its last home. This carriage had followed closely upon their own and had been accompanied by two of Fred's male servants. The two carriages had woven their way northwards under the high, pale sky of late July. The route was similar for the first half of its journey to that taken a week or two earlier by the funeral cortège of Lord Byron, but there were no respectful crowds waiting to touch the casket. They could not hurry, for the horses needed constant rest and the roads, as they reached the north, were not good. The carriage, with Fred, Jane and Polly arrived in Salton on the evening of the twenty-fourth. For the last few miles they had followed the coastline. The glinting silver sea had never been far away, and sometimes when the road was on the clifftop they saw ruffle after ruffle of curly foam arrive on vast, deserted sandy beaches. They had gone through Salton village and been greeted by old Taylor, who had been apprised of events by a letter sent through the local militia. Fred had put 'the keeper of Salton Delevinge', not knowing to whom he was addressing himself.

But the person who came forward when they arrived at the only inn in Salton village and were surrounded by a crowd of curious onlookers, was a sober-looking old man who seemed truly sorry about their mission. Jane remained in the carriage, dreading the crowd of villagers when the second carriage would arrive. They had resolved to say nothing to anyone of her relationship to the deceased, unless they were asked, and it was to her great relief that the old man undertook to wait for the hearse and send a boy on ahead with them meanwhile to show them the road to the hall.

'There'll be beds for ye,' Taylor had said. 'I allus keep a few rooms for Mr Charles.' And he added turning to Fred – Jane was leaning back, hidden by Polly, against the hard seat, leaving Fred to follow the old man's directions – 'I've dug him a grave by t'owd mausoleum –

he were there in't winter – aye, I nivver thowt he'd be back so soon. I mind him well as a little lad with his bonny red hair, that I do.'

Fred thanked him, and their carriage went on along a lane that led out of the village, through a wood and then turned along an old drive with a lodge gate surmounted by twin eagles.

The path, now neglected and overgrown, caused the horses some stumbling. There was a salty tang in the air and the sea could be heard not far away and the summer trees were also soughing in a faint breeze. As they turned finally, the boy trotting by their side, Jane saw a strange building – incongruous in the pastureland around – rear itself up like a tiger. There was a tower that was open to the sky and a ruined wing to its left and an older wing, more ordinary, with a steep roof and chimneys of an Elizabethan design, standing on the nearside. All was absolutely still and she caught her breath as they descended from the carriage. She turned from left to right, seeing the waving grasses and a lane with a hedge-row that arched above it on each side and then back to the yellow-brown stone of the only roofed-in part of the hall, now itself covered in ivy. She shivered and shut her eyes for a moment. 'No, it's all right,' she said to Fred, who had sensed her sudden start. Not even to Fred could she say that she had seen this landscape before, and these fields and the tower in the dreams she had had. But there was no menace about the place now as she saw when she walked with Fred to the large, studded door. Only when she looked up at the tower did she feel odd. Once all this must have been an enormous estate, a vast mansion.

Had her mother been here, then, towards the end of the last century? What had it looked like then? The door was open. Mr Taylor had seen that the room they entered was at least clean and, in a moment, there arrived, from the inner door, a woman who, with her, 'Eh, Sir. Eh, Miss, you'll be ready for a bite,' obviously expected them. She brought in bread and cheese and kept reassuring them that Taylor would soon be back. He had been out all last evening at 't' grave like,' and 't'parson would be over tomorrow.' She seemed incurious about who they were, but perfectly clear as to why they were there. Also, unlike a southern woman of the same class, she did not adopt an obsequious manner and talked to them both as though they were of the same rank, more or less, as herself. Taylor had clearly briefed her and Jane found her rough kindliness a comfort and was glad to be shown to the 'guest' chamber. 'I've swept it and found some sheets from the lodge. Mr Charles didn't keep much here,' she said. 'He slept upstairs – his things are there. They say the old lord's cousin is coming over soon and they're going to pull down all t'rest of hall.'

Jane knew that Fred had communicated with Charles's father's cousin and family. They had shown no inclination to follow the body of their relative to see him buried. Indeed, they had seemed relieved that nothing was to be expected of them. Nothing had been heard, either, from Colquohoun.

'Oh, it was a grand place once, Miss,' the woman was saying. 'I can't remember mysen, but my mam told me.'

Jane murmured something, not wishing to appear rude, but she excused herself to Fred after she had had her box brought down for her and set Polly to unpacking what she would need, and went into the grounds behind the occupied wing, grounds that she knew sloped down to the sea. She closed her eyes for a moment and leaned against an old oak tree. She could not let herself think too much or she would go mad. She longed for the burial to be over.

What was left was not Charles and now she strove to imagine the real Charles, who had lived here all his childhood and been here earlier that year. Her mother *had* been here. It was not a dream. The events of the last week or two seemed to flash upon her inner eye like a magic-lantern show – the shadows round the bed cast by the candles where Charles lay dying, his whisper, the little locket with her picture, which was to be buried with him. Daisy's voice saying, 'Put some flowers for him, Jane, for me,' Mrs Ogilvie weeping when she heard the story from Fred – and then the long, long journey. Was it a madness to bury him where he wished? To come all this way out in the wilds to find an almost ruin and a summer day that was somehow out of time? It seemed to be the wrong season for a burial and the wrong season for Salton Delevinge, which needed winter branches and owls and cold moonlight to be credible. She was here at last – but with the wrong person. It was the right place though – the place of her vivid dream: the eagle she had seen in her dream was one of the stone pair at the lodge gates. There was no linnet, and the sparrow she had dreamed flying in the eaves must have been life itself, come in and out of an open window – the passage of a man's life.

Until she was back in London she must take a hold of herself. She could not mourn him properly here – it was not her place, or her mother's. Only he belonged to it. She was his sister, but she was an interloper. She had loved him, but her love had not saved him. What right had she even to mourn this man whose spirit she had loved?

Dazed, she went out across a mossy terrace with the lowering tower behind her and followed the ivy-hung hedgerows and passed a little wood where she heard the sound of voices and came out onto a little embankment and saw, in the distance, that the tide had gone out, leaving a smooth, sandy strand pocked here and there with what looked like sea coal. The sun was still quite high in the sky and all was peaceful and she knew that her mother had walked this way and it was her mother, above all, whom she was mourning. They would bury Charles nearby and she would say goodbye to him, but she was thinking of, and mourning, and – yes – even greeting her own mother, in this wilderness. She could scarcely believe that Charles was in that coffin in spite of seeing him there in London. Something she had never understood, some feelings long buried that had perhaps led her to Charles, some inability to remember Mama – all this was suddenly there in her mind as she stood now on the desolate beach and with it came a strange release. Those different worlds of her own past and her mother's far away past, and Charles Fitzpercy's more recent history, came together like an explosion in her mind as though she were holding one of those children's toys they played with at festivals called detonating bon-bons, and the little flash of gunpowder had released a gift. But this gift was not of sweetmeats, but of bitter herbs which she must consume before she could be free. She had never really known Charles, or her mother. If Charles were there to walk with her instead of lying in that grim coffin which she had known was following them and tried not to see, she would, at last, have had the opportunity to love him as Mama's child. 'Jennet,' she heard her mother's voice say, 'Jennet, you have a little brother.' She was back in Bedon and her mother was holding a small, wailing bundle. Her brother Edmund who had stayed so short a time and whose death had frightened her as a child. 'Jennet'. *She* had said Jennet? How could she have forgotten that? She stood there, looking over the far horizon, but not seeing

345

it – seeing only her mother. So her mother had stood here – she knew it – and so Charles had stood not long ago, but just as irretrievable as her mother's past. It was all past. His body was here in the present – was probably being carried even now to its place of burial, and she must just endure this present which would itself join the past when all ceremony was done. Somehow she must find a way to make sense of it all. 'I've brought him home, Mama,' she murmured and turned and saw the little stream which came down from the fields onto the shore. She felt a vast peace as she walked back – no longer agonized and sad. Some story had come to an end here which his committal to earth only sealed, but had not itself brought to an end. It was the living who buried the dead. The dead would stay alive in the minds of the living if they could be properly mourned. Curiously she wanted to thank someone or something. She had been blind and unseeing, wrapped up in her passion and love, eager for experience, eager to put the past behind her. But it had not been put behind. It was the *Now*, and all a part of *her*. She felt old, a little weary, but calm as she went in to Fred and prepared herself for the morrow.

The mausoleum stood, half broken-down in the clearing, gloomy and ugly, but the grave of Charles Fitzpercy had been freshly dug in the open by its side. The mourners were few: Mr Taylor – who, with some young men from the village who remembered Charles – had dug the grave when the news had come from London; the youths themselves and a few women; the housekeeper, a bailiff, who had turned up at the last moment, three young gentlemen who had arrived that morning and said no word to anyone or to each other, Polly – and Jane Banham with Frederick Digby. The parson no longer

346

served the house or the hall, but had ridden over from the town to do his duty and was shortly, with relief, to ride back. The mound of soil they had dug for the grave was black, and the turfs to be placed over the grave once the coffin had been lowered, were green with summer grass. Jane was holding a small wreath of lilies and roses she had gathered herself in the overgrown gardens. She had also picked some wild flowers and bound them round with ivy. She was thinking of Daisy who had wished to share in the funeral garland, and she was trying to pray for Charles. Fred had ascertained that the ground in front of the funeral monument had been sanctified long ago when the first Percy had been laid there, and there had been no objections to the rather unorthodox laying to rest. Jane had placed his locket in the coffin when they left London, but had taken the picture of her mother out. At last, Charles no longer needed a mother. But *she* wanted her mother's likeness and it was now reposing in her own locket round her neck.

She had not wept and had remained calm, in spite of the sorrows of the day. It was a brother she was mourning now, and she was thinking of him, not of herself. Fred stole an anxious glance or two at her now and then, but seemed satisfied that she would not break down. She looked over at the young men and saw that one was Archie Colquohoun. Now the priest was at the words: 'Man that is born of woman hath but a short time to live, and is full of misery. He cometh up, and is cut down like a flower; he fleeth as it were a shadow, and never continueth in one stay . . .' The coffin was being lowered and Jane stared at it. Still she could not believe Charles was in it. Then as the priest spoke the words she had dreaded: '. . . take unto Himself the soul of our dear *brother* departed', the people began to take small handfuls of earth to throw on

347

it, and 'ashes to ashes, dust to dust', and there was a jolt as it found the bottom of the grave, and she stooped with the others and stood up and sprinkled a little handful of earth. Then moved to the head of the grave as the man went on speaking and she threw down the posy of wild flowers. She would put the wreath over the closed-in grave – these flowers were for Daisy and for all who had loved him. One of the young men was turning away, tears on his cheeks, as the rest of the small company muttered the Lord's Prayer, along with the priest. She tried to think of Charles as he had been, not as the shut-in body which, even now, the parson was saying had been delivered out of the miseries of this sinful world. Charles. Her brother. She murmured prayers, silently, for her mother and for him. If there were a heaven, surely those two could be united at last? Then it was over and the gravediggers moved forward to accomplish their task and Fred was standing by her and the others had gone. Expect for Mr Taylor, who was saying: 'He went to t'chapill last time he were here. Never went usually, and he came here when I was lugging stones. Poor Mr Charles. He were only young – I mind him as a babby, that I do.'

The present Lord Percy's bailiff stayed to drink a glass of claret and nibble a biscuit, which Fred had sent for from the inn. There was nothing more to say, but the bailiff seemed anxious that the family should not be held to account for not having known of Mr Fitzpercy's whereabouts or for failing to arrange or attend his funeral. However, he did not seem to take any umbrage for Mr Digby's overseeing of the latter. Indeed, he seemed relieved and quite grateful.

'There is just one little matter,' he said before he left. 'His present Lordship is not prepared for the name of the

348

deceased upon the gravestone – which is, after all, within the Family livings – to appear as Fitzpercy. The man was called Entwhistle by the Family.'

'Mr Charles's name was the name of my mother,' Jane said, overhearing this. 'My mother was Elizabeth Stone. That was Charles's real name.'

'Indeed, indeed?' replied the bailiff, raising his eyebrows, staring at Jane and brushing crumbs from his cravat all at once.

'But my brother,' said Jane firmly, 'was known as Fitzpercy – I think I should like there to be some recognition of that. I shall of course pay for the grave and for its upkeep.' She marvelled at her own voice which seemed, to her, to sound like the voice of Henrietta or Snetters. 'I thought, "Charles Stone known as Fitzpercy",' she suggested.

'I shall have to enquire – yes, I shall enquire,' said the gentleman.

'I believe my brother was friendly with one of the family,' she went on. 'A Mr Alexander Percy of S – House.' She had remembered the name which Mr Farquharson in Hampstead had once mentioned to her.

'Indeed – yes,' said the bailiff, and made to beat a hasty retreat, after thanking Mr Digby for his hospitality.

'We are off tomorrow,' said Fred. 'I shall, of course, pay your employer's servants for the services they have rendered to us. It was Mr Charles's last wish that he should be buried here – we are only fulfilling that – we could not wait for permission from the present Lord Percy. I hope you will convey that message.'

'Of course, Sir.' The man's manner had changed slightly after the magic words 'Alexander Percy' had been mentioned. Then he was off.

'I hope that is the last we ever see of them,' said Jane.

'Jane, are you sure you are well? You look a little pale?' said Fred.

'No, I am all right, Fred. I want to leave this place now.'

He left her to her thoughts and later she said 'Goodnight' to him and went off with Polly to the little room to lie down, if not to sleep.

It was only much later, back in London when Salton was in danger of becoming another dream, that Jane said more to Fred about Charles. She remembered that line little Miss Landon had tossed into the conversation, it seemed years ago, at Vine House. 'She is far from the land where her young hero sleeps.' It was not quite true. Charles was with her wherever she went, but not a dead man, nor a lover, nor a sad ghost – but part of Mama, Mama's child. The funeral had been in the wrong place for Mama, at the wrong season. Salton was not a place Mama had ever loved, she was sure. The Salton of her dreams had been full of menace and dread and fear – Mama's Salton. Whoever that dream had come from, it had come from the past. The presence of Fred, who had taken so much out of her hands, enabled her to know it *had* all been real.

He urged her to take a holiday and offered Vine House once more where she could go with the boys for their summer vacation. It would, he thought, take her mind off her grieving, and his servants could amuse the children if they got too much for her. Mrs Ogilvie needed a rest too. The latter had sat for hours thinking over the past and trying to fit in her knowledge of the young Elizabeth Stone with the revelation of that past.

In his letters Hal seemed equally stunned. Jane had not, of course, mentioned anything about her own special

350

feelings for Charles, but had alluded to Louisa Collins's sister-in-law's mother, old Mrs Smith, and the link with Charles through this. Hal was concerned for his niece and most grateful to his friend Frederick Digby for taking matters in hand. Jane had not yet told him about the journey to Salton and the funeral. Neither could she tell Hal – who had never wanted to talk about his sister – of her own feelings for her mother. The obscure sense she had had of a 'shape' in her head – the shape of her mother and of her mother's past and of Charles was too obscure to convey to anyone.

She resolved to read through Charles's papers and notebooks which had been brought in a trunk from Fred's house in Bloomsbury and were waiting for her at her uncle's. Her own writings seemed trivial.

When she did finally summon up the courage to read the poems of which the books were full, she found very little of a personal nature. All was expressed in images and symbols which were the more powerful for not being too explicit. There were descriptions of young men, it was true, but they were set against classical landscapes for the most part. A separate notebook contained his 'Gothick Pieces', and these eluded her. They were of uneven quality. Powerful descriptions of states of mind and visions of a meaning beyond the everyday world almost gave the impression that they had been composed after opium, but they were written in a clear back hand. Some of them were, she was sure, of dreams he had had. Perhaps they had both inherited this capacity for dreaming of great beauty and power. Yet he had scribbled over many of them: 'Work this up' or 'What does it mean?' and they were sketches for poems or essays rather than essays themselves. His work would need a good deal of editing and she doubted that she was the person to do it.

351

Mr Bruce or Mr Hood should be approached, she decided. There was no one long sustained piece, except for the last thing he had written – which was itself unfinished. In it he seemed to envisage a world where events on earth were paralleled with events of another world of souls who had reached beyond the world of the senses to a realm of spiritual powers. She was troubled and half baffled.

Finally, she wrote two letters, one to Mr Hood (who Fred said would be the best person to help her), and one to Charlotte Howard, asking if the offer of the post in the Fulham school in the autumn was still open. She did not tell even Fred of this until she had heard from Charlotte.

Her uncle wrote again, this time with the news that they intended to stay in Paris en route from Italy in late October or early November. In his letter her uncle also mentioned Philip March who was, he said, now editing a magazine for emigrés in Italy, an idea which Mr Leigh Hunt had had before him. There was apparently a large circle of readership for such an undertaking. 'Why do you not join Edith and me?' urged Hal. 'You will be in need of a change after all you have been through. Your aunt and I are very conscious that we have not been of any help to you at this difficult time.'

But Jane preferred to go to Vine House. Somehow Italy or Paris, at the moment, would be too far from her preoccupations. She did not want her feelings to be jerked away from her in case they returned unresolved. Now was the time to live calmly and quietly. Perhaps it would be a good idea to put together some of her own unpublished pieces – Fred was always urging her to suggest it when she consulted with Hood about Charles's work. She must keep busy. Enforced idleness would be no answer. She owed it to Charles to keep going. But she often woke in

352

the early morning and would think: What is to become of me? Often, too, she would find herself thinking of her own father, who had seemed, somehow, set apart from his wife and her children. He, too, was to be mourned. Surely he must have known about Lord Percy and his wife's past, if not about his wife's child? How sorry she was now for him, that reserved, but kind, man, who had rescued her mother and done his best to make her happy. Perhaps she was more like her father than she had supposed? 'Dear Papa, forgive me,' she murmured at night when sleep would not come. 'Forgive me for being thoughtless. If you are anywhere now in this universe except in my head and memory, forgive me for not having loved you enough.'

Mrs Ogilvie found her sitting before her work-table with its ink-stand and the smooth quire of paper as yet untouched since Charles's death.

'I think you need a change, Miss Jane,' she said severely, but kindly. 'It's all been too much for you. I heard you creeping round last night. Were you unwell?'

'No, Mrs Ogilvie – it was just that I could not sleep.' She shifted the inkwell an inch or two and then put it back in place. 'I must work. It is no good my sitting here thinking about – about Mama – and my brother – '

She looked down at her notebook – it seemed so long ago, but was only a few weeks since she had sat planning her next article. Would the other publication want that? The thought of living here with the family forever when Uncle Hal returned, with only memories of Charles, filled her with foreboding, even if she were ever able to write again.

Mrs Ogilvie stole away and Jane forced herself to start a letter to Mr Hood, and then to begin to copy the poems in Charles's notebook. At least it was work, and she

353

began as carefully as she could to transcribe his writing, which itself gave her a pang, remembering his short letters to her which she had kept in her jewel box. A year ago now and all the world was dark. It was no good promising yourself you would be brave and look to the future. The days had to be filled.

She worked for a week at the copying. The calm that had come in Salton began to desert her. That had been an acceptance of the past. This now was a fear of the future. Hal's eventual letter did not help. How could it? He was sincerely sorry about her brother, but too far away from any knowledge of her mother to understand the situation of her troubled heart.

Snetters offered, in a long letter, to have Jane back for a holiday in Norfolk. Jane knew she would have to see her one day and would have to discuss her mother with the older woman. There might be something more she could tell her of Elizabeth Stone's life, but it was not yet time. She replied to her, saying that she was to go for some time to Hertfordshire and that she was thinking of taking up governessing in a private academy in the autumn.

Slowly the idea of some expression of her grief, which would be worthy of both Charles and her mother, began to crystallize in her mind. It was Salton that began it. She kept seeing the place – the distant wild cliffs and the wood and the strange, ruined hall – and seeing the child Charles living there. What if she could write of that – a story that would enter into the mind of a child reared in such a place? She let it lie in her mind having a sure instinct that she was not yet ready to write it.

Fred had left her alone, had taken up the task of settling Charles's estate, such as it was, and conferring

354

with the distant cousin about a gravestone. She had left it to him.

The boys arrived back from Mr Macdonald's, looking forward to their stay in the country. Jane begged Mrs Ogilvie to accompany them, but she said she preferred to stay in the London house with Emily. Polly would go with Jane, and Fred's servants would help to oversee the lads.

'They're a right handful, Miss Jane. I do hope you are well enough to take them on. I know Mr Digby's a real gentleman and gey helpful, but it won't be much of a holiday for you with those three. Thank goodness their mama and papa are to return soon.'

'Never mind, Mrs Ogilvie, it will take my mind off other things – and I need some fresh air and walks – it will be just the thing for me,' she replied, trying to convince herself.

A letter from Charlotte that very morning had pleased her. Her friends would still be delighted if she were to join them in their venture, but were not yet quite sure of their financial position. The idea of independence was attractive, but Jane knew it would mark a change in her life. Charles would recede and recede as the duties crowded upon her – she saw it happening and was already anticipating it. She scolded herself: You must not live in the past. Your mother is dead and Charles is dead – you must work, you must work . . . Somehow the idea of working in the Fulham Academy was not as attractive as continuing to write. Yet she did not want to stay in London. What should she do? Must she burn all her boats? She hesitated before writing to confirm Charlotte's offer and was still hesitating when she arrived in the mail coach in Hertfordshire with Polly and the boys and saw the familiar brick house and the gardens, mellow in the

355

late August sun. Fred, having been there for some days, was waiting for them all in the courtyard.

'I have good news from Hood,' were his first words to her. He seemed determined to be cheerful and ceremoniously shook the boys' hands. 'Sausages in the kitchen for you, my lads,' he declared. 'And you can see the stables and go out with young Jones tomorrow.'

Fred had their holiday all worked out for them, and Polly and Jane went up to their rooms. Jane determined to discuss Charles's poems and even her own idea with Fred that evening. She had brought the notebooks with her.

'But why did he write to *you*? I wrote to him – Mr Hood – two weeks ago with the idea. I suppose he thinks that women are not worthy of replies?'

'No – no, I saw him in London before I left – the fellow is in love and full of his Miss Reynolds. I mentioned your plan and he said he would write to me, as I told him you were to visit here.'

'It is kind of you, Fred,' she said. She felt a little uneasy with him now that life had resumed its accustomed ways.

'We shall talk it over after dinner. I see you wish to be business like. How is your writing going along?'

'At first I felt I could never write again, but then I *have* been thinking about a story. I'd rather not talk about it until I see how it is shaping; it seems sometimes a sort of disloyalty to write of him as though he were just a figment of my imagination. But I am not writing of Charles, but of an imaginary child in that place, Salton. I will think about it whilst I am here, Fred.'

It was only one evening after the boys had gone up to what Fred called their quarters – they had been romping round like young colts at last free of school and the Town – that Fred returned again to the subject of Jane's own

356

work. He had deliberately avoided the subject of Charles, apart from the mundane details of the possessions and the papers and the arrangements over the gravestone, and Jane had been glad. She was still in that limbo of regret and shock and had consciously decided not to allude to other feelings to Fred. Her state of mind was curious. Her dreams had been of standing on a shore and seeing a small boat go out further and further away from her towards a distant horizon and watching it go without a word or a sign as it became a speck on the rim of the earth. And in waking life, even as she sat with Fred over a simple meal, she seemed to be to herself on a shore, alone. Only with difficulty at first did she make conversation. Fred was tactful and talked of his garden and his house, waiting for her to say more and resolved that if she did not, he would remain silent. He urged again that she collect her pieces together, even as he agreed with her that her new idea was good. She looked at him in the fading evening light and felt he, too, was remote and that the shore she stood on was a solitary one. Then – 'I have decided to work for Charlotte Howard,' she said at last, her face averted and her hands fiddling with a little twig of vine stripped of its grapes that lay untouched on her plate. Fred poured her a glass of his best brandy and was silent for so long that she thought he had not heard, or was angry.

'I must work – I feel I must repay Uncle Hal's kindness – I can't imagine sitting for ever in his house when he returns – and if I hadn't come to London I expect I should have been working in Norwich. Snetters would have found me some wool merchant's family.'

'But if you go to the school you will not be able to go on with your writing,' said Fred. 'Is it that Philip March's decision not to take any more from you has made your

357

mind up for you? I think Hood *is* interested in your stuff, you know. He is rather whimsical, but he has a good head on his shoulders and he told *me* he was interested. If you could add a few pieces to the ones you already have, that would probably impress him and he would take some more.'

'It is not just that – I must keep busy. It – hurts less, when I am busy.'

'Yes, I know,' he said gently.

They were walking round the garden at the back of the house the next day. Johnny had been climbing the wall over by the park and had fallen and scraped his knee and Jane had made a fuss of him. The other two boys were in the stables with the coachman and planning a fishing expedition on the morrow. 'They are happy, I think,' she said. 'It is good of you, Fred – the little one does miss his mother.' She tried to stop thinking of mothers and little boys. How *could* her mother have left her own son even if she had expected eventually to rejoin him?

'They will soon be back,' replied Fred. 'I remember feeling very sorry for myself at that age when they sent me away to school. But I suppose it cannot have done too much harm in the end.'

'I used to wish I were a boy,' said Jane. 'Papa would have liked a son.' She was thinking, and if I had been a boy, what should I be doing now? I *should* have liked Fred though, as a friend.

'I suppose that if we had to work for our bread as the common people do we should not be plagued with questions about what we should do with our lives,' Fred said, looking thoughtful. 'They wanted *me* to go into the Law – and then when I decided against that, to go into the Church – a living near here – I think I could have done it – but, of course, I took it too seriously. Then I wanted to

358

farm and I'm still interested, though my brother is the one with the land. All I can do is keep an eye on my City investments and *cultiver mon jardin*. I'm ashamed when I think of all there is to do in the world. But I didn't want to be a soldier or a missionary or in politics. I ought to have taken my legal studies more seriously – what a misspent youth. Or perhaps I should have stayed and caroused with all those bachelors in Oxford.'

'You seem a little low in spirits yourself,' offered Jane, glad to talk of someone other than herself.

'Oh, Jane, this summer has disturbed us all – I'm not made of rock, you know.'

'What you did for me was – something wonderful – how could I have got through it all, Fred? If I thank you it sounds ridiculous and you didn't even know him, you needn't have gone with me, helped me. I *do* thank you, Fred. I seem to have grown old to myself in the last few weeks – everything has been turned on its side – I was foolish – no, don't disagree – I *know* I was foolish. Perhaps now I can learn to live soberly and find some place for myself. I think sometimes, but it is egoistic, that I was destined to meet him, that it was a lesson for me – but what could it have been meant to tell me? I can't forget him. I know I shan't ever forget those feelings – but why did it have to end like that, Fred? Charles was punished, but did I have to be punished, too?'

For answer Fred said: 'Don't grow up too quickly, Jane. Youth is over before we know we are a little wiser, and we go on making mistakes. I wanted to say it before – but it was, it seemed selfish – what I was telling you in London before you discovered your brother. I have to say it again because it would be wrong for me to be perpetually at your side when I can't ever ask you to marry me. But I wish I *could* ask you!'

359

'Can't we still be friends? You are not like Philip – what if I'd gone away with Philip or become his mistress? – I know it could have happened – because I was miserable. Then I would have felt even worse and should have denied the feelings I had for Charles.'

'Can you not feel for him now as a brother, Jane, and mourn that? It is hard, I know – '

'Oh, yes – I *do* feel now he is a brother to me in my mind – I am mourning a brother now, not a lover, Fred – I should still mourn him if I had never felt what I did, but it is all such a waste and that seems selfish, too. It was *his* life and I wanted him for myself. Is love always so selfish?'

'I am sorry he died – and angry he died, but I am glad he was your *brother* – how could I not be glad? You have been doubly orphaned,' he went on. He wanted to say, I love you, even if I should not. I do love you. He wanted to say, I shall wait for you but you cannot wait for me. Life is hurrying you by and we shan't be able to sit here together year after year, for you will go away and someone else will claim you. Some young man who will expunge your Charles in the end, through sensuality or marriage. Instead he said: 'It is not a brother you need now, Jane.'

He looked at her tenderly and she lowered her glance. He said, a little shyly, 'Clara, you see, was never independent – she depended upon men for her feelings of worth. That is why I know you must carry on with your work, and go to Miss Howard's, if you must, but I don't advise it.'

'You are right – you are talking to me as though we were equals.'

He stood up and made up his mind to speak as she remained sitting on the little rustic seat. 'I love you, Jane Banham, and I have no right to love you – and especially

360

after all you have suffered. But I say "I love you", though I am not free to say it. You are my equal in love.'

'I *would* live with you, Fred,' she said timidly. 'I know you are not like Philip – you don't divide the world of women into the virtuous and the fallen. One day I could live with you, Fred. I like you so much – but my feelings are all in a whirl.'

'Of course.' He sat down and took her hand. 'I should not have said it – forgive me. I care for you, I shall always care for you, would never desert you. I am *proud* of you. I should not trouble you with my feelings – you must not tempt me. Of course I want to live with you but how can I speak of these things? You probably think I am an old man! Well, I am seventeen years older than you, I admit – I know that even if I were free, you are a radical in these matters of men and women – we should have a lot to teach each other . . .'

She was upset and squeezed his hand. She felt there was a key somewhere to all this confusion, but did not know where to look for it or what sort of key it was.

'It is better for a time that we do not see each other,' Fred said, keeping her hand in his. Jane felt desolated.

'I suppose you are right,' she said, and her voice trembled. She needed comfort and there was, apparently, no comfort anywhere. She felt she had lived years and years since the day when Charles had told her he could never love her. But had she wanted him to love her, or only to accept the feelings she had for him? Something was still developing within her, she knew, the 'shapes' of her mother and her mother's past and of Charles. Yet here stood Fred, a live person, a man – who said he loved her!

She wanted – had always wanted – a marriage of two minds. Could she ever find a man whose mind would grow into hers and into whose mind hers might grow? Fred was interested in her mind as well, though she knew he wanted her body, too. She felt his nearness and her own virgin state acutely. 'I understand,' she said finally, not sure whether she did.

He tried to speak lightly now. 'Come – let us go and round up those boys and fill them with plum cake, and *I* should like some tea. Tell your Polly to bring it into the library for us, and the lads can go and fill themselves up in the kitchen.'

Johnny came running up then and Fred saw how the child took Jane's hand and how she bent towards him and listened solemnly to his talk and how the child trusted her. It made him long even more for her, but he resolved to put away any daydreams he had had of one day seeing her as mistress of Vine House for it could not be, and he must leave her alone to find her own life and future without him. He must not ask her to live with him either. The world would find no excuse for her and would be too strong for them both. If she had been anyone but Jane! But she was Jane and must be allowed to be free. He recognized, with astonishment, that he was lonely, he who had always been so self-sufficient – for he had had to be, even as a young man, aghast at the failure of his love and his marriage. Yes, he was lonely. And he desired her with senses sharpened, not dulled, by the passage of years.

He wished that there had been some revolution in Jane's emotions, too, now that she had been cruelly forced to admit that her love for Charles Fitzpercy could not have been consummated even if he had lived – doubly impossible because of the man's nature and also his relation to her. And indeed had she not said to him: 'I am mourning a brother now, not a lover?'

To keep his spirits up, he resolved to move heaven and earth to hurry up young Hood and get him to commission an edition of Charles's poems. That would keep Jane busy and enable her to understand her dead brother the better.

When Jane had gone back to London he sat alone in his quiet house and considered divorcing his wife. He had grounds in plenty, but they were distasteful to him and he did not blame Clara. Somehow or other he had failed her. Someone else might have been able to keep her. And divorce was a prolonged and difficult business and would drag her in the mud. He did not mind for himself, but for her it would be a future existence of moving from *pensione* to *pensione* away from many of her friends, the prey, as she grew older, of irresponsible young men who thought a divorcee was easy game. If he had been going to do that, it should have been years ago when she had first left him. It did not matter so much in Italy, of course, amongst the expatriates there and in France, but she would probably have to cut herself off from England for good. Perhaps she would not mind that. He had always paid her an allowance – and even stinted himself – because he felt he was the cause of her miseries. If there were anyone else, of course, who would want even now to risk it and marry her, he would divorce – but he did not think there was. What a hypocrisy all their laws were, when all he and she had both wanted was love. But it had never worked. Even at the beginning he had seen he had made a mistake. Jane was not the only person to have mistaken the object of her passion.

Jane found it difficult to work on her return to London after she had taken the boys back to Dr Macdonald's. Jimmy was to go to Eton next half. All that was to be arranged when Hal returned. The date fixed for that

363

return was to be mid-November. Hal had decided to buy a house in a pleasant suburb away from the city smoke and to leave Lincoln's Inn Square where his house was only rented on a short lease from a barrister friend. This was communicated to Jane in a long letter which was waiting for her on her return from Vine House. He had various plans – a house with extensive gardens whither he might go daily to the City, keeping a *pied à terre* at his office for those nights he had to spend in London. His plans were detailed and Edith, he said, was delighted. Italy had transformed her health and little Betsey was as brown as a berry. It was a miracle, and he intended to take no more risks on their return. Privately Jane thought that the absence of housekeeping and the absence of the noisy boys might have been just as responsible for the change in her prospects. Edith had had a good long rest!

The days passed quickly as September saw the summer to a gentle close. It was misty, but not cold, and the inevitability of winter was not yet a fact. Two months, three months, since the death of Charles and no one had been apprehended. Neither had Jane cared to visit Rebecca or Daisy. They belonged to what seemed now another age, another time. Instead she wrote to them thanking Daisy for all she had done. There had been a letter from Farquharson, a kind and good letter which had made her cry. They had heard the story of the attack and its consequences when they returned to London from his wife's parents in Hampshire – it had been reported in the *Chronicle*. Jane replied but decided not to acquaint the couple with the fact that Charles had been her brother. What good would that do anyone now? She felt listless and it was an effort to settle down to her writing which had just reached the stage where ideas had to be moulded into actions and scenes. It would need a Scott or a Byron to do justice to her brother. But she would try.

She struggled to imagine the rough lives of the cottagers and the moors and the village and the ever-present sea at Salton, and to follow the growing boy, with all his sense of being abandoned, amidst his awakening feelings. It was difficult to imagine the life of a boy and she almost gave it up, but gradually something seemed to be shaping under her pen of which she was not completely ashamed.

Hood's letter came as a surprise, and a welcome one. He commissioned her to select what she thought the best of Charles's poems for a small limited edition which he was willing to publish. It would be a difficult undertaking, but a more thorough perusal of them ought to help her own story. She had the battered trunk they had brought from Charlotte Street to Fred's house and on to her, and one day after receiving Hood's letter she sat down to begin to go through it all again. There was so much, and much of it indecipherable – notes, bundles, rewritings. She began with the easier notebooks and saw, with fascination, how he had developed his themes. He had read avidly, and in French, too, and the poems were interspersed with jottings. There were, however, no letters he had received and no sketches of letters to anyone. Probably he had burned them as he went along. Apart from his writings he would seem to have had no existence. There was no record of gambling debts or appointments, no proper journal, but there was a little exercise book written in France with remarks upon destiny and Napoleon and much annotation of philosophical themes. His education had not been neglected.

She wrote back to Hood accepting the commission and sending him the old piece on the City churches. It was long enough and would give him an idea of her style. She added a new ending – a short paragraph on mortality and

365

the forgotten dead. Fred had wanted her to gather together her own pieces and when she re-read them they seemed to emanate from an unknown person, a hopeful, excited, surprisingly confident person. She must have changed, for no longer did London seem to her to be full of unknown adventures, nor her own life full of promise. All that was over. London – or life – had been too much for her, she felt. She had been untried and ardent and found life full of interest, and that enthusiasm had been conveyed in her little sketches. How long would it be before she could ever feel that enthusiasm again? The idea of Charles had spurred her on, but she had had other feelings even in the midst of her infatuation for him. Would even those feelings never return?

She decided to pay a visit to Henrietta and Charlotte for she had not set eyes on them since Charles's death. She had written to Charlotte about the funeral but had said nothing of her true relationship to Charles. She would not take Polly with her but would order Uncle Hal's carriage and go to Fulham in a respectable convey-ance as befitted a future governess. She must accept that offer at least. There would surely be time to work on Charles's poems after the day's tasks were over. She would put aside her own writing for the moment and wait for the settling of her feelings before she began the second draft of *The Boy on the Shore* which she was still deter-mined to write one day. The trouble was that the real Charles kept obtruding himself into her vision of him and she was frightened of traducing him. A story was a story, but when the inspiration came from a lived life, it was hard to know how to present it. Only by losing the 'real' Charles for ever would she write that story to her own satisfaction, as a memorial to him. And the real Charles who had died in her arms seemed dreamlike. Dreamlike now as a lover, exorcized by his burial, but as a brother the source of fresh pain.

'My dear,' murmured Charlotte when Jane was announced. They were in the first-floor room with the balcony and Henrietta was not in evidence.

'I am sorry I did not come before and you must tell me if I am in the way,' she began.

'Jane, you are thinner – that terrible experience – if you do not wish to speak of it, I will not. Of course you are not in the way. It is my little hour of rest. Henrietta is playing some music to the boarders. We have got a new teacher of painting you know.' Charlotte was nervous and Jane saw it stemmed from embarrassment.

'I don't mind speaking of – Charles,' Jane replied as firmly as she could. 'I'll tell you all about it one day – but I really came about your offer. You see, I believe I am to be taken on to help edit Charles's – Mr Fitzpercy's – writings, by Mr Hood. Please do not think me disloyal to the *New London* but – '

'I think we must talk of the *New London* – and of Philip,' replied Charlotte and she disposed herself on a small sofa near the window and patted the chair next to it. 'Sit down, Jane. Of course you must not mention the word disloyalty when Christopher had the gall to tell you you were not wanted any more. Philip had grandiose ideas for that issue.'

'I have never seen it. I have been much away.'

'You have never seen it because it has not come out!'

'Why? What has happened?'

'Philip had decided to start up this new thing in Italy – did you not hear? – a journal for emigrés, à la Hunt. Christopher moved to Waterloo Place and then Bruce left us. Then Christopher found he could not meet his bills. He wrote to Phil. And do you know what the reply was?

367

"Let us forget the *New London* for the present. Come over to Italy with me and we will edit the *New Florentine* together!" Of course Christopher does not want to go abroad. He is a very English sort of person. All that languor and laziness! So – it is just – *finito* – all over – and Philip is there in Italy running around collecting copy from hundreds of poets who have declared themselves desirous of publication. He even touched Landor for some money. No wonder Chris is angry – and you too, my dear – you are better out of it all. I always thought you ought to write something more expansive, from your heart rather than your observation.'

'Yes, that is what I am trying to do now,' replied Jane, a little at sea in all this information, which cast a new light on Philip March. Had Italy gone to his head? But there was more to come. Charlotte seemed agitated.

'You cannot imagine what has happened to Phil. It's common knowledge now, I believe. He has conceived a grand passion and gone completely mad.'

'Who? An Italian lady?' Jane was remembering the stories of Byron and his Italian love.

'No, no.' She paused. 'The lady is the wife of your Mr Digby, I believe.'

Jane was about to say, He is not 'my' Mr Digby, but the stronger import of her friend's words then caught up with her. 'You mean – *Clara* Digby, Fred's wife?'

'The same.'

Jane got up in agitation and walked to the window and looked out at the new houses going up with their stucco shining in the sun. She turned round again to Charlotte. 'But I do not think Fred Digby knows,' she managed to get out. She must tread carefully.

'It is not the first time the lady has conducted herself indiscreetly,' Charlotte went on. 'But I have never known

Phil to lose his head before. It has been going on for several months I gather. He is doing no harm to her reputation as she has none – but it seems to have advanced beyond mere dalliance – well, to put it plainly – ' She paused. 'Has your uncle said nothing about it in his letters?'

'No, but he would not wish to gossip. Edith might, but would not think it perhaps suitable for my ears.'

'It was a shock,' Charlotte said and got up again and went to stand near the chimney-piece. 'It seems the lady is *enceinte* – and what will happen now?' Charlotte blushed.

'She is still married to Fred!' cried Jane.

'So the infant when it comes will be a little Digby,' said Charlotte grimly. 'What a confounded *pagaille* Phil has landed himself in. He is living on her, must be, for he will have used up his funds on this new venture. So, there he is – living on Fred Digby's money. What do you think Digby will do when he discovers?'

'I don't know,' replied Jane, feeling rather weak. How tasteless. Yet if Philip March really loved Fred's wife . . . Why should we not ascribe the finer emotions to others? He must be in love with her, he who had been so careful not to get trapped. 'I believe she is still very attractive,' Charlotte continued. 'The sort of woman men like. Why has Mr Digby not divorced her years ago? He could have done.'

'I believe he is still quite fond of her, and was sorry about his failure to make her happy. And, of course, it takes years to get a divorce.'

'Others would call him a fool,' said Charlotte. 'We had someone like that in our family and there was no end of a fuss. The family paid her off to get rid of her reputation.

369

Reputations are catching, you know. It was one of my uncles – some woman had bewitched him.'

Jane was silent, thinking of her own mother and how the story might appear the other way round, so to speak. Charlotte was never so haughty as when she spoke of her noble relations.

They drank a little tea and then Henrietta came up towards the end of Jane's visit.

'You have heard the news?' she asked brusquely.

'Yes.'

'What do you think of it then? Philip is a fool in my opinion. That woman will never make him happy – nor he her, I shouldn't think. I cannot understand why that Frederick Digby has never disowned her.'

'Surely we must not be too hard on our own sex,' suggested Jane. 'After all, she was not happy, and perhaps now she is.' She was thinking that Philip had certainly found someone who was 'ruined' and wondered whether it mattered. Jane also had the impression that perhaps Henrietta was now less desirous for her to join the school, though Charlotte still seemed to want her.

'Now we have Mr Fuller for drawing we should be able to charge more for the term's board and so we could afford more leisure for ourselves and another governess,' said Charlotte, looking to her friend for confirmation.

'Are you sure you really wish to undertake this work, Jane? It is different for two dried up spinsters like us – surely you will hope to marry,' was Henrietta's reaction.

'You are not dried up,' was all Jane said at first. Then, 'If you think I would not be up to it . . .'

'No, no – but your writing?' Henrietta went on, 'Let us say we wait until Christmas to see what our bills are like. We could not yet offer you very much.'

'And now it is my turn to go down to the pupils,' said

370

Charlotte briskly. She squeezed Jane's hand affectionately as she went out.

'How do you think she is taking this news of my brother?' Henrietta asked as soon as a decent interval had elapsed.

'She was fond of him, certainly – but as you once said to me, "Charlotte will never marry." '

'Were you very cut up over Mr Fitzpercy?' asked Henrietta.

What could Jane reply to that? The secret of their relationship was something she was going to keep to herself. It would come out later, as these things were liable to, through some mixture of gossip and speculation.

Henrietta persisted. 'How did it happen? Was it some-one he knew who killed him?' She was cruder than Charlotte.

'Some ruffians attacked him – we do not know the reason why,' replied Jane.

'Was he what they call a "Greek"? – Julia hinted that,' said Henrietta.

'I suppose so.' Jane's voice trembled a little but she kept her composure. Soon after that she rose to go.

'We shall let you know definitely by Christmas, about the post. Your uncle will want you at home when he returns. Oh, and tell him we could take the youngest of the boys next year. We're planning on teaching some small boys – not for boarding – the girls' mamas would not like it – but we've had various enquiries about a day school. It seems many families are moving out of town in this direction.'

'Uncle is thinking of settling in Richmond or Highgate or Blackheath,' said Jane, glad to turn the subject of conversation away from Charles. But Henrietta returned to Frederick and his troubles.

371

'Do you think Fred Digby will *do* anything?'

'What can he do? He's not the sort of person who would fight a duel over his wife,' said Jane.

'Good grief, I hope not – he'll probably be glad to be rid of her if she and Phil are cohabiting. You can do what you like in Italy – so long as you are English!'

On arriving home there was a letter from Fred. It was simple and to the point: 'I have had a letter from Philip March. He tells me he is in love with my wife and wants to take her on for good. But he has no funds! By the next post one from Clara – she says she is "not well". I may have to go to Italy very soon. When does your uncle Hal return?'

Uncle Hal and his wife were expected back within three weeks and Jane's life would be so much less free. She was looking forward in a way to their return, but also aware that once they returned she would not be able to see Fred on the old footing. Perhaps once he was in Italy, Fred would send Philip packing but it seemed unlikely. Fred was morally strong, and intelligent, but would even he offer Philip money to keep his own wife? What difference would it make anyway? He would still be married to Clara. There had been a full-length portrait of her at Vine House kept in one of the downstairs rooms that no one seemed to visit. Jane had seen it and mused over it a little. It had been painted on her marriage, about fifteen years before. Most men would have turned it to the wall. It was a strange relationship, that between Fred and his wife, yet Jane was beginning to feel that all human relationships were strange.

Fred was the only person in the world to whom she was close. She did not know what she was going to do or say but she must see him before he left. Accordingly, she

372

walked alone to Bloomsbury Square the next afternoon.
The sun had gone in and there was a light rain. The plane
trees were now beginning to turn yellow and an autumn
wind had rustled the fallen horse chestnut leaves into little
drifts. A few boys were gathering conkers in the square
gardens. Another winter on the way. Would she be always
remembering a lost brother, lost as soon as found, as the
seasons changed? The remembrance seemed daily to
change into the memories of a *brother*, a complete
beloved brother, now lain to rest. All her earlier feelings
for him were remembered but they were not *felt* as they
were remembered. Perhaps it was better so, but it was
sad.

Fred himself opened the door to her. He had been
expecting her, knew she would come.

'Do you have any more news?' she asked as soon as he
had taken her cloak and was standing looking at her with
a strange expression in his eyes. He turned away and
gestured her into the small sitting room. Then, 'She is
pregnant you know. After all these years. It's unbelieva-
ble – but perhaps that will make her happy. You know, in
law, it will be my child?'

'Yes. Fred – I came to say – ' She stopped for a
moment. Fred went up to the fireplace, and, after a
moment, said, 'The servants are all away or out. Come sit
by the fire. What a mess, Jane, what a mess!'

'Fred.' Something in the way she said it made him stare
at her, trying to decipher her expression.

'Fred! I want you to – to love me . . . Help me, Fred. I
don't know what to do. I keep thinking of my brother –
and then of you – and even of Philip. Give me a chance
to make you happy, Fred . . . because I want what you
want, Fred. I do. I want to be a real woman – '

He stood looking at her steadily. 'We must not. I can't

373

marry you, dear Jane. Not legally, you know, unless I divorce Clara – and that is a long business.'

'*Because* you cannot – and *because* you would not think me wrong to want it. You didn't think my feelings for Charles were wrong. You understood. Oh, Fred, you will go away and my uncle will return and I must – must know that I am not an oddity, that there is nothing wrong with me, Fred.'

'There is nothing whatever wrong with you, Jane. I should feel angry about all this business in Italy, but I don't. I'm worried, but not angry. I must see it all out.'

'Fred – when are you going to Italy?'

'Soon. I think I *must* go.'

He seemed somehow not unhappy, but dejected, lost, looking into the glowing coals and not at her.

'Help me just once. You can help me – and I you,' she said. She had not known that she was going to say what she was now saying. She had not deceived herself about why she had come but had not known exactly what she must do. Now she knew.

'Are you sorry for me, Jane?'

'No – I am not sorry. It is no one's fault. We are as we are . . . You've made me need you, Fred,' she went on and moved towards him and looked up at his face. 'Something is coming to an end – or a beginning,' she said. 'I don't disavow anything I felt before – for Charles. How could I? All these months – how long is it Fred, since we met? Nearly two years! It was the same day I met Philip March at my uncle's, and the same evening I met you – and saw my brother.' She paused for a moment and saw his face soften. Fred was not Philip and he was not Charles, and he was restraining his feelings out of notions of duty and honour. She must not fail now. Her senses were stirred by him; a sort of recklessness in her blood mixed too with past suffering.

Fred, the man who loved her, she knew he loved her, was so close and she wanted to make him happy by making herself happy. If Fred rejected her now she would not see him again. What was still left to her, though, was her independence – and if Fred did not reject her, where would that independence be? She would take the risk. The desire for experience was part of it, but also all the promptings of her better self. Fred wanted her. She knew that. She put her hand on his shoulder. He looked down at her as now she looked at him steadily. So different from Charles. Different but very dear to her.

'Make love to me, Fred! On that bed where you made me lie when Charles died, when you wiped my hands.' She put her arms round him.

'I'm not made of stone, Jane. Do you know how I love you and how I want you, day and night? I'm always thinking of you and imagining you're beside me. You mustn't tempt me. *I* should be asking *you*. *You* should be asking *me* to stop. That is how it should go.'

'Yes, I know,' she murmured and she took his hand and kissed it. 'And if that is how you want it, I will stop.'

'Mrs Smith said you were a gypsy,' he said. And then: 'You are a warm-blooded creature, gypsy or no. Would you love me, Jane? I think you might. If I took you upstairs and then where should we be? Is that what you want? Is it?'

'I am, maybe, naughty, but I am not a fool,' she replied. 'Am I not worthy of a little experience?' And she was thinking, Now I must go through with it. Love will make me live again and make Fred live again, too. She could see only a little way ahead. The rest was all dark. 'It is because you love me,' she said. 'Ever after, whatever

375

happens, *you* can ask *me* – if you let me ask you, just this once.'

Oh God, please let her be able to take from Fred, let him want to give to her, the way she wanted to give to him now. Desire was like a river and if it were once undammed it would flow on for ever. Fred must find her through the senses or she would be lost, whirling round on a little piece of water before the dam gate.

He sighed and traced her lips with his finger and she shivered. Then he kissed her eyelids and took her hand and kissed her knuckles. Then he drew her to himself and kissed her mouth and she felt her whole body tingle with the expectation of that continued kiss, and warmth seemed to flow out from her fingertips.

'Must it be on that bed?' he whispered.

'Yes – please let us go there.'

She abandoned herself to him as he sought now her mouth, now her neck and kissed her ear and cheek. She had to raise herself a little on tiptoe as he was a good deal taller, and she thought, How strange, but how pleasant. He smells of brandy and cigars.

Fred put his arms round her and together they walked slowly up the stairs in the silent house and to the little room where she had lain that terrible night.

'Oh, I do adore you, Jane Banham,' he murmured.

'Please, Fred, take me and – love me,' was her reply.

He was almost unmanned at that, for he loved her spirit as well as wanting her body and when he felt that young body, slim and ardent, lying so close to him in the half-light that seeped through the blinds, wonderingly he gazed into the depths of her eyes until she began to caress him.

He was much stronger, much more passionate, than she had imagined in her wildest dreams of this moment – but so was she. 'Receiving' love became irrelevant, for they seemed meshed together in some passionate dance. Oh, how ready she was to accept him, how close she felt to him in some almost impersonal love, as though they were both of them dipping into some overflowing well. Was this then what they called passion? The thought went through her head even as her last defences melted away. Not that, she thought, there had been any needless resistance. Oh this was wonderful, her skin against his, entwined, still rocking . . . She smiled, and when she opened her eyes and looked once more into Fred's she saw tears there. He stayed close to her, breathing more quietly now and murmured something and hid his face against her breast. 'Why did you smile?' he asked. 'Lovely Jane, why did you smile?'

'Because it was so good,' she replied. 'So good – just so right – oh Fred, I can feel you do love me. I feel I could love all the world.'

She tightened her arms around him again. 'Now you have burned your bridges,' he said.

'Yes – because I wanted to.'

'You are wonderful,' he said and gently stroked her arms and smoothed her hair and kissed it and wound it round his fist.

'You made me happy,' she said. 'So happy. I wish I could stay here for ever.'

Fred looked at her and after a moment he said, 'You gave me such pleasure.'

'It was you,' she answered, and thought, It couldn't have been like that with anyone else. And she thought as they lay looking at each other, silent now, It is Fred who is in my arms, Fred, and all the puzzles of existence seemed less puzzling.

'Why does anyone ever want to get up?' she said. 'But I shall have to go, dear, sweet, clever, clever Fred – '

377

'I don't want you to go,' Fred groaned. 'I wish you would stay with me for ever, Jane darling.'

'You will go to Italy, and soon Uncle Hal will return. At least I have had this. I was selfish – will you forgive me for tempting you?'

Yet there was a smile in her voice. At least for an hour or two the complications of their circumstances had receded.

He was thinking, She is made for love. She will go now and find that with others. I cannot hold her. 'If there should be any result of – this – ' he began.

'You mean if I were to find myself with child? I suppose it could happen – what would you want Fred?'

'I should want you and your baby with me in the country. You would live with me. You wouldn't desert me, would you?'

'Then I should be your mistress – I suppose I *am* your mistress now.'

'It is a ridiculous word,' he said. 'How can you be my mistress if I don't pay for your pretty dresses – though I would love to pay for them.'

'And I should like to buy *you* handsome things with the money from my stories.' She sighed. 'I'd like to load you with smoking jackets and signet rings and cravats and everyone would say – she is a wicked girl – debauched – '

'No,' he said. 'You are a good girl and a good lover – what a pity – '

'What?'

'That we cannot *marry* – oh God!'

'Would you still want to marry me?' she said in a small voice.

'Oh, my love – if I didn't before I would now – and I did and I do,' he whispered.

378

'Can't we just be lovers, Fred? I don't want to be owned.'

'I would *like* to be "owned",' he said. 'But you would never be tamed. You have all sorts of things in that mind of yours that I want to understand. You are a revelation. Highly unusual.' He was smiling now. 'Let me look at you again.'

'What time is it?' Rain had darkened the room.

'My clock says five-thirty, I think. Let me look at you by candlelight – ' He lit a candle and stared down at her as she lay on the narrow bed where she had lain before. 'You are so beautiful. I had forgotten how a young woman could look.' He put the candle down on a little table and sat on the bed and kissed her shoulders. 'And yet,' he said, 'it wasn't the most important thing – and so there will be other revelations. I should like to have you sculptured just as you are. Time changes women – and us all – and I should love you if you were not as you are – but, just to remember, your body in bronze, so I could see it every day. So young. I'd put it in a special room and gaze on it.'

'*Don't*, Fred – I don't want to be a statue.'

'But what else could I have?' he said.

'We can't know the future,' she said, sitting up and beginning to button up her petticoat.

'I am not jealous of your Charles any more now,' he said suddenly. 'He was your first love and always will be.'

'And you are my first *lover*,' she said. 'I feel so energetic – is that what lovemaking does to women?'

'Ah – you tire men out. Though you should be *quite* tired yourself!'

The bubble of happiness which Fred had brought her stayed floating above her head as they sat for a moment by the fire in the small sitting room. Yet strangely, it did

379

not blot out the memory of her brother. She had not been able to save *him* – but if she were to have a baby from Fred, she knew she would never desert *that* child!

Am I heartless? she thought. I can still mourn Charles, but this is so different. How can our coming together in the flesh, Fred and I, make such a difference? But it does, it does! Why am I not sad since everything is in the balance – my life and his? 'I believe you when you say you love me,' she said at last. 'Before, I never expected to be loved, I suppose, but I don't think I could be happy now if I had not loved before – and been unhappy before.'

Fred sat in the armchair that had been his father's and Jane leaned against his knees as he stroked her hair. He was thinking that it was a very special coming together and one he could not have had years ago. And she was thinking – I am glad Fred is older than me – it gives me an advantage.

She smiled again at her thought. But how could pleasure be absorbed into life? Was it so powerful because it was forbidden and unusual? I am an adultress, she thought. And I don't care.

'I shall not tell anyone – don't worry, Fred,' she said. 'Just consider what Uncle and Aunt would think!'

'They would not believe it of me,' said Fred.

'Nor of me.'

'Then we are in a private conspiracy.'

'I know what I want to do now,' she said. 'I've made up my mind – I shall write and write and write. I think I know how I shall do my story of Salton – for it's my mother's story, too. I must think about Mama and why she came to grief. *Was* it love, do you think?'

'Jane, you frighten me – when I think of your mother – and of you.'

'But I am not like Mama,' she said. 'And you are not

like that Lord Percy. I expect he wanted to have his cake and eat it.'

'Well, don't I?'

'No – I forced you to eat the cake. I'm so lucky that you wanted it. So lucky.'

Her genuine wonder touched him, but he was frightened still. He did not regret their lovemaking, for it seemed to stand quite separately, like a beacon. But he regretted his own circumstances.

'Now you must go,' he said. 'And I shall write to you from Italy, whatever happens.' He was thinking, I shall *have* to divorce Clara – but he knew that marriage was not really in Jane's mind.

They clung together for a moment before he let her out. A hansom cab was in the square and he called it. 'Look after yourself, Jane, my sweet.'

'And you, darling Fred.' He held her hand for a moment and then she was in the carriage and waving to him and then she was gone.

He could not believe it. He went upstairs to the room where they had lain and sat on the bed and put his head on the pillow which still smelt of her hair. Oh God! – this made everything so much harder. He should not have done it. But he was rather proud of himself. It had been a success. Let tomorrow wait.

Jane's feelings were to fluctuate like powder in a clear water bottle, tipping round and round, sometimes clear, sometimes cloudy. Overwhelmingly though, she was incredulous at her transformation. She thought of Fred's tenderness and his strength and his passion. Something had made her mind up for her and she had walked blindfold but to the right place. Charles would have approved. She knew Charles would have wished her well and, as she thought of him, she saw him in a new light, quite apart from his relationship to her – lonely and gifted and maligned. Loving someone must surely extend one's sympathies to others, and she felt that.

Charles had been a person who too had loved and made love passionately and dangerously. How powerful it made you feel to give by receiving. 'I don't care – I don't care,' she said aloud as she stood brushing her hair and staring at herself in the glass, and she meant she no longer cared whether the claims of passion could ever be reconciled with common sense and the claims of ordinary existence. She was young; she was happy. *She* had made it happen. She had dared to learn her true nature. Now she could leave it all to Fred, herself in his safekeeping whatever happened in the world outside themselves. The face she saw reflected had suffered, perhaps from her own fault. But no longer had she any doubts about her instincts.

Yet, giving up her hard-won semi-independence, slight and precarious as it was, might be another matter. She had wanted the floodgates of passion to open their waters over her and she had not drowned but been borne along in the current. Fred had been borne along with her. She ached for Fred to be by her side again but still she could not forget that women were not free – particularly if they had abandoned themselves – and the world was not full of Fred Digbys. How lucky she had been to find him. Oh she must never lose him now, never!

There was nothing she would be able to say to her uncle and aunt about herself, or to anyone else. In spite of Hal's kindliness and tolerance, he would not understand. Of course, if she had been a young man she thought, there would have been nothing remarkable in her conduct. Men were expected, nay even encouraged, to sow their wild oats; women, never.

She did not want always to be powerful, to command, to be in control – just not to be commanded by anything or anyone not freely chosen by herself. Fred had chosen her. He, more than her equal in intelligence and her equal in passion, had chosen her. She put down her hairbrush and thought back to all Fred had done for her in July and after, without expectation of reward or even of gratitude, and loved him for it. He had made a nightmare bearable, trusted her, understood her. And he had not 'seduced' her. She had seduced him. But then that mattered no longer, for his initiation of her into the mysteries of sensual love had made them true equals, both givers and both receivers.

Later, she went to her bureau and took out a piece of paper given to her by one of Uncle Hal's clerks. On it were the details of her own private income. It was little enough, but it was her own. If the worst came to the worst she could refuse any longer to be kept by Hal, however hard it would be. She imagined working, as young men worked, as a clerk or a notary, but there was no place for women there. All her intentions might come to grief if she found herself pregnant. Her own mother had worked in harder circumstances than hers. Her own ideals might still be shipwrecked on the reefs of necessity. Well, she would at least have tried, even if she could not be entirely free.

She pulled Charles's notebooks towards her and began to read again, and now, as she read, she recognized that he, too, wrote of love and clothed in images and metaphor the riot of his senses. She read on, that day and for the next six. Nothing arrived from Fred and when she took a short walk with Polly by his square she saw the blinds still drawn. He would be in Italy, from where Uncle Hal was returning in two weeks.

383

She sat on at her little table and, in the gathering winter, she began again the story of the lonely boy on the Salton strand.

Hal's boys had been given leave from school to await their parents' arrival and the whole household was agog. Everything that could be cleaned and brushed and washed and wiped had been cleaned and brushed and washed and wiped. Polly and Emily and Cook and William and even Mrs Ogilvie looked as though they had gone through the same process. Jane had moved her table and books back into her own room and gone early to Covent Garden for flowers. There had been no sign of Daisy, so Jane had bought chrysanthemums from another stall, and their scent filled the downstairs rooms. Jimmy and Tommy and Johnny were excitedly rushing every minute to the windows to see when the carriage should arrive. They had heard of the safe arrival on the coast and now the travellers could be expected any minute.

Jane looked in the glass. Did she look different from when Hal had left England? The same face looked out of it as she had seen before, but thinner – the eyes darker, the hair more fashionable. Would they have seen Fred? He had been due in Florence ten days ago, so it was possible. Henrietta had said Philip had gone back to Florence with Clara Digby, and the English colony there would be sure to know.

Mr Simpkins, the head clerk from the City office, was also waiting to greet his master and she found him in a state of great excitement when she went down to the first-floor drawing room. He had remembered, even so, to bring her newspaper for her and presented her with it courteously.

Jane took Johnny aside, for he was getting too excited,

and suggested a game of chess. The candles were lit and she had been beaten by Johnny and they were just about to begin another game when they heard the sound of horses' hooves and a 'whoa there' and a jingle of harness and then silence. Jimmy and Tommy ran down to the door that gave on to the square and the others followed more decorously. Emily opened the door and suddenly the entrance hall was filled with people – Betsey's squeals could be heard and Hal's loud, cheerful voice and there was the sound of trunks being dragged in and the voice of the coachman and his deputy. Johnny went running down too, and Jane stood for a moment alone. She drew a deep breath and then, judging that the children would have been greeted, went slowly downstairs, her hand on the banister. How very long ago it seemed since she had set sight on her tall uncle and his wife and now she saw them looking up towards her, their faces wreathed in smiles.

'Jane – my dear Jane!' shouted Hal. 'My – how grown-up you look – Here's your cousin Jane (to Betsey) and Edie – here she is!'

Her aunt was sitting on a chair in the hall, her children standing round her, jumping up and down with excitement, except for Jimmy who was rather quieter and had grown so much that his mama declared she could not believe it.

Jane went up to Edith and kissed her and Hal shook her hand as though it were the village pump, expressing his great happiness over and over. Edith looked a new woman and Betsey had grown into a tall, beautiful child, her hair dressed *à l'Italienne* and a fashionable cape round her shoulders. Mrs Ogilvie had happy tears in her eyes. The old clerk was then presented and the children told to come down to supper in an hour whilst the trunks were taken up and then there would be presents. They were a happy family, reunited once more. Other talk could wait.

'Well, my dear, we thought we'd find you with a beau or two,' said Hal cheerily. 'We'll talk about that other business later – a bad business – we were shocked, I can tell you. And Mr Digby – he's in Florence. We saw him just before we left.'

Jane's heart struggled up into the cage of her chest like a puppet jerking on a string. But she composed herself.

They were sitting after dinner eating nuts, and Hal had had the port brought up for Simpkins and himself and refused to let the ladies out of his sight. Ogilvie had been prevailed upon, too, to join the party.

'It's like Christmas,' said Tommy, on his mother's lap and quite unlike the tough little schoolboy he usually was.

'There's no hurry, madam. You can take up the reins slowly,' Mrs Ogilvie was saying to Edith. 'It won't take me and the maids – and the new girl – long to settle you all in.'

'You heard about the new house?' said Edith. 'We think we've found just the thing. A nice new villa – quite grand, they say – in Blackheath. A large garden for the boys, and so convenient for the City – but I shall believe it when I see it,' she said to Jane.

The din was indescribable. Only a family who liked each other and one whose master was of a radical cheerfulness could have made so much. Jane was looking at Hal and thinking, Yes, there is a look of Charles there – how could I have missed it? Hal was turning to Simpkins.

'How are Digby's investments? Nothing bad I hope. It came to my mind we'd promised to look into that matter of spices, but he didn't seem to want to talk business last week. I can't blame him.'

386

Edith gave him a warning look, as though to say: Leave that till the children have gone to bed, and he changed the subject.

Jane went to sit next to her aunt when coffee was brought in. Little Betsey was almost asleep and muttered something in Italian when Jane offered to put her to bed.

'Mr Digby said he had seen you and you were well,' said Edith. 'Poor man, I don't know what will become of him – '

'Why? What has happened?'

'Of course, you won't have heard the news – well it is very sad.' She lowered her voice. 'I will tell you when Betsey is settled.'

Jane took the child, now awake once more, and went upstairs to the newly cleaned old 'nursery'. Betsey looked too big now for a nursery, but was finally tucked up there without too many complaints on her part, and Jane went down again. She paused before the drawing room door, and then went in. The boys had gone, too, to their old schoolroom, bribed by the presents which were to be taken up there. Polly came in for a moment with some more coffee and looked across at Jane. They had said little to each other recently. Polly had been busy and Jane had not wanted to discuss the summer with anyone. Mrs Ogilvie was talking to Edith now, but broke off when she saw Jane. Hal was before the great grate with a pipe and with Mr Simpkins sitting stiffly on a Windsor chair at his elbow. Jane went and sat down by Edith.

'My dear – you must tell us all about it – you must have had a dreadful time,' said Edith. 'Hal was amazed – he is still not quite over it – but, there, it's all over now.'

'Yes,' Jane said. 'It was a terrible business.' She wondered how much Mrs Ogilvie had ever guessed about her feelings for her brother.

387

'And you went up to Salton with Mr Digby? How kind he has been. He looked quite ill in Florence last week.'

'Tell me what has happened,' Jane began. Her aunt had the most infuriating way of changing the subject. But she looked very much happier then when Jane had last seen her. Plumper, and with a better colour.

'His wife – Clara – ' Then she stopped.

'Yes – I was told something by Miss Howard,' Jane said once more, patiently.

'She *died* last week, my dear. They are putting it out that it was a decline, but, of course, we knew she – was – in the family way. It was Mr March who had got her to run away with him – met her in Rome . . .'

But Jane stopped her. 'Aunt Edith, you are saying that Fred's – Mr Digby's – wife is *dead*?'

'Yes. I'm afraid so. It is all being hushed up, but we met him just before we left – he'd hurried to Italy when he heard about the affair with March. It was the last straw, I expect. They'd been around Rome and Florence quite flaunting themselves – of course, they talk quite openly of these things in Italy. I'm sorry if I have spoken indelicately – I keep forgetting, dear, that you are unmarried. I must not gossip. Of course, I suppose it is a mercy, the poor woman was rather old for a first child. The villain has gone to pieces, they say. He decamped after the husband arrived. Then Mr Digby fetched him back! Everyone was saying he would stay to bury her and then revenge himself on Mr March – but I don't think that could be true. You remember, dear, last year, people were talking about her. We met her in Rome and Mr March was with her, but of course, we didn't think much of it – '

'She died having a baby?'

'No, no, it was a miscarriage, and something went wrong

afterwards. We had not known she was "in that condition". But she died quite suddenly – I don't know what happened after the funeral to that young man. Poor woman! If she'd had a child from her husband maybe they wouldn't have separated.' Jane said nothing after listening to Edith but went to her room to write to Fred. He must be in a terrible state. The widower and perhaps the real mourner. Fred, who had once loved his wife.

That very morning Jane had received confirmation that she, at least, was not 'in that condition' and she had thanked heaven for it. Poor Clara – at last to have achieved happiness and then to have everything taken away. Why did she have to die? It should have been Philip who died. How dangerous it was to be a woman. But then – and strangely enough it was only then! – she realized that Fred would now be free.

It took several days for the house to return to normal and by then Jane had told Hal in greater detail – although suitably edited – about her discovery of Charles Fitzpercy, and they discussed his relationship to her and to Hal. Hal kept saying, 'God bless my soul, poor Betsey – poor boy – I can't believe it.' When Jane had told him also that she was editing his poems for another review and that she herself no longer wrote for Mr March's, he shook his head.

'I'm afraid the young man took too much upon himself,' he said. 'Still, Janey, you got your little pieces in print.'

Wisely she said nothing about her new literary plans and cut her account of Salton down to a minimum.

'If I had only been here . . . What a time you must have had – aye, well, it's all over now. But then there's poor Fred's lady?'

Now he was 'poor Fred'.

'And between you and me, I'm a bit worried about his investments. There were problems over the imports. It's about time I got back to work.'

'You mean Mr Huskisson and the new bill?' she asked.

'Bless me, where did you hear about that?'

'Oh, Simpkins brought the papers faithfully to me. I tried to understand it – money seems to be a very peculiar property.'

'It is, but I've hopes of righting all that. Tell me now, how have the boys been? No real trouble? I knew you wouldn't say even if there were.'

'Johnny took a little longer to settle, but I think they've learned something, Uncle.'

'You've grown thinner, Jane,' he observed. 'I suppose it was all that trouble in the summer.'

'He looked like Mama,' she said, and brought out the locket with its little miniature. 'This is the picture he had.'

He took it from her and peered at it. 'That's how I remember her,' he said finally. 'It's my sister all right. Thank God Father and Mother never knew.'

She took it back from him.

'Mrs Ogilvie says you've been a great help,' he said, clearing his throat and glad not to dwell on the sad story. 'Now you must enjoy yourself! You've been neglected, but we're grateful for all you've done. What about a little holiday back home? You must be tired of London! And then by spring I've good hopes our new house will be ready.'

'I am quite happy, Uncle. I want to go on with the editing I told you of.'

'All work and no play,' he observed. 'Edie met some of her mother's family out in Italy. They're coming back home – lots of cousins – they'd launch you in London all right.'

390

'Thank you, Uncle, you are very kind, but I am really a bit old now for being "launched",' she laughed.

'We shall see, we shall see,' he replied.

She felt under an obligation to appear as if nothing had happened to her. What was it to them but an unfortunate incident from the past? Even Fred's tragic married life was 'a pity'. They were kind and tolerant, but they were not her sort of people. She must hold out for her independence. She went back to her work. She had not known what to write to Fred, so had just sent a short note to Bloomsbury Square to greet him on his return. 'Dearest Fred – I am thinking of you. I am so sorry about Clara. Jane.' She added a postscript: 'There is nothing else to worry about,' and underlined it. At least Fred could be spared that.

'Letters for you, Jane,' shouted Tommy, a few days later. He came rushing up the stairs making the most of his specially granted holiday. There were two letters. One with an Italian frank and another from London.

She took them quickly from the child. Fred's handwriting on the foreign one. Still abroad then. Upstairs to her room for blessed peace. The children were shouting around the house – their parents had brought them mock swords and uniforms and the air was constantly cut to invisible ribbons with the dashing swordsmen's slicings and parries. In her room the sounds were muted. She shut the door, sat on her bed and opened the letter from Fred. He must know she had heard his news from Hal. Yes – he assumed she had, for his note began: 'You will have heard the news . . .

I think I have now done my "duty". Jane, will you marry me? Not because of what happened in Bloomsbury Square – though

391

I should like to repeat that! Now that I *can* ask you, I am afraid. If I waited, I should be even more afraid. It is not Clara's death, but that I fear you have regrets. In spite of your feelings about the relations between the sexes – in spite of your brother – in spite of my bereavement – there is nothing else I want in the world, it seems. Write to me – can you give me hope? I return about the thirtieth if all can be settled here. Dearest Jane, will you trust me? I want you only as you are – if you will take me as I am. Tell me all you are feeling now – be honest with me. Your own Frederick.

Her immediate feelings were of great joy. She held the letter lightly in her hands – such a small thing to decide a lifetime. Another thought, which she could not help, followed in the wake of her first happiness. Would marriage to each other risk that glimpse of perfection which she had experienced as she lay in Fred's arms? She was thinking not just of herself but of him. Would being Fred's wife spoil her for being his love and his lover? But another thought came quickly: Fred knew about marriage – who better? – and yet he wanted to risk his life with her. She read his letter again and a few tears splashed down over his words. Fred trusted her, so she must trust herself. That was it. The tears were succeeded by smiles, even as the former lay on her cheeks. Oh but she was happy. And she so *liked* Fred. And Fred would not want to 'own' her like a chattel. He knew there was a little corner of her heart which she must keep for herself so that growth and change might take place. She thought of him sitting in some *pensione*, alone and perhaps afraid for the future, his youthful hopes buried with his wife. Fifteen years could not be cancelled in a day or a month. Her own first love too had been buried: perhaps they had more in common than they had realized.

With a start she found she had been sitting holding the

two letters for over an hour, and so bestirred herself to open the other which turned out to be from Hood. Yes – he accepted her plans for the edition of Charles's works. It had even struck him as strangely apposite that they should be presented to the public by a woman. He trusted her taste and so did his friend, Telfourd. Meanwhile, she must be encouraged to continue with her own writing. It was not often that youth and femininity could combine to produce work whose merit lay in the personality of its progenitor, whose very artlessness concealed art, etc, etc.

She smiled again, wryly this time, over her 'femininity', but his letter cheered her. They wanted to print her pieces. They were a corrective to the gloomy and Puritanical apparently, and to the bombast of those who attempted tragedy when only a rueful irony was within their grasp. Decidedly she must appear as something different from her real self in her work, unlike what *she* saw as her real self. What would Hood think of *The Boy on the Shore*? Well, she would see.

She held both letters and wondered whether she had to choose between the different promises they held out. But why should she? Why should she not go on being herself, and if she were lucky and hard-working, go on being published, even if she were married? Lots of married ladies wrote even if most from necessity rather than choice, it seemed.

She wanted both these lives. She did not overestimate her own talents, she knew her own limitations. Praise could not really alter that. Did she, though, know her own limitations in matters of the heart? She thought again of Fred's ardour, which she had deliberately aroused, and she was sure there were more secrets of that sort which they could reveal to each other. Oh, yes! Thank God Fred was older than she. She could not imagine loving a man of her own age. Seventeen years older was just right. Men, she thought, needed longer to grow up and by the time she was his age she would be glad of a sober companion. She laughed a little at this rational idea of marriage, but it was true, nevertheless. Fred had sowed his oats long ago and was still capable of love. There was no one to turn to for advice except Fred himself. Charlotte and Henrietta would say, 'We always said you would marry, Jane', and Uncle Hal would be astonished, but secretly relieved. The thought of Aunt Edith's cousins who would 'launch' her was profoundly depressing. If she were to marry, it must be quickly, with no more time for appraisal and agonizing and introspection. But she would write to tell him what he was taking on!

What had Hal said about Fred's investments? Perhaps he was going to lose some money. That would be perfect – then she could earn some herself and they could live simply, grow their own vegetables, eschew society! She laughed at herself. It was true she had had enough of London. She wanted, yearned, for country air and a house where she was not a guest. And married to Fred there would be no going governessing. If she were to be a governess it would be to her own children, hers and Fred's. And at that thought she felt solemn and a little afraid. But the soul had many mansions and there were empty rooms to be filled with Fred and Fred's children. She began to look forward in both senses of the word.

My dear Fred (she wrote), I hope this will be waiting for you on your return from Florence. I have been thinking about you all the time since we parted on your doorstep (even when interrupted by drives with Aunt to replenish her supply of linen, and games with Betsey, who has grown into a nice girl but one who needs constant entertainment).

Darling Fred, we women are not supposed to reveal our

394

thoughts and feelings even to a possible 'suitor' – especially if we want him to marry us. But there is no need for me to reveal myself is there? I would rather talk to you than write a letter – and that is a great compliment, for you know I love writing letters.

I know, too, just how you are feeling – or I believe I do: full of sorrow over your wife, and filled with horror at the cruelty of death. Let me help you to bear it if I can, dearest. I want to care for you and to make you happy again, for you have made me happy again. I have been thinking a great deal about love and about men and women, especially about women, strange to say, and how women with strong passions may be made to suffer for them if they try to live like men do. I think we all need a centre to our lives, men and women both. I know I do. But all you want is a Yes or a No, isn't it? How could the answer be anything but Yes? Oh, *Yes*, Fred, I love you and I need you and I want you. Will *you* marry *me*? Ever your own – Jane.

Fred found Jane's letters when he arrived, weary, from Italy a few days later, his mind still full of the images of his wife's burial and his scene with Philip March, who had expected at least a furious reception and got a sad but courteous conversation. Both men had been at the funeral, for Philip, having been asked to return by Fred, had gone to the Protestant Cemetery with him. Then they had parted, Philip to Rome, immeasurably afflicted and guilty, and Fred to England, knowing that to each a chapter of his life was over.

Fred read Jane's first letter and then sat in his study, hardly daring to open the second. He had read a business communication from Simpkins, who warned of some reduction in his revenue, but he was too tired to worry. He took Jane's letter up to bed with him. No one apart from the servants knew of his return and he gave himself one night's grace before confronting the morrow; placing the unopened letter under his pillow, he fell immediately into a deep sleep.

In the morning, a Saturday, he opened the letter over the coffee his servant brought in to him and began to read. Then he read it again. Then he went upstairs and changed into his best suit, went downstairs, read it again, and went out.

He was awash with tenderness for Jane, for that dear, angry-spirited girl and ached to hold her close. He would call round at Hal's – it was not far – and ask her to walk round the square gardens with him. It must all be settled. He could not wait now. Funerals, sadnesses must be over – he vowed he would make her happy – he *knew* he could make her happy. He prepared himself for Hal's astonishment, for he was sure she would have said nothing to him or to her aunt. He had better make a pretence of 'asking for her hand'. They would do the *convenances* – but no announcements for the gossips. A special licence, perhaps, and a quick wedding – St Pancras Church maybe – somewhere impersonal. Or would she want a great to-do? Surely not.

He was agitated when he pulled on the bell of number seventeen and spoke nervously to Polly, who had opened the door. Edith was in the morning room.

'It's Mr Digby, Ma'am. He says is Mr Stone at home? He would like to see Miss Banham.'

'Oh dear, I am not decent and Hal is upstairs. Poor Mr Digby – his wife, you know.' She was muttering vaguely to herself and was just about to go towards their visitor when she saw Jane bound down the stairs like a boy and into Mr Digby's arms. She stood stock-still with astonishment.

'Forgive us – we have something to discuss,' Fred said. 'We shall be back in a moment. I thought a little walk – in the square?' he said to Jane.

They were both through the door, Polly standing open-mouthed, but smiling.

'Polly, what is all this about? I thought he wanted to see my husband.'

'Oh, he'll be back, Ma'am. I expect he's asking her to marry him,' said Polly, overcome with giggles.

'Polly! What has possessed you?' Hal was leaning over the banisters. 'I thought I heard Digby. Has he come about his investments?'

'Hal, please, come down. It's Jane – Polly says she is going to marry Fred Digby. Will you please come down!'

Jane had run out bare-headed and there was a nip in the air. 'There,' said Fred. 'Sit down.' He sat down next to her on a bench under the almost bare branches of horse chestnuts that spread over Lincoln's Inn Fields. 'I just wanted you to say it – then I can tell the world. I read your letter only this morning – I was afraid to open it last night. Jane – you will marry me? Oh! Jane!'

She almost teased him. 'Knowing all my radical opinions about men and women?'

'Knowing you!'

'Fred – I must ask you, too – it is only right. Will *you* marry *me*?'

'Yes, Jane.'

'Then – yes, of course, Fred,' she said, and put her arms around him.

'As soon as possible?' he murmured, his face now in her hair as she turned towards him again.

'Yes, Fred.'

'Why are there tears in your eyes, Jane?'

'From joy. Now I can dare to be happy.'

'Oh, my darling one.' Fred stroked her hair which fell down her back for she had not even had time to put it up.

397

'Your uncle's feelings will have to be consulted, I suppose. Your aunt looked positively aghast!'

'Perhaps they will want us to wait because of – '

'She has not been my wife for five years, if you mean Clara – it makes no difference.'

'All I want,' said Jane, looking up at him again, 'is to find myself on a nice comfortable bed with you and I want to go to live in Vine House. I have seen some very comfortable beds there. Oh Fred, I just want you – and if marriage is the price I pay for you, then I'll pay the price.' At this he took her in his arms. Two barristers out on an early stroll from Lincoln's Inn gaped at them as they sat under the trees and one even looked at his watch as if to ascertain that it was indeed morning – such a public exhibition in the light of day and the man looked a gentleman too!

Their kisses left them blinking and dazzled, but eventually Fred and his future wife got up and walked slowly, arms entwined, back to her uncle's house.

In the end it was not St Pancras Church which was the scene of their nuptials but the little church next to Vine House. Hal insisted on a wedding breakfast, for, once he had ascertained that this was, indeed, Jane's wish that she marry Fred Digby, he said he would bear the costs. He had only one niece and he was determined to support her decision. Folk might gossip, but with the Stone family behind her and the financial arrangements secure and the two of them apparently so much in love, what else could he do?

Jane refused a dowry – she had her little competence and hoped her writings would bring in more. Fred sold his house in Bloomsbury Square and some land he owned nearby, which was bought up for building on by Mr Cubitt

398

at a very good price. All Jane's friends came to the wedding, which was a simple affair early on a Saturday morning, New Year's Day, 1825. The three boys behaved themselves and were delighted to renew their acquaintance with the stable lads. Charlotte and Henrietta came, and Fanny Kelly, and from Norfolk Sybil Snetterton, in her best grey gown. Mrs Ogilvie celebrated her retirement the same day and called in at Hertfordshire on her way to Scotland, where she was to settle for good. Polly was in the bridal procession, too, and was to stay on as maid to Jane. And Daisy had been specially asked – and came – and was admired by a village lad.

A few 'rattles', friends who had shared Fred's schooldays and student days, were also present, and his sister, too, who seemed to approve of his choice. Mr Thomas Hood and Mr Harrison Ainsworth also attended, but not Mr Bruce, who was dallying not far away with the lady who had been so shocked by Byron's death in the summer.

Fred said little when he gave a toast to his bride, except, 'Hearts have triumphed.'

'You will be retiring from London, then, Miss Banham?' said Mr Hood.

'Yes, Mr Hood – the better to continue with my writing,' she answered.

'Mr Digby wants you to continue, then?' he asked, with some surprise.

'My husband,' replied Jane, with some asperity. 'My husband is most insistent that I do so.'

'I see he is a kindred spirit, then,' said Mr Hood with a bow.

'And wants to retire to the country, too,' said Ainsworth, who looked even more handsome and bore an air of success like an emblem before him.

'Oh, yes – London is too much for us both.'

'Then you will read Mr Wordsworth together,' said Hood. 'He is said to be good for the complexion.'

'Ah, the days of our youth are the days of our glory!' said Fanny Kelly.

'Youth's a stuff will not endure,' replied Jane. 'You must excuse me – I must go to my husband now.'

'"There are two things which excite my imagination,"' quoted Fred, as he watched her unbind her long hair that evening when the wedding guests had all departed. '"The moral law within me and the starry heavens above me." And a third thing of my own,' he added. 'The woman I love.'

'I love you,' she said in the middle of the night to Fred.

'And I love you, beautiful girl,' he said, smiling. 'And I shall demand of you your wifely duty once more.'

'Ah – if you will perform the "duty" of a lover, then,' she replied.